EVERNIGHT PUBLISHING ®

www.evernightpublishing.com

Copyright© 2016

Evernight Publishing

Editor: Katelyn Uplinger

Cover Artist: Jay Aheer

ISBN: 978-1-77339-047-5

8 AUTHOR ANTHOLOGY

DARK CAPTIVE: MANLOVE EDITION

Everyone has a dark side…

Ransomed by Doris O'Connor
Collecting His Debt by Angelique Voisen
I Love the Way You Hurt Me by James Cox
Shanghai by Pelaam
Taken by Michelle Graham
Get Off Hard by Lea Bronsen
Uninvited Love by L.J. Longo
Runner by Kai Tyler

RANSOMED

Doris O'Connor

Copyright © 2016

Chapter One

This was almost too easy. Perry whistled under his breath as he extinguished his cigarette end under his boot, and snapped on his gloves. When he'd first been given this assignment he'd thought it would take considerable skill to lure Danvers O'Flynn away from his ever present bodyguards. Senator Seamus O'Flynn's golden-haired only son went nowhere without the two steroid-induced hunks of muscle, after all, but Danny boy had been surprisingly inventive. Perry had been watching the boy a week now, and for the third night running he'd given his muscle-bound apes the slip, and disappeared into the seedy underbelly of London's Soho area. Judging by the wet sounds and male groans that came from the alleyway the boy had disappeared into moments ago, he was engaged in his favourite pastime—sucking dick. Perry's own cock stiffened as he listened in. That boy sure seemed to know what he was doing.

Finding out that Danny boy was gay had been an unexpected pleasure. There had been no mention of his proclivities in the intel Perry had been given. Danvers was, after all, engaged to be married to Melissa Beauchamp. Her billionaire father was behind the push to get O'Flynn into the running for the next presidency, and the main reason why Perry was stalking his daughter's fiancé.

The pretty O'Flynn boy was nothing more than a pawn with a high prize on his head. They couldn't get to Melissa, but they sure could get to him. Perry's lips curved in disgust at the machinations of the rich and richer. Money made the world go round, after all, and it seemed neither parent cared much for what their offspring might make of this arrangement. The two of them would make picture perfect babies, for sure, always assuming Danny boy could actually get it up for the blonde Barbie look-a-like. Having witnessed the lad's enthusiasm for the other sex, Perry had his doubts in that regard, and the pictures he'd been able to find of the two of them together showed Danny boy to be polite and attentive to his fiancé, but nothing more. If Perry had to guess, the high class Melissa would have rather slummed it with Danvers's bodyguards.

He barely suppressed a snort of amusement at the thought. Airhead heiress and brawn for brains would work well. Certainly better than Danny boy and her. For some reason that Perry didn't want to delve into too much the thought of Danvers with her didn't sit well.

The boy had brains for starters. You didn't get a PhD at Harvard unless you were a clever piece of cute ass.

Perry flattened himself against the wall as Danvers's latest conquest exited from the alley with a satisfied smirk on his face. He had no business noticing the boy's cute ass, nor wondering why Danvers seemed satisfied in simply servicing the men he met up with. As far as Perry could tell, those jerks never returned the favor. This asshole certainly hadn't, and glaring at the man's departing back, he entered the dark and dingy alleyway that ran between the buildings. The streetlights barely illuminated the entrance, and he waited a second for his eyes to adjust. Danny boy was mid jerking himself off, and froze when he noticed Perry blocking his exit way.

"Don't stop on my account, boy. I've been enjoying the show thus far."

Hand wrapped around his slim, yet surprisingly long dick, Danvers relaxed and resumed his hand job. Already, beads of pre-cum glistened on the tip of his peen, and Perry swallowed hard. He had the insane urge to close his hand over the boy's and finish him off. In his mind's eye, Danny boy was coming hard all over his hand, before he dropped to his knees in front of him, to enable Perry to shoot his own load all down Danvers's slender throat.

Fuck knew where those thoughts were coming from. Danvers represented a nice, big paycheck for Perry—that was all. Perry always kept his hands off the merchandise. As they were usually female, he never had a problem with it, but this guy—who now shot him a saucy look from under his long eyelashes—yeah, he was getting to him.

Keep your mind on the job and out of your trousers.

His mental pep talk did little to rein in his wayward libido. Clearly it had been way too long since Perry had taken one of the boys at the club for a ride. *All work and no play make Perry a horn dog.*

He smirked at his thought processes and willed his erection to deflate as Danny boy came in a wide arc of the white stuff. It splashed against the wall, and Perry experienced a moment of regret at the sheer waste of it as the air around them thickened with sexual tension and the unmistakable odor of sex. Eyes screwed shut, breaths seesawing in and out of his chest, Danny boy braced himself against the wall with one hand while he continued to milk the last few drops of spunk out of his dick.

Perry cleared his throat, and with a sheepish grin in his direction, O'Flynn's son tucked himself back into his designer jeans, and zipped them up.

"Has your Mama never told you not to make a mess, boy?" Perry asked, as he closed the distance between them. He was a good head taller than the lad, and considerably brawnier than him.

Still, for a studious type, Danvers was in surprisingly good shape. He clearly worked out, and he had the lean, toned form of a swimmer, with powerful shoulders, and biceps that flexed as he ran a hand through his shoulder-length mop of blond hair, and a smile that could seriously make a man forget he had a job to do. It lit up his youthful face, and made his baby blues crinkle up at the corners. A dimple appeared in his stubble roughened cheek, and Perry was hard pushed not to smile back at him. Danny boy seemed to have abandoned the clean shaven, almost angelic look he gave off in the rounds of propaganda pictures he'd been involved in in the States prior to his departure. Dressed in the ever-present designer jeans, and with a tight tee showing off his toned torso, he didn't look like the spoilt rich kid his file purported him to be. No, this was a man who knew exactly what he wanted, and that seemed to include Perry, as Danvers made no move to disguise the fact that he was checking Perry out. When his gaze lingered longer than was necessary on Perry's groin, he barely resisted the urge to place his hands over the area. It would only serve to draw more attention to the fact that he wanted the kid. And despite the intriguing tattoos on Danvers's arms, compared to Perry's life experience

Danny boy was just that—a boy—and merchandise.

"She sure did, Sir, but I never was a very good listener."

The unexpected title Danvers bestowed on him, caused his cock to give up all pretense of behaving itself, and punched forward with a speed that made Perry feel almost lightheaded, as all his blood shot south. Seeing Danvers's smirk increase as he noticed Perry's reaction, only served to piss him off more.

He had a job to do, dammit, and this unexpected attraction that had sprung up between them would only complicate matters.

"Oh, *Sir* likes it when I call him that, it seems."

Perry took a deep breath in to swart the inherent urge to take the boy to task for his sassy mouth. Now was neither the time nor the place to do so.

"If you want me on my knees you only have to ask," Danny boy said.

Perry closed the distance between himself and the insolent pup in seconds. When he noticed the gloves on Perry's hands some of the boy's bravado left him. He swallowed hard, and took several steps back until the rough fence at the bottom of the alley stopped him.

When Perry pulled the syringe out of his pocket, and yanked the protective tip off the end with his teeth, his crystal blue eyes widened in horror. Danvers's sudden fear thickened the air between them, and Perry smirked as he jabbed the needle into the side of the boy's neck.

"There's only one thing I want from you, pretty boy, and that's the Beauchamp money." Recognition dawned in the boy's eyes, seconds before the sedative took hold, and he slumped.

"Thatta boy." Perry pulled a flask of whisky out of his back pocket, and upended it down the front of Danvers, to further the illusion of the lad being overcome by drink. Shoving his shoulder under the other man's armpit, he pulled Danvers's arm around his neck and grasped his hand while grabbing him round the waist. Perry proceeded to drag him along, with Danvers mumbling incoherently under his breath, as they rounded the corner and emerged into the bustling night life.

A cop duo appeared, doing their rounds. Perry smiled, and rolled his eyes.

"Can't hold his drink, officers. Don't worry. I'm taking him home, where he can sleep it off. He won't be any trouble."

The uniformed officer nodded, while his female counterpart spoke into her intercom, and then they both turned their attention to a ruckus breaking out across the street. It seemed a gaggle of inebriated punters had taken offence of being asked to leave this particular establishment, and the guys at the door were getting heavy with them.

Perry didn't envy them their job. In what seemed like a hundred years ago now, Perry had once been a bouncer. Until he had been approached by his current employer, and offered a far higher *salary* for taking care of Z's *problems* than working at any door would have ever earned him.

Zion—that wasn't his real name either—seeing Perry's potential had put him on more and trickier assignments, when he realized that crossing the line wasn't a problem for Perry. While he didn't get off on the violence and the killing like some in Z's employ, Perry sure enjoyed a good fight. The thrill of the chase and his prey's ultimate surrender could only be surpassed by a good session at the club, and as his painfully hard cock was proof, it had been far too long since he indulged in that pastime.

He dodged the crowds milling about in the

pedestrianized area, as he continued to drag Danvers along, while whistling *Oh, Danny Boy,* to himself. His very own Danny boy seemed intent on saying something, and increasing his steps, to hurry them along, Perry only half listened to what Danvers was trying to say.

Fuck it. I should have given him a higher dose. He's sure coming round fast.

As he would have attracted too much attention, however, had he carted a completely unconscious man around with him, he would just have to hope Danny boy wouldn't start shouting for help, or some such nonsense.

Instead of crying for help, he seemed to be muttering something else.

"Won't work. Let me go."

Perry smirked and hoisted the boy up more, his car now in sight.

"You better hope for your sake it will, boy, because you're no use to me otherwise."

They finally reached his car, and before Danvers could come round fully, Perry surreptitiously applied the pressure needed to the boy's neck to render him unconscious. He deposited him in his car with a grin, and strapped the lifeless form into the seatbelt. Unbidden, his hand lingered on the surprisingly soft skin of his nape as he arranged the man's head on the head rest and laid the seat down to stop him from lolling about. If he took much more care with him than he would normally have done, it was only due to his need to keep the cover of tending to a drunken friend. It had nothing to do with the need to touch the boy.

No fucking way.

Chapter Two

Dan came round in a dark room, naked, bound, gagged, and with a brass band seemingly having taken up residence in his head. Even the slightest movement meant cymbals clashed inside his skull, and he winced. Panic held him in his grip, as the events leading up to him being in this predicament crystallized slowly. He'd slipped away from his bodyguards, determined to scout out the local talent and have some fun. Being a relative unknown in London had helped in that regard. Without the muscle-bound hunks by his side, who simply screamed *VIP*, he'd found it easy to blend into the crowds. Something that had pissed off dumbass and brawn-for-brains, as he'd called his bodyguards in his head—much more suitable names than Sam and Rogers, in his opinion.

Each early morning, when he returned to the hotel suite, they threw their version of a hissy fit, threatening to cart him back to the States. Dan knew it was all talk, however. Firstly he was a grown man, who could damn well do what he fucking pleased, and secondly, they would have to admit their utter failure to *keep him in line* to Daddy dearest and Melissa's father to boot. Neither man would take kindly to that, for sure.

Dan bristled anew at having overheard that conversation between his father and future father-in-law.

Harry Beauchamp had been very clear.

"If that boy insists on making this foolish trip, Sam and Rogers will go, too. I've invested a lot of money in this coming marriage, and I will not go and see it wasted. This is great publicity for our campaign, and shows you as the perfect family man."

Seamus O'Flynn had tried his best to soothe the ruffled feathers of the man, who held the senator's future in his beefy hands. It was a match made in heaven really. Dan's father had the clean cut image needed to become the next president, and Beauchamp had the financial means to get him there. Personally, the mere thought of his father in the White House turned Dan's stomach, because he would be no more than a puppet for Beauchamp's dealings, and as the man had made his fortune in far from legal means, it didn't bode well for the future of the country should their plan succeed.

His marriage to Beauchamp's daughter was another spoke in the well-oiled propaganda machinations. Dan had done his best to wriggle out of it, but short of coming out publicly and announcing that he was gay—an action which would mean that he would never be allowed to cross the threshold of the family home again—there wasn't much he could do about it.

While there was no love lost between Dan and his father, he couldn't just abandon his little sister, not with Mama next to useless. Karen was at that difficult age, not quite a teenager, but itching to grow up and make sense of the world. She looked up to him, relied on him. Were he to leave, Seamus would only poison her innocent mind with his bigoted ideas.

Dan scowled into the darkness and yanked at his restraints in a futile attempt to get free. It was useless. Whoever had tied him had done so with care and precision that would have put any Shibari Master to shame. The rough hemp of the rope his assailant had used didn't budge even an inch, yet didn't restrict his circulation either.

In any other circumstance, Dan would have found this helpless situation most arousing. It fed into all of his dark fantasies, and unbidden an image of the man he'd met in the alley jumped out at him. Dressed entirely in black, the guy had simply oozed leashed aggression, and dominance, and had been the main reason why Dan's instincts had let him down. He had instantly responded to the other man, and he hadn't seen the danger until the guy had pulled out his syringe. Disappointment set heavy in his gut. The one man he might have actually allowed himself to truly submit to, turned out to be after him, for what exactly… Cash, most likely. Not the first time Dan wished he hadn't been born into a wealthy family. While it had afforded him the best education money could offer, it had certainly not brought him any happiness.

A match struck in the room, and his garbled thought processes came to an abrupt stop. The light from that point seemed far too bright in the dark room, and briefly illuminated the rugged features of the man in the alley, as he used it to light his smoke. The man's azure eyes crinkled up at the corners in seeming amusement, and Dan stopped breathing for the moments it took for his captor to run his gaze leisurely over Dan's naked body. It was a far too fanciful thought, but Dan could have sworn he could feel the other man's gaze almost like a physical caress. Sweat broke out on his forehead with the sheer will power needed to not have his cock rise to the occasion, when his captor's gaze rested on that particular part of his anatomy for a fraction too long. The man's full, sensuous lips kicked into a knowing smile, and then the room plunged back into darkness with a flick of his hand when the match burnt out.

Dan sensed the man step closer, his spicy cologne and the smell of tobacco a helpful tracking beacon of his movements, because the man seemed to move with the stealth of a large cat. Soundless, dangerous, a predator on the move ready to devour him. That thought alone should have Dan screaming for help, but he instinctively knew that it wouldn't do him any good. Everything so far spoke of a professional hit, which begged the question as to why Dan was still alive. He had seen this guy's face, so it was fair to assume he wouldn't be alive for much longer.

His captor appeared to be pacing to and fro, if the slight air displacement wafting over his naked skin was any indication. Goose bumps broke out on his exposed flesh, and Dan yanked at his restraints again. The hemp chafed along his skin, the slight burn far too arousing under the circumstances. The bed dipped, and swallowing his curse, Dan forced himself to simply carry on breathing. The cigarette end glowed bright as his captor took a long drag. He blew the resulting smoke into Dan's face and when Dan coughed, the other man's dark laughter washed over him.

"Not so sassy now, are you, Danny boy? Shame really, I was rather looking forward to occupying that mouth of yours." He yanked the gag out of Dan's mouth and he pulled a much needed drag of air into his lungs.

"Fuck off." Dan growled the words through clenched teeth and his unknown assailant laughed again, seconds before he clamped his large hand around Dan's balls, and squeezed. Pain shot up Dan's body, hot, hard, intense, and he screwed his eyes shut, and bit his lip to stop himself from crying out. Through his closed eyelids he noticed the room get brighter, as the man torturing his junk appeared to have switched the lights on.

When his captor ran his hand up Dan's shaft to pull on his piercing, Dan couldn't stop his grunt of what … pain, need, he wasn't entirely sure which, as the guy changed from a painful squeeze to a soothing caress.

"You're full of surprises, Danny boy. Tell me, what shall I do with you?"

That question made Dan open his eyes to look at him and his breath stalled in his lungs again at his first proper look at his assailant.

The harsh fluorescent lighting played over

features seemingly cut from granite. Stubble graced the man's jaw, adding to the mean, dangerous look. Shoulder-length black hair framed a harsh face, from which piercing blue eyes regarded him solemnly. Try as he might, Dan couldn't look away from those intense blue spheres. The man's gaze pulled him into his will, and when he stepped up the up-and-downward slide on Dan's cock, that body part stiffened in response. The guy noticed, of course, and increased the motion. Dan swallowed hard when his captor ran his thumb repeatedly over his slit, gently manipulating his piercing in the process. Dan's cock jumped and hardened further, and he couldn't stop his groan of pure need as he lifted up his head to watch the other guy's beefy hand work his dick with unerring precision. It meant he was fast hurtling toward an orgasm he neither wanted, nor needed. It was humiliating to know how easily this *criminal* manipulated Dan's body and mind it seemed, as he dropped his voice to a growly whisper which shot straight to Dan's balls.

"Stop fighting it, boy. This one is a freebie. Let it go and show me how pretty you look when you come for me."

Dan shook his head and desperately tried to think unsexy thoughts as the stranger's dark head slowly lowered toward his dick.

"No, fuck, I... Jesus, yes, please, don't stop. Yes!"

Hot lips closed over his dick, and Dan saw stars when his captor swallowed his dick whole, until his nose buried in Dan's pubic hair. He grazed his teeth along Dan's shaft on the way back up, adding to the pleasuring pain the stranger inflicted on him, because he chose that moment to squeeze Dan's balls again. Nipping at his piercing with his teeth, he licked along Dan's slit, now wet with pre-cum, and released his cock.

"Please…"

Dan didn't care about begging right now, because this guy had him so worked up, that he was going to explode if he didn't finish what he started, which had no doubt been his captor's intention, because he blew across the wet tip, and withdrew with a wicked grin up at Dan.

"Please, what, boy? Ask me nicely if you want me to continue."

The guy sat back, crossed his arms over his massive chest and chuckled softly. Dan yanked anew at his restraints, which proved utterly useless, of course. He was trussed up like a Christmas turkey, and there wasn't a thing he could do about it.

At least the guy's question brought Dan back to his senses, and, shaking his head to clear it off the lust-filled fog, he did his best to glare at him.

"What the hell do you want from me? If it's money, you're barking up the wrong tree."

The man's eyebrows rose to his hairline, and Dan sucked in a sharp breath when he pulled a jackknife out of his pocket, and flicked it open.

"What are you going to do with that?" Dan had to ask, and his breathing grew even shallower, when the guy smirked and shrugged his shoulders. It was hard to tell with him sitting down, but judging by the width of those shoulders, and the biceps straining against the black t-shirt, which lovingly hugged this man's body, accentuating his muscled physique, he had to be well over six feet tall. He clearly also either worked out, or, as was more likely in his line of work, was used to manual labor. You needed strength to heave unconscious victims about, after all.

"That's entirely up to you, Danny boy. You play nice and give me the answers that I need, and I might let you live. If you don't … well … it won't end well for you." He smirked, and setting the tip of that lethal looking knife to Dan's skin, traced the outline of his tats. Up and down his side, over and around his biceps, up his shoulder, and over the writing on his pecs and down to his other side.

"Interesting tats, boy. Any special meaning behind these?" He retraced the path his knife had just taken, while he dug the tip in slightly more, still not breaking the skin, yet leaving definite scratches behind. The slight pain pitched Dan right back into his aroused state, and his dick twitched against his belly.

"Hmm, my boy likes a bit of pain, it seems. How utterly delightful. Now answer my question. These tats—"

"Are for my mom and sister." Dan blurted the words out, interrupting his tormentor, and that painful, yet sensual path the knife took stopped, right over his breastbone, where Dan's heart seemed determined to burst through. It was pounding so hard he felt faint, or maybe that was due to the loss of blood to his brain, because it all seemed to have rushed to his erection. His pre-cum left a wet mark on his abdomen, and he was so hard he was sure his cock would snap in half if he didn't get relief soon. Which surely meant he was fucked up in the head. Then again, that was the general assessment from Daddy dearest anyway. When he'd found his teenage son masturbating to gay porn, he'd sent him away to be *cured.*

Dan had played along to enable him to get out of that hell-hole, and had since chosen to keep that side of him private. Clearly he was more fucked up than he thought, however, because this whole being at this stranger's mercy turned him on beyond all measure. He ought to be screaming to get away, not melting at the touch of this criminal.

"Ah yes, one isn't well and the other one is blossoming into a nice young woman."

"How the hell do you know that?"

His captor simply smiled, traced the tip of his knife over and around Dan's nipples now, and then brought it lower, until the flat side of it rested against the base of his erect cock. It should have killed his erection dead, but the inherent threat had the opposite effect on him.

Dan couldn't take his eyes away from the sight of that knife resting against his shaft, and cold sweat broke out between his shoulder blades.

"Please … Sir … I don't know what… God, please do something."

Chapter Three

The boy's husky, needy words, delivered through clenched teeth, as though they cost him dearly, meant Perry's already hard dick pressed painfully against his fly. When he'd brought the senator's son here, stripped him, and tied him to his bed, it had been with the sole intention of taking the required pictures to get his father to pay up. That old weasel couldn't afford a scandal, and the photographic evidence he'd collected on his golden boy only son going down on men in alleyways, should have been more than enough ammunition to get O'Flynn and most especially Beauchamp to cough up the cash. Perry didn't need to touch the boy, yet he couldn't help himself either. The tats and the piercing had been a delightful surprise, as has had been the young man's immediate reaction when he'd come to. Not fear at being restrained, but unwilling arousal, which had meant that Perry had stayed in the shadows, watching silently, and eventually stepping up the game by making his presence known.

He'd have expected tears, whining, promises of giving him all the cash he wanted to set him free, but not *this*. Instead the boy had been angry, and the instant attraction that had sprung up between them was simply too potent to ignore. Danvers's instinctive reaction to Perry exerting his dominance, his responsiveness, and his fearful arousal at the little bit of knife play, Perry couldn't help but indulge in … *fuck*. He hadn't expected that.

Neither had he expected the stony wall of silence coming from both O'Flynn and Beauchamp. It was late afternoon in the States now. They would have received the e-mail, and demand to deliver the goods by now, yet there had been no response whatsoever. Zion was not happy, and that wouldn't end well for Danny boy here.

His phone beeped with an incoming text, and leaving the knife where it was for now, he flicked a glance up at the man at his mercy and smirked.

"Best not move, Danny boy. It would be a shame to cut such a pretty cock."

A strangled groan escaped the boy, and every muscle in his body locked tight, as he took shallow breaths in a seeming effort not to move. His cock remained as erect as ever, the broad mushroom tip wet with Danvers's arousal. *Such a fucking turn on.*

Perry swiped the screen and frowned at Zion's message.

Fucker is not responding. Time to step this up and send him a body part.

Suppressing a sigh, Perry typed his response.

Surely, it's too early for that. It's not been twenty-four hours yet.

The response was as damning as it was immediate.

Do it, now. No one gets away with ignoring me. Besides, he's high profile, and you know what that means.

Perry knew that only too well. The longer they kept him, the higher the chances of being found by the authorities. It was the main reason why Perry had taken Danny boy here back to his house, rather than one of the abandoned warehouse locations he would normally use to store someone temporarily. At least that's what he'd told himself, when he'd heaved the unconscious man out of his car and into the cellar under his house.

Perry lived alone in a ramshackle building that had been in his family for several generations. The affluent suburb location meant that, generally speaking, folks ignored each other, ferreted away behind their iron gates and thick hedges, something that had worked in Perry's favor. He was as sure as he could be that no one had seen him bundle the senator's son inside his house, and the cellar was soundproof and impenetrable. Built to withstand a nuclear attack, thanks to Perry's eccentric grandfather's belief that the end was nigh after Hiroshima, it was the safest place anywhere.

Thus it made sense to bring the boy here. Avoiding discovery had been the sole motive for his actions, not the need to keep Danny boy close to him. No fucking way.

The soft curse coming from said male meant Perry shifted his gaze from his phone back to the prone body of his captive, and taking the other man's cock in a firm grip, he picked up the knife again. Danvers's breathing sped up again, and his hands balled into fists, the knuckles white with the force he used.

"Tell me, is there a reason why your father and Beauchamp are ignoring the ransom demand for you?"

He kept his voice even, as though the answer didn't matter to him one iota.

"Cause I gotta tell you, boy, it would be a shame for you to start losing body parts to get your old man to cough up the goods."

He flicked his gaze up to the young man's face, and something twisted inside in his chest when their gazes collided. The boy was clearly terrified, the scent of his fear a potent aphrodisiac in the air, and a direct contradiction to the hard, pulsing shaft in Perry's hand. It seemed Danny boy got off on danger, which went a long way to explaining why he'd been so reckless to seek out sexual adventures in the back alleys of Soho. After all, he had to know he was a target. Why else would he travel with bodyguards?

"Cat got your tongue, boy?" Perry lined the knife up with the bottom of Danvers's pretty cock, and smiled at the youngster. "Maybe giving good old Dad his precious boy's cock on a platter will get him to cough up the cash. What do you think?"

An all-over body shiver was his response, and Danny boy turned an interesting shade of gray, his blue eyes riveted to the knife.

"You wouldn't?"

The strangled question made Perry smile, and to further fuck with his prey's mind, he pumped his hand up and down the length of the other man's shaft while he hooked the tip of the knife into the piercing. The action stretched the circumcised head, and Danvers hissed through his teeth. He jerked in his restraints, and if that was possible grew even harder in Perry's hand. What a fascinating development that was.

Continuing his slow measured strokes designed to keep the other man at boiling point, Perry grinned.

"I so would, if I thought it would get you to talk, but, you, my boy, seem to be enjoying this playing with fire a little bit too much. Besides, it would be a positive waste to ruin such a pretty cock, not to mention the awful mess it would make on my bed." His grin deepened when Danny boy glared at him, and he let go of the other man's junk. "No, I think, a finger will do for now." Shifting position, he sliced through the rope securing Danvers's left arm to the headboard, and unraveled the hemp from around his arm. The red crisscross marks left behind on the pale skin made him smile, and he automatically massaged the limb to ensure circulation returned. When the other man fought against him, he used his superior strength to pin him back down.

"Fuck you." Danvers's returning sass was rather delightful.

"Oh, I may very well do that yet, boy."

Danvers fisted his hand and swore when Perry uncurled each finger, and then set the knife to his ring finger.

"I wonder what your airhead fiancé will do when she opens the box to find your severed finger? That's a mighty fine, distinguishable cygnet ring you got there. Engagement present, was it? Too bad you won't be able to wear a wedding ring once I'm done."

A snort was his answer this time, and Danny boy's blue orbs seethed in anger.

"Have at it. I have no intention on wearing her ring, ever." He bit his lip as though he'd said too much.

Perry put one knee on his arm to keep it in place, grasped the other man's wrist, and lined the knife up with the first knuckle.

"Good, this finger it is then."

A thin line of blood appeared under the sharp edge of his knife, before Danvers caved with a strangled cry.

"Wait, Jesus. I'll tell you what you want to know."

Perry released the slender hand, and lifting it up, licked the thin line of blood away. Danny boy's life essence exploded on his taste buds, and they both groaned.

"You're one sick bastard, aren't you?" Danvers asked.

Perry shrugged, and purposefully glanced down to the other man's still erect cock.

"That makes two of us, it would seem."

A faint blush stained Danvers's high cheekbones at those words. It made Perry's chest feel tight with unwanted emotion, because right now he was torn between fucking this insolent young man raw, or cutting him loose and protecting him from those who wanted him harm.

Danvers surprised him again by nodding.

"So, I want you. Stockholm syndrome in progress. That doesn't mean jack shit."

"If you say so. However, you might wanna get your money back for that Harvard education, because I'm pretty sure that would only happen had you been my captive for some time." He grinned at Danny boy's sharp intake of breath. "In other words, you want me as much as I want you." To prove his point, he adjusted his rock hard dick away from the zipper of his pants, and when he looked back up again, it was to see Danvers lick his lips. His blue eyes had darkened to almost black, and Perry picked up the knife again to distract himself from the wanton promise in those orbs. He had a job to do here, *dammit*.

"Talk, boy. My patience is wearing mighty thin."

Danvers yanked at his restraints again and fisted his freed hand by his side.

"I tried to tell you when you jabbed me with that syringe thing, it's no use. If you want money, you should have gone after *her*. Neither Daddy dearest nor Melissa's father will cough up a penny for me."

His words wobbled slightly as though it cost him to admit that, and giving into the disturbing need to soothe the man in front of him, Perry wrapped his hand around the clenched fist and squeezed.

"Why not? They send you over here with bodyguards, after all. Clearly, you mean something to them."

Another gruff laugh came from the man bound to his bed.

"I'm a means to an end. Melissa needs a baby daddy for the bastard she is brewing in her belly.

Beauchamp needs a puppet in the White House, and Daddy dearest needs Beauchamp's money to get him into office."

Danvers delivered that news in a flat monotone as though he didn't care one way or the other, but when Perry grasped his chin to make the boy look at him, he caught the glimpse of pain in the other man's blue eyes, before he blinked and masked them.

"I see. What do you get out of all this?" Perry asked. "It must be something, or you could just walk away?"

"What do you care?"

In answer, Perry slapped the man's balls and a strangled groan came from Danvers. Sweat broke out on his brow, and he had trouble breathing, when Perry followed that assault by squeezing the sensitive parts hard.

"Watch your mouth, boy. You're in no position to give me sass, and if you were mine, these"—he squeezed harder still, until tears swam in Danvers's eyes—"these would be locked away in a chastity belt with a vibrator stuffed up your butt and set on high until you've learned your manners."

More pre-cum leaked out of the end of Danvers's cock at those words, and Perry smirked. The boy was definitely submissive and a bit of a pain slut to boot. What fun he could have with that, had they met under different circumstances.

"What do you say to me, boy?" he asked.

"Sorry, *Sir.*"

The intonation Danny boy put on the grudgingly delivered title meant Perry had to hide his grin behind a cough.

"Better, boy. So, again, I ask you, and I expect an answer this time. What's in it for you?"

Chapter Four

How to answer that question without baring his very soul—that was the question. By far more disturbing, however, was the way Dan had to fight not to unburden his baggage onto the broad shoulders of his captor. The man's icy gaze held him spell bound, and he got the uncomfortable sensation that this man could look right into his soul, which should have been a ridiculous notion. He didn't know this man, and he couldn't forget that this *criminal* had kidnapped him, tied him up, and…

Fuck!

Was it assault when everything this man had done to him had made Dan so hard he could pound concrete with his damn dick right now? The urge to wrap his free hand around his cock and jerk himself off was almost too much to resist. He also knew, however, that Sir wouldn't let him. The more he bestowed that title on his dark-haired angel of death, the easier it became. Besides, he had to call him something, and he highly doubted he would ever find out this man's name. If he did, he would no doubt kill him, which should have turned his arousal, his deep-seated need to get to know this man, to see how far this chemistry they seemed to share could go, dead, but the opposite was true. The longer he stared into the depths of Sir's oceanic eyes, the stronger the need to tell him everything became.

After all, he could read no judgement in the other man's eyes, just quiet patience, mixed with that underlying danger which made this whole situation such a turn on.

"I'm a patient man, Danvers, but it's not limitless, so I suggest you start talking. Otherwise Daddy dearest will start receiving your body parts, and if that doesn't work, then you, my dear, will be feeding the pigs."

He crossed his arms over his massive chest and quirked one eyebrow at Dan.

"You'll be doing that anyway. I've seen your face. I'm not that stupid to think that you will let me live when I could identify you," Dan said.

A humorless laugh was his reply, chilling in its lack of emotion and ice cold dread snaked up Dan's spine. Strangely enough, it finally caused his dick to deflate and his captor winked at him.

"Ah, you're finally starting to take this seriously then. Talk, boy. Or, my face will be the last you ever see. I'm assuming you at least care about your mother and sister." He traced the outline of the angel tats along Dan's sides again. "Maybe I should send your body parts to them?"

Dan swung wildly with his free arm, determined to do some damage, but the other man was too fast for him. He ducked the fist aimed at his chin easily enough, and simply stood and out of Dan's reach.

"Temper, temper, boy. I see, I'll have my hands full with you, if I decide to let you live."

Closing his eyes in frustration, Dan barely swallowed a growl, and the stranger's dark laughter washed over him. Giving in to the inevitable, Dan shook his head.

"Keep my sister and mother out of it. Mama is too ill to cope with this shit, and Karen has her whole life ahead of her still. They suffered enough at…" He clamped his mouth shut again, and shook his head when Sir gestured for him to carry on.

Dan refused to say anymore and the amusement left the other man's eyes.

"Still guarding the O'Flynn secrets? Okay, let me guess. Daddy dearest is an asshole, only concerned with furthering his career, which includes maintaining his squeaky clean image. Am I on the right track so far?" he asked.

When Dan kept silent, he smirked.

"Your silence speaks volumes, boy. I'm assuming Daddy either doesn't know or refuses to acknowledge you're gay, and he's using that to what … force you into marriage to the Beauchamp cunt? No, that doesn't make sense … no, don't tell me." He held up a hand when Dan was going to say something.

"I'll figure this out. I like puzzles, see. You said she's pregnant and needs a baby daddy, so that's clearly where you come in. Beauchamp wants O'Flynn to get into the White House, so that he can use him for his own ends." He smirked when Dan couldn't help his sharp intake of breath. "Oh, come on, everyone with an ounce of brain can see that. Money talks, after all, and Beauchamp's alliance with O'Flynn gives him respectability, further enhanced by marrying his daughter off to you. But that still doesn't explain why you're going along with it. You could strike out on your own, after all. Renounce Daddy dearest … which leaves lil' sister. You don't want to leave her, do you?"

Dan blinked away unwanted tears as images of his sweet little sister filled his brain. He swiped away the resulting moisture with his free hand, only to find his captor watching him. It was the quiet compassion in his darkening eyes that robbed Dan of any further resistance.

"You're wrong, you know." When the other man's eyebrows went up, he rushed on. "Not about Karen. You're right. I would do anything to spare her from becoming another pawn in Seamus's power games. She's away at school right now, so she's protected from all this crap. Mama insisted she'll be sent away to a girl's school in Switzerland. I didn't agree with her at the time, but I guess boarding school is preferable to being subjected to the atmosphere in the house. Seamus is obsessed with getting into the White House. A gay son will never do, nor will an alcoholic wife, never mind Daddy dearest is the one who drove her to the bottle in the first place."

Dan flicked a glance up at the other man, but if this was news, and as far as Dan was concerned it had to be, because Mama was never seen out in public due to her *illness,* then he hid it well, because his expression gave nothing away.

"He thinks he's cured me, you see."

That at last, got a reaction, because the big guy swore.

"Fuck, no, don't tell me. He put you in one of those camps?"

At Dan's nod, a string of most inventive swearwords came out the other man's mouth, and despite the situation, Dan laughed.

"Yeah, it didn't work, of course, but I let him believe it did. What Seamus O'Flynn doesn't know, he can't get his ass in a twist over, but there is no way on this earth he'll send money to you for my ransom. If he gets evidence that I'm gay, he'd rather I was dead, I am sure, and Beauchamp is even worse. I never met a bigger bigot. So, if it's money you or whoever employs you wants, you're plain out of luck."

Another text came in in on the other man's phone, and Dan's heart beat faster when he saw the grim expression on the guy's face.

He texted a reply, ran a hand through his hair, and shook his head.

"You're wrong, you know." He fixed his dark gaze on Dan, and something in the depths of those blue orbs made Dan's chest feel tight. Regret, anger, and some other emotion that he couldn't figure out. It caused a cold sweat to run down between his shoulder blades, nonetheless.

"Your father did respond, and he pissed off my *employer* ... big time." He mimed quotation marks around that one word with a grim smile. "Want to know what he said to him?"

Dan didn't really, but he found himself nodding anyway.

"I have no son."

Even though he'd expected that response it still hurt. Far more than it ought to, surely?

"I have orders to kill you, boy."

Was it regret he heard in that deep timbre or was it just wishful thinking on his part? Dan couldn't be sure, as his mind fogged over in horror, and he shut his eyes against the sight of his captor picking up his knife again. The bed dipped as he sat next to him, and Dan flinched at the gentle touch of the man's calloused fingertips across his jaw. Soft lips brushed across his, and when the other man's tongue licked across the seam of his mouth, Dan opened to him instinctively. Sir, it felt right to call him that right now, gave a satisfied grunt, and fisting one hand in Dan's hair, took charge of the kiss in such a way that Dan's cock surged back to life with a speed that made him glad he was lying down as all the blood left his brain. The idle thought occurred to him that at least, he'd die with a hard on, and he couldn't help the sob that seemed determined to escape from deep within his soul.

Breaking off the kiss, his captor's deep voice floated over him.

"Open your eyes, boy, and look at me."

Dan couldn't *not* obey that gentle demand, and when he did, he saw the first genuine smile on the other man's face.

"Good boy, that wasn't so hard now, was it?"

Dan rolled his eyes in answer and the other man laughed.

"Oh, I do like the sassy ones." He ran his fingers along Dan's jaw and then lower, until he could wrap his large hand around Dan's throat.

"What's your name, Sir?" Dan had to ask. After all, he was about to die, and it wasn't as though he could rat on the other guy to the authorities.

"Perry, but no one calls me that." He paused, and out of the corner of his eye Dan could see him pick up the knife again. "I'm sorry, boy, but I have to do this."

Dan nodded and shut his eyes, not willing to see his death coming. There was some movement, the hand on his throat cut off his air supply, and then nothing but pain until he slipped into the blessed oblivion of darkness.

****

Perry punched the steering wheel in disgust, picked up the folder of pictures, and exiting his car, threw his keys at the hovering valet. He walked up to the fancy club which housed Zion's head of operations, nodded at the bouncers, and went in search of the man himself. He found him having a private lap dance in one of the booths, and crossing his arms over his chest he leaned against the wall to wait for the girl to finish.

It seemed ages before she stopped gyrating on the man's lap, and at a click of Zion's fingers, got to her knees, and proceeded to suck his erect dick.

"Is it done?"

Three little words, which made Perry's gut churn anew, delivered as they were without any compassion for the young, vibrant life which the man had put an end to with one text.

In answer, Perry handed him the thick envelope,

and he shut his eyes, as Zion pulled out the first gory picture. Throat cut, the senator's once so beautiful son, lay in a pool of his own blood. Perry resisted the urge to inspect his fingernails. He felt dirty, used, and deeply unhappy. Emotions, which battered his soul. Emotions, which he'd never had to deal with in previous kills.

"You sent these to the relevant people?" Zion asked, and Perry gave a sharp nod.

Zion shut his eyes, and moaned his release, as the perky redhead between his thighs seemingly got him off. Pulling a wad of cash out of his trouser pocket, he stuffed it inside the girl's tiny top, and waved her away.

"Thanks, Trixie, back to work."

The redhead hurried away, and Zion gestured to the seat next to him.

"No, thanks, I prefer to stand," Perry said, and Zion's oriental eyes drew together in a frown.

"Don't think I like that tone, Robson. You've been pissy about this assignment from the start. Something bothering you about this?"

Perry shrugged and ran a hand through his hair, feigning a nonchalance he was far from feeling. It took every ounce of self-control he possessed to not rearrange the guy's smooth features with his fists, truth be told.

"Not a fucking thing," he said.

"Good. I'll make sure these'll hit the newsstands first thing. That should put a nice dent in the senator's bid for presidency. That asshole will rue the day he said no to me, and Beauchamp too. Might not have got to him directly but this will hurt his plans anyway."

The evil smirk that played across Zion's face confirmed what Perry had suspected all along. This had never been about the money for Zion, but Beauchamp had clearly pissed him off in the past, and this was his revenge.

He pulled out a thick envelope stuffed full of cash, and flung it at Perry.

"Gave you some extra, 'cause I reckon you'll wanna lie low for a while, right?"

Perry stuffed the envelope in his leather jacket, and nodded.

"Yeah, I'm going to ground. I've had enough of this shit."

Zion's eyebrows shot to his hairline, but he didn't question Perry further, just waved him away.

"You'll be back when the cash runs out."

Perry didn't bother to grace that with a reply. Instead he made his way out of the heaving club. He had a wrong to right, and in doing so, maybe he could erase the horrific pictures in his mind.

Chapter Five

Dan came round with a gasp, surrounded by light.

"Well, fuck a duck, I made it to heaven after all."

A familiar chuckle penetrated his consciousness, and he gasped at the voice of the man who killed him.

"Afraid not, boy. If it was heaven, you'd have just earned yourself a one way ticket to hell, I reckon."

Perry's amused face appeared in Dan's vision, and his heart turned into a jackhammer, further reiterating the fact that he'd not only said those words out loud, but that he was still very much alive.

"What? How? You killed me?"

He grimaced at the croaky quality of his voice, and, again, Perry's laughter washed over him.

"If I had I'd be lousy at it. No, you, my boy, are very much alive, if slightly altered."

"Altered?"

Belatedly Dan realized that he was neither restrained, nor naked anymore, and the bed seemed to be gently rocking. A quick glance around confirmed that he appeared to be inside the cabin of a ship. The large portholes showed there to be nothing but blue sky, sun, and an endless expanse of water around them, but that couldn't be. Ignoring the quietly intense man by his side, Dan scrambled off the bed, and promptly froze when he caught sight of himself in the mirror on the wall.

A much thicker beard than he'd ever allowed himself to grow covered the lower half of his face. His long hair had been cut off, and what was left of it was an almost military short brown.

"What the fuck have you done to me?"

He spun to glare at the other man, and swallowed

hard when Perry shrugged, and handed him a passport.

"Say hello to the new you. Danny Golden, that's you. Lecturer, and on your honeymoon, with yours truly." Perry pointed to his broad chest, and then shut Dan's mouth for him with a wink. He hadn't even realized it had fallen open, and much to his disgust even that slight touch sent tingles of awareness across his skin.

The air thickened between them with sexual tension, and Dan took a step away. To buy himself time he flicked open the passport. There, his new image stared back at him. Danny Golden, indeed.

"This says I've got green eyes. How?"

Perry pulled a contact lens box out of his shorts and held it up.

"You will have a different eye color with these."

"Son of a fucking gun."

Perry laughed and in the next instant tugged the fake passport out of Dan's hands and taking him by the elbow, steered him back to the bed.

"Sit down, before you fall over, boy. You've had a shock." He walked over to the minibar, pulled out a bottle of eighteen-year-old Macallan single malt Scotch whisky, and poured them both two generous measures. Dan swigged his back without hesitation and the welcome burn as the liquid slid down his gullet to warm his stomach further reiterated that he was very much alive, still, and most importantly free. Free of the name which held him back, free of all the baggage, and…

"Fuck, what about Karen. She'll think I'm dead, she'll ... umph." Perry's large hand clamped over his mouth and stopped his frantic exclamation. He fought, of course, but it was useless. The other man was too strong for him. All Dan achieved was to find himself pinned on the bed with Perry on top of him, and his struggles ceased when he realized what the object poking against his groin was.

"Yeah, I want you boy, but I shan't force you. Not this time." Perry smirked at Dan's sharp intake of breath which made his nostrils flare, and he took his hand off his mouth. Bracing himself either side of Dan's head, he pushed his lower half further against Dan's cock. Naturally his dick stiffened in response, and Dan couldn't help his groan.

"Will you look at that, my little subbie wants me too, it seems. What ever shall we do about that?"

Dan shook his head, and Perry frowned when he brought his hands up and placed them against the man's firm pecs. Damn, there wasn't an ounce of fat anywhere on this man's body, and the vest top Perry wore only served to accentuate the muscled physique underneath.

Without any conscious effort on his part, Dan let his hands wander over Perry's torso, and the other man groaned when he lightly pinched his nipples through the thin fabric of his top.

"Heaven help me, I want you too, *Sir.*"

Perry's dick twitched against his, and before Dan could say anything else, Perry dipped his head and kissed him. Unlike the earlier kisses they'd shared at what seemed a life time ago now, this one reeked of possession. When Dan groaned, Perry took the kiss deeper. Teeth clashed and tongues danced with each other, as the kiss turned ever more passionate. Perry only broke away briefly to yank his top off him. Taking Dan's hands by the wrists he pinned them high above his head, and then used his top to tie them together. He smirked when Dan put up no resistance and claimed his mouth in another passionate kiss.

"I've brought my toys, but if I don't get to fuck you soon, I'll explode. It's been fucking torture, waiting for the drugs I had to give you to wear off." He pulled back and something like remorse crossed the man's features, as was confirmed by his next words. "I'm sorry about keeping you drugged, but it was the only way I could get you out of my house and onto the cruise. Folks simply thought you had one too many, see."

"Did you put me out when you pretended to kill me too?"

Dan hated the wobble in his voice as he recalled that terrifying moment he thought Perry was cutting his throat. Again, Perry surprised him by dropping a kiss on his neck, right where a slight soreness remained.

"I had to make it look real. Zion wanted Senator O'Flynn's son dead, and I had to kill *him*. I figured you wouldn't miss him much."

While that was certainly the truth, pain sliced through his heart at the thought of his little sister. As though he'd read his thoughts, Perry rushed on.

"Karen knows you're alive."

He sat back to study Dan, when he bucked underneath the taller man, and nodded.

"She doesn't know the particulars, and she doesn't know of your new identity, but she does know you're not dead. She is a very bright girl, who will go far in life. I said you'll get in touch when you're able to, and not to listen to the news."

Dan swallowed hard, and shook his head in wonder.

"You did that? For me?" he asked.

****

The wonder in the boy's voice and the way his beautiful blue eyes widened in seeming astonishment soothed the niggling doubts in Perry's mind. He had done what he had to do. The dice had been cast from the moment he'd allowed his personal feelings to interfere in this job. From the first time he'd seen Danny, witnessed the first alleyway blowjob the boy had given, heard his laughter, and seen his smile, Perry had known this was more than just a job.

Had the senator coughed up the cash, he'd have simply sent the boy back to his father. While Danny had seen his face, the drugs he had been given, coupled with the ones he'd have pumped him full of to send him home to Daddy, would have ensured the younger man would not have been able to give a coherent account of what had happened to him, let alone come up with a description to enable the cops to find Perry. It was the same cocktail of drugs that kept the boy out of it for the last two weeks, while Perry had got everything set up to create this new identity for both of them.

It wasn't the first time that Perry had disappeared from view, but it would be the last. He'd saved enough cash to live off for a while, and besides there were legitimate ways of earning a living, which should hopefully keep him off everyone's radar.

When Zion found out that Perry had not only disobeyed his orders, but taken off with the senator's son, there would be hell to pay. Perry counted on the fact that Zion's needs for the kill had been met anyway, and hopefully that would stop the man from wanting Perry's head. Time would tell.

Of course, if Danny should decide to squeal, then they would both be dead men walking. And if his sister blurted the limited amount she knew…

"Sir?"

Danny's hesitant question forced Perry away from those depressing thoughts, and he smiled.

"I did it for me, as much as I did for you."

Another sharp inhale from the man pinned underneath him. One that turned into a groan when Perry flexed his hips so that their cocks rubbed against each other. That action sent delicious friction rippling along his peen but it wasn't enough. He wanted, needed to fuck his boy, to exert his dominance, and to confirm the fact that he hadn't made the biggest mistake of his life in letting the younger man live.

"What do you mean, you did it for you?"

The panted question, coupled with the needy, shaky quality of the other man's voice, made Perry get even harder. He would leave a wet stain on his boxers at this rate. He also didn't miss the fact that Danny still had his arms raised above his head. He'd only tied the boy's wrists together. They weren't secured to the headboard, yet, he'd chosen to follow Perry's orders regardless. His willing submission was a heavy aphrodisiac indeed. Instead of answering him, Perry dipped his head and ran his tongue along the faint mark left behind on the boy's neck. To make it look more real, he'd cut the skin slightly. Not deep enough to do any real harm, but enough to make it look as though he'd sliced Dan's neck. Copious amounts of fake blood had completed the task. It had been the devil of a job to clean up, but the end result had been worth it.

Freedom for them both. Hopefully—a future—together.

Gooseflesh broke out over Danny's skin, and the deep throated moan the other man gave as Perry continued his gentle exploration down along Dan's collarbone, until he could bite one flat nipple through the thin layer of the shirt his subbie was still wearing.

The little nub hardened instantly and Dan hissed trough his teeth. Pinching the other nipple with his fingers, Perry briefly lifted his head and smirked up at him.

"Do you want to discuss my reasons, or shall we just fuck?"

Dan groaned and shook his head.

"I've always said talking is overrated. So, for the love of God, fuck me already."

Perry hid his grin and bit down on the nipple lovingly outlined by the now wet fabric of the man's shirt.

Danny boy flinched, and groaned when Perry lifted off him completely.

"I shouldn't fuck you at all, if you can't ask me niccly, boy."

"Sorry, Sir, please. I want you."

His eyed widened when Perry stepped away and shrugged out his clothes. His insolent pup licked his lips when Perry's cock sprang free, and Perry rubbed his hand up and down his shaft for some much needed relief. Pre-cum seeped out of the swollen head of his dick, and having swiped his thumb through it, he stepped back up to the bed and held it up for his subbie.

"As you've remembered your manners, here, have a taste, and tell me how much you want my cock."

Danny wrapped his full lips around the digit and it was Perry's turn to groan at the way the boy wrapped his tongue around that finger, and sucked in an erotic imitation of sucking peen.

Perry slapped the other man's thigh, and Danny let go off his thumb with the most adorable pout.

"Enough, boy. Next time you can suck my dick. Right now, I need to fuck you, and you're wearing far too many clothes still." He picked up his ever present knife off the bed stand and Danny's breathing sped up further.

"I see you remember my favorite toy?"

He laughed at Danny's nod, and taking the knife to the hem of the man's shirt, sliced it clean off of him, until it lay in tatters around him. For old time's sake he traced the boy's tats with the knife briefly, and then brought it down to Danny's crotch. He was tenting his shorts most satisfactorily, and grunted his need, as Perry traced the outline of the boy's cock through the fabric.

"Such a pretty cock." Abandoning the knife, he reached inside the waistband, and pulling the shorts and boxer briefs away, he grasped hold of his subbie's dick, while he yanked the clothing further down and out of his way. Danny helped him by lifting his butt and kicking the material the rest of the way off, until he was gloriously naked in front of him.

Using his teeth, Perry grasped hold of the other man's piercing, while he pumped his hand up and down the long shaft a few times. That organ swelled and pulsed and Danny's hips lifted into every stroke, telling Perry how close his subbie was to exploding. In truth, Perry wasn't far off shooting his load either.

Jerking off in the shower to images of Danny boy's full lips around Perry's junk had been a piss poor substitute for the real thing. Especially as it wouldn't have taken much persuasion on his part to simply fuck the boy while he'd been out of it on the drugs. Perry wasn't such a bastard, however, that he would take anyone without his consent, let alone a man he'd been half way in love with ever since he'd first laid eyes on him.

Love was the stuff of fairytales and romantic fools. Tender feelings had hitherto held no place in Perry's life, but like it or not, he couldn't ignore the tight feeling in his chest every time the boy's baby blues landed on him, nor the very palpable evidence of how out of character he had acted around the boy. Still was for that matter. Why else would he have chosen the cover of a married couple on their honeymoon for this cruise? He could have just left the boy somewhere with his memories scrambled, but that would have meant he'd have been at the mercy of anyone, and no one was going to touch this man's soft skin, or drink in the little sounds he made in the back of his throat as he hurtled toward release.

Danny boy was his, dammit.

"How close are you, boy?" he asked and flicked a glance up his new subbie's delectable body. He would have such fun exploring every dip and valley of those hard muscles, and seeing his boy squirm as he tortured him a bit, before he let him come, again, and again, and again. It was one of the many reasons he had chosen a cruise to the Bahamas, rather than taking a flight. Besides, the best place to hide was in full view of people. No one would expect the two of them to be on an Ocean Cruise liner, and the state cabin afforded all the luxury and privacy they needed to establish the boundaries of their future relationship and to truly get to know each other.

And he sure as fuck hoped they had one and this wasn't a completely one-sided deal. He didn't think it was, but that could just be his ego talking.

He went down all the way, and Perry grinned around his mouthful of cock, when Danny boy screwed his eyes shut and shook his head. Grazing his teeth along the other man's magnificent shaft as he came up, he licked up the spicy essence leaking from the head of his lover's dick, while he fondled Danny's heavy balls. They drew tight, further signaling how much on the edge the other man was.

"You'd best not be coming before I'm in that gorgeous ass of yours, boy."

"No, Sir, but, please, hurry. I'm so damn close. I need you inside me."

Those husky words were music to Perry's ears, and he wasted no time in pushing the other man's legs up to his chest, while he scooted lower and sucked Danny's balls into his mouth.

"Fuck, please … I can't." Reaching up, he squeezed the base of Danny's shaft to stop him from orgasming and licked his way down toward the little puckered hole he needed to claim. He nibbled and licked around it, and worked the tight ring until Danny boy relaxed enough for him to slip his tongue inside. Dan made an unintelligible sound, and Perry stepped up his efforts to tongue fuck the other man's ass to prepare him for taking his cock.

"Please…"

Perry withdrew his tongue, and pulling Danny boy's ass cheeks apart, spat right into the tiny hole, before he came up for air and reached for the lube.

Dan watched him through hooded eyes, cheeks flushed in his arousal, and perspiration covering his skin. Such a beautiful sight that it made him wish he could prolong this moment, but if he didn't bury himself balls deep in that tight ass soon, he'd disgrace himself.

Lubing up his fingers, he squeezed a generous dollop into the boy's crack and then used his slick digits to work the lube inside. Danny's moans increased and his cock stood tall and erect, the head so swollen it had to be painful. Perry dropped a kiss on the thick tip, and Danny groaned.

"I know, boy, soon. Let me just prepare you."

"Fuck that, just do me already. I'm good." The most fascinating all over body flush spread over his subbie and Perry raised an eyebrow.

"Sir, *please,* make me yours."

Perry's heart gave some very suspicious bumps at that plea, and when he looked up, it was to see the same raw need he felt reflected back at him. It might just be the circumstances talking here, but he'd fucking take that look and run with it.

He somehow managed to roll a condom on with trembling fingers, slathered yet more lube along his sheathed length, and then lined his cock head up with the little hole calling him.

"You plead so nicely, boy. Let me in."

Perry pushed in slowly, and Danny let out a shaky breath. The tight ring of muscle gave way and he swore under his breath, as he bottomed out in the warm clasp of his lover's butt.

A keening sound came from Danny, and bracing himself on his hands to keep his weight off him, he pulled out, until only his thick head stretched the tiny hole. Seeing Danny all stretched around his dick robbed him of what little control he had left, and he thrust back in.

Dan groaned his name, and it was all the permission he required to set the pace he needed to chase his rapidly building orgasm.

"Fuck, yes. I'm … argh."

Perry increased his thrusts in and out of other man, as Danny exploded in a seemingly never ending arch of jizz, which covered both their abdomens. Their gazes locked, and Perry gave himself over to his own release, brought on by the rhythmic clenching of Dan's asshole which sent shockwaves along his dick. As he filled the condom, Perry claimed Danny's mouth in a kiss that he never wanted to end, before he lost the ability to hold himself up and collapsed on top of his lover.

Spent, gasping for breath, he rested his head on the other man's sweat slickened chest, Danny's staccato heartbeat an echo of his own thundering heart rate. When his vision cleared and the feeling returned to his limbs, he gently withdrew his softening penis from the other man's ass, and rolled off him. Having disposed of the spent condom by tying it off and throwing it in the waste paper basket, he reached across to untie Danny's arms, and dropped another kiss on his lips.

It was meant to be a mere brush of his lips across Danny's but the boy surprised him by grabbing hold of his hair and pulling him down for a longer kiss. Perry gladly relinquished control for the few precious moments that kiss lasted, because the sheer passion behind it took his breath away and made his heart sing. It was a kiss which promised so much more, as though Danny, too, needed this contact, and when they finally broke apart, both of them were grinning like fools.

"What was that for, boy?" Perry asked, and Danny's cheekbones turned pink under Perry's close scrutiny.

"Nothing, everything." When Perry pulled back better to study him, Danny boy blushed even more.

"That encompasses a whole lot, boy. I'd like to think it was for the sex we just had, but I know I can do better than that. I usually last longer, for starters."

Perry's grin deepened and that insistent flare of hope inside his chest blossomed into a raging inferno when Danny shook his head, seemingly outraged.

"The sex was awesome. I came so fucking hard I'm still seeing stars. If that wasn't you at your best, I dare say I won't be able to walk at all once you do show me your best." He dropped his gaze to Perry's collarbone as he spoke and the sweetly submissive tell meant Perry felt himself harden anew.

Danny's eyes widened when he noticed and a coy smile appeared on his face. It deepened the cute dimples in his cheeks, and Perry pulled him back in for another kiss that left them both breathless again.

"You can count on it, boy."

"Count on what?" Danny asked and Perry laughed.

"Not being able to walk when I'm done with you. Though, I have to tell you." He paused and, grasping the other man's chin, tilted his head until Danny had no choice but to look at him. "I may never be done with you."

"You won't?" There was such a hopeful note in the younger man's voice Perry felt ten feet tall.

"Nope. Look, I … shit, you can tell me to fuck off, but I want to explore this thing between us. And I don't want you to feel obliged to stay with me, because I didn't kill you, or any of that nonsense, but because you want to be with me."

Danny pulled in a sharp breath, and when he scooted away from him, Perry's black heart shattered into a million pieces. He could swear he could hear the tiny parts echo through his soul, but he made no move to stop the other man.

"And if I don't want to stay with you, what will you do then?" he asked.

"Nothing."

"Nothing? You expect me to believe that?"

Danny's voice had risen much higher than his usual cadence in his agitation, and sighing, Perry swung his legs off the bed and yanked his shorts back on. It didn't seem right to have this conversation when he was buck naked. Not that Danny seemed to have any problems with his own nakedness. No, the boy sat there in his birthday suit, to all intents and purposes not affected at all.

"You asked me earlier why I did what I did, and I'll explain my reasoning now. I've been toying with the idea of getting out for a while now. I just didn't have a reason to, until I met you."

Danny boy gasped and Perry nodded.

"You didn't deserve to be pulled into the power

games involving your father, Beauchamp and my former employer. I don't know the details and I'm sure I don't want to know, but this whole thing was a set up to get back at Beauchamp. It was never about the ransom, unless you count your life, and I was not prepared to let that be ransomed. I don't kill innocents let alone those I…" He couldn't bring himself to say the words out loud, and ran a shaky hand through his hair instead. Much to his surprise, Danny intercepted that move and when he looked at him, the other man's blue eyes had softened from their previous icy glacier to the soft warm baby blues, Perry would so miss when they were hidden behind the essential green contacts.

"Don't clam up on me now, Sir. Those that you what?" Danny asked.

Putting his heart and his very life on the line to be trampled all over, if the other man didn't feel the same way, Perry said the words burning a hole in the fabric of his soul.

"Those that I care about, okay."

"Only care? Seems to me you went through an awful lot of trouble for me, if you only care about me." The boy had the audacity to wink at him, and Perry held up one finger.

"Keep up that sass and your ass will be a nice shade of red before I let you go, boy."

Rather than be chagrined by that, his Danny boy smiled, and flipping over on his belly, presented his ass. Perry groaned and his half erect cock surged to full mast when the younger man wiggled those perfectly shaped pale globes at him.

"Do your worst then, Sir, because I have no wish to go anywhere."

"You don't?"

Even to his own ears, Perry's voice sounded

hoarse and he sat down on the bed, before his suddenly
shaky legs failed to support him any longer.

Danny turned on his side so he could face him,
and the utter sincerity he read in the other man's eyes
took Perry's breath away.

"No, I don't. You're not the only one who wanted
to get away, and couldn't. You've given me a new start, a
brand new life away from my father's toxic influence. I
never thought I would achieve it. At least not for years to
come. Not, until Karen came of age and was free to make
her own decisions. I was going to help her break free
then, if she wanted my help. You made this all happen so
much sooner, and for that reason alone I want to stay.
Besides, with everything else going on, I know I'll sleep
better at night, knowing that I have you to watch over me,
Sir."

"Right."

Perry was beginning to sound like a caveman with
the monosyllabic responses which seemed to be the only
sounds he was capable of producing right now. Then
again, he would appear to have an elephant sitting on his
chest, because the simple act of getting oxygen into his
lungs seemed extraordinarily difficult.

"I guess what I'm trying to say and seem to be
making a hash out of is that I *care* about you too, Sir. A
damn great big deal, and I want to explore this thing
between us, too. After all, we seem to be on our
honeymoon, right?"

Danny winked at him, and then rolled back on his
front.

"So, will you please punish me as you see fit, Sir,
and show me what it means to be yours?"

All the little broken pieces of his heart slotted
back into place as Perry brought his hand on his boy's
ass. The action left a very satisfactory hand print behind,

so he did it again, and again. When his hand tired, Perry switched to using one of his flip flops, and soon enough Danny moaned into every stroke, while he pushed his hips into the covers in a seeming effort to get off. Perry, too, was once again hard, and after delivering one last resounding swat to Danny's glowing butt, he threw the footwear on the floor and massaged the hot flesh.

A deep throated groan came from the man on the bed, and, abandoning the stinging globes, he pulled Danny's head around so that he could kiss him.

The sheer desperate need in which his subbie kissed him back told him all he needed to know, and breaking the kiss, he rested his forehead on Danny's and smiled.

"You do realize that I'm not ever going to let you go now, right? I own you, boy."

Danny smiled.

"I'm counting on that, Sir."

The End

www.dorisoconnor.com

COLLECTING HIS DEBT

Angelique Voisen

Copyright © 2016

Chapter One

The Debt Collector

Eight o'clock and right on the dot, Carter Slater strolls out of his apartment building whistling a tune under his breath. Like the night before, he looks perfect, or close to it. He curses, nearly slipping on the wet sidewalk. I almost yank my car door open and give myself away, but Carter manages to right himself at the last second. Looks like all his punishing college football training—three hours a day, five days a week, is paying off.

I savor those few precious seconds when he checks for his phone and bends down to pluck it from the sidewalk, giving me a perfect view of his tight ass and the powerful muscles of his calves and thighs. Number forty-seven of the Red Sharks is a looker.

Blond, blue-eyed, and a good old Catholic boy, Carter's a Greek god in human skin, except he harbors a secret that can wreck all he's worked hard to achieve. Carter plays for my football team, and he's already made that one grievous error that will ruin his career. You see, I know everything about my golden boy. All his flaws, dirty little secrets, and the needs he's ashamed of. I know the name of the town where he grew up in, the fact Carter left the home the moment he turned eighteen, and even the name of his first mutt—everything on file, but records can only tell me so much.

When he sleeps, I capture him through my lens, nestled in the nook of the ancient oak tree strategically right outside his bedroom window. Sleep eludes Carter lately though and I know the reason why.

Carter picks up his ringing phone. "I'll be there in fifteen minutes."

It's a trap. I want to walk up to Carter, grab his shoulders and shake some sense into him. Better yet, I want to lash his wrists to my bedroom and convince Carter he needs no one else but me. Too bad, Carter's wasting his hopes and his heart over a fucker who plans on dishing real hurt on him with a couple of his buddies. Carter gets into his ride and continues humming under his breath.

For a moment, he pauses, looks around, and every muscle in my body freezes up. I grip the wheel of my old Mustang until my scarred knuckles turn white. If Carter sees me, he'll run straight for the hills without looking back.

I'm not a good man, and I've never pretended to be. The truth is written all over my skin, in ink and scars. Most people have the tendency to look away when a monster is peering back at them from the dark and Carter is no different.

Shrugging, Carter starts his engine and after five minutes, I follow at a discrete pace. Taped to the dashboard is a yellowing piece of paper, an old piece of news long forgotten by most of the world, but I don't forget easy. I know each word of the article by heart.

Chief Phil Slater, Carter's father, the chief-of-police, ruined my life ten years ago when he sentenced me to a ten-year prison sentence over a simple drug bust. Only one thing kept me going while I festered behind bars and left behind my humanity. There's an outstanding debt between the chief and I.

Carter is mine and I intend to collect my dues. My golden boy's hell on wheels today, passing all the red lights. His excitement almost rubs off on me, but I remember my purpose. In the back of my trunk lies rope and tranquilizer darts. An extra gun for emergencies, but I hope it will never come to that.

"You're about to find out I'm the lesser evil, baby," I keep my car a quarter of a mile away from his.

Carter parks his car by the curb of a noisy bar. I park mine three cars away and Carter doesn't suspect a thing. His focus is completely on Rodrick Gibson, backstabbing fucker and teammate, and the guy Carter bared his heart to a week ago. They trade jokes, but it's all an elaborate play to distract Carter.

Envy and rage colors my vision red the moment Carter brushes his fingertips over Rodrick's arm. Rod draws away and tries to brush it off with a joke. Carter doesn't see two of Rod's sniggering buddies hiding behind the alleyway, toting matching baseball bats. These juvenile brats think they're hard assess, pretenders who'll croak and plead in the end, when the real monsters come out. I don't bother knowing their names, because they're all walking dead men. Rod, I'm saving for the last, because I want to wring every last scream out of his scrawny throat.

I get out of the car, my footsteps barely making a sound on the gravel. Rod begins to pull Carter into the alley, pretending to tug at his shirt for a kiss.

"Let's go someplace private," I hear Rod say.

I crack my knuckles. Adrenaline sings in my

veins. I lose it when Rod teases the first ragged scream out of my Carter. A muffled groan follows and I announce my presence. Thrashing on the ground, Carter tries to get up, but Rod delivers a vicious kick to his ribs. Carter coughs out blood and I nearly crack, but these fuckers don't deserve a quick and easy end.

A ring of bruises begin to show around Carter's neck. A cut on his forehead leaves a trail of blood down the left side of his face. Cronies one and two smack the heads of the bats on their palms, wearing identical sneers on their faces. Each time the aluminum slaps flesh, Carter cringes, knowing it's his flesh about to take a beating.

"Three against one seems fucking unfair, boys."

They jerk at the sound of my voice, like guilty children caught doing something wrong. Rod's cronies eye me up and down, their resolve shattering when I pull out the revolver from the inside of my jacket or maybe they glimpse what I look like under my hoodie. I click the safety off, and put my finger on the comforting trigger. With the silencer and the noise from the bar, no one is going to hear us.

"Better move along asshole, if you know what's good for you," Rod threatens. "You don't know who you're messing with."

Wrong. I know every little detail about the fucker Carter's holding a torch for, including where Rod and his loved ones live.

"All bark and no action, pup?" I pull the trigger and Rod howls.

Blood begins to spread across his jeans and I smile. Some of my fellow inmates back in prison say my smile is the worst part of me, not my impressive collection of scars. Rod's two accomplices back away, abandoning their bats. A second's hesitation can mean dire consequences, but my mind is clear of doubts, of morals. Two pulls and two more screams add to the cacophony started by Rod's original score. They drag their sorry-ass bodies on the dirty gravel, leaving a trail of blood.

Police sirens wail in the background, annoying the hell out of me. Someone saw and tattled. A bystander perhaps, but it doesn't matter. My scarred lips twist in distaste. Enduring more time behind bars is not in the itinerary, enjoying my prize is. I aim my faithful Colt right at Rod's groin, the perfect target.

"Don't kill them. Please," a voice rasped.

I whirl, brows furrowing, to find my golden boy, a tad bloody and banged up, leaning against the brick wall. Looking like a miserable piece of pummeled meat, his amazing blue eyes are blazing with strange conviction, some silly notion of chivalry. Even like that, Carter looks no less perfect, swollen lips practically begging me to take them.

"They deserve to die." I state the obvious truth, unsure why I bother to explain myself.

"They do, but you're better than that."

Some call me the Debt Collector, a cleaner, a monster, but Carter says I'm better. What a hoot. I let out a bitter and hollow laugh. "You don't know a single thing about me, golden boy."

I'm about to prove my point, to give Rod a new hole to worry about, but Carter's words stop me cold.

"You saved me. I know enough."

The idiotic confidence of youth stuns me, shouldn't mean a thing to me, but from Carter's lips, they feel like the Ten Commandments. I wonder if he'll come to regret those words. Easy to mistake me for a savior now, when one's on the verge of being beaten to death. Dizzy from the beating, Carter can't see all too well in the dark. Once he's inside my well-built prison, he'll learn what I really am. If Carter's smart, he'll accept our roles as captor and captive, and take what I plan to give. Fuck, thinking about the things I want to do to him makes me hard, even now.

The sirens grow distinct, too close for comfort. Three bullets for three bullets, easy-peasy, but for some reason, the colt feels heavy in my hand—an alien feeling. Warning bells go off in my head. Carter is trouble, but I'm too deep in this hole to pull myself out now. I never leave a kill unfinished, but tonight is the first for everything it seems. Besides, no one will connect me to these boys. Disappearing is what I do best.

Ignoring the groaning bodies, I walk to Carter and hunker down. His eyelids flicker, like he's fighting to stay conscious. Did his internal circuits start to scream "stranger danger" in his head? Carter's mouth opens, closes, as if he's trying to form words, but can't. Fuck, everything about him drives me mad, especially that mouth. I can imagine Carter putting those perfect lips to good use, wrapping themselves around my dick.

Leaning forward, I steal a kiss, the first of many. I taste copper and mint on his breath, a heady combination. To my shock, Carter responds. It's out of reflex more than anything else, but I savor his compliance, like we're sharing a dirty little secret the rest of the world can't begin to comprehend. When I pull away, he lets out a cute little moan. Wanting more, I imagine. I tuck my gun away, keeping one eye over Rod and his crew, still moaning in pain. Perfect.

Despite his bulk, I heft him with ease over my shoulder. Run my hand over the well-formed muscles of his calves.

"I'm not your white knight, golden boy. I'm your worst nightmare."

I'm not sure Carter hears. By the time I place him

carefully in the backseat of my car, he's unconscious. Whistling, I get back to the driver's seat and slot the key in. I didn't even need to use any rope, or the tranquilizers. A police cruiser arrives on the scene fifteen minutes later, according to the news, but I'm well out of the way then. Behind me, Carter stirs, moans in his sleep, and I smile.

Mission accomplished, but I'm far from done collecting my debt.

I drive back to my place, to a lesser known neighborhood in the city I'm pretty sure Carter and his ilk doesn't know exists. Night is when the underworld truly comes alive. Hookers ply their trade, hanging by lamplights, stalking their prey. Dealers lie further in the shadows, if you know where to look for them. No one notices me drive by. According to police records, the real me died in a prison fight, body buried God knows where. I like to think of it as rebirth, a second chance, a golden opportunity.

Further I go, until I'm on the outskirts to a former housing development abandoned in the 90s. My ramshackle house is no different from the others on the street, but it's the perfect base of operations. For one, the houses are far apart. No one can hear Carter scream, or if they did, no one will care. The chief won't think to look for Carter here.

I park the car in my garage, get out, and take a few seconds admiring my conquest.

"No one's coming for you, golden boy. You're beyond salvation now."

Chapter Two

Carter

"Where the fuck are you hiding, you useless piece of shit?"

Slamming doors, a loud crash, and the sound of splintering wood follows Dad's voice. Heavy footsteps thud on the hardwood floors, meaning he's wearing boots. Not hard to imagine all that hard leather colliding with flesh. I cringe, making myself as small as possible. The dark can only hide and protect me for so long. My heart beats so hard against my chest I'm certain sooner or later it will burst. I taste bile in my mouth and my breaths come out short.

Rubbing my clammy hands together, I look at the shelves above my head for anything I can use as a weapon. What use is defiance, if it will only make him madder, and the punishment worse?

His footsteps come to a sudden halt. I can practically hear his heavy breathing outside the closet door. The door hinges creak, the suspense ratchets my fear into another level and he knows it, savors it while he spouts biblical passages, telling me he's doing this for my own good. I imagine I'm victim number thirteen in a B-rate horror movie, about to meet my maker in the form of the axe-murderer, except this is real life. Mine.

The door opens all the way. The light hurts my eyes, illuminates Dad's looming figure above me. I don't know how long I've been here, hiding, while he wrecks everything in sight. Dad's not usually like this. He was much better when Mom was alive, or so his deputies say when I come visit him in the station, bruises peeking from the sleeves of my jacket.

"Little fucker, there you are." His eyes gleam

black under the bright light. On hands and knees, I back away, retreating to where, I have no clue, but his hand grabs a handful of my shirt and tosses me out. The force of his throw sends me sprawling on the carpeted floor. My ears catch the awful sound of leather slithering from his belt loops and I know what's coming for me.

"Did you think I wouldn't know you kissed another boy, you little fag?" Dad slaps the leather against his palm, the impact making me wince. I look up, angry, ready to fight, except all my resolve withers. There's another man standing beside Dad. He's young, and handsome, except for the sneer on his face. I know him, or I thought I did. My gaze slips past his face. He's wearing a football jersey with a familiar number and name.

"Rod," I whisper. "Help me. Save me."

Rod's lips, lips I imagine kissing, curve into a knowing smile. It's the kind of smile a hunter gives to his prey before going for the kill.

****

I jolt up, awake, and all my aches from the beating flare up. Sweat coats my bare back. I look down, uncomprehending, seeing bandages across my chest. I'm wearing unfamiliar jogging pants. I clutch at unfamiliar sheets, heart thumping hard against my chest at the old nightmare.

"Fucking nightmare given a new face-lift," I mutter to myself.

The awful moment rewinds in my head—Rod closing his hand on my wrist, the grip hard enough to bruise, and his breath against my ear, telling me we'll take this somewhere private. I remember feeling giddy with excitement, sensing a secret kind of promise in Rod's rough handling. Playing football hadn't just been a way to appease my dad, I loved the punishing exercises.

61

It's the reason why I play linebacker. Rod hisses out a word, wrecking all my fantasies of that evening. *"Faggot."*

What came after? Muddled images fill my head. Rod wanted Bron and Barry to break my legs, when someone else intervened—my mysterious scarred savior in a black hoodie, carrying a gun. Head swimming in pain, I couldn't make out most of his features, but I do remember the way his slate-gray eyes burned in his sockets and that smile—if you can call a crooked line a smile.

Something's broken in him, I had thought back then, but what does it say about me, when I silently willed him to do it? Pull the trigger. End Rod, Bron, and Barry's lives, because the world will be a much better place without dicks like them and my father.

I let out an involuntary shudder, and pull the blanket over my shoulders. A blanket, I note, that isn't hospital issued. I know, because I spent plenty of time there in my childhood.

Panic sets in me. I survey my surroundings, taking in what I find with a nervous swallow. Boarded windows, peeling plaster, and pieces of clobbered furniture decorate the space that smells of time and neglect. A single flickering light bulb illuminates the space. Even the frame of the metal bed I lie on is a rusted black monstrosity, but the sheets and pillow smell like fabric softener.

"Don't panic, Carter. Breathe. Think." I breathe in and out. Silently count to ten in my head. *I'm in a serial killer's den,* is the first thing that comes to mind. Then again, I possess a vivid imagination. I swing my legs off the bed, or try to. Something cold and thin tightens around my left ankle. A chain, I realize a second later.

"Are you finally awake, golden boy?" A deep

amused voice says from somewhere in the room.

Suppressing the urge to scream, hurl obscenities, or make demands, I focus on the source. My gaze finds one corner of the room I didn't notice earlier, the one spot where the light doesn't reach. A figure sits on a run-down armchair too small for his size.

"Have you been watching me all this time?"

"What do you think? I like to fucking admire my prize."

"Prize? Me?" I let out a hollow laugh. If only this stranger knew the truth. I'm no one's treasure. "Come out where I can see you. Please."

Instinct makes me add the last word and it works. I settle for sitting on the edge of the bed. I know I can't go far with the chain restricting my movements. He rises from the armchair and I silently take stock of my captor. On the floor, I notice the same black hoodie he wore hours, or can it be, days ago? He's a behemoth, a monster in a plain black tee and faded jeans.

Six-feet, broad-shouldered, black ink and white scars cover his golden skin. Every inch of him is roughly hewn muscle. He has a sinewy kind of build that's not earned from the gym but from hard labor. Intense iron-gray eyes stare back at me from a face that could have been handsome, if not for the minor imperfections—a nose broken a couple of times, and a strange crisscross of white scars dissecting his nose and left cheek.

One look and I know he's a real predator. Quiet menace emanates from him and even my father pales in comparison to this guy. He doesn't need words or to use those massive fists to make his point. The only difference? The old terror that renders me into a mess when my father comes into a room is absent here.

"Are you going to kill me?" My voice sounds calm, strange, like my mouth and body no longer belong to me.

He reaches me and my heart thuds in fear and incomprehensible anticipation. I look up at him, daring him to make the next move. Logic defies my action. Any rational being will fight and claw his way to freedom, but I'm not one of them. My dad says I'm born wrong, not just because of my sexuality, but my internal mechanism isn't the same as everyone else's.

This stranger says I'm his prize, helpless, and his to toy with, but that's not entirely true. Bruised and bloody, I knew there's something broken in him, because I see myself in him. I don't even know his name and he might know everything about me, but we're alike.

Grabbing my chin, he tilts my head up, so I'm looking into his face. Christ, those eyes. They tell me secrets I don't want to know, and call to all the dark parts of me I make sure to hide from my father, my teammates, and the entire world for fear of discovery.

What did it matter? I told my very own angel of death to spare Rod, Bron, and Barry. If they live, my secret would come out, and ruin my career. I tell myself I play football to get back at my father, to prove I can make something out of myself, but despite all that, I'm still that scared little boy, eager to please. Where did that get me? I tried to be what my family wanted—good little Catholic boy, loyal son, everyone's golden boy, but I'm tired of being what I'm not.

My father will hunt me down if word gets out about the truth he's worked so hard to hide, even though we haven't spoken in years. The chief's done with teaching lessons. He'll make certain I'm lying in the dirt.

Did I even love Rod, or is what I want the allure of the forbidden?

I don't have anything to lose. I'm free and it feels fucking good, amazing even.

"You shouldn't be looking at me like that, golden boy," he says, voice harsh.

I can hear the longing in his voice, and the pain he tries to hide. "How am I looking at you?"

"This isn't going the way I fucking thought it would. I thought you'd have more fight in you."

"You saved me," I state, but he frowns, furrowing his dark brows, not understanding. "You almost sound disappointed."

He barks out a laugh, the sound like gravel, but it sends a flutter in my belly. Fuck, but he's exactly my type. The kind of guy I go for, because I'm sure he won't disappoint in giving me the kind of sex and right amount of pain I crave.

"I didn't save you because I want to be model fucking citizen of the year. You're mine, golden boy. Mine to torment and tease, break apart and build back up again."

I let out an involuntary shiver, triggering his jagged smile, bringing my attention to his mouth. There's a pearl-like scar on his bottom lip. They're thin lips, cruel lips not made for kissing but taking. God, did I want them, to taste him and his heat. He only needs to look down, to see my dick pressing up against the jogging pants. Did they belong to him too?

"Kiss me. Please." The words tumble out of me before I can stop. I don't know what's wrong with me, why I choose to flirt instead of finding possible escape routes. When he touches my cheek with his large callused hand, I lean into it, like a needy cat denied of touch for so long.

"What the fuck is wrong with you?"

"I ask myself that question every day." He moves his hand past my cheek, fastening his fingers on the nape of my neck, squeezing, wrangling a moan from my lips.

"Kiss me." I repeat. This time he doesn't deny me.

"Stand up." I rise to my feet, shaky, aware of his hand burning like a brand on the back of my neck, so possessive, so certain. He bands one arm across my waist, tugging me close until my flesh touches his. There's nowhere to run, but into his embrace.

"Kiss—"

"Shut the fuck up." He takes my lips before I can draw breath. All tongue and teeth, it's a punishing kind of kiss, the right kind. Yielding, responding, I bite back, catching his scarred lower lip with my teeth. I rub my body against his, and yes, I feel the bulge of his jeans pressing against the cotton fabric of my sweats.

He pulls away first, nostrils flaring, reminding me of a wolf caught off guard. "You make a habit of kissing strangers, golden boy?"

"Why do you call me that?" I ask, panting, although all we've done is kiss.

"Don't like it?" He peels his lips back, baring white, slightly crooked teeth. I almost expect canines to emerge. He brushes his rough stubbled cheek against mine, breath brushing against my left ear. "You're fucking perfect."

"I'm far from that. I'm the exact opposite. Perfect outside, dirty inside, that's what my father always said."

"Your father." He snarls at the word like it's a curse, before continuing, "Is a walking dead man."

"I don't want to talk about him. Not when you're holding me like this."

It's odd, to be able to look into the eyes of someone else bigger than me, to be able to fit into his arms like we're made for each other. I'm a romantic, I know, and I doubt the word "romance" exists in this stranger's dictionary. I can't exactly call him my captor any longer if I'm a willing accomplice. Hell. I don't even need Stockholm Syndrome for him to break and tame me.

"Who knew it would be this easy to own you, golden boy?"

"Own me?" My heart skips a beat. Nothing about him screams safe, sane or consensual, but every muscle in my body feels alive and my blood sings with adrenaline. The way I react to his every word and deed stumps me, frightens me, but it's too late to stop now.

"It's not just your body I want, golden boy. By the end of this all, your heart and soul will be mine too."

"Greedy bastard, I don't even know your name."

"They call me the Debt Collector."

"That's what you want me to call you?"

He steals a kiss from me without warning, but the moment his mouth descends on mine, my insides melt. Electricity of the carnal variety zips down my chest to my thickening dick. It's crazy the way my body reacts to him, but I can't help it. He's like a drug. Once I get a taste, I want more.

"Insolence tastes fucking fine on you, golden boy." He pulls away, and shoves me back on the bed.

"I thought you were going to fuck me?" My voice sounds whiny to my own ears.

"Not when you're like this, when you're thinking about that fucker whose dick I should have shot."

"Rod?" I stare at him, speechless. What right did he have, to be jealous? He's not even my anything, yet anyway. The world didn't have a label for what we have—this bizarre relationship.

"Don't think of going anywhere, golden boy. If you run, I'll chase you down and teach you a lesson you won't fucking forget."

I cross my arms, glaring at him. To make my point, I tug at my ankle. "Oh yeah, I have plenty of appointments to keep. People to meet."

"You have a game this Tuesday—three days from now, classes to attend, and a paper to submit," he lists my chores, tasks I can't remember, using his finger to count them off.

Sitting up on the bed, I open my mouth, close it. How can I forget about the game? Three days from Tuesdays—which means I've been out for a day. Guilt rams into me when I think about the rest of my teammates. I narrow my eyes in realization.

"How long were you watching me?"

"Nightmares plague you every time you sleep, but when you don't dream, you almost look like a fucking angel, golden boy. You can't imagine the number of times I wanted to enter your window and bury my cock into you until you woke up."

Fear, the real kind, crawls down my spine as the gravity of the situation hits me for the first time. I swallow, feeling his huge hand wrapping around my throat. He applies some pressure, not enough to bruise, but to remind me who holds all the power here.

"You won't hurt me, Collector." How I manage to say those words without an ounce of hesitation stuns me and him. It's in my nature to shove back when someone pushes me.

He thumbs my racing pulse, regarding me. "Maybe I ought to stuff that smart mouth of yours with my cock to shut you up."

"Go ahead, baby. You can't imagine how I've missed the taste of cock. I have a feeling yours won't disappoint."

Hand not leaving my neck, he uses his other to mutely unbutton the top of his jeans. With my hands free, I assist him the rest of the way, unzipping his fly. No boxers or briefs. He lets me pull out his dick and for a couple of seconds. I can't do anything but stare. Massive, long, and erect, I don't think I've had anything that huge in me.

"Having second thoughts now, golden boy?"

It irks me each time he calls me that, and he knows it. The fact he waits for my answer confirms my suspicion. If he's waited so long to kidnap me, he'll want to play with his new toy. This isn't a game. I know that. Those huge hands are capable of easily breaking bones, or strangling me to death, but for some reason, I feel safe with him.

"No." I hold his gaze. "And my fucking name is Carter. Do you need me to spell it out on your dick for you?"

Chapter Three

The Debt Collector

I remember Cater asking me if I'm disappointed. Far from it, because in all the scenarios I imagine in my head, none of them headed this way. I know Carter has guts, possesses steel in his back bone, but fuck, I didn't think he could be a defiant little hell cat. Licking my lips, I meet his blazing baby blues. I plan to wait a couple more days for Carter's bruises and cuts to heal before sinking my dick into his tight little ass, but that plan flew out the window the moment he put his hand on the zipper of my jeans.

Fucking hell, I don't know why I let Carter affect me this much. Each time he does something off script, it makes me want him even more. I nudge my leaking tip between his lips, half wondering if he'll bite.

"Show me how much you want my cock, baby." *Baby.* Carter called me that first. A mocking term of endearment, but it feels right on my lips.

"It would be my pleasure, Master, Sir, Debt Collector, whatever your real name is."

Christ. This kid has a bite to him, but I never back away from any challenge. I push my cock head into his mouth, insistent. Carter flicks his tongue out, licking away my pre-cum with relish, as if he's enjoying a nice ice cream cone. I shift my hand from his throat and sink them into his gorgeous crown of golden hair. Like this, he's perfect.

I let him run the show for the next couple of minutes, marveling at his skill. Most men I've fucked didn't like sucking cock. They can make all the fake moans they want, trying to please me, but in the end, it's all scripted.

Carter is the genuine deal. The intense expression on his face captivates me. He traces me from crown to root with his tongue, while I harden with each lick. Carter reminds me of a greedy kitten, his pink tongue darting out to explore every inch of me. He teases a groan from me when he takes my left ball into his mouth, applying suction, before giving my right one the same attention.

"That's enough playing around." Carter pauses, looks up at me, as if waiting for my next command.

A part of me wonders if this is some elaborate game he's playing. Is he waiting for me to let my guard down before making his escape and bringing the authorities on me? I doubt he'll go to dear daddy though, judging by the pure undiluted hate on his face whenever he mentions the chief. *Curious indeed.*

Carter finally opens his lips wide, gagging at the size of me at first, before continuing with unerring grace. He bobs his head up and down, applying delicious suction with every inch. Clearly, Carter has practice. The thought of Carter letting someone else use his mouth pisses the hell out of me, but never mind. After tonight, Carter won't want anyone else but me.

Heat slams into my chest and groin. Balls close to bursting, I tug at his hair. His eyes widen, jaws growing slack.

"I'm taking over."

Carter lets me take control, and it's a gift I'm not about to abuse. I fuck his mouth, and begin with slow thrusts until he's comfortable with my size. His mouth feels amazing around my dick, like a wet suction of heat.

"Take all of me in, don't spill a drop," I command with panting breaths. Carter's eyes blaze, the pupils turning a darker shade of blue, like the calm before the storm. The determination there is enough for the pressure building inside me to break. Gripping his hair, I shoot my load down his waiting throat. Closing his mouth over my softening dick, Carter takes all of my cum, leaving no mess behind.

"Fuck."

Carter smiles at the word, like it's a compliment.

I growl at him. "We're far from done, golden boy."

"How do you want me?"

"Stay like that." I kneel between his legs, another first for me, but the look of shock on Carter's face is worthwhile. Not waiting for his reply, I yank his jogging pants down. Blue and black covers his thighs and calves. More bruises bloom against his ribs beneath the bandages, making me wish I didn't hesitate pulling the trigger on Rod and his two buddies.

I plant kisses on the insides of his thighs, nuzzling his half-erect dick. Carter draws out a shaky breath and cups my cheek, mimicking my gesture earlier, his discomfort evident.

"Why do you have to do that?"

"Do what?" I blow against his glistening tip, just to hear the moan slip from his perfect lips.

"Be so fucking nice?"

Frowning, I lick away his pre-cum. "I'm far from nice, golden boy."

"No one has ever," Carter falters. "I mean, usually the guys I've been with just—"

I silence him with a kiss on the side of his cock head, knowing what he's about to say. Dark alleyways, quickies in the men's bathroom in a dingy bar downtown—I know all of Carter's usual haunts. Why he picks those places. There, no one can recognize him. To them, he means nothing, just a needy boy eager to please.

"You don't have to worry, baby. After I have you, no one else can touch you."

"What do you mean by that? Don't make promises you can't keep." He looks a lot older than his twenty-one years when he utters those words. The soul peeking at me from those baby blues is battered and ancient. Some of the puzzles begin to click into place. Takes me long enough to figure it all out too. The hospital visits in his file, the covered-up visit from social services—all of them lead back to his father. Blood rushes to my brain. Rod's not the fucking problem, he's a small fry, because the one who did all the real hurting is the chief.

"Collector, the look in your eyes scares me," Carter murmurs, hand sill on my cheek.

I touch his hand with mine, pry his fingers away and examine each one. Some of his bones are crooked, probably didn't have the chance to heal right. Carter takes his hand away, as if he knows what conclusion I come to.

"Broken boy, golden boy, you're fucking perfect the way you are. Don't let anyone tell you otherwise, especially not that fucker you call father."

Carter cringes at the word. I kiss each of his fingers in apology, with every intention to right all my wrongs.

"Collector—"

"James."

He stares at me for a couple of seconds, disbelieving. I can't remember the last time I tell anyone my real name. *Ages, practically a lifetime ago.* My employers don't need a name for when all I do is collect debts and clean after their messes.

"James," Carter says softly, dragging out the word as if he can taste the syllable.

What the fuck is Carter doing to me? Before I start to lose my mind and start having second thoughts, I give Carter a blowjob he won't forget. Can't remember when I did this either, but it's like riding a bicycle. Each time I draw out for air and take his cock into my mouth, Carter's moans become more needy and loud. Every sound he makes hardens my own dick and draws my balls close to my body.

Carter lets out a tell-tale shudder and I pull away, using my hand to finish off the job. I take his lips again, so Carter can taste me and him combined in my mouth. When I pull my mouth away, he moans into my mouth.

"Give it to me, baby. Your release. Do it now."

My words and a pinch to his tip are enough to hurtle him over the edge it seems. Clutching at me hard, Carter's nails dig into my shoulders as he screams himself ragged, unleashing his load all over my hand, spilling some over my shirt. Bleary-eyed, he watches me put my fingers, still wet with his seed, to my mouth and lick them dry. His eyes widen in surprise when I undo the chain around his ankle. Escape is the last thing on his mind, both of us know it, but I hope he understands this is a sign of my trust.

I won't let him escape. I mean every word. Doesn't take a genius to escape from this house, but its part of my skill set to track people down and give them a lesson they won't forget. Most of my employers aren't creative, preferring a body part or two, nothing vital until its necessary, but that's not what's in store for Carter. Pain is easy to give. Demanding submission and consent is much better.

"I'm going to bring food from the kitchen. Bathroom's out the hall if you need to use it. There are extra clothes and towels there."

I get the hell out of there before Carter says another word or does something to shake my control. Slamming the door shut behind me, I expect movement, but I hear none. Fuming, I stalk back to my own room.

There are no locks in the house. Carter can walk out of the front door if he wishes, but I don't think he will. I collapse into my own bed, raising a hand over my eyes.

Nothing went according to my plan today. Carter's dangerous, toxic even, because he's capable of stirring up something in me I thought was long dead. Each time I come up against him, I'll lose a piece of my armor. A bad thing, considering emotions hinder a killer, but Carter sees something good in me when I think I'm beyond saving.

I'm the villain in this piece, so why do I feel like Carter is the one holding me captive?

****

Carter

I make another round of my room, peer out at the slivers of light able to penetrate the boarded up windows and sigh. After yesterday, James seems to find every excuse to avoid me. Hell, when I wake up this morning, there's take-out on the dresser by the bed. My bandages are fresh too, which makes me wonder why he didn't wake me. Did I go too far yesterday? Why did I care, and why the hell am I still here? A prisoner with a way out doesn't hesitate. He chooses freedom no matter what.

"What the fuck is wrong with me? Scratch that, what the fuck's wrong with James?"

The sudden knock on the door makes me jump. I watch the door, hoping James will come in, and be ready to talk, explain what the hell will happen next. Christ. Does he need an invitation?

"Come in."

"I'm leaving lunch here." Before his footsteps fade away, I run to the door, and yank it open in time to see his broad back retreating from my sight. "Fuck it, James. What kind of kidnapper are you?"

I say the first thing that comes to my mind and it works. Turning, James wears a frightening expression on his face, like he's seriously considering strangling me to shut me up. Swallowing, I remember the feel of his huge hand around my throat, the feel of his thumb rubbing against my pulse. With long quick strides, James is on me in seconds. I take a hesitant step back when he pulls something from his back—a colt, the same one he used on Rod, Bron, and Barry.

"You won't shoot me."

The gun roars, creating a hole on the scarred wooden floor. Sweat rolls down my back. James is dead serious.

"Don't tempt me," James warns and I wisely shut up. "Why the fuck haven't you left? The front door's unlocked. You want my car keys too, or something?"

"Why don't you put that guy down, big guy, so we can talk?"

James' scarred lip curls in distaste. Talking things out is clearly out of the picture. "I'm heading out, if you're still here when I come back, I'm putting a bullet in that thick skull of yours."

He turns his back and walks away, not waiting for my answer. I silently fume for a couple of seconds, too angry to formulate a sassy reply.

"I thought you said I was yours," I yell to his retreating back. This time my bait doesn't work. James keeps on walking.

"I fucking changed my mind. Who the fuck wants a broken toy?"

James' last remark really hits home. I sit on the edge of the bed, gripping the rusted frame. Fuck this, but the solution seems clear. Eventually, I pluck the brown take-out bag James left behind, consume the burger in seconds and furiously munch on the fries. Carb overload makes me lie my head down.

When I wake, sunlight no longer filters through the boards. I rub at my eyes, taking a couple of seconds to remember where I am. Not my tiny studio apartment, but James's house. God. I'm only here for two days, yet that world—college and football, feels like a world apart. Did I stubbornly stay, because I no longer want that world? Here with James, time seems stuck in a limbo.

If I head back, time will resume and it's back to my usual routine. Be the golden boy who has it all. I fumble my way to the doorway and flick the switch open. The flickering bulb draws my attention to the items on top of the chest of drawers beside the bed. Feeling numb, I walk to the drawer. The clothes I wore during my disastrous date with Rod are folded in a neat pile, smelling like the same fabric softener used on the bed sheets. All the blood stains are gone, I realize with some surprise. To the right of my clothes are the rest of my belongings, including my wallet, cell phone and car keys.

With trembling hands, I pick up my cell. The battery is dead, no surprise, but I have a feeling there's a bunch of missed calls and messages waiting for me.

"You really want me to leave, huh?" I whisper to the empty room. "Well, message well received, bastard."

I don't waste any more time. Stripping down, I bring the borrowed shirt to my nose and sniff at it, like some kind of pervert. It smells a little of James. Wanting a reminder, I keep the shirt and dress back into my old clothes. I make my way out of the room, pause by James's bedroom to knock, but there's no response. Usually, he keeps it locked, but this time, the door is wide open. Pushing my way in, I glance around, wondering what I'm searching for. Like the rest of the house, his room is a place of careless regret. Dirty clothes, old pizza boxes, and empty beer bottles litter the floor. In a cabinet,

I don't find clothes, but more guns and an impressive collection of blades.

The yellowing newspaper clipping on the cabinet door catches my interest. Staring back at me from the photo is a young man. It takes me second to recognize James, sans the muscle mass, ink, and scars. The smaller picture next to James in cuffs and a prison uniform is someone I recognize—my father.

I quickly scan the article, breaking out into a cold sweat after I finish reading.

"Is this why you took me, only because you want revenge over my father?"

There's no one in the room to answer. My temper flaring and ready to burst, I walk out of James's room, down the flight of stairs, and walk out of the door. The cool night air tickles against my clothes, my skin, and I notice there's no one in sight. James's nearest neighbor must be miles away, making his place close to perfect for kidnapping unsuspecting young men, hiding bodies, or whatever else James does for a living.

What makes it worse? My car is right on the driveway.

"Fuck this." I pull out my key and get in the driver's seat, heart racing. Breathing exercises don't work this time around. Slotting my key into the ignition, I start the engine, eager to go fast, to drive away as far as possible from this hell. It takes me an hour to get back to familiar streets and neighborhoods.

If James is really after my father, it's my job to play the good son. To ring him up, warn him, but I want the bastard dead as much as James.

I choose to keep on driving, not stopping until I reach my apartment building. On my way up the lift, my neighbors make small talk, completely clueless I was missing over the weekend. Back in my apartment, I feel no relief, so sense of comfort. I plug my phone into the charger and the messages start popping up, demanding why I didn't attend practice, why I'm not answering my phone.

"This is the life I want to return to?" I end up in bed, hoping this is all a bad dream, that when I wake, James's scarred face will be looking down at me.

Chapter Four

James

It's Tuesday night and I'm back to square one. I didn't know what I expected when I came back home after finishing a job for an old client. Carter waiting in his room maybe, still demanding answers, but didn't I want him out of my life? Yet here I am, glutton for fucking punishment, waiting on the curb of his apartment building. I check my wrist watch, frowning. Half an hour to game time and it's unlike Carter to be late.

Something's not right and my instincts never lead me wrong.

Might be a bad decision, but I get out of the car. Old habits make me cling to the shadows, and in minutes I'm climbing up the old oak that has a perfect view of Carter's bedroom. No lights inside or sounds of life. Pulling my revolver out from my holster, I shoot at the glass and punch my hand through the broken shards the rest of the way to reach the latch. I clamber in, searching for clues.

In the closet, Carter's football is missing. Did he slip out without me knowing? Growling under my breath, I climb back out the apartment and head back to my car. I drive to the university stadium, nearly getting a speeding ticket, but I manage to slow down before the copper catches me. I leave my car in the empty lot. At this time, most of the crowd is inside.

I'm about to head for the stadium when a familiar profile catches my attention. From where I'm standing, it's not hard to pick out Chief Slater, even out of his uniform. Carter has his golden hair, but Carter has his mother's eyes, not the chief's black ones.

Jaw tightening, my hand creeps to the revolver

tucked in my belt holster. The chief is taking a phone call, back turned. So easy to walk up to him and pull the trigger. I can imagine bits of his skull and skin flying, his eyes widening in recognition when I blow his brains out while I tell him I'm fucking his son.

I'm close enough to hear the fucker say to the caller, "Yeah, my boy's playing tonight and I have a feeling he's finally getting scouted. I'm so proud of him."

Funny how the chief manages to say that with actual pride in his voice. I remember the heavy weight of his merciless black eyes and the sharp cut of his cuffs as he slaps them on my wrists. In my mind's eye, I see Carter's crooked fingers, recall the toneless way he says, *"Perfect outside, dirty inside."*

I grip the butt of the colt so hard, I'm sure the metal will bend and break, but only humans are capable of doing that. The chief begins walking away, still chattering about how God's gifted him with the perfect son. Each step he makes dampens the pleasure of shoving the barrel of my gun between his eyes and shooting at close-range.

"You're better than that."

Too late now, I loosen my hold on the colt and place it back in its holster, breathing hard. Carter's done it. Sunk his hooks deep into my skin and soul, and I can't undo the damage. Cursing under my breath, I light a smoke with shaky fingers. Once I'm ready, I go into the stadium, only to see number forty-seven isn't playing on the field. Carter's no where in sight. What the fuck? Carter couldn't have run, because all his belongings are still in his apartment. I stalk back to my car and slam the door shut, thinking, trying to calm the fuck down. I stay there, unmoving, until one-by-one, the car park empties out. I waste a couple of hours, driving around the city, restless, unsure of what to do next. By the time I head back to my place, it's three in the morning.

Weary, I drag my sorry ass into the house, pausing at the sound of movement. I whip out my revolver, clicking off the safety only to see Carter descending down the stairs, taking two steps at a time. He comes to a halt several inches from me, for some reason, he's mad.

"Where the fuck have you been? I've been waiting for you for hours."

I stare at him for a couple of seconds, wondering if he's a hallucination. I tuck my gun away. To check, I close the distance between us and tug him close for a kiss. I can almost taste his frustration, but he yields under the force of my kiss, like I know he would. He winds his arms around me, and I deepen the kiss, wanting more.

"Why the fuck did you come back?" I ask, releasing his mouth. "There were scouts in that game."

I hold off telling Carter I nearly put a bullet in his father's head. Plenty of time for revelations later, when he doesn't look like he wants to bite my head off.

"I don't give a fuck, I never liked football anyway."

"Don't fucking lie to me if we're doing this, whatever the fuck this is."

"I'm not." Carter bites his lip, looking guilty. "I played to get back at my dad."

He looks me in the eye now. "I can choose to be whatever I want and pick whoever I want. This is my fucking life too."

"You want to be with the man who kidnapped you?"

Carter grabs a handful of my shirt, presses his forehead against mine, and closes his eyes.

"You also said I'm perfect. The answer is 'yes,' James," he says simply, and it's good enough for me. His blue eyes twinkle with playful mischief and I remember Carter yelling at me days ago, asking why I didn't make him mine. Well, its time to make good on my word.

I tug at his shirt. "Upstairs, baby. I intend to fuck you so hard you can barely walk in the morning."

We stagger our way upstairs, tugging and stripping at each other's clothes. By the time we reach my bedroom, we're both nude. Carter stares at me, every imperfect scarred inch of me, and licks at his lips like I'm good enough to eat.

"Baby, you're fucking one of a kind."

"Well, I hope so."

I push Carter against the edge of the bed and he draws his knees up, parting his legs to show me how hard he is for me. Grinning, I settle between his legs, blanket my body over his, and take his mouth. Carter's sweat-slicked and smooth muscled flesh feels amazing against mine. I make a path of kisses down his neck, feeling his fingers into my hair.

"Fuck, James."

"Damn right, baby. If you're good, I'm going to sink my dick into that tight ass of yours."

The dirty talk makes Carter groan and tug at my hair. I close my mouth over his left nipple, sucking until the bud hardens. Carter groans and the sight of the imprint of my teeth on his tanned skin looks fucking amazing.

"You're going to be my fucking canvas, Carter, because I want to see all my marks on what's mine."

It's a good thing Carter likes some bite to his pleasure, judging his thickening dick pressing up against my stomach. I leave a mark on his right nipple too, before making my way downwards, nipping and sucking my way until I reach his dick. By then, I can tell Carter can't hold out his climax any longer.

"Don't you dare come without my permission, baby," I warn, intent on teasing him. Swirling my tongue around his cock head, I lick away his pre-cum. He groans, rocking his hips to my mouth and I slap at his thigh, chuckling.

"Behave, golden boy, or I'm bending you over and covering that perfect ass of yours with my handprints."

Carter stills and I take his dick between my lips, bobbing my head up and down until he's steel-hard and near bursting. I draw out my mouth, kiss him on the mouth and continue pumping his prick with my hand.

"Come for me, baby."

With a shuddering breath, Carter explodes all over my hand. This time I put my fingers to his mouth. Without needing to say a word, Carter licks them dry. I get off the bed and pull a tube of lube and spare condom from my bedside drawer. After rolling the condom over my shaft, I take position between Carter's legs. I lube my fingers and apply a generous amount into his opening.

He groans, squirming, and I push a finger into his puckered hole, then a second. I stretch him wide, preparing him for my access.

"James, please."

"Patience, baby. I'm not exactly small."

"Don't remind me." Carter moans.

I push my cock head into his opening. Then the rest of my prick, slow and steady, until I'm fully sheathed inside Carter. He whimpers and I lock my fingers around the flesh of his hips. Carter's inner muscles clamp around my shaft, like a fist around my heart.

"Fuck, you're so tight for me. Breathe, Carter. Relax. I'm going to make you fly soon."

Carter obeys and I begin to move. I start with slow strokes, until Carter becomes used to me and I pick up speed. Locking his arms around my neck, Carter kisses his me and heat rams into my chest and groin. I piston in and out of Carter's waiting hole, moving faster and deeper, seeking to breach his most intimate places.

Shifting the angle of my thrusts, I know I hit his prostate because Carter's eyes fly open and he lets out a loud gasp. Carter digs his fingers into my shoulders and I aim for his sweet spot repeatedly. Reaching between our bodies, I begin gliding my fist up and down his shaft.

"James, I'm close," Carter confesses.

I'm near to bursting too. Hammering into him a few more times, I growl against Carter's ear. "Come together."

I slam into his slick opening one more time, and hurtle us both over the edge. The world narrows its scope to the two of us, until all I'm aware of is Carter's body linked to mine. I can practically feel his soul, tethering itself to mine and cleansing away some of its taint.

"Fuck," is all I manage to say. Carter screams out my name, emptying his load into my hand and chest.

Head reeling, waves of pleasure assault my body. I explode into the condom, and draw my dick out of his ass. I collapse against Carter, feeling his hand rubbing the curve of my back. We stay like that for a while, trying to regain our breathing.

"Fuck," Carter agrees, with a little laugh.

Recovering, I dispose of the condom, and come back to Carter with a washcloth in hand. Irrational fear hovers at the back of my mind—somehow, I'll return to an empty bed and house, but Carter's there, flashing a lazy smile at me. After cleaning us both up, I join Carter in bed, pulling him up. Carter settles against me, the curve of his back pressing against my spine, and lets out a purr. He reminds me of a large predatory cat. *Mine.*

I hate to ruin the perfect moment, but I can't help

but ask. "What the fuck's going to happen tomorrow?"

Carter places a hand over mine, beginning to stroke my scarred knuckles thoughtfully. I'm beginning to think Carter has no answer, that he'll tell me we'll take one day at a time, but he turns, so we're facing each other. I rest my hand on his waist and tug him close so he can feel my dick, ready for round two.

"I have classes tomorrow."

"I know."

He grins at that. "Next year I'll finish my four-year course. I'm telling my coach I'm quitting football. Also, make some room, because I'm moving in."

I furrow my brows. Does Carter understand what the fuck he's saying? Pretty greedy of him to want it all, but then if he's ready to risk it all, I can't argue. A decent fucker will tell Carter this is all a bad idea, that he should go live his twenty-one year old life and forget all about me.

Too bad I'm also a selfish bastard. Fate threw Carter under the wheels of my ride, and I don't intend to let him go anytime soon. I tried that. Practically gave him the keys to his freedom, but he came back here of his own accord.

What right did I have, to turn him away?

"It's a long drive from here to the university," I say. I know from first-hand experience its useless trying to dissuade Carter when he's made a decision, but its fun to tease my golden boy.

Carter has an angry ready. "Doesn't matter, because I only have one year to go and after I graduate, we'll figure it out together."

"You make everything sound so fucking simple, golden boy."

He kisses me on the cheek. "We'll work things out somehow."

"Fucking right, baby."

The End

www.angelvoisen.blogspot.com

I LOVE THE WAY YOU HURT ME

James Cox

Copyright © 2016

Chapter One

"Here, I am the boss. I am in control. I am master. You are slave. I own you for the duration of your sentence." I stared out at the new prisoners in their light blue garb that made them look like a sea of choppy waves. "You play nice with each other and your stay here will be pleasant. You make trouble and you go to the pit." I pointed to a lone building at the edge of the large stone prison. "Anyone can sneak in there and take advantage." I walked the first line, staring at each man and glaring. Some cowered, others watched me in defiance and a few smirked. You'd think they'd be the problem. No, they'd fit in just fine around here. It was the shy ones that often contemplated escape from the hellish life here or suicide. "It takes all manner of men to run this prison but I'm the one who's going to work your ass if you cause chaos, is that understood?"

"Fucking fag."

Ah, I was wondering when they'd start in. It was the tallest in the bunch, dark hair, scar on his chiseled chin, and a slightly crooked nose. "You got a problem with gays … number forty-two fifty-three? You ain't nothing but a number and a hole to me."

"Nothing some matches and gasoline won't cure." He said and garnered a few laughs.

"That's good. Funny, right?" I smiled and before the expression fell I took out my slick, black baton and slammed it against his knee. He cried out and went down. I followed with a smack to his back and another on his ass when he was face down in the dirt. I pressed my foot into his spine and waited for him to struggle then I slapped his ass again. He cursed before going still. "You like to burn faggots do you? Best not to mention that again to me or I'll tie you up and let each man here have a go. We have an understanding?"

The guy spit into the grass. "Fuck you."

"You're not my type." I gave his back another hard slap with the baton.

"Okay. Okay!" He hissed out.

"Good boy. Now get your ass back on the line." I stepped away and waited from him to join the others. "Anyone else want to comment?" I made my way to the last man. A few feet away stood enough guards to bring them all down. It took a few years for them to accept me and twice as many to get them to respect me. When I got promoted it took another few years before they all followed my lead without question. It was a long fucking uphill battle but here I was. Respected, in charge, followed and most of all, getting paid to keep these fuckers from the world. I spun on my heels and faced them. "This is your first day of hell, boys, best not piss off the devil."

****

They were sharks, predators, swimming in a sea of fish looking for their next meal. It was the best analogy I could come up with as I stood by the door. There were fifty prisoners taking yard time and I knew which ones to watch for trouble and which ones to watch to keep safe.

Most of the new guys kept to themselves. The big guy that liked to mouth off was already in with the fucking skinheads. There was one man I had to watch though and not just because he stirred my cock. No, this guy had prey written all over him. He was on the shorter side with that orange-red hair that was only associated with the Irish. He stood by the fence staring out and looked about as sad as a puppy without a toy. His fingers rested in the wide holes of the wire fence. His back was completely unprotected and from how attractive he was, that be an invitation some wouldn't pass up. I took note of his number, fort- two eight eight, splayed on the back of his blue uniform, and scanned the area near him. Some men liked other men, some just wanted a warm hole and others, well, some others just liked trouble. I spotted that one from where I stood. His name was Carver, and he was in here for what his name suggested. Only he preferred to cut on women. Pathetic ass was always on my radar. I walked along the fence which signaled my men to be on alert. I saw a few of them perk up as I moved toward the new guy that oblivious to the danger. "Forty-Two Eighty-Eight." I shouted.

He didn't even turn around.

"Carver."

The tall, tanned man paused.

"You best not be moving toward that boy." I kept advancing. "I know you don't want to spend a night in the pit with those hungry coyotes sniffing at your bleeding ass." The threat was hollow but he didn't know that. He also wasn't that smart because we didn't have coyotes in these parts.

"Just making some new friends, Devil."

I nodded and paused, hand on my baton.

He smiled, showed off crooked teeth then stumbled back the way he came.

Fucking disgusting bastard. I glanced at the redhead and jerked when his very bright green eyes were on me. They were wide, probably with fear and his plump lips parted as he breathed heavily through his mouth.

"Don't turn your back on them." I gave him that bit of advice when blood stopped rushing down between my legs.

The young man nodded and leaned against the fence. I didn't move too far away, just enough. My gaze lingered on him and I knew the moment my break began I had to find out about him. Nothing sexual, no, I wanted to know what he was in here for and if he could defend himself. It was purely for work purposes. Mostly.

His name was Seamus McGregor, obviously Irish, if the red hair and green eyes hadn't given his heritage away. He was twenty-eight years old. A good twelve years younger than me. Not that it mattered, this was just to keep him safe in my prison. Yup, that's all it was. I stopped arguing in my own head and went back to reading his file. I was in an office, last one at the end of the hallway, where most of the records were kept on an ancient computer. Seamus was five foot eight and had no known aliases. No spouse. His term was six months. No previous records, not even a fucking traffic ticket. I scrolled down to the large letters that spelled out crime. Mr. Seamus McGregor was convicted for the crime of grand larceny. So, the sexy redhead was a thief. Maybe he was innocent or maybe he was a bad criminal. The point was he didn't exactly scream crazy fuck that should be in prison, like Carver. I closed the file down and went back to work.

Mr. Sexy Irishman was in his cell. It was a cramped space barely big enough for the bed, if you could call that lump a bed, and a toilet with a tiny sink. The bars were solid and made a resounding sound when hit. I knew because I'd been here during the riots a few years ago. Fifteen men got free on account of a new guard that didn't know his ass from his elbow. He was sent to the hospital with stab wounds but survived. Ten escapees were captures without issue. Two were caught outside the fence. And one, Carver, managed to go three days before we caught him. It added another year to his sentence. We were fucking lucky no one died. Now, when something clanged against the bars it instantly caught my attention. You had to be alert and focused, so thinking about Seamus McGregor was liable to get me in trouble. Too bad my body wasn't listening. My cock was uncomfortably thick in my uniform pants as I stopped near Seamus's cell.

His head jerked up from where he sat on the bed.

"You okay in there, boy?"

"He's going to kill me."

I lifted a dark eyebrow. "Who is?"

"Carver. He said my ass was his and that if I didn't bend over he'd cut on me like he did those women." Seamus sounded genuinely scared. "I don't belong here. I'm not … I'm not like them."

He was either a fantastic salesmen that could sell me a sweater for my dick, or he was telling the truth. "Stay away from him then." I knew it was a dumb thing to say. There were only so many places to go in prison and most of them weren't exactly friendly. Showers, yard time, mess hall, and occasionally the library or the laundry. All of them were ripe for being jumped despite our best efforts to keep the violence to a minimum.

Seamus scoffed. "He's a psycho!"

I couldn't argue with that.

"He's going to hurt me." His head fell and I heard him take a deep breath.

"He tries to hurt everyone. Stay near the guards

and you'll be safe."

He didn't answer and I didn't say anything else. We staid quiet for a few minutes before I walked on. I couldn't linger at a prisoner's cell without arousing suspicion. Besides, it wasn't protocol.

Even though I went through the rest of my shift, my mind wouldn't focus. I finished up and returned home to a sparse apartment. A cold bed that was rarely slept in and a furry black cat. I fed Cat. Yes, that was his name. He was a rescue. I found him outside the building the day my parents and little sister died in a car crash. I was feeling heartbroken, he was feeling hungry, we've been perfect roommates ever since. Too bad he wasn't the company I was looking for tonight. Tonight I wanted a man … one with red hair to pull and green eyes to go wide as I fucked him.

Chapter Two

It was a long night of masturbation, erection inducing dreams, and a cold shower for breakfast. I rushed to work, taking the train and walking one block to get there. It gave me enough time to clear my head, too bad that space filled with a naked redhead. Why the hell was I so obsessed with him? Okay, obsessed was a bit harsh. Maybe preoccupied. Yes, he was hot, but I wasn't some teenager that couldn't keep my fucking cock in my pants. I was just lonely and a sucker for a sweet guy. That was all. I hadn't been to the BDSM club in the city for at least a year. That's all this was. Still, when I came on shift, after getting ready, I found myself on his cell block. The doors were open and each blue-swathed prisoner was lined up on one side. The left side had the shower right now. I scanned each face and smiled when I saw Seamus. He was holding a towel and a bar of soap while staring around with wide eyes. Yeah, prison showers didn't invoke good thoughts. I'd seen them go bad enough times. However, I planned on staying in there to keep him safe. Being gay, I usually stayed away from that area. Not because I couldn't handle myself around naked men, I'm a fucking adult, but because it tended to make everyone edgy, including my guards. This time, they'd have to deal with it.

The shower was a double-wide hall with drains in the center, showerheads near the ceiling, and half walls to give the prisoners that illusion of privacy. I stood near the door and another guards stood at the other side. My gaze may have drifted toward Seamus. Okay, my sight was stuck on him as he pulled his shirt off and stepped behind the wall. He made the motions of taking off his pants. I glanced away to count each head and be sure there was nobody wandering around. Of course, I found myself back where I started, watching Seamus. Water dampened his hair making it darker like a red moon in a night sky. Shit, when I started getting poetical it was time to back the fuck off. I made it a point not to stare anywhere but in his direction. It lasted about ten minutes. But this time when I looked back he was staring at me. Our eyes locked for a second and I swear everybody else in the room faded away. Then Seamus blushed and went back to washing his body. Damn, I could have been jumped and went down smiling.

Shower time ended only moments later. The men were in towels and dripping or fully dressed depending on how they felt about having their ass used by the other prisoners. We usually kept that fraternization to a minimum, but where there was a will there was a way. I led them out, counting aloud cell doors as they clicked closed loudly. I came to Seamus's cell and stopped abruptly. He wasn't there. He wasn't in line where I'd seen him not a minute ago. "Fuck."

"Come on baby. You'll like it." Carver's soft voice was sickening.

The other guard was busy breaking up a scuffle, probably designed as a distraction. I bypassed the two men yelling at each other and went right for Seamus. We had procedure, a system, and I blew them all to fucking hell when I stepped between the men. "Carver."

He looked startled and then suspicious.

This close I could see the lines around his eyes and a scar beside his lower lip. "Back the fuck off."

"Aw, now, I was just making friends."

I pulled the baton out, well aware, that at this distance I wouldn't be able to get a good whack. If he had a shank, I was in for a bloody night. "He's not interested in friendship and you're out of line."

"Just staying away from the fight." He smiled.

Fuck it. I swung the baton against the side of his leg. He went down hard and hunched like he was about to suck my cock. "Did I fucking stutter? Get your sorry excuse for a dick back in line."

"Sir?" The other guard jogged over.

"Fight under control?"

"Yes." This guy was the youngest here with thick blond hair and a nice mouth. I always noticed a man's mouth. "Good, take Carver back to his cell. I'm placing this one in the pit."

"O-Okay."

I waited for them to walk away, or in Carver's case, limp away. Another set of guards followed. A few of them gave me a look. Yeah, Yeah, not routine. I wasn't letting Seamus get raped just because he wasn't a cold-blooded bastard.

"I didn't do anything."

"Shut up." I grabbed him by the arm and dragged him along. "It's to keep you safe."

"Oh." He went quietly after that.

It didn't take long to traverse the corridors because I avoided the crowded ones where other men were getting ready to strip down and wash. The yard was empty at this time, void of life which gave it this eerie quality. It always reminded me of some kind of horror story, zombies or some apocalyptic shit. I walked toward the shack like structure. It was made of steel though, thick walls and a door with locks on the outside. I had the master key and opened it up. There was no bed here. No lights. A toilet that was being held together by rust. Chains on the walls that would give a man limited freedom. There were names scratched into the old paint that were half faded over the years. That's it. A steel box, a toilet. The pit. I pushed him gently into the space but left the door open. I was reluctant to leave which should have been my first clue that this was a bad idea.

"Thank you." He spoke softly then leaned against the wall. "Why are you helping me?"

"I'm an idiot." It sounded better than saying I'm being led around by my cock.

Seamus snorted. "I doubt that."

"Why'd you do it? The larceny?"

He paused as if he'd been caught all over again. Seamus nibbled on his lower lip and then dropped his gaze. "I was starving."

That's what they all said. I was starving so I stole. I was horny so I raped. I was bored so I beat that man to death. I'd heard it all and then some.

"I lost my job. My ex stole everything out of our shared bank account and anything of value from our apartment."

I sighed.

"It was stupid. I knew it was wrong but I just kept thinking about my growling stomach and how I was all alone and…"

Damn it, he could be lying. I didn't think he was. Not by the way his head was down, his shoulder drooping and his bare toes curling into the floor. He wore his crumpled blue shirt and trousers. They looked too big on him. His hair was darker when wet. A few strands flopped onto his forehead when he looked up.

"I don't expect you to believe me. I'm sure you've heard enough excuses."

"I have."

Seamus nodded.

"I also think you're telling the truth." I stepped into the small room and eased the door so only a sliver of light from outside made its way in. "You don't have family that can get you out of here?" Legally, I meant.

"My older brother's a marine, off in Afghanistan or Iraq. Some top secret stuff. He's all I got and … and I don't want him to see me like this. A criminal."

Aw, hell. "I'll leave you in here and make sure you get fed. It'll keep you away from Carver for a few days." I grabbed the short chains on the wall that ended with cuffs. "I have to lock you in. Protocol."

He nodded and lifted his hands over his head.

"Once the door close, the chains will loosen and you'll have more freedom to move around."

"I'm not a bad person, but I'm sure you've heard that before."

"Yup." I stepped up to him and grabbed the first cuff. His wrist was warm and soft under my fingertips. The loud click of the cuff locking seemed to echo in the small space. I'd never noticed how hot it was in here. Not until this moment with my body inches from Seamus.

"So, then tell me why you're helping me, Devil."

"I told you already." I shifted to his left side, held his wrist and placed the other cuff there.

"I don't think you're an idiot."

"Oh but I am." I said softly, staring down at Seamus. My breath came out in puffs and rushed across his face. "The biggest kind." My voice went down to a whisper. "If I wasn't already in charge of hell, I may just be heading there today." Then like the idiot I claimed I was, I kissed him. I shoved the door closed with my foot and it loosened his chains. His arms fell to his sides with a rattle. I forced his mouth open with mine. My tongue swept inside, along his teeth and deeper still. The kiss was intense. I knew my lips would be red and swollen from the sheer pressure but I couldn't help myself. Seamus was an irresistible temptation. I kept kissing him, falling deeper into the void and then he leaned his body against mine. I swear I heard angels singing. Fucking hell, it hadn't been that long since my last fuck. I was acting like a randy teenager. I pulled away and Seamus followed.

"Please. Please." He murmured and placed his lips back on mine.

This kiss was just as wild. I held his head in my hands and angled to send my tongue deep into his mouth. Seamus moaned and pressed harder against me. Shit, I could feel just how horny he was. His cock pressed against the flimsy prison pants and against my hip. I thrust against him, forgetting everything but that wonderful burst of pleasure from between my legs. I jostled my hands between us and quickly unzipped my black uniform pants. My cock bounced out, hard and beyond ready. I stopped kissing Seamus long enough to open the button. His hair was silky soft against my fingertips. I grabbed handfuls and forced him to his knees. Idiot flashed through my mind again but it was quickly replaced by blowjob. I wanted this sexy redhead's lips around my cock. Now.

"Devil," he moaned.

The chains rattled as I gathered his wrists in one hand. I used the other to direct his head. My dick was only inches from his mouth. I took a deep breath as he opened wide. "Suck me." It was an order, given with a harsh tone and no chance of flexibility. Seamus was going to take my shaft into his mouth. There was no negotiating. My tip was without foreskin so when his breath rushed over it, I felt the tingle through my entire body. My cock was stiff, pointing upward like it was making a choice. My balls were low hangers, the left lower than the right but they were still stuffed into my pants. Only my shaft was unconcealed and ready to be slathered with saliva.

Seamus closed the gap.

The groan that came out of my mouth was decidedly high pitched as he wrapped his lips around my tip. I stared down, watching as he lathered the bulbous head with his tongue and poked at my slit. "Yes. Yeah. Seamus." I tugged his hands higher, making them taut and under my full control. Then I used my other hand to push his head closer. My cock skimmed along his teeth, gently until his mouth widened. I pushed inside without hesitation until I hit the back of his throat then I eased out. His tongue lapped at my hot, hard flesh for a moment then his green eyes rolled up to stare at me. "Oh hell, I'm going to fuck that pretty mouth so hard." I pulled on his arms as I shoved his head forward. He had no choice but to take me in, deep, deeper. I felt his throat around me and nearly cried out. Warm. Wet. Sucking at my flesh like it was candy. I held Seamus tightly in my grip, he couldn't move as I pressed my dick further down his airway. Pulses of pleasure seeped up my body. I hauled the shaft out and thrust back in. He started to gag so I jammed my cock deeper. Seamus coughed and struggled to free his hands.

"Devil." His voice was raspy and weak.

I ignored him and plunged forward again into his open mouth. Air rushed over my dick then that warm saliva eased the way. I started pumping into him, deep, shallow, deep, shallow. It was a rhythm that I couldn't control but seemed to be instinct. He felt so damn good. My head fell back as my fingers dug hard into his wrists. I had no doubt he'd be bruised after this. I liked the idea of my mark on him. Seamus sputtered, inhaled quickly, and I thrust my shaft hard. It was brutal. Too much. I knew it was but I couldn't stop myself. Other than the gasps and sputters Seamus didn't even protest. I don't think he did. I tugged on his hair and propelled deep. The orgasm was sudden. One minute I was on that edge and the next I was careening through the air. "Oh. Oh. Yes." The words were whispered. My mind shut down for a few beautiful seconds as sperm shot out of my slit and down Seamus's throat.

The climax faded too quickly. I wanted it to last but it had been too long for me. Thus, an issue when single. I opened my eyes, unsure of when they closed and stared down at Seamus. He was gasping, a bit of cum rolled from the corner of his mouth. One cloudy drop landed on his shirt. His prison shirt. Motherfucker, I just got a blowjob from a prisoner. It was like suddenly the lust haze was gone and my mind was clear again. I really was a fucking idiot. I let go of Seamus's head and his hands. He landed on the floor, still trying to catch his breath. "I-I." Nothing came to mind, so I pushed my softening cock back into my pants. I zipped up as I opened the door. The chains retracted, pulling Seamus to his feet. He stood there watching me. I couldn't get away fast enough. I rushed from the room, slammed the door closed, and leaned against it.

I was going to be fired. All the hard work over the years lost to a blowjob. They might even place me in here. I'd share a fucking cell next to Carver. I had a hard time breathing as I walked away from the tiny shack. What if I was turning into the nasty fucks that I was supposed to guard? The question stayed with me, lingering in my mind like a stubborn hard-on.

****

Even as I finished my shift, I fought with myself. I'd never done anything like that before. All the years here, with sexy men and ugly ones, shower time and not so much as a half mast. Now, suddenly I'm hard when I step through the doors and forcing inmates to blow me. What the fuck had happened?

By the time I made it home, I'd come to the

conclusion that it was Seamus. His attraction, his soft green eyes, and his sad story. He leaned against my unbreakable wall and the fucking thing crumbled. I should give myself in. I should apologize to that young man and be arrested for being a sexual deviant. Cat's meows pulled me out of the fog. I fed her, and ate cold, leftover chicken as I stood by the window. The prison was in this direction. I couldn't see it but it was there. The night concealed any glimpse I would get. Still, I stared, thinking of Seamus chained in that room with my cum filling his belly.

Chapter Three

I spent all night thinking about him, so when I walked into work it was like a dose of cold water. No one approached me, no one threw me in a cell to rot. I dressed in my uniform, the spare one because I was more than sure there was some dried cum splattered in the other pants. I smiled, waved to other guards, and went about my duties as if I hadn't gotten a blowjob from a prisoner the day before. Sure, some prisons operated like that but not this one. We were clean, figuratively speaking. I felt dirty and yet my cock started to thicken as I stepped out into the yard. Each step had my body itching to undress and I fought off the urge just as fiercely. I was a man not an animal. I opened the pit door and heard the chains clinking until a dark figure was drawn up to his feet.

"Devil," he whispered.

I shuddered and left the door wide open. Sunlight beamed into the dark room and showed new scratches, Seamus's name and a smiling emoticon. I eased the door closed halfway, not wanting anyone to overhear our conversation. Not likely because the yard was empty and the other guards on duty in the prison. "You're a first time offender and I violated your rights, your … body. I'm sorry. If you want to speak with the warden I'll take you there right now." There. My fate was sealed.

"The warden?"

"To explain how I … hurt you."

Seamus blushed. "Devil, I loved the way you hurt me yesterday." He squeezed his bottom lip between his teeth.

Oh, I hadn't really thought of that scenario. "You did?"

He nodded and glanced at the ground. "I hadn't

done anything like that and it was … well, it was what I was missing. I think. Someone in control because clearly I suck at making decisions." He spread his arms indicating the dark, dank room. "But I liked sucking you." He blushed harder.

I was going to hell. Devil or not, I was going to the deepest, darkest, worst hell in existence and I was not going to regret it. I stepped up to him. He was dressed the same as yesterday but his arms were over his head, chained and his legs were spread hip width apart. His red hair dried wild making him look feral and gorgeous.

"Devil, you in there?"

"Fuck." I spun around, hoping the shadows hid my tented pants. "Yeah, just checking on our latest pit resident. Everything okay?"

"Fight in the cell. One man busted up, won't talk." The guard speaking was Billy Lee. A good southern boy that was as loyal as he was smart.

"On my way." I said then whispered to Seamus. "I'll come back."

"I'll be here."

I snorted and walked out, closing the door softly. He liked the way I hurt him. It blew my mind pretty far from the poor bastard bleeding all over the infirmary floor. I just hadn't expected that. Anger, regret, maybe some denial but wanting more? The medical offices all had thick doors with bolts and large windows showing the empty yard. My gaze strayed to the lone shack as I walked in. "Hey Doc, he okay?" The injured prisoner was one of the new guys. Middle aged, Caucasian, black hair, and in here for attempted murder. I knew his case because Billy Lee was waving it under my nose like a fly.

He grinned when I grabbed his wrist. "This here's Max. He got himself punched in the face and his ribs bruised."

"Who's his cell mate?"

"Empty, which is why him getting all bloody is a bit of a mystery," Billy Lee said.

We walked up to him as the doc checked his ribs. Max was a fit guy, lots of muscle and tattoos. "Who did this?" I asked and wasn't expecting an answer. His nose was bleeding still, kind of crooked like maybe it was broken. His ribs were turning a swollen, ugly shade of yellow.

"Want me to set him up in the medical wing?" Billy Lee asked.

"Nope because you did this to yourself, didn't you?" Everyone stared at me. "The ribs had to be the sink, it's the only thing you can hunch over and ram against. The nose was … the bars? The wall? I don't think you meant to hit hard enough to break the sucker though."

"That ain't fucking true," Max shouted.

"I think it is fucking true. You see, there's no cell mate and none of my other pets were out of their cages. There's also this tiny note at the very bottom of your chart, you see it there." I pointed to the folder in Billy's hand. "Says you're fucking addicted to Oxycodone. So the way I figure it, you beat yourself up to get the pain killer that doc has in a syringe right now." I glanced at the short, glasses-clad doctor who had to be nearing sixty. He nodded. "So, how's about we keep that junk away from his veins and send him to the pit?"

"There's somebody in the pit."

Fuck. He's right. "Solitary it is then … with chains so he doesn't hurt himself again."

"That ain't fucking right!" Max struggled against the handcuffs that tied him to the bed.

"Well, Max, if everything in life were right I'd be a millionaire and there'd be world fucking peace."

"And I'd have three wives." Billy Lee snorted.

The doc cleaned up his nose, which wasn't broken, and bound his ribs. Then we walked, okay slightly dragged, him down the stairs to solitary. That room wasn't as bad as the pit. Here there were other occupied cells and a guard came in every few hours to count heads. Max was still bitching when we cuffed and left him.

"This job ever going to get boring?" Billy Lee asked as we walked down the hall to prepare these fuckers for yard time.

"The day it becomes boring is the day my ass is quitting and I'm becoming a drag queen."

Billy Lee smiled. "I think you'd make a mighty fine looking woman."

I slapped his ass, which made him turn a shade of red. Banter over, we went to let the animals out to play.

****

Yard time was uneventful, fortunately, because all I could think about was Seamus's ass. Actually, Seamus in general. He was quietly sitting in that room all day. I hadn't heard a shout or yell or even a protest. It was like he was punishing himself for his crime. That made a potential lover pause and think a bit. Is that what we were going toward? Lovers. Granted, there was a bit of a conflict issue with him being a prisoner and all. Maybe with dinner I could talk to him. Get to know him. I had an hour break and it occurred to me I could spend the entire time with him. I liked him which in and of itself was a scary concept. Ah, fuck, what the hell was I doing. I stopped in front of the door, tray balanced in one hand, keys jingling in the other.

"Devil?" Seamus's voice was soft and near the door.

Was he pacing? Waiting for me? I shoved the key

in the lock and steeled my spine as I turned it. Light flooded the small room and Seamus covered his face with a wince. I left it open, enjoying the way he hunched and huddled. He looked ... vulnerable. "I brought you food."

"Thank you." He shifted toward a darkened corner and those green eyes popped open. "I didn't think you were going to come."

There was a crude joke on the tip of my tongue but it was lost as Seamus stood. He was shirtless, the pants low on his hips and dipping below his belly button. Shit, all my morality was waning thinking about Seamus naked. "I was debating that myself." I placed the tray on the floor then edged the door closed so only a wedge of light bathed the room. "This is not the smartest moment in my life." I reached out and placed my hands on his hips. The chains rattled as he leaned his back against the wall. "But I did shove a condom in my pocket this morning and a packet of lube. Kind of like the size of the ketchup ones on your plate. You can be my condiment."

Seamus snorted.

"Also not my best day for humor." I slithered my fingers under the rim of his pants. "But I am going to make you scream until I have to cover your mouth and fuck you harder."

Seamus visibly shivered.

"You have a problem with that?" I tugged on his pants before he could answer. They flopped over his tented crotch and puddled at his feet. "Very nice." I glanced at Seamus's erection. He wasn't fat but long and curved. He had a thick vein crawling up the side and a tip covered in wrinkly foreskin. He had a slight shine to the end, smeared pre-cum. I reached down and wrapped my fingers around him. "Do you want me to touch you?"

"Y-Yes." Seamus's head fell back.

"Beg me."

He glanced at me, green eyes hooded and looking sexy as a well fucked man. Soon. Very soon. "Please, Devil, touch me." He blushed.

I stroked him from base to tip. My thumb rubbed along the foreskin. I tugged on that stretchy bit of flesh and he groaned. "Do you want me to suck you?"

Seamus whispered to low for me to hear.

"What did you say, boy?"

"Yes. Please. Please, Devil, suck me."

I grinned then lowered to my knees. They protested being on the cold, hard floor but I continued. Up close with Seamus's dick gave me a great view of his slit, and the drop of sperm at the hole. His foreskin was eased back showing his almost pink cockhead. I licked my lips then went in for the attack. His salty skin glided against my tongue as I took him a few inches in.

Seamus's hips came off the wall. He gasped loudly before the chains rattled and his hands were in my hair. It wasn't long enough for him to grip but he sure as hell tried. "Oh, please. Please."

I did like the begging. I sucked harder and wrapped my hand around his shaft, stroking it. His practically jumped into the air. His body came off the wall, his hips jerked forward sending his dick into my throat. I gagged a moment before relaxing and taking him all the way. His balls slapped at my chin so I cradled them in my hand and wiggled my tongue around. The gasping got louder as did the throbbing in my ears. I pulled back, saliva dripping down my chin and onto my uniform. "Look what you made me do." I mumbled and stood. There may have been a grunt as my knees complained.

Seamus was blushing so hard he was practically as pink as his shaft. "I'm sorry."

"You will be." I winked then opened the door

more. The room was brighter and Seamus's chains tighter. He was strung along the wall taut and naked. Fuck, I was so rigid staring at him, memorizing the vision. His long, lean body stretched. His cock was practically weeping saliva and pre-cum. The pants were bunched around one leg and his toes were curled. "This is a good look for you." I said and then opened my belt. He watched me, breathing heavy as I unbuttoned my pants then eased the zipper down. My dick was stuffed behind a pair of boxers. The moment I pulled my shaft out he gasped and nibbled on his bottom lip. "You want this?"

Seamus nodded.

"I didn't hear you beg?" I pushed him to the side and landed a hard smack on his ass cheek.

He yelped. "I'm sorry. Please, please I want you."

"What do you want me to do?"

"Put your cock inside me." He pressed his lips together.

"You forgot to say hard or slow." I gave him another swift spanking.

"Hard. Hard!" He shouted.

I halted. "Good boy." I spun him around completely so the chains were twisted, his hands pulled tightly above his head. I spread his legs with my own and gave his ass a gentle rub. I knew the touch stung from my previous firm smacks. There was no rush as I pulled the condom and lube out of my pocket. I made him wait, worry, anticipate, soak up the nervous energy in his body. I opened the lube and squirted the entire contents onto my two fingers. "Wider." He shifted his legs further apart but the door didn't let the sun shine this far inside the room. I spread his cheeks with one hand and then shoved both fingers into his ass.

"Fuck." Seamus tensed. "That's cold."

"No complaining." I eased my digits completely

inside, spreading them and the lube.

Seamus moaned and his head fell forward onto the wall.

"You blushing again?" I said, mimicking the rough movement I was about to make with my dick.

"Probably." He muttered and moaned.

I pulled my fingers free and wrapped my hand around my shaft. Damn, I was so fucking ready. My cock was a fat bundle of excitement. I could hardly contain myself at the thought of pressing inside him. He was gorgeous, sweet, a blushing submissive that was quickly driving me out of my mind. I opened the package with my teeth and rolled the plain white condom on. Once sheathed, I grabbed my dick and pressed the tip against Seamus's well lubed hole. "Hard."

"Please."

"You going to scream, boy?" I asked and then eased the tip inside.

Seamus didn't utter a sound. He gasped and his entire body tensed. The chains rattled as he grabbed them and he used that for leverage to push back.

I dropped my cock as inches disappeared into his hole. Warm. Wet. So fucking tight. I grabbed his hips as pleasure danced up my spine. "Don't scream." I didn't want to get caught. "There will be other time I'll want to hear you scream." And there would be. I knew the moment my dick slid inside him that this wouldn't happen once. I wanted more and what I wanted I worked hard to get. My shaft eased deeper, the lube helped spare Seamus pain as I penetrated.

"Devil," he whispered, it was slow and guttural.

I shoved deep and we both gasped. It was fate or coordination or some shit. I pulled out and then back in. My hands holding his hips forced him to take what I was giving. There was no stopping this, not that Seamus protested. He let out small moans and groans as I fucked him. Over and over, I plunged and pillaged like a motherfucking criminal. My body slapped against his and the chains would occasionally rattle over our heavy breathing. Then the orgasm slammed into me. I bit his shoulder to keep from crying out. Not drawing blood but leaving my mark. My balls emptied into Seamus and I couldn't keep from calling his name. So much fucking ecstasy swam through my veins that I was practically high. Then the orgasm began to diminish as did my hardness.

I kept my shaft in Seamus as I reached to his front and tugged on his cock. Two long pulls and he was coming. Seamus chanted my name as cum splattered on the wall. It sprayed his body, my hand, and littered the floor. When he finished, there was nothing but gasping and thundering heartbeats. I stepped back, my softening dick fell free of him. "Seamus." I kissed the angry red mark on his shoulder and tugged the condom off. It landed somewhere in the corner, probably beside the packet of empty lube. He untwisted his body, facing me as I tucked my shaft back in. By the time I glanced at him my belt was secure and I looked like a pillar of authority.

"Devil."

My gaze drifted from his green eyes down his body to my cum that was now dripping out of him. "I'm going to leave you like this, naked, cum dripping down your thighs, door open just enough to keep you chained to that wall. I'll return in a few hours. Be a good boy and don't scream, I'll let you suck my cock when I come back." And then I left him just as I promised.

Chapter Four

A tight ass improves your whole day. I went through the routine with a bit of pep in my step. If anybody noticed, no one said anything. But I felt awesome, the lingering effects of a good fuck were awesome. There was no fighting, no dark hallway kills, and best of all, not even a black eye. It was rare that we didn't have two men going at it, fighting that is. Usually it was just a quick beef but sometimes it was more sinister and at the end we'd have a body on the ground with no witness. Today, was a good day, great, fucking fantastic. I smiled at Billy Lee who was taking a few prisoners out for yard time.

"You got too much energy today."

"You think?" I stepped outside to the sun shining down and the sounds of exercise equipment clanging. The shack was quiet, looking deserted and lonely but I knew better. The man inside was well fucked and probably asleep with a smile on his handsome face.

"What put you in this mood?" Billy asked. "I want me some."

I nearly choked on my spit. "I don't think you're going to get a thrill out of my fun."

"Something gay?"

I winked at him.

"Well, fuck. You got some." He grinned. "Good for you."

I gave him a pat on the shoulder and walked along the fence with my hand on my baton. Although I was feeling invincible, I knew I wasn't. These weren't wild dogs I was paid to watch. I moved my gaze along the many thieves, murderers, and criminals about. Pacing made the time go faster. I went from the door to the fence and back again. Over and over, creating a shallow ditch along the dirt. Billy Lee started getting the prisoners lined up and I was his backup. It took near an hour to get all the animals back in their cages and once that was done the prison echoed with noise. Shouts, insults, propositions, all yelled from one cell to another. I used my second break of the day earlier than normal and made my way to the pit. It was all quiet. The sun was setting which gave the exterior an eerie mashup of shadows. I eased the door open quietly and the soft light engulfed the room.

Seamus was pulled from the floor to standing with his hands above his head. He must have cleaned up with the plastic cup of water from his tray because his thighs were clean of my jizz. The food was gone but so were the clothes. He was still naked and squinting at me. His cock was soft against his thigh, looking like a pornstar about to be primped for the show. I closed the door and the room instantly went dark. It sent a thrill between my legs not being able to see. One step, two then three and I bumped into him. I reached out, touched his firm chest and then dragged my hands along his flesh to his wrists. The cuffs came off with a brief snap. Seamus's left arm fell to his side then his right. We stood there in the darkness, nothing but breathing and the feel of his body against mine. He was getting firm too. The poking was enough evidence of that.

He closed the distance between us and pressed our lips together, or tried to. But he missed and wound up kissing the side of my nose.

I chuckled and adjusted so our mouths met. He was so beautiful, even in the dark. Seamus kissed like this was the last touch of his life. He put all his emotions and strength into this. I took control, plunged my tongue inside and pressed him against the wall. "I want you again." I said between kisses. They were practically tame now. Lips against lips. Both red from pressure and damp from saliva.

"I'll beg if you want me to."

Fuck. I took his bottom lip between my teeth and squeezed gently. "You have no idea how much I want to force you against this wall and plunge deep." I groaned and pressed my forehead to his. "I don't have any more lube or a condom or time." The promised blowjob would have to wait. I knew it. If he stayed in here too much longer there'd be questions and attention we didn't need. "Get dressed, Seamus."

He frowned. "But…"

I stepped back and found my way to the door. Groping in the dark gave me a few seconds to compose myself. I waited there, in the threshold of the pit as Seamus rustled clothing behind me. "I'll find a way to get to you again." I whispered. "There are ways to get you naked. Maybe a private shower."

Seamus stepped beside me, dressed in rumpled clothes and wild red hair.

I turned and placed handcuffs on him. My back was to the prison as they clicked in place. "Seamus."

He glanced at me, lips still puffed up from our kiss.

"Fuck." I braced my legs apart and blocked the door with my body. If anyone was looking I was just standing here, most likely but who the hell was watching the pit now? No one, I hoped. "Open my zipper."

He grinned and handcuffed, did as ordered.

"Take my cock out." I braced my hands on my hips to keep up appearances even though Seamus was reaching into my pants and wrapping his hands around my dick. He eased the shaft free. "I want you to use your hands, Seamus. Just your hands. Make me cum."

He swallowed loudly and then cupped each side of my cock and stroked.

It was a quick, messy motion that had me fighting to moan aloud. "Fuck. Yes." I pressed my lips together and tried not to giveaway the events taking place. This was fucking crazy. Someone could see. Someone could watch us, report us, hell, there could be an escaped prisoner sneaking up on me this very moment. I didn't care. I focused on the motion of Seamus' hands and the feel of pleasure growing. "Motherfucker. Bend over and suck me. Now."

Seamus bent at the waist and wrapped his lips around my dick.

I nearly lifted to my toes. My body was alive with sensations and exploding nerves. "Come on, boy. Suck harder. Get me off. Now." I couldn't hold back the groan as he complied. Then I was coming. My body tensing and sperm spurting into Seamus's mouth. I came quickly, spitting out white ribbons of cum onto his tongue. When I was done, I gulped air and whispered, "Tuck me back in." My voice was husky, strained from trying to keep quiet.

Seamus tucked my shaft in my pants and slowly zipped me up. I looked like any other guard in this prison. "Good boy." I grabbed him by the cuffs and pushed him out ahead of me. No one knew what just happened but us and it thrilled the fucking hell out of me. I kept Seamus ahead of me, knowing he was hard. "Keep walking to your cell. I'm going to be staring at that beautiful ass as we walk."

He had a bigger sway in his hips.

His cage came too quickly. Seamus went in and turned around, facing me with a lick of his lips.

I removed the cuffs and stepped back. "Close cell 104." I shouted. The dark bars slid between us. "I want you to lay in that bed, take your dick out and jerk off until your cum is bubbling out and dripping all over your hand." I winked at him. "I'll see you tomorrow." I waited a heartbeat for Seamus to go to the cot. The lights dimmed in each cell for the night. Just as I turned to walk down the hall I saw him tug his pants down and his firm cock flopped out. What I wouldn't give to be in that cell watching him right now. Despite two orgasms in one day I still wanted him. I continued down the hall, gnawing on that thought.

Chapter Five

Seamus had a six-month sentence which had my attention this fine spring morning. After feeding Cat and shoving down some cereal, I drove to work in my electric car. Yes, I was environmentally conscious. Anyone who wasn't looking to save the planet was an idiot, in my opinion. Anyway, I was thinking of Seamus like I had been most mornings this week. He was broke, alone, and would be out in a few months. It dawned on me as I was sitting in traffic that maybe … maybe he'd come stay with me. It was a hell of a jump from fucking in a dark room in prison to living together. Too big of a jump. I blasted the radio to some rock music the entire way to work to keep my mind occupied.

The prison was stirring more than usual at six in the morning. I put on my uniform as quickly as possible and secured my baton when the alarms went off. "Where and what?" I yelled to Billy Lee who opened the gate ahead. Two more guards were behind me.

"Fight. Mess."

Batons and Tasers were out as we approached the area. I could hear the shouts, the grunting, the slap of flesh on flesh. "Back up, now!" I yelled at the nearest prisoners. Some went to the wall, hands up, legs spread, looking over their shoulders. Billy Lee and I ran in first, we unleashed the baton against any limb we could reach. There were about ten prisoners in the melee. "Get to the fucking wall."

"Back off." Billy Lee shouted over the chaos.

One guard came to join us, then two and finally the fighting stopped. The last three guys dropped their fists, blood sprayed just about everywhere. "Get the fucking doctors." I winced at all the sanguine on the floor and the walls, even on the tables. "Fucking idiots. Get to the wall." Three of them shuffled off. That's when I noticed the body on the ground. "Damn it. Get the doc here now, we got one down." It was probably a damn distraction, the fight. This had to be the real target. The blood spreading under the body was forming a puddle, too much for a beating. Shank, most likely. I placed the Taser in my belt and used the baton to ease the guy all the way over. "Fuck." The word was a whisper but the gasp wasn't. "Seamus." I landed on my knees in the next heartbeat and shoved my hands over the leaking hole in his gut. His blood was warm, wet and covered my hands too quickly. "Where the fuck is the doctor?" He was going to die. Someone had stabbed him in the gut and used the fight as a distraction. Footsteps sounded as I pressed to help stop all the blood from seeping out of him. "Fuck, shit, Seamus?" His eyelids were closed. His chest barely rising. He was going to die. The thought struck me like lightning and it was just as devastating.

"Here, right here," Billy Lee shouted.

Two men in white coats ran toward us with a nurse pushing a stretcher.

"He's bleeding out," I screamed at them, still holding his wound.

"Stomach stabbing, we need his blood type and an ambulance now." The doctor closest gave orders.

I barely heard as I kept my hands firmly down and stared into the face of the man I fucked yesterday. It hurt my chest to think of him gone, honestly, it did. I'd seen blood before, seen death too and it had hit close to home, but Seamus. We were just starting to get to know each other. This shouldn't have happened. I helped lift him to the stretcher and off in the distance I heard the wailing sirens of the ambulance. They rolled him from my touch, shoving padding under his shirt to staunch the blood flow. I stood at the entrance of the prison, watching as they placed him in the ambulance. I swear I saw his eyes bob open once but maybe that was wishful thinking.

"Devil?"

I glanced at Billy Lee. "What?"

"The prisoners are secure. Doctors are seeing to those injured."

"Good." The doors closed and the siren started screaming into the quiet morning as it pulled away.

"You're covered in blood, Devil."

I glanced down, realizing that my uniform was nearly soaked through at the chest and knees. "Fuck." Even my hands were getting crusty with dried blood. I walked through the hallway and the closer I came to the guard lockers the further the sirens sounded. He'd be okay. I had to tell myself that. Maybe it would be true. He'd be alive and have a scar and that was it. He was young and healthy. That had to count for something. I changed, throwing the clothes in the trash bin and showering in the guard's private shower before placing on Billy Lee's uniform. It was slightly tighter around the arms and chest, I was bulkier than him. Then I went back to work, slightly dazed as I thought of Seamus lying on the surgery table being put back together.

****

"Who did it?" My voice was quiet and calm as I asked. We stood in the empty locker room after a hellish few hours of work. There was still no word on Seamus's condition.

Billy Lee glanced up. "Started the fight or the one who stabbed that guy?"

"Both." I said darkly, knowing it was a threat to my career, hell, my freedom.

He lifted a dark eyebrow and pinched his lips before answering. "You seem awfully upset about this beef that got hurt."

I didn't answer.

"The new guy started the fight. The one that gave you trouble his first day here. From what I know, he did it to get in good with Carver. Don't know why Carver wanted to kill the guy but … what are you thinking of doing?"

"Teaching."

"Devil … why? I'll help you because God knows Carver deserves all the pain he can get but tell me why now? He's killed before."

"He hasn't killed. Seamus might make it."

Billy Lee nodded. "Ah, so you have some kind of … what, gay crush on him?"

I frowned. "Really, gay crush? As opposed to a straight crush."

"Shit man, I don't know the gay terms. I'm asking, as your friend mind you, what the fuck is going on."

I was going to get fired and probably sentenced if Billy Lee ever told. Still, I trusted this bastard, maybe more than I should. "There's something going on there. Between me and the beef … Seamus."

"A prisoner."

"I know. I know. It just happened."

Billy Lee shrugged. "Good enough for me. Just don't start going into details about that shit."

I grinned. "First you spread the ass cheeks…"

"Fuck!" He slugged me in the arm and took off out the door before I could retaliate. Besides, I had to save my energy for someone else.

Billy Lee took Carver out of his cage. He was being sent to solitary for starting the fight, which he denied as he was led away. His hands and feet were chained together. He was shuffled into the small room in the basement of the prison. The moment Billy Lee pushed him inside I followed with my baton. "Carver."

"Ah, shit. The fuck is this."

"You stabbed him, didn't you?" I asked as Billy Lee stood at the door with his Taser out.

"I don't know what the fuck your talking about." He leaned against the wall, with his feet bent.

I slammed the baton down on his ankles. I think the bone cracked but I couldn't tell over the way Carver cried out. "You stabbed him, and I want to know why."

"Fuck you."

"Wrong answer." I brought the baton down on his calf.

He cursed, pulling away but he had nowhere to go and the cuffs kept him from having much movement.

"Want to try again?"

"I'll sue you, asshole. You'll be fired, put in here, and then I'm going to shove my cock up your ass while the other fuckers get in line."

I rolled my eyes. "Like I haven't heard that threat before, Carver. Now, let me issue one of my own. I'm going to make you feel pain. So much pain you're going to cry and beg. When I'm done you won't be doing a fucking thing to anyone, ever again. You'll be found in the yard…"

"Laundry would be better." Billy Lee said from the door.

"Good. The laundry. You'll be found there, beaten, and bloody. Maybe even one ball swinging solo. Just another prison attack. We'll have iron clad alibies."

He looked nervous now, his eyes slightly wide and his lips parted. "The fuck, man. You're a cowardly prick."

"And you … shouldn't have stabbed my boyfriend." I used the baton across his face, spraying blood along the wall. It was the first time I'd said that about Seamus, giving him a title meant something. I didn't ponder it long enough because I was busy trying to inflict the most agony I could on Carver, and in the back of my mind I wondered sadly if Seamus would live to hear those words.

Chapter Six

"Carver has a broken jaw, nose, and ankle. He's got one testicle crushed, a bruised spleen, three fractured ribs, and enough welts to cover forty percent of his body. How does that even happen?" The warden asked with a caress of his gray mustache.

"How does what happen, sir?" I asked, acting the fool. "I'd rather not know about the testicle bit."

The warden snorted. "Neither would I. Eh, it couldn't happen to a nicer guy. He implicated you and Billy Lee but you're both on camera walking the halls. We'll have some inquires, but since Carver has a history here and no family, it'll probably blow over in a few months. I'm placing you both on leave just until this is over with. Think of it as a paid vacation." The warden's glanced around the room and to the open window where yard time was starting. "Out with you and for fuck's sake don't talk to any reporters that come sniffing around."

Billy Lee grinned. "Yes, sir."

We walked out of there with our heads held high and a gaze between us. Carver would be in the medical area for the next few months, unable to do much more than groan. Revenge was beautiful. Oh, and most important, I learned just minutes after the fucker was found in the laundry that Seamus was alive. He came through the surgery, which was a hell of a relief on my part. I nearly stumbled and had to hold onto the wall when Billy Lee told me. He was alive, patched up, and spending a few weeks recovering in the hospital. He'd have a gnarly looking scar but the blade missed all the vital organs. I wanted to see him, to visit, and maybe hold his hand but that'd look sort of suspicious. A prison guard going to sit with a prisoner who was stabbed?

Yeah, I'm not that dumb. Although Billy Lee liked to say that was still debatable. I had a few weeks off, Seamus wasn't going anywhere, so what else could I do but track down his brother?

Marine, red hair, green eyes, and a crooked nose, his name was Rupert. He was a handsome guy but not as good looking as his brother. It took some strings to find out Seamus's brother was in Iraq, coming home in ten months. It took even more greasing to get a phone call with him. I told him about Seamus, what had happened, the arrest, the sentence, the stabbing, all of it. I called myself Seamus's new boyfriend but failed to tell him what I did for a living. When we hung up I felt better than I had since I first saw the redheaded beauty in his prison garb. Now, all I had to do was wait another five months for Seamus to be released which was down to two because of the stabbing.

The vacation time was slow moving despite going fishing with Billy Lee three times a week and rearranging the apartment twice. I also took Cat to the vet, which she enjoyed so much she scratched up my arms and took a bite at the veterinarian. It took three months but it dragged like a dog's ass on the carpet, which was why I had a feline. Cat was happy to have me home, I think. She only tried to trip and kill me twice, so I think that's a good sign. She slept on my chest and sometimes my back, purring away like a broken sex toy. Work wasn't the same when I went back. Carver was still in the medical area with new anal soreness and it seemed like the ankle didn't heal properly, so he'd have a permanent limp. His days of ruling the prison were over. Seamus did return but not for near another month and even then he was kept segregated. That was the one place it'd be suspicious for me to stop by. So, I bid my time, did the work, joked with Billy Lee and teased him about fucking a guy. Life was on hold…

And then it was Seamus's last day of prison.

I waited outside the prison in blue jeans and a plain black t-shirt. The sunglasses were big and the hat pulled low. I was using my Harley which had been tucked away in storage waiting for the warmer weather. I leaned against my bike with my arms crossed and stared at that door like the release process would magically go faster. Hell, I had no idea if this was going to work, anything between Seamus and I. He was a damn prisoner. It still irked me that I went so low as to fuck him in the pit. What the hell had been going through my mind? It still made me nervous, thinking back. What if somebody did see? Would they pressure Seamus to turn on me? I had no idea if I could trust him that much. But what's that saying, you never know if you don't try. Yeah, well, I was fucking trying.

The thick gray door opened and two guards escorted him out. He looked nervous, fidgeting with his shirt, clamping his bottom lip between his teeth. They walked him to the tall gated fence with the razor wire on top. He glanced around, gazing right past me and toward the rather dusty road sprouting spring grass on either side.

"Looking for a ride?" I asked once the guards began to move away.

Seamus jerked his attention back to me. "D-Devil?"

I'd never seen him smile so wide before. "You're here?"

"Where else would I be?" I straightened and uncrossed.

"I …" He started walking toward me, the smile still in place. "I just thought I'd be walking to the closest town. I didn't think I'd get an escort. And on such a nice ride." He blushed when he came close enough to see my tented jeans.

"Not to town, handsome, to my apartment."

His expression fell. "Your … apartment?"

"Where else can I take all your clothes off without the threat of being fired?" I swung a leg over the Harley and shoved the helmet on then handed the other to Seamus. He hesitated a moment before taking it.

"This is crazy."

"I like a little crazy in my life." I started the engine, the roar echoed in the grassy fields surrounding the prison.

"You're a prison guard." He threw up his hands. "I was only recently a prisoner. Granted, I don't have anywhere to go and I like you. Hell, I like you a lot but…"

"We figure shit out as we go," I interrupted him. "And no more stealing."

Seamus hopped on the back and wrapped his arms around me. "No more fucking men at work."

I grinned. "Deal. Now, let me take you home and hurt you."

His laugh sounded over the Harley's rumble as we pulled away from the prison. "Someone once told me not to piss off the devil in hell."

"Then you best get on your knees and start sucking when we get home."

Seamus hugged me closer. "Home."

The End

www.authorjamescox.weebly.com

SHANGHAI

Pelaam

Copyright © 2016

Chapter One

Inhaling deeply, relishing the scent of leather, sweat, and musk, Noah wandered aimlessly around the club. Nodding at some men, ignoring others, he prowled the floor, constantly glancing left and right. The Leather Slipper was popular, upmarket, and had a solid reputation for good reason. Neither he nor Blake allowed anyone or anything to get out of hand.

Not only did they both maintain a presence there, they had security men, almost indistinguishable from their patrons, also patrolling the club. The result being, that on those rare occasions when something started to escalate, it was snuffed out almost immediately.

"Good crowd tonight." Blake greeted Noah with a wide grin. "Dance floor's full, half the dungeons are in use, and there's quite a few around the benches. Best of all, no idiots."

"So far. Don't jinx us." Noah nodded his gaze darting left and right.

"Oh, just in case you're interested, that blond's by the benches. You might want to take a walk over there." The feigned air of innocence from his best friend only served to make Noah bark a laugh, rather than get angry.

"Blake, I love you like a brother, and I truly appreciate you don't want me to sit at home all alone, huddled around a single candle. But I assure you, I don't. But no one is going to replace Thomas any time soon. When that drunken idiot lost control of his car, he didn't just kill the man I loved, he killed a part of me as well."

"Look, bro, I know you've encased that great big heart of yours in concrete, but just remember your movies. It was a scrawny little kid that pulled a sword from stone and went on to be king of England."

This time Noah snorted out loud, but at the same time he knew he was going to go and look anyway. There was something compelling about the blond. Something he'd glimpsed in eyes as blue as the sea he loved to sail on. The blond was fighting his own inner demons, just as Noah was. *No one can blame me for Thomas's death. No one except me. He wasn't just my husband. He was my sub. I should have gone and picked him up. Maybe we'd still be together. One way or another.*

"No one, least of all Thomas, would want to see you live the rest of your life in self-imposed isolation and celibacy. Jeez, Noah, you haven't even had a casual date in two years."

"I'm not isolated, I come here most nights and I still have my interests during the day. I'm just not interested in sex." The replies were stock and Blake rolled his eyes as usual.

"Every single man in this room could turn their attention on you and you'd still be isolated." Blake sighed and then punched Noah's left bicep. "Go take a look at him. I think he's one that the phrase 'still waters run deep' was probably written for."

Noah watched Blake merge into the crown and frowned. For Blake to make that kind of comment, he'd clearly made a study of the man in question. *Perhaps it's time I checked out the benches.*

Keeping back, Noah scanned the groups of men around the benches and frames. There were some singles, those looking for the right Dom or sub, most were established couples who came regularly. Even so, the blond stood out like a beacon in the mist.

Noah estimated he had maybe six inches in height and a good hundred pounds on him, but the blond was not a scrawny kid. Slender he might be, but he was also toned, his muscles screaming of diligent workouts. He stalked around aggressively, but every sub that approached him was sent away. *You act like a Dom, you're fooling most, but not me. A good Dom will see right through you and unless they're really willing to take you on, ignore you. You exude trouble, but I could break through that.*

Leaning against a column, Noah watched the blond. His gaze often flicked from the scene being played out to the couples around him. Frowning, Noah peered harder, taking in when the blond's body language changed, working out for himself what caught the blond's attention. *As butch and aggressive as he acts, his attention is on the fem sub.*

Scrubbing a hand over the stubble on his chin, Noah pursed his lips. *It's all there, if anyone wanted to take on the challenge. But you won't let them will you? Not easily. You'll fight every inch of the way. The question is, why? What happened to you to make you like this? Fuck it! What am I doing? I'm not interested.*

Turning sharply, Noah headed away from the benches, but even as he did, a tiny voice deep in his mind shouted out. *Liar.*

Chapter Two

Peering over Pita's shoulder, Noah gave an exclamation of triumph as the blond's image came up on the membership database. "That's him."

"He causing problems, Boss? You want his membership canceled?"

"No, no." Noah patted his man's shoulder. "Nothing like that. Something—something Blake said about him." Pulling out his cell phone, Noah jotted the pertinent information down. It wasn't as if he was going to knock on—he looked at the name again, Finn Halliday—Finn's door.

But he could make a few discreet enquiries. Just quench his curiosity. *Curiosity. Yeah. Right.* Noah grimaced. The little voice in his head was becoming a nuisance in regards to his interest in Finn. Looking down at Pita, the furrowed brow on the man's face forced Noah to smile. "Nothing to worry about. Thanks for finding him."

"If that's all, Boss?"

"Yes. That's it. Thanks." Noah strode toward the door. He needed to get out fast. Before any more questions could be asked. *I'm an idiot. Even if I wanted to consider another sub, why would I pick him? Thomas was perfect. Everything I ever wanted. This one would be trouble all the way.*

Despite his misgivings, Noah still ran a check on Finn. Of course, that only told him Finn had a secure job, a good credit rating, and no criminal record. Noah sighed. *I want to know more about Finn, but I already feel like a stalker. I can't justify, even to myself, the use of a private investigator. At least not now. I'll see how he deals with an approach by a Dom. Who knows? I may be completely wrong about the whole thing.*

****

"You're looking hot tonight. Haven't seen you in that harness for quite a while." Blake's feigned innocence only made Noah snort.

"I felt like wearing something different. I haven't worn a harness, so I picked this one." Noah aimed for casual nonchalance but he failed as miserably as Blake and they hugged, laughing in the way only long-time friends could.

"Fuck, you look good enough for me to want to take you home. For you I'd be versatile." Blake slapped Noah's shoulder. "Well … maybe." He winked and they laughed again. Noah had to admit, the banter was just what he needed to help break the building tension.

"Yeah, right. Well, let's see if this blond is in tonight and what he does when a Dom approaches him."

Blake pursed his lips. "I know I pointed you in his direction, but don't be surprised if he declines you as vehemently as he has all the others."

"Do you know something about him?" Noah leaned closer to Blake, certain his friend wasn't confessing all he knew.

"Okay, look. I'm dating a guy who doesn't come here very often. He's pretty private and doesn't want all eyes on him until we're sure this is really going places. I'd like to think you'll be meeting him soon."

"That's awesome. Congrats. You deserve a break. But about Finn—"

"Finn? You've been doing your own digging." Blake smirked, wagging a finger.

Busted. "Just preliminaries. Fuck, I felt like a stalker. So give it up. What did your friend tell you?"

"Homophobic family. Tossed out on his ear. No

steady relationships. Something major happened with the last boyfriend, but Finn won't talk about it. Clams up. Maybe he's not the one for you."

Blake's concern was obvious and Noah smiled. "Believe me, bro, if he doesn't push all my buttons, I won't be bothered pursuing someone with a broken past. Up to now I never thought of anyone but Thomas. It's taken me a few days to realize I've thought of Finn and, even more, I've thought of me. Noah, the man. Not the businessman, not the image I project at the club, but plain old Noah."

"Nothing plain or old about you, bro." Blake laughed, and then grew serious once more. "I'll wish you luck then. I have a feeling you're gonna need it."

So do I. "Thanks, Blake." Noah infused his smile with more confidence than he actually felt. "I'll keep you posted.

Wandering around the club Noah could at least feel a little less like a stalker as he thought over what Blake had told him. A bad relationship would certainly explain Finn's prickly demeanor. *I guess it just depends on how acrimonious the break up was as to how difficult Finn will be.*

Noah gave a mental shrug. *I'm pretty laid back unless I'm immersed in a scene. No good me trying to pre-empt how he'll behave. Just go with the flow.*

Finding a comfortable niche, Noah watched the various couples. Two Doms were working one sub, his mouth wrapped around one Dom's solid cock as the other paddled his ass. Another couple were using a flogger, and at the end, a sub was manacled to chains dangling from the ceiling. A flash of platinum caught Noah's eye and he moved deeper, working his way through the crowd,

Sure enough, it was Finn. The man seemed mesmerized with the scene. The sub everyone was watching wore male lingerie–matching pink bra and panties—and black hold ups with a pink lace trim. His silver stilettos had to be at least four inches high, but he owned the scene.

He and his Dom pushed everyone's buttons as the Dom prowled around his captive with a flogger, occasionally flicking it over him, while the sub kept silent, glaring at his Dom, the tension building. When the Dom pulled his sub's hard cock free, there were more than a few groans. But when the Dom started to fuck his sub, a look of ecstasy lit up the sub's face, and a lot more of the gathered crowd openly groaned.

Choosing the moment very carefully, Noah made his move, circling around Finn so the blond wouldn't see him until Noah had already reached him.

Stepping in front of Finn, Noah smiled. "My name's Noah. I've seen you around here quite a lot. Always alone. Care to have a drink with me?" Despite the softness of Noah's approach and tone of voice, Finn jerked as if he'd been touched by a cattle prod.

"Not interested. Piss off." Recovering quickly, Finn glared at him.

"You may not be interested in the subs sniffing around you, but that's natural since you're a sub yourself." The flash of fear that flickered in Finn's eyes took Noah by surprise. Without thinking he reached out to him. Finn shot out a fist, catching Noah solidly on the nose. Grunting Noah stepped back, touching his nose gingerly. It was bleeding, but not badly. One of his security men appeared within seconds.

"You okay, Boss? You want me to throw him out?" The man eyed Finn as he would dog shit on the sole of his shoe.

"No. Just a misunderstanding." Noah shook his head, taking a perverse pleasure in Finn's shocked look.

"That's right. I'm *that* Noah. This is *my* club." He took a step closer to Finn, as if the crowd around them no longer existed, his gaze locked on the other man's. "You and I will meet again. See you. Soon."

Turning on his heel, Noah strode away. Going into the upstairs offices Noah examined his nose carefully in the mirror. The door slammed open and Blake rushed in.

"I just heard from security. Fuck, Noah, what happened?"

"Something triggered a really defensive reaction in him." Noah shrugged. "Don't know what."

"And that's it?" Blake voice rose sharply. "He fucking assaulted you."

"I scared him. Don't know what I did, or even said, but the fault was mine. Won't be caught like that again, though." Easing away from the mirror, Noah perched on the edge of his desk.

"You're kidding, right? Come on, bro. Surely you're not going there again?" Blake flopped into a chair, staring at Noah as if a second head was emerging. Noah just laughed.

"He's got a good right hand, I'll give him that much." Noah gently touched his nose. *I've had worse. More the shock. Fuck! Something scared the beejeezus out of Finn.*

"You've got it bad. I never noticed before. Noah, be careful. He's not Thomas."

Sighing heavily, Noah met Blake's worried gaze. "I know that. I think that may be why he caught my attention. If he looked or acted like Thomas, I would never have noticed him. Closing his eyes, Noah thought back to what he'd seen, and the way Finn had reacted to what he was watching. Opening his eyes, he smiled at Blake. "I think I'll run a more in-depth check on Finn, and then make him an offer he won't refuse."

"How can you be sure?" Blake leaned forward, his elbows on his knees.

"Like you said. He assaulted me. Somehow I think Finn will do almost anything to avoid that going public. Especially given where it happened." Noah grinned at Blake. "Did I mention I might take a week off? I quite fancy a break."

"I'm sure you did." Blake stood up, came over to Noah, and hugged him. "Don't get burned, bro."

"Don't worry. He surprised me once. This time it's my turn."

Chapter Three

Taking the letter from his box, Finn groaned softly. *What else could I expect? He said he'd see me again. No doubt with me in the dock and his solicitor all over me like a rash.* Finn shivered as Noah's image seared into his mind: tall, powerful, and confidence oozing from every pore. A true alpha male from the top of his close-cropped head to tip of his steel-toed boots.

Shaking his head as if to force himself to change the direction of his thoughts, Finn sighed. *Shit! I didn't realize just how much about him I noticed.* Steeling himself for the inevitable, Finn went into the house and through to his lounge. Unable to wait any longer, Finn tore at the envelope, his hands shaking, then pulled out the letter that would seal his doom.

And sat heavily in the armchair behind him.

It wasn't the court summons as he'd expected. It was a politely worded *request* to visit Noah aboard his yacht, with the underlying threat that failure to agree would result in a court case with all the media circus to go with it. This time Finn shuddered for entirely different reasons.

No. Fucking. Way. I don't want anyone knowing anything about me. Apart from which, how would the other engineers react to not only finding out I'm gay, but go to leather clubs? Slumping in the chair, Finn stared at the ceiling as if divine intervention would come forth in a blaze of celestial lights and heavenly choirs if he waited long enough.

"Fine. You want me to visit your yacht, I'll visit it. But that's it."

****

Even Finn, who wasn't a sailor, knew Westhaven

Marina was the largest marina in the southern hemisphere with more than two thousand boats of all kinds. *And I have to find my way to a yacht.* Finn grimaced and peered at the map Noah had included with his letter.

Looking up from the map, Finn spotted a man in jeans and white muscle t-shirt heading toward him. He was a striking figure with his deep tan and long, dark hair, Finn instantly thought the stranger seemed entirely at home in the marina and wondered how much of the dark tan owed to being outside and how much to his heritage.

"Excuse me—"

"The name's Luca. You Finn?"

"Yes."

"The Boss thought it might save time to have you met. Follow me." Luca didn't wait for Finn, turning sharply and heading back the way he'd come.

Scowling, Finn ran after him and fell into step behind him, although Luca's long legs meant that every few steps Finn was forced to trot a little to keep pace, which did nothing to soothe Finn's growing anger. However as he gazed at the yacht they were intending to board, a frisson of fear inched down his spine.

Oh. My. God. The boat—yacht—was huge. Finn had guessed Noah was rich, but the craft he stared at looked as if it belonged sailing the Caribbean with film stars at its rails.

"This is it. Welcome aboard." Luca strode up the steps leading onto the yacht.

Giving himself a mental shake, Finn followed, stomping up the stairs, forcing himself not to be intimidated by the size and magnificence of the yacht.

There was more than one deck, and Finn looked around at the spa pool, luxurious recliners, and comfortable eating area.

"If you wait here, the Boss will be down in a minute." Luca indicated the upper deck, only half the length of the one he was on. "He likes to be hands on. Does a lot of the sailing himself, although we always have a trained man as backup."

Folding his arms, Finn tapped his foot, his irritation growing by the second. However the tapping stopped when Noah made his appearance. As many times as Finn had caught a glimpse of him at the club, they paled into insignificance when seeing him clearly as he descended a flight of steps.

Wearing nothing except a pair of white shorts and deck shoes, Noah's muscular build was displayed to perfection. His broad, furred chest led to solid abs and a dark treasure trail drew Finn's gaze lower. The shorts did little to disguise the size of Noah's cock and Finn shivered as he imagined it fully hard.

Forcing himself to raise his gaze, Finn could now appreciate Noah's tattoos: a full sleeve on his left arm, and *ta moko* on his right arm and thigh. *Shit! He's got the grace of a tiger.*

"Welcome aboard. I'm glad you chose to come." Noah stopped close to Finn, but Finn refused to step back.

"I came here like your letter demanded of me. So is that it? Do you want compensation?" Finn jutted out his chin, snapping the words at Noah.

"Of course." Noah smirked.

"How much?" Finn steeled himself for losing a chunk of his savings.

"You aboard my yacht, spending a few days with me." Noah turned to wave at a man who's been leaning over the upper deck rail. The stranger returned the wave and vanished from sight.

When the yacht started to move Finn stared for a

moment at Noah, losing even more precious seconds processing that Noah wasn't kidding. They were leaving the marina.

"Not a fucking hope." Whirling, Finn bolted for the stairs, but Luca barred his way, a smirk on the big man's face. With an incoherent snarl of fury, Finn lashed out. But his punches were blocked and, with arrogant ease, Luca took him to the floor, pinning him down.

"You took the Boss by surprise. But not me. Don't fight. You'll lose."

At the icy menace in Luca's clipped tone Finn stilled instantly.

"Good." Luca immediately moved away, standing with his arms loosely at his sides as if ready to tackle Finn again.

"You might as well enjoy the trip. You've already said you don't want anything going public, sailing with me is the compensation price I want for the assault." Noah stood beside him, his hand extended. "You never know. You may even come to like me."

Rolling away from Noah, Finn got to his feet unaided and gave Noah his most contemptuous glare.

"Not a chance. You're all the same. It's all about you. Take, take, take, no giving, and toss aside—" Finn clamped his lips shut. *Calm down, calm down. There has to be a way off the yacht.* "My work will expect me in on Monday. I won't feel any differently toward you then as I do now."

"Actually, the owner of your firm's a client, as well as a personal friend. I told him *not* to expect you Monday. He's given you a whole week off. To spend with me. No one will miss you, no one will look for you. While you're aboard this ship, you're at my beck and call. Get used to it." Noah shrugged and headed back toward the bridge.

"You can't just—just *kidnap* me." Finn yelled after Noah.

"You mean s*hanghai* you." Luca smirked at him, despite Finn's best snarl.

"You agreed to come aboard. I just feel like a nice sail. She handles beautifully, you'll enjoy it. Far better than paparazzi, sideways looks, and no privacy, all of which will go hand in glove with my bringing a charge of assault against you, don't you think?"

Deflated, Finn stared after Noah's broad back, his gaze dropping unbidden to the flexing and relaxing of Noah's ass cheeks as he jogged up the steps. *I'm not out in work and the last thing I want is anyone looking into my private live. Fuck, Noah, the bastard.*

****

"Would your husband have approved of this?"

At Finn's yell, Noah stopped. Turning slowly he looked toward Finn who stood, arms folded, almost hugging himself. A riptide of anger threatened to sweep Noah away, but he withstood its onslaught, regaining full control before slowly advancing on Finn.

Sweat glinted on Finn's brow, a drop snaking down his temple. A primitive urge to lick it flashed through Noah but he kept his face coldly neutral.

Fear and defiance warred in Finn's eyes. Although Finn balled his hands into fists, he made no attempt to lash out at Noah, even when Noah purposely loomed over him, invading his personal space, forcing Finn to look up at him to meet his gaze.

The tiniest flinch was all that betrayed Finn as Noah reached out. Noah slid his hand through Finn's hair, its silkiness heating Noah in a way he hadn't felt since losing Thomas. Fisting his hand behind Finn's head, capturing a large handful of the hair, Noah applied gradual pressure, pulling down.

Their gazes never wavered or broke, even when tears filled Finn's eyes. They slid down his cheeks before Finn finally, with aching slowness, dropped to his knees.

Leaning down, Noah only stopped when his face was so close to Finn's he could smell the salt of the tears. "I know what you want. What you need. What you *crave*. It's all right here. Right in front of you. I'm here when you want me."

"I'll never want you." Finn choked the words out.

"You will. You already do. I can see it, smell it—"Noah darted out his tongue and licked away a tear—"taste it."

Releasing Finn, Noah spun on his heel and walked away without a backward glance. Reaching the steps up to his bridge, Noah stopped. "You have a suite below. Down the stairs, third door on the left. All the rest are locked. If you want food, use the intercom. You can reach me by pressing one, or the kitchen by pressing two. My kitchen staff are on call twenty-four hours a day." Without waiting for a reply, Noah took the stairs two at a time and didn't look back.

Chapter Four

Anger and frustration bubbled over in Finn, born as much from feelings for Noah that he refused to give a name as much as the way he'd been effortlessly imprisoned on the yacht with Noah. Needing an outlet, Finn swept his hand across the bedside locker, sending the lamp, clock radio, water carafe, and glasses to crash onto the floor.

Next was the bedding. Snarling, Finn dragged off the comforter and sheets, tossing them away from the bed, and then threw the pillows across the room.

There was a dressing table and stool set against the wall backing onto the bathroom. With a yell of rage, Finn slammed the stool into the mirror, smashing it completely. Then he stopped, staring at the damage he'd caused, a flush of shame shunting his anger aside.

"What the fuck is wrong with you?"

A solid slap sent his senses reeling and Finn dropped to his knees holding his cheek. Noah glared down at him, his face little more than a frozen mask. Movement caught Finn's eye and he saw Luca standing in the doorway, a look of disgust on his face.

His attention moved almost immediately back to Noah who still stood over him. With a wordless growl, Noah grabbed Finn and yanked him to his feet.

"Fucking brat."

The shake Noah gave him even rattled Finn's teeth and he almost fell again when Noah roughly shoved him aside.

"Give him another room. I have an appointment arranged for tonight that I can't miss. I may cut short the rest of the trip."

"Yes, Boss."

Finn's shoulders slumped. Fight and defiance—his mainstays—suddenly weren't enough. Nothing seemed capable of filling the void that threatened to consume him. An image of Noah staring at him flashed into his mind and Finn felt as if he'd taken a gut punch. *I saw the look in his eyes. He's despaired of me. He's throwing me away already.*

"I'm not wasting my time clearing this room after a bratty tantrum." Luca kicked at the bedding strewn on the floor. "Tomorrow, you get your ass in here and clean it yourself. Did you trash the wardrobes too?"

"No." Finn looked over as Luca opened the sliding door, and then scowled. "Ward*robes?*" He'd only seen the racks of shirts and pants on either side. His breath caught in his throat as Luca pulled the rack with the men's clothing forward and then out to the side. The wardrobe went much deeper than Finn imagined and a second set of clothing was revealed.

"I didn't know that was there." Finn peered inside.

"I guess the Boss didn't get chance to tell you about it." Luca stroked a hand down a black dress. The gesture caused the dress to move and light glinted off the sequins around its neck and hem. "He has good taste." Luca sent a scathing glare in Finn's direction. "Usually."

Taking a few steps forward, Finn spotted shelves with hats, wigs, shoes, and a large cosmetics box.

"I'm staying in here. I'll clean up now." Finn glanced over at the dressing table. "Could I have another mirror? Even just a small one?"

Tilting his head Luca gave Finn a long, hard stare before nodding slowly. "I'll find you something."

Finn tried for a smile, something he wasn't used to doing. It must have worked as Luca shook his head and smiled back. "Gimme ten. I'll be back."

Nodding, Finn focused his attention on the clothing. Almost in a trance he headed over and looked through the selection. Several long ball gowns took most of the space, a couple of skirts, one long, one short, and a few tops from formal to funky. It was an Aladdin's cave of treasure. *How did he know? How* could *he know?*

Luca was as good as his word. Positioning a free-standing full-length mirror next to the dresser, Luca cocked his head at Finn. "I'll just say this. I've worked for the Boss for years. He's a good and honest man and he was devoted to his husband. That was a low blow and will have hurt him. Don't lead him on. He doesn't deserve it. He hasn't been quite the man I knew. Darkness. There's darkness inside him."

Finn swallowed against a lump in his throat and nodded. "Thanks."

"Look, I'll clean in here." Luca waved at the devastation. "You might want to go up on deck. Noah'll be with the skipper. Sailing's his release. Apologize to him at least. Go!"

Hesitating only for a few seconds, Finn hurried from the room. Making his way up onto deck, Finn peered up at where Luca had told him Noah would be steering the ship. His head and heart warred constantly.

Those I thought would love and care for me have let me down before. Tossing me aside as if I was worthless and twice I've clawed my way out of the abyss and proved them wrong. I don't think I could take a third betrayal. But why go through all of this? Noah recognized something in me only one man's ever seen, and he won't have told anyone.

Licking at his lips, Finn rocked back and forth, frozen in an agony of indecision. So caught up in his own world, it took several seconds before Finn realized Noah stood at the top of the stairs looking down at him.

"Did you want me?"

There was no anger, no accusation, and a wave of shame crashed over Finn. "I–I came to apologize and—to say—" Finn stopped, trying to draw in enough breath to dispel the dizziness that threatened to overwhelm him. He didn't even see Noah descend the stairs. A strong arm encircled his shoulders and the raw need to lean on Noah, to accept someone else's strength, sliced into Finn.

"Let's go and sit down." Noah's voice was reassuring enough for Finn not to voice an objection as they walked to the stern of the ship where large, circular daybeds, complete with overhead canopies to provide shade, were positioned beside a large spa bath.

Noah eased Finn down before sitting himself, ensuring there was space between them. Finn wasn't sure he knew the right words to say. Instead he shuffled to his left until his arm brushed against Noah's.

"Talk to me." Noah didn't move away from him and Finn nodded.

"Don't turn back." Finn almost stumbled over the words, but he got them out, staring resolutely at the spa bath.

"Look at me and tell *me*."

Almost hyperventilating Finn turned his head, just enough to see Noah. His expression was unreadable, his face betraying nothing. "Don't turn the boat around."

"If we don't turn back tonight, you'll be on board for the duration of the voyage. If you trash one of my rooms again, you'll pay for it. They don't come cheaply."

"I—I'd like to spend some time with you." Finn grabbed the last of his courage with both hands and glanced quickly into Noah's eyes. They were still dark and brooding, but now Finn saw also heat and triumph and he wished he could dive into them.

His heart skipped a beat when Noah offered a

brief smile. The man's face transformed. He'd been darkly handsome enough, but the smile—*dear God, I'd beg to see that look again.*

"I'll let my skipper know. As much as I like piloting my yacht, this trip isn't entirely about me."

Stunned, Finn stared after Noah who stopped a few feet away and looked back at him.

"If you want to relax up here, maybe take a dip in the spa, go and get changed. I'll be around. But there will be a *penalty* to pay for destroying the bedroom. You can be sure I'll collect." Noah continued on, ascending the steps and getting halfway up before Finn galvanized his legs into moving.

Shivering at the chill of Noah's words, Finn didn't run for the hills. Instead he raced back to his room, pulled out the wardrobe and studied the contents carefully. Still feeling unable to fully be himself Finn picked a pair of swimming briefs first, then hunted in the inner wardrobe.

Unsure what he was looking for, Finn gasped out loud when he saw exactly what he wanted. *It's perfect. It's gorgeous.* Pulling out the multi-colored kaftan, its random sequins caught the light and glittered beautifully. Finn fingered the sheer material before slipping it on. Almost transparent, the garment was a perfect fit, skimming the top of Finn's thighs.

Hugging himself, Finn shut the wardrobe over and stared at his reflection. *Please. This time.* Swallowing hard, he went back inside, through to the shoe racks, and selected a pair of white kitten heel sandals. They were a little tight, but Finn didn't care. *I won't be wearing them too long.*

Walking around his room for a minute or two to familiarize himself with heels, Finn headed out to join Noah on deck. Approaching the daybeds, Finn didn't miss the hungry look Noah gave him, the big man's gaze roamed over Finn's body leaving his skin tingling in its wake. Then Noah's eyes were shuttered again and he gave Finn a curt nod.

Perhaps this time, Finn stood a chance.

Chapter Five

Sitting and relaxing after dinner, Finn mused on how the day had gone. The time had passed easily enough. Noah had acted more like a new friend than a prospective lover—or Dom. Although very attentive, Noah only touched Finn as a friend might, even when they'd both been in the spa.

They'd eaten dinner below deck in an immense dining room, the meal as good as any top restaurant fare, and now Finn toyed with his coffee cup wondering what would happen next. The uncertainty gnawed at him. If Noah noticed Finn's growing agitation, he didn't comment.

Finn glanced across the dining table at Noah. Finn had even been permitted a few moments where he piloted the huge craft, albeit with Noah and the skipper at hand to help him if needed.

All in all, once he'd settled, Finn had found Noah an extremely knowledgeable and generous host, although Noah spoke very little and kept a distinct distance between them. *He hasn't asked about my past. Not once. I still wonder just what he's going to demand of me.*

For a moment, Finn wished things could just go on as they were, but Noah's words kept coming back to Finn. *"I know what you want. What you need. What you crave."* And Finn was reaching the conclusion that if any man did, it was the one sitting opposite him, calmly drinking coffee as if Finn hadn't trashed one of his bedrooms.

"May I tell you a little about me?" Finn clasped his hands together on the table and Noah's gaze flickered from them to Finn's eyes.

"If you wish. I promise you this, Finn. I will take

what you owe for the room. You understand that? But I won't pressure you or chase after you. You will come to me. Because you know I'm what you need." Noah's voice was quiet, but there was no mistaking the steel behind the words and Finn nodded.

"My dad was a man's man." Finn sketched quotation marks in the air. "But although I wasn't uber macho, I still thought he loved me, his only child. But when he found out I'd kissed a boy he threw a fit. And me—with all the arrogance of a seventeen year old—told him I was gay and proud. An hour later I was gay and homeless. I couldn't believe my own father would stop loving me just because I liked boys, not girls. But I wasn't going to let it stop me. I managed to flat with some older mates, finished school, worked my ass off to get through university and I am proud of where I am in that respect. As to the rest..." His defiance died away, his voice softening.

"If you don't want—"

Finn held up a hand to stop Noah. *He might as well know it all.* "My sex life was one train wreck after another, until I finally found a Dom. I thought we were a good match, and that he loved me until I found out the hard way that he wanted a butch sub. One full of attitude and aggression. Well, I have plenty of that, but that's not all of what I am. I thought to surprise him one evening. I wore a dress, makeup. But he'd been drinking and brought a couple of friends around. Fuck, he was furious."

Shivering, Finn wrapped his arms around himself. "They laughed. I was humiliated, but worse yet, *he* was humiliated. As well as I can defend myself, he still beat me, ignoring my safe word and my pleading, and then threw me out. So I swore, no more. Never again. No one and nothing would ever hurt me. Ever."

Noah leaned forward and briefly rested his hand on top of Finn's, the heat permeating the chill Finn felt.

"If I didn't think we had a future, I would never have started this." Noah's voice dropped in timbre. "You're as far removed from Thomas as I could possibly imagine, but I can assure you you're not a substitute for him. I can also assure you that I'm not looking for an *uber macho* sub."

Hope warred with fear. *Can I possibly trust him?* He shook his head, his body trembling in a mix of want and dread. "I don't—I can't—"

"Let me give you something with no strings attached. Okay? You don't have to do anything in return."

"What?" Finn could hardly speak, his throat was so tight, and his cock so hard.

"This." Noah peeled off his t-shirt with deliberate slowness, revealing his hard abs and furred chest. Finn's gaze riveted on the nipple piercings. A small silver anchor dangled from the one on the left. "Move the chair away from the table and take your cock out, Finn."

As tempting as it was, Finn shook his head. Noah advanced on him. Sliding his hands into Finn's hair as if to caress Finn's scalp Noah yanked him to his feet instead.

"Do not defy me." Noah's voice was hard, his face close enough for Finn to feel his hot breath and smell the coffee Noah had drunk.

Looking into Noah's eyes, Finn's instinctive resistance melted in the heat of Noah's gaze. Releasing him, Noah stood back, arms folded. Not taking his eyes off Noah, Finn unzipped his pants and pulled his cock free. A soft whimper escaped him as cool air swirled around his heated flesh. Sitting down, his hand hovered close to his dick, but he didn't touch.

"I want to see you come. That's all I ask of you. Touch yourself, let me see you give yourself pleasure." Noah moved out of Finn's direct gaze and Finn shivered. "Touch it, Finn." Noah's voice, dark and seductive came from close to Finn's shoulder.

Finn wrapped his hand around his shaft. Moaning at the touch, he stroked slowly, giving a twist of his wrist as he flicked his thumb over the slit. His belly was already tight, his balls ached, the need to come almost forcing him over the edge before he'd barely begun. Instead he slowed his movements even more, spreading his legs wide. Delving into his pants, Finn carefully withdrew his ballsack, cupping it in one hand while he continued to stroke with the other.

Breath hitching Finn stroked harder, his body shook as he raced to his release. Noah's name was on his lips as jets of creamy seed splattered over his pants and onto the floor. He almost toppled out of the chair from the force of the full body jerks, but Noah was there to rest an arm around his shoulder, grounding him.

"Beautiful. As I knew it would be. Goodnight, Finn. Luca says your room is clean and ready for you."

It took a moment for Finn to realize Noah wasn't joking, he was already at the door before Finn rallied enough brain cells to make a desperate sound, extending a hand to Noah.

Pausing at the door, Noah stared intently at Finn, as if weighing him up. For the first time, in more years than he cared to count, Finn prayed. Prayed that Noah didn't find him wanting and threw him aside.

"Tell me what it is you want." Noah remained where he was, but his voice was softer.

"Not alone. Not alone. Please." Finn forced the words out, his defenses still railing against allowing himself be vulnerable.

"You don't want to sleep alone?" Noah folded his arms. "Tell me, Finn. I need to hear *you* tell me what you want."

"I—I don't want to sleep alone. I want to sleep with you." The words seemed to tumble from Finn's mouth, but he meant them. Every. Single. One.

"Sleep. That's all it will be. You understand? I knew you were broken. I didn't know how broken. I still think we can have a future, but I won't be pushed, rushed, bullied, or cajoled. Understand?"

It was almost more than Finn could have hoped for. Nodding, he rose shakily from the chair. Only then did Noah come over to him.

"It was intense, I should have thought."

Focusing on tucking himself back into this pants, Finn nodded, the concern almost undoing him. "I'm okay."

"Follow me." Noah didn't touch him, just turned and retraced his steps back to the door.

Still wobbly, Finn followed. Noah's room wasn't even on the same level as his. The vastness of the yacht took Finn's breath away. He trailed behind Noah down another set of stairs, along a passageway, and finally into a huge bedroom.

"There's a bathroom through there." Noah pointed to a door to the right of a large mirror. "I'll be in my en suite if you need me." Noah went to the mirror and slid it aside. Peering over Noah's shoulder, Finn saw similar rails of clothing as in his room, but the far end opened out into a bathroom.

"Thanks." Finn scurried quickly into the bathroom, itching to be out of his clothes. Kicking the pile aside, Finn spent a minute working out the shower before luxuriating in the hot spray. *Of all the things I ever imagined, being dragged off the street, kidnapped, and taken away on a boat did* not *feature.* A slightly hysterical giggle broke free. *Instead of a pirate or buccaneer, I have a Dom willing to make me his cabin boy.*

A thrill of arousal skittered down Finn's back, his skin breaking out in goose bumps despite the heat of the shower. *Dear God, I don't remember anyone—or anything—that did that to me. Could this work? Noah thinks so.* Finn chewed at his lower lip.

After their fight, he'd made sure to find out all he could about Noah. Honest, industrious, and off the market since getting married, despite the death of his husband. *He knows what it's like to really hurt. I hurt him, too, but he didn't react. Didn't lash out at me. Fuck, I'm getting hard just thinking about him, even after that mind blowing orgasm.* Refusing to touch himself a second time, Finn diverted his attention to getting clean.

Chapter Six

Tossing his clothes aside, Noah stepped into the shower, poured a generous handful of shower gel into his hand, and worked his cock, which had been achingly hard from the moment Finn had drawn his out. He couldn't shake the image of Finn stroking himself, and kept his lips firmly shut as a moan threatened to burst free.

Not that he'd hear me, but better not to take chances. I don't want him thinking he was my personal erotic show so I could get off. Nice sized cock, a perfect handful for me. An image of Finn on all fours flashed into Noah's mind and he came hard. His seed splattered the glass of the cubical and was quickly rinsed away.

Coaxing out the last of his release, Noah leaned his head on the wall of the shower in the aftermath of his climax, letting hot water cascade onto the back of his neck and down his spine.

When his wits returned, Noah finished off his shower, drying himself thoroughly before snagging a pair of snug, black boxers to wear to sleep in. Returning to the bedroom, Finn was waiting for him, sitting on the edge of the bed. Although he was wrapped in a voluminous robe, Finn was agitated about something. His body was too stiff and his gaze darted around the room until Noah emerged.

"You need something to sleep in?" Noah hazarded a guess and was pleased when Finn nodded.

"Is there—is there anything in my wardrobe?"

The hopeful tone wasn't missed by Noah and he smiled, nodding. "Yes. Yes, there is. Come on."

Back in Finn's room, Noah waited in the room, sitting on the bed while Finn trotted back and forth bringing out the clothing to make his decision. Noah had made sure there was even a choice of sleepwear. Nightshirts, pajamas, but those outfits which seemed to capture Finn's full attention were the full length nightdresses. A choice of cotton or silk and a range of colors, they drew Finn like a moth to a flame. One in particular.

His decision clearly made, Finns shrugged out of the robe and replaced it with the nightdress. Noah clenched his hands into fists at the glimpse of Finn's toned ass, but he had no intention of breaking his own promise. *He makes the move.*

"What do you think?" Finn pirouetted before Noah, a small, shy smile playing around his lips.

"I think you look exquisite. Is there anything else you need?" Noah wasn't going to lie, but he wouldn't be swayed from his path no matter how entrancing Finn looked.

"Oh, wait." Finn scurried back and Noah rose to his feet curious to see what Finn wanted. A smile tugged ineffectually at the corners of Noah's mouth when he saw the slippers topped with a black ball of fake fur.

"I don't know how you knew." Finn looked down at himself and then back up at Noah, wonder in his eyes.

"I study people." Noah shrugged. "I'm glad I was able to judge correctly."

Finn approached him and Noah remained unmoving, despite the temptation to take Finn in his arms, to show some emotion, Noah kept them at his side. However he briefly closed his eyes at the demure kiss to his cheek.

"Thank you."

"Let's go to bed shall we?" Noah was pleased to see Finn's nod. *We might have a chance. If Finn's willing to trust me.*

Chapter Seven

The day had passed so quickly, Finn could hardly believe it was evening already. Tonight he wanted to dress for Noah. Knowing exactly what he was looking for, Finn went through the rack of dresses and pulled out the epitome of a little black dress. The dress's scooped neckline was lined with black diamante, as was its hem.

Laying it on the bed, Finn went on a treasure hunt to find everything else he wanted; a necklace with several strands of pearls and a glittering centerpiece, a wig in an upswept style, long black gloves, and high heels. Now for the underwear. Although there was a pair of gorgeous black stockings, Finn decided against wearing them as they needed suspenders and tonight Finn didn't want to tantalize. There were other things on his mind.

Selecting a pair of hold-ups, that only left the bra and Finn selected a beautiful black lacy one. Satisfied, he sat at the dressing table to go through the cosmetics box, applying his makeup carefully.

Finally ready, Finn headed to the dining room. Walking across the room, Finn felt like a million dollars as Noah stood quickly, his gaze heating in seconds.

"You look amazing. Please, sit down." Noah indicated the seat opposite him.

"Not yet." Finn took a deep breath, already starting to shake. "You were right, Noah. You were—are what I want. What I crave." He slid to his knees. "Please. Sir." It didn't seem possible, but Noah's eyes darkened further.

"Are you sure, Finn? Don't start something you really don't think you can follow through. I'll punish you for trashing my room, but that's different to being *my* sub."

"I trust you." Finn could only manage a hoarse whisper.

Rising slowly, Noah came and stood beside him. "We'll see shall we? I need a word."

"Phoenix." Finn hoped he'd be like the fabled bird. That he, too could rise reborn from his own ashes.

Moving from the dining table, Noah settled himself in a comfortable chair positioned to look out over the ocean. Kicking the footstool to the side of the chair, he patted his thighs. "Come here."

Rising fluidly to his feet, Finn approached Noah, kneeling on the footstool to that his upper body was across Noah's lap.

"Comfortable?" Noah ran his hands over Finn's back in soothing circles.

"Yes."

"A dozen. That's all. That will suffice. I don't think you can take more. Understand? If you can't even manage that, use the safe word and I'll stop. Immediately."

"I understand." Finn tried to relax, but was aware of his rigid posture. There was no way Noah couldn't notice, but he didn't say anything. Instead he ran his hand along Finn's back, down to the back of his knees and back again. He related the movement several times before hitching the dress slightly with each upward move. Finn thought he heard a soft groan at the revelation Finn wasn't wearing panties.

"Beautiful. Noah ran his hands over each bared cheek, before squeezing them hard in turn.

Finn trembled, but wasn't afraid as Noah tapped a finger down each cheek. The first slap was almost a pat, the second hard enough to sting. As much as it smarted, the residual was good, a combination of heat and prickle that went right to the need simmering along Finn's nerves.

By the third, his ass cheek burned, abandoning that cheek, Noah repeated the actions on the other. When the next blow was delivered, Finn anticipated the sweet sensation that followed the discomfort of the slap.

As with everything else, Noah had judged correctly what Finn was able to endure, and at the twelfth slap, Noah stopped immediately. He helped Finn to stand, holding him against his chest as Finn sobbed against his shoulder.

"Are you all right?' Noah spoke quietly to him sending warmth to comfort Finn.

"Yes. Just a little more intense than I imagined."

"Here." Noah stepped back. Shrugging out of his jacket, he peeled off the pristine shirt and used it to dry Finn's tears as well as the mascara that had run down his cheeks. "Better?"

"Yes." Finn locked his gaze with Noah. Wrapping his arms around Noah's neck, Finn pulled him into a kiss. Deep and passionate, their tongues sliding urgently against one another, the kiss left Finn panting heavily in its wake.

"As much as I may want to, I'm not going to take things farther tonight." Noah eased Finn away from him. "We've already had an intense session and I think anything else would be too much too soon for you. Tomorrow I'd like to show you my playroom. And I'd like you to wear the long black nightdress with the side splits."

It wasn't a request, it was an order and Finn recognized it instantly. The way Noah's voice dropped in timbre, Finn's cock hardened, but he nodded. Part of him was tempted to push Noah, but he already knew it was be pointless, and Noah was right. Anything more would be too much for him. *But I can hardly wait for tomorrow.*

"I ruined your shirt." Finn tried to lighten the mood a little, and Noah nodded.

"It was well worth it. I can get another if you want?"

Stepping back, Finn ran his hands over Noah's solid chest, the hair soft under his fingers. "No. I like the view."

"I'm glad. Up to eating yet, or would you like to sit a while?"

"I'm ready to eat. I need to keep my strength up." Finn batted his lashes and Noah flashed a rare smile.

"We both do."

Chapter Eight

Excitement and anticipation made Finn tremble as Noah led him to the playroom on the lower deck. Finn was amazed at how well-stocked it was. Noah touched his elbow and indicated a set of manacles hanging from the ceiling. Finn studied them. Taking a deep breath he nodded.

"Yes."

His hands were pulled above his head and thickly-lined metal cuffs were shut around his wrists. At this point Finn knew better than to speak until Noah directly addressed him.

"Comfortable?" Noah asked, his face an emotionless mask.

Finn tested the bonds and nodded. "Yes."

Noah glared at him. "Sir," he corrected.

A bolt of lust seared through Finn "Yes, Sir." He dropped his gaze and waited for Noah to speak again.

"I'm rather glad there's another similar outfit to this one in the wardrobe." Noah fingered the silk nightdress. "This one will be unwearable after the session."

Although the nightdress was ankle-length, both sides were slit up to Finn's hip. Noah dropped to one knee and ran his fingers up Finn's legs, a light, teasing touch that left Finn wanting more.

Standing, Noah ran his hands over the crisscross of ribbon that ran from the scooped neck to the naval. With agonizing slowness, he pulled them apart, just enough to bare Finn's nipples to his gaze.

Trying not to wriggle, Finn kept his gaze directed downward, waiting to see what Noah would do next. He bit back a moan as Noah licked each of his nipples before taking one into his mouth, pushing Finn's nipple bar through the nub from side to side before easing away.

Straightening, Noah settled a finger under Finn's chin, urging Finn to raise his head and held his gaze. With the same deliberate slowness Finn now recognized as part and parcel of the man, Noah licked the thumb and forefinger of the other hand.

Releasing Finn's chin, Noah played with Finn's piercing before capturing his other nipple with the dampened fingers. He pinched the helpless nub and Finn's chest arched outward, as much as possible in his restrained position.

As if intending to soothe the hurt, Noah bent forward, lapping at the peaked flesh before giving it a sharp nip. Finn gasped, twisting in the padded manacles.

"Good." Noah nodded. Sliding his hands around Finn's waist, Noah moved them down to palm an ass cheek in each hand, his face so close to Finn that he could almost taste Noah.

"You're very beautiful. I want to use you. Give you pleasure. Take it. Do you feel up to the challenge?"

"Yes, Sir." Finn would have got down on his knees and begged if he wasn't manacled to the ceiling. The heat in Noah's smile threatened to incinerate Finn.

Noah squeezed Finn's ass hard and pulled him forward roughly, crushing Finn to his naked chest. When Noah thrust forward, Finn felt Noah's erection stabbing against him. For a moment Noah simply ground against him, the cotton of Noah's boxers and the silk of Finn's nightdress the only things separating their cocks.

While Noah continued to grind against Finn, he also lifted the nightdress until cold air wafted around Finn's bared ass cheeks. Finn bit his lip as Noah's thick fingers pushed between his ass cheeks, pushing and probing blindly at his entrance, never forcing himself in.

Panting harshly, Finn had nowhere to go except to writhe and buck against Noah's solid chest. Wriggling, on tiptoe even with the high heels he wore, Finn tried to move, to spread his legs wider, and to offer himself silently for his Dom to use.

When Noah stepped away, Finn almost called out to him to come back but quickly clamped his lips shut. Noah went to the rack on the wall and selected a flogger. Finn shivered as Noah played with the black leather falls before stalking back toward him.

Noah wielded the flogger expertly, even through the nightdress, Finn felt its sting on his back and down his thighs. Instinct finally made Finn try and avoid the blows as his skin increasingly tingled, growing in sensitivity, but Noah moved away before Finn was unable to endure any more. Trying to draw in air, Finn hung limply, panting harshly.

Raising his head Finn looked at Noah who didn't look as if he'd exerted himself. Other than a sheen of sweat across his collarbone, and an erection trying to force its way through his boxers, Noah appeared as calm as before the session began. Letting the falls of the flogger slide through his fingers, Noah advanced.

For a few seconds Finn thought Noah was going to use the flogger again. Instead he came close and licked away the tears that had snaked down Finn's cheeks.

Turning away, Noah re-hung the flogger and moved along the wall pushing at what Finn had assumed was simply decoration. Instead a drawer slid out. Noah picked up a familiar tube—*lube. He's getting lube.* It was all Finn could do not to cry out his delight, especially when Noah removed his boxers.

Advancing on Finn, Noah stalked back toward Finn, stroking himself slowly. He stopped in front of Finn, and nuzzled his cheek. Finn's breath hitched as

Noah kissed his collarbone, pressing a trail up to Finn's mouth before claiming a hard kiss.

Finn welcomed Noah's tongue as Noah pillaged his mouth ruthlessly. By the time Noah eased back, Finn was panting, his chest heaving to draw in enough breath. Noah caressed his cheek before moving to stand behind Finn.

Anticipation zinged through Finn, his skin tingling as Noah ran his hands from Finn's ankles to his upper thighs and down again.

Finn trembled at Noah's impatient growl, then gasped as a sharp tug on the nightdress was followed by a loud tearing sound. Cool air hit Finn's ass, then his cheeks were pulled wide apart. A choked-off cry escaped him when Noah thrust his tongue against his entrance,

"I want to hear you." Noah's voice, deep and guttural sent another wave of goose bumps along Finn's skin and he shivered. This time when Noah's tongue probed as his opening, Finn moaned loudly.

Finn tried to spread his legs when Noah cupped Finn's balls, still tongue-fucking him. Sagging in his restraints when Noah moved away, Finn tensed quickly when Noah slid his cock along the crease of his ass.

"Do you need a ring?" Noah whispered hoarsely in Finn's ear and he nodded frantically, certain he'd come the moment Noah tried to enter him.

Returning to the still open drawer, Noah took out a cock ring and fastened it securely. That wasn't all he held. There was also a condom packet.

"In the future, I want to do this bareback. I want to watch my come drip down your legs. But for now, we use these."

A jolt of lust and arousal hit Finn so hard he was sure he'd have spilled his load if it hadn't been for the cock ring. *I want that, too.* He stared unblinking as Noah rolled on the rubber, slicking it with more lube.

Finn tried to push his ass back at Noah willing his lover—his Dom—to mount him. But Noah simply slapped each cheek so hard Finn gasped, but there was pleasure in sharp edge of pain.

One finger pushed inside him, quickly followed by a second. Finn jerked as Noah found his prostate and moaned his encouragement. The fingers withdrew and Finn then felt the blunt head of Noah's thick cock push at his opening.

"If it's too much, tell me." Noah whispered in Finn's ear, biting the shell. Then he shoved forward.

Finn cried out, and then focused on relaxing his body, trying to push back, to take every millimeter of Noah's thick cock. Looking up, Finn saw that his knuckles were white around the chains as he clung desperately to them. Finn gasped as Noah withdrew completely, only to cry out as Noah thrust deep inside him.

After several achingly slow thrusts, Noah was buried balls deep in Finn's ass and Finn panted while he adjusted to the incredible feeling of fullness.

"Ready?" Noah's breath caressed his ear and Finn shuddered.

"Yes, Sir."

"Do you want to be fucked hard?"

"Yes, Sir. Very hard. Fuck me, fuck me, fuck me."

In response Noah eased back fractionally and jabbed forward, repeating the actions until he was almost fully withdrawing and slamming back inside. The pounding was all Finn could have wanted and he whimpered, clenching his inner muscles around the solid pole of Noah's flesh impaling him.

The air filled with musk, sweat, and pre-ejaculate

and a harmony of the chains, Finn's moans, and Noah's deep grunts. The force of the thrusts forced Finn onto tiptoe each time, and finally he was lost in the pleasure.

Noah bit randomly at Finn's shoulders, the nips sharp enough to add another level of pleasure for Finn.

"This is what it's like to be mine." Noah growled harshly in Finn's ear, but Finn lacked the breath or ability to reply. He let his head drop back, shuddering in ever increasing ecstasy.

For all his roughness Noah didn't ignore Finn's need. Wrapping the silken nightdress around his hand, Noah grasped Finn's dick in a hard grip and pulled hard in time with the powerful thrusts.

Free-floating in bliss, Finn was barely aware of Noah releasing the cock ring until he convulsed hard as his climax slammed into him. He came with a scream of Noah's name, harsh gasps, and painful tension in his arms as he pulled uselessly on the restraints.

Noah bit down hard on Finn's shoulder and Finn shuddered again as Noah growled low and deep, filling the latex that separated them. Letting his head loll back against Noah, Finn smiled.

Finn couldn't help but murmur his loss as Noah eased from his body, but Noah quickly returned to kiss Finn softly, release his arms, and scoop Finn into his arms. Noah carried him to the oversized back at the far end of the room. Laying Finn down, Noah stretched out alongside him.

"We'll rest here for a few minutes, and then I think a dip in the spa would do us both good."

"Mmm, sounds good." Finn nestled close to Noah, sighing in contentment as Noah wrapped his arms around him.

"I think I'll have a full breakfast this morning." Noah kissed Finn's brow. "I've a feeling I'll need to keep my strength up."

Squirming enough to be able to look down at Noah, Finn kissed him tenderly. "Thank you. For everything."

"A rocky beginning, but I think we've hit calm waters now." Noah winked.

Rubbing his nose against Noah's, Finn laughed. "So do I."

"I'm glad. You were worth fighting for."

"Even though you had to fight me to win me." Finn shifted to sprawl fully across Noah, wriggling with delight as Noah palmed his ass cheeks proprietarily.

"To the victor the spoils. Here's to new beginnings." Noah rolled their bodies and sealed his lips over Finn's.

When they parted, Finn smiled down at Noah. "I'm looking forward to the rest of my voyage with you."

Noah rested a hand on Finn's cheek. "I want this to last way beyond a few days, Finn. I'm looking long term. When we get back, nothing will change for me. It isn't a case of you being yourself here where there's just the two of us. I want you to be you when we're home."

"Even in your club?"

"*Especially* in my club. I don't want to hide you. I want to walk around the club, my collar on your throat. I want to see everyone's eyes on you, desiring you and envying me. I want to display you and know that no matter how many gaze at you, when the end of the night comes, it's my bed you'll be in, my arms holding you, and my name you scream when you come."

"Oh, fuck, *Noah.*" Finn buried his face in his lover's neck, grinding hard against him. Even though he'd just had the most intense orgasm in his life, he was already getting hard again. Not just from want was said, but the possessiveness that dripped from every word

Noah uttered. *He* is *everything I've ever craved.*

"But for now, just relax. A little later I may show you some other toys in my playroom. If you're very good."

Finn lifted his head to gaze down at Noah and smiled. "Anything you want, Sir." Even as he tried to settle, a surge of insecurity tried to assert itself. "What *will* happen once we're back home, back in the real world?"

Noah wrapped his arms tightly around Finn reacting to Finn's anxiety. "I don't have to be in the club night after night. It's not my only business. I also have a lot of real estate providing a very good income. There's a lot more to me than the club, just as there was a lot more to you than your aggression. I'm not asking you to give up your work. There'll be things you want to do or places you have to go without me. That won't interfere with what we can have. I'd like us to do what any other new couple would do. Go out to dinner, movies, and, when you're ready, be at my side at the club. I've been in a dark place a long time. It's time I came into the light."

There was sincerity to Noah's words that warmed Finn, chasing away the chill of apprehension. *Noah knew me well enough to know what I needed even before I came aboard his yacht. I instinctively trusted him in the playroom. He never really lost his temper with me no matter what I said or did.*

"Be patient with me?" Finn gazed into Noah's eyes.

"I have oceans of patience."

Finn let Noah pull him into another kiss. *Noah's already accepted a part of me no one else did. For the first time in my life I can truly be who I want to be.* Finn smiled at Noah as the kiss ended. "Here's to our future then."

Gripping tightly to Noah, Finn sealed his lips over Noah's and infused every ounce of his passion into his kiss. *I feel like I've finally come home. I can actually see a bright future with someone who accepts me for who I am at my side.*

"May it be long and happy." Noah panted out softly as Finn eased back.

Nodding, Finn let Noah roll their bodies. He was ready to start a new phase in his life.

The End

www.evernightpublishing.com/pelaam

TAKEN

Michelle Graham

Copyright © 2016

Chapter One

The stench of sex and despair hung in the air and the memories nearly forced Diego to abandon his post. Damn Villa for giving him this assignment. Not once since pulling Diego from The Warehouse years ago had the boss asked him to go back. Though Diego ached to just walk away, his exit strategy wasn't ready yet. He was stuck here. Determined to get the job over with as soon as possible, Diego took a deep breath through his mouth and pressed on into the dim corridor.

At the third door he stopped and turned to the young man behind him. Diego guessed that the kid might have been seventeen or eighteen. Though tall, the kid was too thin, giving him a slightly stretched look. Ribs and hipbones jutted out. Scar tissue formed a letter T and the number eighty-six on his upper right arm. His dark skin was chalky and dull and years of inactivity had left poorly toned muscles under his skin. His face appeared gaunt, diminishing his boyish features.

Diego looked into the kid's eyes. What might have once been a beautiful chocolate brown had been rendered dull and devoid of any emotions. The eyes of someone who'd lost all hope. Clenching his jaw, Diego glanced through the window into the room, and his heartbeat kicked up a notch at the display of implements laid out on the table. The sight of a paunchy, half-naked man stretching quickly doused Diego's excitement. It was for the best.

Diego vowed he would never again give into the darkness and become like the lowlifes who frequented The Warehouse, paying Villa to have their way with kids forced into sexual slavery.

Turning away from the window, he unlocked the door and shoved the boy inside. Then he relocked the door and stood guard with his back to the window, trying not to think about what was happening in the room.

At first he only heard low murmurs and the rattle of chains, but then the unmistakeable crack of a whip made Diego flinch. The cracks were followed by brief cries that grew louder and more ragged as the treatment continued. Each cry stabbed into his head. Each crack of the whip peeled away another chunk of the barrier he'd put around his memories.

Despite his instructions and better judgement, Diego turned to peer in the window when the cries became full-fledged screams. Bile rose in his throat at the sight.

The boy was chained to the wall, the skin on his back a bloody mess. Individual whipmarks couldn't even be made out anymore. As Diego watched, the paunchy middle-aged man raised the whip and brought it down again. The boy's scream jolted Diego into action.

He threw the bolt and whipped the door open, stalking inside. The coppery scent of the blood assaulted his nose and he eyed the older man with disgust.

"What the fuck do you want? Wait outside until I'm finished here."

Struggling to keep his voice calm, Diego said,

"You're going to kill him if you don't stop."

The man laughed. "I pay to be able to do what I want. *Whatever* I want. With an older one like this Villa's willing to take the risk. Now get back into that hall before I chain you up, too."

Diego stared at the man for a moment as he fingered the knife sheathed against his thigh. Straightening, he turned toward the door and nearly made it back to the hall when the whip cracked and drew a bone-chilling scream from the boy.

The rage in Diego burst free and he pulled the knife from its sheath. He turned and threw it, satisfied when it found its mark at the base of the man's skull. As the man's body dropped to the ground, Diego rushed forward and fumbled to undo the boy's chains. When he'd succeeded, the boy collapsed with a groan.

"Hold on a minute," Diego said as he surveyed the room. He couldn't take the kid out of here completely naked. The older man's clothes hung from a hook beside the door. Diego grabbed them and rushed back to the kid's side. He used the undershirt to pat the wounds, eliciting pained whimpers, but it soon became clear he wouldn't be able to stop the bleeding before someone else came along and discovered what he'd done. Diego struggled to get the young man into the shirt, which hung like a huge sack on his slight frame. Unable to do anything else to protect the boy's dignity, Diego stood.

"We've got to go. Can you walk?"

The boy shook his head. Diego's thoughts raced as he reviewed the locations of the guards and the exits out of the building. If he could get the kid outside, he'd be able to get to his truck and take off. It wouldn't be easy carrying the kid but they'd be dead if they stayed where they were.

Mind made up, Diego withdrew the knife from

the dead man and wiped the blade clean before slipping it back into the sheath. He then withdrew his pistol, attached the silencer, and checked the magazine. Crouching, he grabbed the boy and hoisted him over his shoulder in a fireman's carry. It was easier than it should have been and Diego cursed Villa again. Taking a breath, Diego headed to the end of the corridor.

When Diego opened the door, the guard stationed outside started to turn but Diego dropped him with a shot to the head. He managed to get into the exit corridor before encountering anyone else.

"Hey, you! Stop!"

Diego whirled around with his gun already aimed. He squeezed off two rounds, killing both guards before either could raise their own weapons. He broke into a slow run as he approached the exit. He slammed the door open and shot the exterior guard. Looking around, he made a quick assessment of the surroundings before deeming it safe to proceed. He ran as fast as he could with his burden, making it to his truck without incident. Though he hated to do it, the easiest solution was to dump the kid into the bed of the truck.

He carefully settled his charge on his stomach. The kid seemed to have passed out and Diego was grateful for that. It would make the drive easier for both of them. He withdrew a tarp from the storage box and arranged it over the boy before he jumped down and climbed into the cab. One last check of his gun, and then Diego drove carefully to the exit, holding the gun down to his side. As he approached the gate, he waved at the guard. The guard held out his hand for Diego to stop.

"Aren't you heading out a bit early?"

"I'm not feeling well," Diego said.

The guard reached for his radio. "Just let me call—"

Diego shot the guard before he could do anything, jumped out of the truck, and pressed the button to open the gate. He made it back into the truck just as he heard shouting behind him. Stomping on the gas pedal, he peeled away from the old building.

When he reached the exit to the highway, he glanced to the back of the truck. Still out cold. The best thing would be to take the kid to the hospital but Diego nixed the idea as Villa would certainly have sources who could lead him to the boy. No, the safest thing would be to get out of Nevada. He'd help the kid get better and then take off. The darker part of him whispered that it might be nice to have a personal slave but as Diego turned onto the highway he told the darkness to fuck off.

Chapter Two

T gradually awakened to soft strains of music and a light scent tickling his nose. He opened his eyes to a dark room with light flickering from somewhere near his feet, but as he began to roll over, fiery pain flared along his back and he cried out. The memory of the guy with the whip brought a sob from T's lips. What had happened? Where was he? This wasn't The Warehouse.

Sheets rustled. Footsteps shuffled along the floor. Sensing someone just in front of him, T cracked open one eye to see the man who'd been guarding him.

"Hey, man. How are you feeling?"

His first attempt to answer produced no sound so T swallowed several times and licked his lips. "Shitty," he said in a hoarse whisper.

"Thirsty?"

T nodded and closed his eyes as the man moved away. He could hear water running from somewhere close by and a second later the man returned.

"Can you scoot to the edge of the bed on your stomach? I don't think you'll want to try rolling over yet."

T managed to squirm over to the edge of the bed though each movement sent a fresh lick of pain shooting across his back. The man held a cup with a straw to T's mouth. The cool liquid soothed him, bringing much-needed moisture to his tongue. "Thanks."

"No problem." The man set the cup on a bedside table and then sat down on the floor near T's head. "You got a name?"

"T."

The man reached out and traced the brand on T's arm sending a shiver through T. "What was your name before they took you?"

Closing his eyes, T struggled with the memory. He'd been T for so long that any memories of his life before seemed like ancient dreams. He searched for something that would tell him what his name had been but came up empty. "I can't remember."

The man bowed his head for a moment and clenched his jaw before looking at T again. "T was your name in The Warehouse. Pick something new if you can't remember."

T attempted to shrug but winced at the pain in his back. What did it matter if he had a name? Why couldn't the guard just leave him be? "I don't know."

"Well how about Tom? Travis? Theo?" The man kept throwing out suggestions but T's head hurt too much to think. Why did it matter? And why was the man so angry about it? "Tex? Tate? Tyson?" T's eyes flew open as his mind produced a vivid image of a cheerful woman. "Tyson?"

As fast as it had shown up, the image disappeared, leaving T exhausted and confused. "I ... sure. I guess." It had been a long time since he'd thought about his family.

"Too long. Let's make it Ty." The man held out a hand. "I'm Diego."

Shaking hands from his current position was painful and awkward so Ty settled for a brief squeeze of Diego's fingers. He closed his eyes and let his head fall back to the bed. Come to think of it, it was a much nicer bed than his cot in The Warehouse. Where had the man—Diego—taken him?

"How old are you, Ty?"

And why couldn't Diego stop pestering him with questions? Especially questions he didn't know the answer to. At The Warehouse, one day blended into another and eventually time lost all meaning. "I don't remember. One of the other guards thought I was getting too old." Ty had been told repeatedly that his youthful features increased his usefulness at The Warehouse, but that had been changing a lot in the past year or so.

Ty expected the man to berate him but instead, the man asked, "Did you ever watch sports?"

A memory of a big TV and men on skates popped into Ty's head. "Hockey."

"Do you remember who won the Stanley Cup?"

Straining to hold on to the memory, Ty tried to conjure up a clear picture of the hockey uniforms as the players hoisted the gleaming cup into the air. "I think it was the Ducks."

"Got it. 2007. What grade were you in at school?"

Ty closed his eyes and tried to picture the school he'd gone to once upon a time. He remembered being excited about finally getting to middle school, but couldn't remember having gone. "Grade five, maybe."

"Okay, so you'd have been eleven and that was eight years ago making you nineteen now."

"Okay." Ty wasn't sure why it mattered, but clearly Diego wanted to figure out the details. The only thing that concerned Ty was the growing pressure in his bladder. "I gotta take a piss."

Diego jumped to his feet and helped Ty get to his hands and knees before backing off the bed and standing on shaky legs. Diego slung Ty's arm over his shoulders and together they walked the few steps to the bathroom. Before he knew what was happening, Diego had yanked a pair of shorts to Ty's knees and was helping to settle him on the can.

"I'll just wait out here but don't lock the door in case you need help." Ty pulled the door closed and left Ty alone with his thoughts.

The bathroom was small but spotless. Nothing

like the grubby room at The Warehouse where the boys had had to shower and shit in full view of everyone else. When he'd finished his business, Ty gripped the counter and stood. He struggled to get the shorts pulled back up. The pain in his back had faded to an intense throb rather than the white hot burn he remembered as the whip had marked his back. Ty turned his back to the mirror, looked over his shoulder and gasped.

Raw wounds filled his back in a haphazard pattern. Some of the cuts looked quite deep and a few were oozing fluid. Ty fought to keep his stomach under control. Of course he'd been whipped before but never as badly and he'd never actually seen his back after a session. There weren't any mirrors in The Warehouse. Ty faced the mirror again and took in his appearance. A fine layer of fuzz grew on the top of his head. His keepers had always shaved his head and any other part of his body where hair grew. Ty barely recognized the person looking back at him. His dark skin looked wrong somehow. Pale.

A knock sounded on the bathroom door. "Ty? You okay?"

"Yeah. Just a sec." Ty washed his hands and splashed some water on his face before opening the door and taking a few tentative steps into the other room, realizing that they were in a motel room of some kind. The flickering light came from a TV along one wall opposite two beds. A table with two chairs stood in the corner near a chest of drawers. Thick curtains covered the windows. The room was simple but tidy and more luxurious than anything Ty had known for most of his life.

"So where are we?" Ty shuffled to the bed and sat on the end. "Why did you take me?"

Diego settled onto one of the chairs and leaned forward, resting his elbows on his knees. He stared at his hands for a moment before meeting Ty's gaze. "That sick fuck would have killed you. I couldn't let that happen."

An image of a man lying on the floor floated through Ty's mind. "Did you kill him?"

Diego nodded. "I had to get us both out before someone found out or you and I would be dead now, too. We're in a motel outside San Antonio."

Ty stared off into space and tried to process everything that had happened. A long time ago, after he'd first been abducted, he'd dreamed of someone coming to rescue him. He'd fought against the men who held him prisoner, hoping for help, but the only thing his struggles earned him was pain. Although some of the clientele enjoyed it when the boys fought back he paid for it. All hope of rescue had drained out of him, but here was someone who'd taken the chance and gotten him out of the hell hole.

"What now?" Ty voiced the question circling his head.

"Now we get you healed up. We're far enough from The Warehouse now that we should be safe here for a while. After that, I don't know."

Chapter Three

As the days passed, Ty got stronger and felt more like a person than he had in years. Diego brought him all manner of interesting foods, admonishing Ty to eat up. Ty rediscovered old favourites like pizza and hamburgers, but enjoyed the Thai and Indian food as well. Diego kept the place well stocked so anytime Ty wanted to eat, he could. Compared to the bread and vegetable soup he was accustomed to eating even having fresh fruit felt decadent.

Food. Privacy. And a companion who respected him. The only thing Ty still missed was the sun, but until the wounds on his back had healed completely, he had to go shirtless and the gashes littering his back would draw too many curious looks. Twice a day, Diego washed Ty's back and carefully applied an ointment to help with the healing.

"These are looking good. You'll have scars, obviously, but they shouldn't be too bad. There are creams that will help."

"Mm hmm." Ty lay face down on the bed, relaxed and content. He focussed on the feeling of Diego's fingers on his skin. Everywhere Diego touched tingled. Ty couldn't remember the last time anyone had handled him so gently. As the contact went on, Ty became increasingly aroused and he shifted on the bed to ease the discomfort of lying with his hard cock poking a mattress.

The touch vanished and Ty let out a tiny whimper. "Don't stop," he whispered.

The bed bounced a bit as Diego stood. With a sigh, Ty lifted his head to look at where Diego stood looking through a crack in the curtains. Getting to his feet, Ty approached Diego.

"What's wrong?" Ty reached out and touched Diego's shoulder causing the older man to jerk away and stride to the other side of the room.

"Don't touch me." Diego's voice carried a hint of a growl.

Ty didn't want to push Diego too hard, but he couldn't figure out why he was reacting this way. "Why did you save me?"

Diego's eyes widened. "Seriously? You think I saved you to have you for myself?"

Ty shrugged. "Why else would you do it?"

"Listen, kid. I'm at least ten years older than you, and I may have dragged you out of that hell hole, but I am *not* a good guy."

Undeterred, Ty approached Diego again. "You're a good guy to me."

In a blur of motion, Diego grabbed Ty's arm and yanked him forward. Ty cried out as Diego slammed him against the wall and grabbed him by the throat. With the older man pinning him against the wall and the wounds on his back screaming in protest, there was little Ty could do. When he looked into Diego's eyes, the excitement glittering in them sent a thrill of fear through him.

"Would you change your mind if I told you that I get off on seeing the fear in your eyes? That I enjoy causing pain when I fuck?"

Ty struggled to draw breath and grabbed at Diego's arm to try and pry the fingers off his throat, but Diego's grip was too tight. It occurred to Ty that he might be in more trouble now than he had been back at The Warehouse. As he fought against Diego's hold, the older man pressed his groin to Ty's, grinding a sizeable erection against him. And then Ty realized that in spite of the fear, in spite of force being used against him, he was just as turned on as Diego.

****

Giving in to his darker desires was something Diego tried to avoid at all costs, but now his self-imposed celibacy put him in danger of going too far. He'd meant to scare Ty, to warn him off. However as Ty bucked his hips up to rub against Diego, the stunt appeared to be backfiring. The fear had faded from Ty's eyes. In its place Diego saw unmistakeable lust.

The kid couldn't delude himself into thinking they could have a relationship. Diego would prove it to him. Diego released Ty's throat allowing the younger man to gasp for breath. Diego pushed on Ty's shoulders, forcing him to his knees.

"Take out my cock."

With trembling fingers, Ty unbuckled Diego's belt, opened up his pants, and allowed Diego's massive erection to spring free.

Before Diego could ask, Ty had dropped his mouth down over Diego's cock. The wet heat nearly had Diego blowing his load. It had been so long since he allowed himself to feel like this. He grabbed Ty's head and forced his dick down the man's throat. God, he loved the gagging sound. He fucked Ty's mouth, wanting nothing more than to empty his aching balls, choking Ty with his cum.

Diego glanced down. Tears trickled from the corners of the kid's eyes and pleasure coursed through Diego's body at the sight. But then he faltered as an old memory assaulted him.

Diego. On his knees. Choking and crying as a man forced his member into Diego's mouth.

With a gasp, Diego pushed Ty off him and stepped back trying, without much success, to jam his dick back into his pants.

"What's wrong?" Ty asked.

"I can't do this." After finally managing to get his pants closed, Diego grabbed his gun and his jacket. "Don't leave. I'll be back."

Without waiting for a response, Diego stomped out of the room, slamming the door behind him.

The isolated motel stood in front of a small, wooded area and that's where Diego headed to blow off steam. Lifting his arm in front of his face, he screamed into the jacket to muffle the sound. When his voice grew hoarse, he turned to the nearest tree and punched it. He ignored the blood and kept going, the pain in his hand growing until he couldn't stand it anymore and then he dropped to the ground.

"You deserve it, you sick bastard," he muttered.

For years he'd managed to avoid situations that could get him into trouble, taking out his physical energy in the gym and not even allowing himself to jack-off to his horrifying fantasies. It had been going fine until Villa insisted on sending him to The Warehouse. The old man had to have known it would be a trigger for Diego. Maybe that's what Villa had been hoping for—an excuse to take Diego out. Had Villa discovered Diego's embezzlement? He'd been very careful to cover his tracks but anything was possible. It just meant Diego had to use his exit strategy a little ahead of schedule.

But the most baffling piece of the puzzle was Diego's decision to bring Ty with him. Having the boy with him meant staying in one place when he should be on the move. True, Villa would have killed the kid, probably sooner than later, but it shouldn't have made a difference to Diego.

Maybe the incident in the motel room spoke to his motivation. Maybe the desire to have a captive of his own had been guiding his actions.

The solution was clear. He had to turn Ty loose

and move on.

Chapter Four

Ty lay on the bed staring at the wall and cursing his stupidity. To come on to Diego had been a mistake. The man clearly didn't want Ty, even though his body had enjoyed Ty's attentions. Ty licked his lips as he remembered the salty pre-cum on the tip of Diego's cock. Ty's cock started to harden again. He needed release.

Jumping off the bed, Ty headed to the bathroom and hopped into the shower. He poured a dollop of shampoo on his hand and began stroking his cock. It was good but he needed more. He turned up the heat on the water and then turned so it struck his wounded back, each drop a sharp needle in his skin.

"Yes, yes!" he hissed. Raising his other hand, he wrapped it around his throat the way Diego had and squeezed. He'd been choked before by some of the men at The Warehouse, but it had never turned him on that way before. Diego managed to turn it into something highly erotic. Ty squeezed his throat harder, picturing Diego's dark chocolate eyes. Pumping his cock faster and faster, Ty finally groaned as he ejaculated onto the wall of the shower. He stood gasping for a few moments. Never in his life had he come that hard.

When his breathing returned to normal, Ty cleaned himself up and grabbed a towel. He opened the bathroom door to find himself looking into the barrel of a gun.

"What do we have here?" The man with the gun was short but solid, with muscles well defined beneath a tight t-shirt.

Ty didn't know how to respond. The man motioned him out into the main room and directed him to sit in the chair. Ty obeyed without a word. The gunman cuffed Ty's hands in front of him, and then took a seat in the other chair, angling it so he could see the door.

"I'm looking for Diego."

Ty didn't say a word. He couldn't really, since Diego hadn't shared anything with him before storming off. For all Ty knew, Diego could be halfway to Mexico.

****

Another minute ticked by on the alarm clock. In his head, Ty started another count to sixty as he watched the man pace the room. The man's agitation seemed to increase with each moment that passed with no sign of Diego. Since forcing Ty into the seat the man hadn't said anything except to mutter in Spanish when he peeked out the curtains every so often. Ty worried about what would happen when Diego returned. Did the man plan on killing Diego?

What would happen if Diego didn't return?

No doubt Ty would end up dead or back at The Warehouse where he'd wish for death.

Either way this man's presence couldn't mean anything good. Ty needed to do something.

"Can I have a drink of water?" The man ignored Ty. So Ty started coughing.

"*Hijo de puta!*" The man moved away from the window and set his gun down on the dresser beside the cups. For a moment Ty considered going for the gun but realized that even if he had enough time, he had no idea how to use the weapon. When he took a cup into the bathroom, Ty leapt off the bed, taking the blanket with him, and flattened himself against the wall outside the bathroom.

The man walked back through the door with the glass and Ty pounced. Whipping the sheet over the man's head, Ty held it in place with the handcuffs pulled up under the man's chin. He jumped on the man's back, locking his legs around the man's waist.

With a roar the man backed up, slamming Ty into the wall. Ty moaned in pain but held on tightly. The man staggered to the side and they hit the dresser. The TV went crashing to the ground along with most of the other things littering the dresser. The man changed direction but tripped and sprawled on the floor with Ty still clinging to his back.

The motel room door flew open and Diego burst in, gun drawn. He checked behind the door, and then kicked it closed and advanced on Ty and the man. He pressed the gun to the man's head.

"Don't move." The man stopped struggling. "Get up, Ty."

Ty disentangled his limbs and stood. Diego felt into the man's pockets and fished out a wallet and keys. He held the handcuff keys out to Ty who took them and freed his wrists.

"Cuff him."

Ty clamped the cuffs around one of the man's wrists, then yanked it behind his back and attached the other one. When the man had been secured Diego looked over at Ty and did a double take, his face flushing a deep red. Ty glanced down at his naked body.

"He caught me coming out of the shower."

"Put some pants on."

"Yes, sir."

As Ty grabbed a pair of sweats Diego turned the man over and pulled the blanket off.

"Santos." The sneer on Diego's face suggested he didn't think much of this acquaintance.

The feeling seemed to be mutual. "Villa's looking for you Diego."

"Why?"

"He wants his money back."

Diego sat back on his heels and ran his hand through his hair. Then he punched Santos until he'd lost consciousness. Diego started tossing all his and Ty's things into bags.

"We need to get going."

Ty pulled on a t-shirt and shoes and helped Diego load the truck. Within five minutes they'd pulled away from the motel.

"Who was that guy?"

Diego exhaled loudly. "He's a guy I worked with on Villa's weapons operation."

"What money was he talking about?"

"I was in charge of cleaning the money from our transactions. When it went offshore. Some of it always went missing into my Bitcoin account. It was part of my plan to get away from him but I guess I didn't cover myself well enough."

Ty nodded as though he'd understood, but everything Diego said sounded like gibberish. "Where are we going?"

"We have to ditch this truck." Diego passed Ty a ball cap. "Put that on and pull it down low."

Ty did as instructed and few moments later they entered the city. Diego drove around for a while and then pulled into a parking structure. Once they'd parked, Diego hopped out and gestured for Ty to do the same. He passed Ty one of the bags and they walked away from the truck. Diego led them into a stairwell and then out of the building. Ty struggled to match Diego's long strides but he was a good six inches shorter and that made keeping up difficult.

A few blocks away, Diego turned into another parking structure. They went up to the third level and headed to a nearly deserted corner. A man stood leaning against a mid-size car. Diego headed right to him and to

Ty's surprise, the two men embraced.

"Ty, this is my friend Danny."

"Good to meet you, Ty." Danny gave Ty's hand a quick shake before turning back to Diego. "I got everything you asked for."

Danny led them to the open trunk of the car. Boxes of supplies and bottled water filled the entire storage area. Danny pulled out an envelope and handed it to Diego. Ty watched in silence as Diego examined the contents. Then he pulled a roll of cash from his pocket and passed it to Danny.

"Good work, as always, buddy. And the stuff for Ty?"

Ty looked over at Danny who reached into the van and pulled out another envelope. Diego examined the contents and then passed them over to Ty. He held a passport, birth certificate, Social Security card, and a driver's licence for Ty Anthony, complete with Ty's picture. Where had they come from? What were they for?

"I don't get it," Ty said.

"Your new identity. You'll need all that to travel or get a job. Danny's got an apartment for you and he'll take you to get a bank account. I've given him enough money to take care of your bills for a year but then you'll have to figure out what to do after that."

Ty's heart raced and he got a sick feeling in his stomach. "But where will you be?"

"I have to get out of the country. Villa will be looking for me and I can't stick around." Diego threw his bag in the back of the car.

"You're not taking me with you?" Ty struggled to breathe properly and felt on the verge of tears. How could Diego just leave him behind?

"You've got to stay here and get your life together. You have a chance to start over."

The tears finally spilled out and ran down Ty's cheeks. "But I want to be with you!"

Diego wouldn't look at Ty. "I don't want you."

Ty lost it as Diego shook hands with Danny again. Ty grabbed Diego's arm but the older man shook him off and pushed him toward Danny. Ty watched through his tears as Diego got into the car and peeled away.

Chapter Five

Diego daydreamed his way to Galveston, trying hard to forget the image of Ty collapsed against Danny, and before he knew it, he had arrived at the private marina where his yacht was docked. He walked alongside doing a quick visual inspection before he boarded and began opening it up. Danny had procured the boat for him but this would be his first chance to use it. He went below into the stateroom and dropped his duffel on the bed. Two small portholes looked out on the sparkling waters of the Gulf of Mexico.

Freedom.

Diego looked over the little bathroom and then the galley, satisfied that the boat would afford him all the comfort he needed. Venturing back to the deck, he checked over the equipment, and then headed back to the car. He made several trips between the car and the boat until he'd loaded all the supplies Danny had gotten for him. By the time he'd finished the sun had begun to dip below the horizon. Figuring he'd be better off waiting until morning to leave, Diego puttered around, organizing cabinets and familiarizing himself with the workings of the boat. In the process he created a list of more things he would need.

I'll pick them up tomorrow and head out the day after that.

****

A week later Diego lay sunning himself on the deck when his phone rang. He checked the call display. "Danny! What's up?"

"I'm glad you're in cell range. Where are you?"

Diego shifted and stared out at the water before turning to look at the marina where his boat was still docked. "Still in Galveston getting … getting some stuff together."

Danny was silent for a moment and Diego rubbed his hand across the stubble on his chin. Though Diego knew he needed to set sail, he hadn't left yet and couldn't quite figure out why he hadn't found the motivation.

"Well you need to get back here."

Diego sat up. "What? Why?"

"Ty's not doing well, man. He hasn't been eating except for junk food and I don't think he's showered since he got here because he fucking stinks. Every time I go, he's just lying on the fucking couch. I don't mind helping him out but I ain't a fucking nanny."

"Fuck." Diego remembered Ty crumpled to the ground as Diego drove away. The kid hadn't been ready but in his hurry to find peace of mind, Diego had abandoned him. It wasn't Diego's problem, but it had been unfair to dump the problem on Danny. "I'll be there around dinner."

****

Hours later, Diego pulled up to the building where Danny had set Ty up. Danny waited, leaning against his car with a cigarette dangling from his mouth. He dropped it and ground it out as Diego approached. "About fucking time."

Diego clenched his jaw. "It's not exactly around the corner." Honestly. Danny was lucky Diego had even made it. He could have been to the fucking Caribbean when Danny called and then Danny would have been screwed. "Just take me up."

When they reached the apartment and Danny opened the door, the stench of BO and something rotting wafted out. Storming inside, Diego spotted Ty lying on the couch in a pair of sweats too heavy for the heat. Empty soda bottles, chip bags, and used tissues littered the floor.

Diego squeezed his eyes shut and clenched his fists. He stomped over to Ty, grabbed the kid's arm, and yanked him to his feet. "What the fuck are you doing?"

Ty blinked and glanced up. That hopeless, lifeless look had taken over the kid's eyes again. Only this time, Diego knew he was the one responsible for putting that look there. His stomach tightened.

"I didn't give you a new life just so you could fucking lie around feeling sorry for yourself." Diego winced. He hadn't meant to sound that harsh.

"Diego?"

"No, it's Santa Claus. First thing you need to do is get your ass to the bathroom and have a shower. Then put on some clean fucking clothes."

Ty hesitated.

"Don't fucking stand there! Go do it or I'm out the door." Diego didn't like threatening to leave but it had the desired effect. Ty stumbled away from Diego and a moment later Diego heard water running.

Diego surveyed the room again and then turned to Danny. "Tell me you put some garbage bags in here somewhere."

"I'll get them."

While Danny disappeared into the kitchen, Diego went to the windows and opened them as wide as they would go, then opened the sliding door onto the tiny balcony. Thank God there was a light breeze. He hoped it would help air the place out.

"Here's the garbage bags," Danny said, thrusting them into Diego's hand. "You'll forgive me if I don't stay."

"That's fine. Thanks for calling."

A couple minutes after Danny left, Ty returned from the shower in shorts and a tank top. He had a smile on his face and was practically bouncing on the balls of his feet.

"Don't look so happy. You need to clean this place up."

"Okay!" Ty took the garbage bag and started to pick up the trash scattered around the room.

"I'll be in the kitchen." Diego went into the kitchen and cringed at the fruit growing moldy on the counter and the glass of milk that had been sitting there for God only knew how long. He set to work cleaning up the old stuff and checking for any food that might still be edible. No luck.

"You done yet, Ty? I want to go grab some dinner."

Ty bounded over with the full garbage bag. "Great! We can dump these in the chute on our way."

They headed out and found a small restaurant in the plaza on the corner. Diego studied Ty as the young man babbled on about … Diego had no clue what Ty was talking about. He could only focus on his lips and the memory of how it had felt to have those lips around his cock. Damn it! He had to figure out how to get Ty more stable so Diego could escape the temptation.

When they reached the apartment again, Diego realized with disappointment that there was only one bedroom. "I'll sleep on the couch," he said. "You take the bedroom."

Ty pouted but Diego insisted and watched as Ty slumped off to his room.

Diego settled on the couch but couldn't sleep. He kept imagining Ty bound and gagged as Diego fucked his ass, or Ty strapped to a bench getting his ass spanked by Diego. Unable to help himself, he took his cock out and started stroking off to the visions. Ty crying as he begged Diego not to touch him. Ty's gasps as Diego choked him.

Ty's back littered with scars that Diego had put there.

It was too much and Diego managed to grab a tissue just in time to catch the load he shot when he came. Disgusted with himself, Diego rearranged his clothes and went to the kitchen for a drink. He heard a scream from the bedroom and raced in.

Ty sat up in bed drenched in sweat and tears. Diego went to sit beside him. "Nightmare?" The kid had had loads of them while they'd been holed up in the motel.

"Can you stay with me?" Ty looked up at Diego with wide eyes. "I feel better when you're nearby."

"I don't think that's a good idea, kid."

"Please?"

Diego sighed. "Fine. Just don't get any strange ideas." He crawled into the bed beside Ty and managed to drift off to sleep.

****

Diego woke in the morning feeling more rested than he had in a long time. No dreams had plagued him as he slept, or at least none that he could remember and that suited him just fine. He glanced down at Ty who had curled himself around Diego during the night. Ty looked very peaceful this morning, almost serene.

Diego eased from Ty's grasp and headed into the bathroom. It needed to be cleaned. He'd have to show Ty later how to do it properly. It astounded Diego how little Ty knew of the world but Diego should have expected that. When Villa had plucked Diego from The Warehouse, he'd been almost as ignorant. But Diego had had a determination that Ty seemed to lack.

Hopping in the shower, Diego avoided thinking about why he'd come back here. About what had stopped him from setting sail that first morning. He was here now so he'd do his best to encourage some self-sufficiency in

Ty before he left again.

That day, Diego made a list for Ty of things he needed to do every day, from self-care to looking after the apartment. He showed him how to plan meals and shop for groceries, as well as some basic cooking techniques. Ty proved to be an eager student, absorbing everything and coming up with intelligent questions about anything he didn't understand. Whenever Diego praised Ty's efforts, the kid lit up, his eyes looking more alive than ever.

Together they made dinner and sat down to eat.

"Diego?"

"Yeah?"

"I wondered how you ended up working for Villa. You're so different from the other guards."

Diego chewed slowly, giving himself time to think. "I'm not as different as you might think."

"You took me out of there. You saved my life. None of the others would have done that."

It took a long time for Diego to answer. "I was at The Warehouse too. I was like you."

Ty's eyes widened. "But how did you get out? And how did you end up *working* there?"

Diego shrugged. "I don't know why, but I had a harder time than most learning to submit. They never really broke me the way they did everyone else. The more they hurt me, the more determined I became that I had to do something.

"One day they took me into the cells with a guy who liked using ropes. I managed to get one wrapped around his neck and strangled him."

"Oh my God! How old were you?"

"I was fourteen. I tried to run but the guards outnumbered me and they had guns. I thought for sure I was dead." Diego paused to take a swig of his beer. Even now, years later, he still couldn't believe what had happened. "Anyway, Villa came to see me and said my talents were clearly being wasted so he offered to train me to be one of his enforcers.'

"Wow."

"Yeah. Well between the money I stole from him and what I earned through investments, gambling, and side jobs, I have enough money to disappear and be out of his reach for good. I just left sooner than I thought I would."

Ty fell silent after that. After clearing the table they did the dishes together. Diego sat on the couch and turned on the TV, flipping aimlessly through the channels. To his surprise, Ty came over and dropped to his knees in front of Diego. When Ty reached out to undo Diego's belt, Diego grabbed Ty's wrist.

"What are you doing?"

"I wanted to thank you for everything you've done for me."

"Christ, Ty! Just say thank you then."

"But I want to do this for you. Please?"

A battle raged in Diego's head. Letting Ty touch him would create a physical bond that would be hard to break later. But it had been so long and Ty was obviously willing. Diego released Ty's hands and then undid his pants. With a smile, Ty crawled forward and took Diego's cock into his mouth.

Leaning back, Diego tried to enjoy the slick warmth of Ty's mouth and his skilled tongue, but he fought against the urge to enact one of his fantasies. As a result, he was only getting partially hard. He pushed Ty off him and stood, tucking his cock back in his pants. "Forget about it. You thanked me."

"Wait!" Ty jumped up in front of Diego. "What can I do?"

"You can start by not being so damn eager!"

Ty paused for a moment before turning away. "I guess if you can't get it up, you can't get it up."

Anger surged through Diego. He strode forward grabbed Ty's arm, and yanked him back. "A minute ago you were all over me!"

"I changed my mind. I don't want to do it anymore." Defiance flashed in Ty's eyes along with a bit of a smirk. "Let me go." Ty tried to tug his arm free but Diego tightened his grip, his cock stiffening when Ty yelped in protest.

Diego took hold of Ty's other arm and slammed him against the wall. His erection surged to full strength. He pinned Ty and wrapped his fingers around the kid's throat and leaned in close.

"I want to hurt you."

Chapter Six

Ty had spent enough time in The Warehouse that he'd learned how to read the johns. When Ty went willingly, Diego had trouble getting hard. But if he had to force himself on Ty? The glorious bulge pressing into Ty's stomach told him everything. Ty was used to playing a role, but this was different. He wanted Diego. Needed him. The choice was easy.

Diego wanted to hurt him? "Do it," Ty whispered.

"What if I go too far?" Diego kept still, but his trembling suggested to Ty the battle that must be going on in the older man's head.

"I trust you."

With a groan, Diego tightened his grip on Ty's throat. Ty struggled and whimpered, getting harder than he'd ever been, until Diego released him. Grabbing the neck of Ty's t-shirt with both hands, Diego pulled until the shirt tore. He turned Ty around and bound his wrists with it before pushing Ty to his knees. Ty resisted a bit, knowing Diego would like it, but ultimately assumed the submissive position at Diego's feet. Then Diego stripped, his beautiful cock standing straight out. He pushed Ty's head back and smacked his face with his cock before trying to push into Ty's mouth. Ty kept his mouth closed and shook his head. Diego squeezed Ty's throat and pinched his nose shut forcing Ty to open his mouth to gasp for air. Diego slammed his cock in.

"That's it, bitch. Take that cock."

Diego gripped Ty's head and pounded into his mouth and throat, setting a frantic pace. Ty choked and gagged but Diego would not relent. Ty felt his own orgasm approaching and knew Diego was close too. It wasn't long before Diego roared and shot his load in Ty's mouth. Ty swallowed every drop.

When he'd emptied his balls, Diego pulled away from Ty and looked down. Though tears streamed down his cheeks, Ty wore a huge grin. Diego's gaze went to the wet spot on the crotch of Ty's sweatpants.

"You came?"

"I came so hard," Ty said.

"Huh."

Ty felt blissful. As Diego released the bindings and massaged his wrists, Ty floated on a cloud of euphoria. Diego lifted him easily and carried him to the bathroom. Diego stripped Ty and set him in the tub, starting the water. Ty remembered Diego muttering something about a walk and then fell asleep.

Ty woke when Diego shook his shoulder.

"You need to get out of the tub and go to bed."

Ty nodded and stood carefully, stepping out of the tub. He took the towel Diego handed him and dried off before climbing into bed. Diego stripped and lay beside him. A contented sigh escaped Ty's lips when Diego stroked his neck.

"I'm sorry," Diego said.

Startled at the emotion in Diego's voice, Ty opened his eyes and looked up at the older man. "Sorry for what?"

"You've got bruises on your neck."

Rolling on his side, Ty gazed at Diego. "I wanted every second of what we did. It gets you off to hurt but I get off on knowing I gave you what you needed. I like being hurt, Diego."

"I'm just like all those other sick perverts who go to The Warehouse."

"No you're not. The fact that you're this upset about it proves you aren't the same."

Ty watched as a variety of emotions flashed over

Diego's face. "Diego, I may not know much about the world, but being at The Warehouse taught me a lot about kink. The whole reason The Warehouse works is because it's a place for people who need that kind of thing. Where it fails is in forcing underage kids to be that outlet. So here's the deal. You need to cause pain and you get off on the fight. I can go along with that. If you ever go too far, I'll say red or go totally limp."

For a moment, neither of them moved. Then Diego lunged at Ty and crushed his lips against Ty's. Ty moaned and opened his mouth to the probing tongue. Diego moved on top of Ty, pinned his hands above his head, and they rubbed their erections together. Then Diego released Ty and stood up. Ty watched Diego go to his duffel and withdraw some zip ties. Ty's belly tightened with excitement. Diego used one of the ties to bind Ty's wrists together. Then Diego flipped him over and positioned Ty with his ass in the air.

A moment later something slapped against his ass cheek, bringing a cry from Ty's mouth. Ty thought maybe Diego was using his belt but he couldn't be sure of anything except the pleasure coursing through him as Diego continued beating his ass. The strikes were hard and stung like a bitch but Ty could handle it.

When Diego finished, Ty heard the distinctive sound of a condom package being opened. A moment later he felt something cool drip down on his asshole. The bed dipped as Diego positioned himself behind Ty. Then Diego pressed against Ty's asshole before thrusting hard and burying himself. Diego fucked Ty's ass the way he'd fucked his mouth. Hard and fast.

"No! Stop it!" Ty yelled and Diego halted for just a moment before resuming his relentless pounding. Ty could feel his orgasm cresting. "Don't make me come! I don't want to come. Oh, God!" Ty lost it, blowing his load onto the bed as Diego roared behind him.

****

Diego left Ty in position on the bed and went to the bathroom. After flushing the condom, he dampened a face cloth and went back to clean Ty up. His stomach twisted when he saw the welts standing out against the dark skin of Ty's ass. "I'll get some of the scar cream."

Ty murmured, sounding content, and Diego marvelled at the sudden turn in their relationship. He wouldn't have believed that Ty would get any enjoyment out of being beaten or choked, but the cumstains on the kid's pants and the bedspread said otherwise. Maybe...

Diego shook his head. One split second decision and everything was fucked up. Villa was looking for him, Ty couldn't function without him, and Diego had no idea what the hell he wanted anymore. He'd planned to sail into the sunset. Alone.

Re-entering the bedroom with the jar of ointment, Diego set to work applying it to Ty's back and ass. He cut the zip tie and massaged Ty's shoulders and upper arms. Ty sighed and cuddled up to Diego.

"Hold on a second, kid." Diego pulled the covers up over Ty and then climbed into the bed. Ty scooted closer and laid his head on Diego's chest. His breathing slowed as Ty drifted to sleep.

Post-coital cuddling had never been something Diego engaged in. Those first few years after he left The Warehouse Diego had seen a string of hookers, finding that he couldn't get any pleasure unless he got violent. And the level of violence had increased until Villa had to come in and clean up a body. Diego had known then that he was a monster. He'd replaced sex with hard work, learning the workings of the business until he'd come up with his plan to leave.

And this teenager had messed it all up.

Awkwardly, Diego folded his arms around Ty and planted a gentle kiss on his forehead. Maybe messed up was just what he needed.

****

Ty responded eagerly to Diego's instructions and before long the apartment sparkled. Diego was pleased but still unsure about where things would go from here. It was clear that Ty expected Diego to stay, but the need to get away weighed on Diego.

"I need to take a walk," he said to Ty. "I'll pick something up for dinner."

"Okay. Thank you!" To Diego's surprise, Ty kissed him on the cheek. "Don't stay out too long."

Diego bolted for the door. Outside, the air helped clear his head a bit as he walked and he could look at his options more clearly.

He could leave Ty, leave the US, and sail off on his own. Diego had always been a loner and he liked it that way. But being with Ty made him think that maybe he didn't have to be alone anymore. And Ty had already shown once that he had trouble functioning without someone taking charge.

He could stay here with Ty and risk Villa tracking him down. They could always get new identities and move somewhere else, but Diego would be looking over his shoulder a lot more that way.

He could take Ty with him. The boat wasn't huge but if they shared the bed it would easily accommodate both of them. There was still a possibility of Villa finding him no matter what, but he didn't see a way around that.

And of course, any scenario where he stayed with Ty could just as easily end with Ty dead.

Stopping for fried chicken, Diego decided that he'd give it one more week and then he'd make a decision.

Chapter Seven

As Diego approached the apartment door, he caught a whiff of cigar smoke and he stopped short. Sniffing the air, he froze. It was Villa's brand. Diego would remember it anywhere. It might be a coincidence but Diego doubted it. He set the bag of chicken down and withdrew his gun.

The scent of the smoke got more pronounced as he closed in on the apartment and he noticed the door was open just a crack. He listened but only heard the TV. Taking a deep breath, Diego kicked open the door and advanced into the room. His chest tightened at the sight before him.

Ty lay bound and gagged on the floor with one eye swollen shut and blood running from the corner of his mouth. Villa sat in a chair behind him, resting his feet on Ty's back. Fernandes, Villa's second in command, stood beside Villa with a gun pointed at Ty.

"Diego, my friend. Glad you could join us."

Not saying anything, Diego kicked the door closed behind him and advanced on the men in the living room. "Can't say I'm happy to see you, Villa."

"No, of course not. I was just telling T here how much trouble you've caused me."

"Drop the gun, Diego, or I'll shoot your little slave." Diego had no doubt Fernandes would follow through on the threat so he set the gun on the floor and kicked it out of the way.

"Sit down so we can have a chat." Villa gestured to the other chair and Diego sat as he ran through several possible scenarios where he managed to get out of this mess. It didn't look good. "Did you know your friend Danny has a boy? Ten years old. We thought the boy

203

would make a fine addition to The Warehouse but Danny sold you out instead."

Diego swallowed. He couldn't blame Danny. No parent would willingly let their child be taken like that. "So what do you want?"

"It's simple. I want my money. You'll give it to me or your little plaything here dies. You've given him some nice scars. Up to your old tricks I see."

"I can't get you the money. It's in Bitcoin."

Villa nodded at Fernandes who pulled a laptop from a briefcase at his side. Fernandes brought the computer to Diego and then stood behind him with the gun still trained on Ty. "We brought you the computer so you could arrange the transfers. You know all my account numbers, I'm sure. If not, they're all on the sticky note inside.

Diego opened up the laptop and saw the sticky. He glanced at Fernandes who stood close enough to see the screen, but far enough away that Diego couldn't jump him. Fernandes was more than willing to help with weapons and drugs, but he got just as queasy as Diego over what went on at The Warehouse. Maybe Diego could use that to his advantage.

"It'll take me a few minutes to get this all set-up and finished," he said.

"Don't take too long or T's time will have run out," Villa said. "Fernandes, make sure he's not messing around over there."

Diego located a word processor and opened it. "What are you doing with that?" Fernandes asked.

"Hit the wrong button," Diego said. "Hold on."

He increased the font size and typed into the program.

Fernandes! Play along and I'll pay you.

Diego's heart thudded as he waited for some

response. When Fernandes didn't say anything or move, Diego continued.

I have $20 million. Half is yours. Plus you can take over Villa's ops.

"Come on," Fernandes said. "Keep working."

"Just a minute," Diego said.

Shoot Villa. Kill him. I can give you all the account info. You can let me go and tell everyone that I killed him.

"Just about ready?" Fernandes asked.

"Almost." Diego glanced up at Villa who sat staring into space and blowing smoke rings. "Now."

Fernandes swung his arm so the gun pointed at Villa. Diego enjoyed the momentary look of confusion on Villa's face right before a bullet lodged itself between his eyes. The cigar fell as Villa's body slumped over.

It was really a bit anti-climactic, Diego thought as he and Fernandes negotiated their terms.

****

Ty stood on the boat deck marvelling at the water spread out before him. He'd never seen an ocean. Had no idea that there could even be this much water in one place. He turned to look at Diego who guided the boat with ease. Ty enjoyed the sun and the gentle mist that blew over his skin as they sped through the water.

When the sun began to set, Diego turned off the motor and dropped the anchor. He drew Ty against his side and Ty snuggled in close. He didn't know what twist of fate had brought them together, but he was so glad it had.

"Thank you again for saving me," Ty said.

Diego sighed. "I don't know. It's not like I gave you much choice." He glanced down at Ty. "Are you sure you're okay with this? With being on the run? Wouldn't you rather try to find your family?"

A part of Ty felt sad that he wouldn't be seeing his family again, but he'd done most of his grieving over that loss years ago. "I'd never be able to fit back into their world," he said. "And I'm happy to be with you. To give you what you need." With a sly grin, Ty slipped his hand down the front of Diego's trousers.

Diego grabbed his arm and twisted it up behind Ty, pushing the younger man against the rails. "You're in so much trouble, now," he growled.

Ty moaned when he felt Diego grind himself into Ty's ass. If this was trouble, he could live with it.

The End

www.evernightpublishing.com/michelle-graham

GET OFF HARD

Lea Bronsen

Copyright © 2016

Chapter One

Giving me the name of Slayton Heines was probably the most ridiculous fucking idea my parents could have. They've had a number of other dumb ideas in their time, but having their kid go by such a stupid name, throwing me to the reckless wolves at school, outdid them all. The neat thing is I used what felt like a handicap to toughen my skin. After cowering for a bit during the first weeks, I fought back viciously and earned respect. So much so that the school bullies started calling me "Slay" instead—a most fitting nickname that has stuck with me since. I'm as hard and cold as the ice I love skating on at the rink. And if you push me just enough, I'm flat-out lethal.

As Slay, I developed my tough-guy behavior and built a reputation in my twenties as the country's meanest hockey player. I climbed high in the ranks of the team, the league, our fans, and sports zines nationwide. They named me "Champ" too. Because that's what I was, a quarter-mile circuit champion. Standing at six-feet-two, not counting the deadly blades under my shoes, I ruled the ice, gave each game all that I had, screwed our adversaries over, and helped bring my team to victory time and time again.

Years have passed since my superstar days. Bad blood, too.

Sighing, I uncork the whiskey bottle, pour some precious drops into my coffee mug, and raise a toast to my surroundings—an old, decrepit ice rink office on the third floor turned one-room apartment, my home after tragedy hit and I lost everything I held dear. I don't exactly like this hole, but it's okay for a semblance of living.

"To life. Fucking bitch." I sip the boozed-up coffee. The hot, harsh liquid sears my throat on its way down. I wince and resist coughing. This shit's been my partner since I became a loner and I'll never get used to it.

Posters of famous eighties and nineties' hockey players decorate the flaking white painted walls. Not much personal stuff adorns the low-lit room except for my two dozen trophies and medals lined on a top shelf. No family pictures, not one homey item to remind me of the years I was a husband and a dad. I simply can't take the goddamn memories. They reappear at night, keeping me awake 'till the booze puts them back where they belong: in the farthest recesses of my mind.

I lean back in my creaking chair, put my boots on a scarred office desk that also serves as a kitchen table, and cross my legs. By miracle, they still feel muscular, as does the rest of me. At thirty-three, I may be a wreck, but I'm a big guy with hard limbs and more strength and virility than I know what to do with.

I've found one outlet, though: following my suggestion for improving the fitness of the current hockey team, the rink owner, Mr. Sampson, installed a boxing bag in the gym. When I'm finished with the miscellaneous tasks agreed to in my contract in exchange for my room—resurfacing the ice, sharpening the players' skates, picking trash after games—I punch away on the bag 'till I'm done and calm, and then I use my right fist to jerk myself off.

That's right. For me, pain and sex go hand-in-hand. Besides the drinking, it's the only way to subdue the hurt inside. When darkness falls and everyone has left, I'll even push my self-therapy a little farther. Naked behind the locked door and with hardcore riffs to drown the sounds in case some stupid fuck ventures back, I'll throw myself against the walls, bang my head 'till blackness nearly shuts me out, and scrape myself until bloody on the rough concrete floor in a desperate hunt for endorphins. All while pumping my cock as if my sorry life depends on a major, extreme release.

The next morning, if Mr. Sampson notices contusions on my face or patches of missing hair, I blame it on "another booze-related episode." It's okay, he knows everything about me—except for my sex-and-pain thingie—and as long as I help him run the rink without drawing too much attention, he tolerates my shabby presence.

I can't say the same about the others. When I'm around the hockey team, coaches and players alike throw me spiteful glances or downright ignore me. They have no idea the loner they so easily scorn is still one tough devil, and should anyone challenge me on the ice, I'd beat them to their fucking knees with the same speed, fierceness, and winner's instinct as years gone by. I haven't lost my skills. I practice when the rink is closed. I'm a killer. The game is in my blood. And they will never take that away from me.

I glance at my watch. Four p.m. In a couple hours, it'll be time to climb into the resurfacing machine and prepare the ice for the next training. Kids aged six to twelve will fill the locker rooms to don their heavy equipment and lace up their skates before hitting the freshly surfaced ice, faces flushed with excitement.

They don't mind me being around and watching. Kids don't condemn so fast. Their parents, on the other hand… I don't have a change of clothes, and with a badly cut black hair, unshaven jaw, and dark, deep-set eyes, I look like a bum. These people have no knowledge of my painful history, yet they put their heads together and whisper with glares as sharp as skate edges. But not directly to my face. No … they're probably sensing that the old champ would bite back with the same ferocity outside of the ice barrier as in the inside. My reputation of brawler has stuck with me all these years…

Pffft, fuckers.

I light a cigarette, close my eyes, and swallow the smoke way down my throat, feeling it roam around in the pit of my stomach before the poison sneaks into my veins and hits my starved brain with a *bang!* Ah, so, so good. Works every damn time, like a shot of heavenly alcohol numbing my senses so very nicely. Or the first round of kill-all blows to the boxing bag, sending a mix of painkillers and adrenaline right through my nerve system.

Yeah, I may be a sucker for these cheap tricks, but it gets lonely after a while. I've lived another life, shared it with dear ones, and known times of love and laughter. I've had the privilege of adoring a daughter, the sweetest thing on this fucking planet.

Coral, my treasured baby angel…

Fate—or whatever you choose to call it—decided that, for some sick and sadistic reason, she didn't deserve to live past her first five months.

I didn't know I could hurt so much from losing a child. The pain shattered me and destroyed my marriage. My wife and best friend, Ella, grieved and then found a new man. Everything that was safe, good, and trustworthy, everything I thought a superstar should get, spiraled out of reach. I broke down and never recovered. Without the kindness, albeit reserved, of Mr. Sampson, I would have ended my days a narc mess in the gutter.

Rest assured, I do not want my past life back. No way can I deal with such an insane amount of worshipping and happiness again whilst all too aware I can lose everything one more time. The only thing this humble guy is asking for, in his miserable second-chance existence, is someone with whom to share a certain passion, a special kind of sex game. I just want to feel alive. Obviously, staying within the confines of an indoor rink day in and day out won't help me meet the right type of person, but—

A knock sounds on the office door.

Startled, I twist sideways and bring my feet down from the desk, tangle them in the chair legs, land on my knees, and nearly kiss the damn floor. In the commotion, the cigarette slips from my fingers and rolls toward the door.

My brain swims. *Fuck, take it easy, man.* Palms flat on the firm floorboards, I stare at the cig's glowing tip for a second and catch my breath that was shocked out of me.

Another knock.

I croak, "Yeah, yeah." My voice has rusted over the years.

It must be Veronica, the concession stand lady and house cleaner. We have a deal, she and I. She brings me groceries, and I clean the bathrooms and locker rooms for her. She says she loathes working in these pigsties more than anything. I can tolerate the male pubic hair on the floor, poop streaks in the toilets, and the sour, suffocating stench left by the sweaty players after a match.

"Coming." I grab my smoke, get up, and pull the door handle.

Sure enough, the plump sixtyish woman, half my size and donning fake brown curls, stands before me with a grocery bag in her arms. My big tough-guy frame doesn't seem to intimidate her.

"Hi, Slay. Are you all right? I heard a noise…" Her squeaky voice reminds me of Mom, who passed when I was a teen. In a way, Veronica is my surrogate mother. Without her, I'd starve to death. I'd rather skip eating a week or two than go out of the building and face the world. Enduring people's stares indoors is difficult enough.

Before I can think of a smart reply, she frowns. "You've been drinking again?"

I shrug and bend to grab the bag from her with my free hand. While she is near, I take a moment to sniff in the smell of woman. She may be twice my age, but a woman is a woman. Her faint flowery scent opens a window into the past, a glimpse of what life once was … happiness, warmth…

Ugh. I blow it all out with a feeling close to disgust.

She steps back, her nose scrunching. "You should quit smoking, too."

Though my heart beats out of tune from the short dive into forbidden land, I choose to respond with humor and maybe even a little affection. "Yes, *Mom.*" Veronica is being kind and helpful—my sole humane company beside Mr. Sampson. I don't want to hurt her maternal instincts. I still keep my tone cool, telling her we'll never be close.

I don't want anybody in my life. I have no heart to share, for it was buried six feet under with my kid. The only form of intimate relationship I'm up for is casual and sexual. Preferably violent with a mutual need to get off on pain. My female partner has to be strong enough to take a beating, wrestle with me 'till we're black and blue and out of breath, and still demand some more 'cause she needs the physical hurt to have her wet pussy clench hard around my throbbing cock.

Old Veronica doesn't qualify.

"I'll be off, then." She tilts her head and squints, her scrutinizing grayish gaze saying she's read something in my eyes. I'll be damned if she's able to undress me and see the cold bastard lurking inside. "Have a nice day. I'll see you tomorrow."

"Yeah. Thanks for the food."

Lips pursed, she turns before looking back at me. "By the way, have you heard they've traded in a new player today?"

"No?"

"They say he's a champ, one of the best in the state."

How did I miss that? My pulse beats a little faster. I may be a reject and cut off from official team activities, but my passion for hockey runs deep. What concerns the players concerns me, and I follow all of the boys' whereabouts from a discreet distance. Not to mention my innate sense of competitiveness has me monitoring their acquired skills closely—I like to think no one has surpassed me yet.

A champ, eh?

Chapter Two

"Slay! Slay!"

Deafened by the *ziiinging* of the skate-sharpening machine between my hands, I look up and squint at the hall light flowing into the tiny room.

In the doorframe stands Greg, one of the young assistant coaches, his blond hair ruffled and eyes wide.

What the fuck? I freeze for a second and shout over the noise, "What's up?"

"You need to come see this"—he sucks in a breath—"there's a fight."

"Where?"

"In number three."

Weird. The players rarely fight. They release their energy on the ice and know fighting in the club is prohibited.

Relieved to leave the stench of burning metal behind, I switch off the sharpener, wipe my oily fingers on a cloth, and hurry out into the hall, grateful for the sudden silence. Though I enjoy seeing a good rumble, I don't want the players to get into trouble.

Greg jogs past a long row of doors, his boots clomping on the scarred linoleum floor. The hall is empty. Everyone must be in the locker room putting their gear on. Practice starts in a half hour, if I remember correctly.

As we near number three, angry shouts sound through the door. Greg stops outside of the room, heaving for breath. He sends me a frightened glance. He's just too young for this job. *Huh.* So when the going gets tough, it's nice to have good ole' Slay on hand after all, isn't it?

With a snarky smirk, I puff my chest and tear the heavy aluminum door open to maximize the effect on the fighters.

The smell of sweat and testosterone meets me like a dense fog. Everybody moves in a big commotion, growling and sneering, fists in the air. What the hell? Who's in charge? And where's Smith, the other coach?

"Hey!" I say using a loud, commanding tone, assessing the situation. Who's fighting who? Where do I step in?

In the center, two raging bodies slam into each other with a *bang.*

That's where I go. Head in, not hesitating. After years of hockey practice on the ice, this kind of hard-punching contact is nothing, even without the equipment. I bend forward with my clenched fists ahead of me and make space between the two fighters, hitting both of their arms and pressing them aside with my shoulders. We're the same height and build, and though they're pissed, I'm meaner and therefore stronger.

The one to my right is Dennis—not really a brawler, so he won't dare swing at me.

I turn to my left. His opponent is a stranger, the new guy? Beneath short, spiked blond hair, brown eyes flare in a face flushed and scrunched with anger. Tattoos cover his arms.

"Back off!" I order, using his slight loss of balance to push him farther backward, away from Dennis.

When his back bumps into another player, he regains his footing and charges me like a raging bull.

Oh, no, you don't. I raise my fists and meet him halfway, forearms hitting his solid chest. The shock propels him backward again while I follow and continue pushing.

Behind him, bodies move aside, out of the way. He stumbles into the wall, his legs buckling against the knee-high bench and causing him to flail. Relentless, blind with rage—or maybe just stupid—he pushes from the wall and prepares for a second round. But I'm ready, hard and unwavering.

When we connect, I sneer at his face, "Back the fuck off!" and push him back again, enjoying this bit of action. For once, the guys see me as the one I was before, a fearless son of a bitch. In a few seconds, years of humiliation have vanished and I'm the one they rely on to restore order.

There's movement to my side. Some players leave for a quieter corner of the room. That's good. If the new guy is the only one too fired up to calm down, I can handle him and control the situation.

In the corner of my eye, I notice Smith, the middle-aged coach with a protruding belly that threatens to pop his shirt buttons. He sits half-slumped on another bench with a hand covering his nose. Is he bleeding? Who hit him? I hope it was accidental, because disrespecting a coach will be cause for banning from the club.

I fix my gaze on the young bull. He slams into me full front with the sound of meat hitting meat. What's got him so pissed? I push him back again, shoving him away from me, my palms on his bulging shoulders. He smashes into the wall. While he's stuck there, I move in close and flatten my chest, stomach, and thighs against his. I hope our intimate contact will embarrass him and provoke him to give up. "Knock it off!" I mutter to his face, my teeth gritted and gaze hard. "What's your fucking problem?"

His barrel chest heaves at a quick rate against mine. Face flushed from the efforts, he refuses to answer but lowers his fists to indicate he won't resist. Sweat pebbles on his large forehead.

I stay in the same position to let him know who's boss. I want him to accept my authority and lower his gaze.

Funny how he remains put, though, his glimmering eyes staring into mine without fear and telling me something I can't decipher. Seconds pass. He accepts our intimacy a little too easily for my taste. And it's in front of the other guys. I don't know many hockey players who would have that kind of balls.

As I linger, his warm breath brushes my lips, his chiseled body feels hot, sweaty, and virile to mine, and for a beat of time, my head spins.

Shit, what's going on with me? I haven't had any alcohol in several hours, so my discomfort has to be due to something else. Am I no longer used to physical contact after living in reclusion for the past years? Or is it just that this new champ is so smart he turns our roles around?

No fucking way. I hold my breath and let go, taking a step backward. Once his heated body is no longer plastered to mine, I turn and face the other players—not just to show I'm the one in control, but to have something to do with myself and not give the new guy the impression he has won.

Dennis and some of the boys stand crossarmed in a group, glaring past me at the new player. Their gaze resembles contempt. Others, who apparently care less about the fight, sit on benches along the walls and put their hockey gear on. A few who have finished dressing leave out the door with their water bottles in hand, their skates making them walk clumsily.

"All right," I address the first group, gazing at the haughty guys one after the other, "somebody want to tell me what happened? Dennis?" I turn my hard stare to him.

Dennis, a mass of muscles with red hair and freckles, flashes his opponent a grin full of arrogance and forms a silent word with his mouth.

"Say that again!" the new guy sneers behind me.

Before I have time to anticipate, he appears like a rocket at my side with a growl and slams headfirst into Dennis, projecting him backward. Dennis stumbles and flails before regaining his balance, supported by his hooting friends, and wraps his arms around the new guy's waist. Punches fly between them with angry shouts. A fist hits the new guy in the face, but he doesn't budge. Stubborn fuck.

Time to stop this one-against-all situation before he ends up on the floor with the others on top. I dive in, catch the roaring lion from behind with my forearm circling his neck, then grab Dennis's arm and bend it until he moans and has to let go. Both of them struggle and resist me, but I have this killer determination inside that no one can surpass, not fucking ever.

When their bodies disconnect, I act on impulse and pull the new guy backward with me to the men's room. Behind a closed door, he'll have to chill.

As I force him to follow me, he turns his head and growls, mouth bleeding, "What the hell are you doing?"

The others stare, some laughing and pointing at him.

"Separating you from them." I throw a glance to the coach, who, with wide eyes and a hand over his nose, looks a bit shaken. "Hey, Smith!"

He lifts his gaze to me, something new in it shining when we connect. Maybe gratitude? Perhaps. I did take care of a rather nasty quarrel. Or respect? Who knows … he's despised me for years.

"You take care of them pricks, all right?" I send a nod in Dennis' direction.

Smith gives a slow nod, telling me that those who took part in the fight will be disciplined.

"Good." Reaching the men's room, I press the

handle with an elbow, shoulder-bump the door open, and pull the young bull inside a small, tiled room containing only a toilet.

"Now." I kick the door shut with a boot and pin him to it, my body blocking him from moving. "What the fuck was that all about?"

He swivels, chin lifted in defiance and wild eyes riveted on me. With each quick breath, his sweaty shirt sticks to his trembling upper body, displaying the chiseled contours of his muscles. He's young, twenty-five maybe, but built like a rock. I bet his abs are a sight, like mine were back in the day. A thin layer of sweat coats his skin, and beads roll alongside his face. A drop of blood prickles from a crack in his swollen lower lip, but he chews on it and sucks the blood.

"You gonna talk?" I step forward until our bodies almost touch, though not as close as earlier. Humid heat smelling of man radiates from him, invading my private space. I don't want a repeat of my previous discomfort—though I'll have to think on that one: what the fuck is it that makes me so wary of him?

Cocky, he tilts his head a little and meets me eye to eye. "You gonna punch me, too?" His voice is husky from the shouting and lathered with sarcasm. I can't believe the strength of his psyche, the stubbornness.

"No, I want you to tell me what happened."

Drawing longer breaths, calming, he glares at me but doesn't speak. What's going on behind those brown pupils? How long is our stare-down going to last?

I'm about to insist when emotion washes over his face, tightening his features. Again he chews on his cracked lip, probably in an effort to control his reaction. "They called me names," he wheezes. His eyes hold an intense glow.

I feel him, feel his pain, but am not going to opt

for gentleness. "You should be able to handle that. You're a tough guy. Deal with it."

"That's what I did."

I shake my head. "Not with a fight. When you sign with the club, you agree to—"

"So insulting me is okay? You tellin' me *you'd* be cool with it?"

"That's not what I said." I sigh. "What did they call you?"

His shoulders slump somewhat, as if the emotion is too much to bear.

Fuck, I hate seeing this young bull like this. He resembles me in my superstar days and deserves my respect. I do feel bad for him. This is his first day with the team and I know all too well what being a misfit is like.

He looks down and whispers, "Fag, among other things."

"What?"

Jaw tightening, he gazes back up with eyes shimmering of hurt. "You deaf or something? They called me a *fag.*"

I swallow his insolence and raise a shoulder. "So fucking what? It's not like it's true. Ignore them."

Something changes in his look, like a somber filter passing over his pupils. "I don't know how they found out. Maybe someone at the other club—"

Then it hits me—what he's telling me is true. But the world of hockey is brutal, unforgiving, no place for a pussy. Laughter bubbles in me, and I can't help chuckling in his face. "Are you telling me you're gay? Seriously? Beefy guy like you? Tats and all? A *homo?*"

His brown eyes slit before he raises a fist and sends it straight to my jaw.

Ouch, didn't expect that. Hit hard, my head

bounces back. I lose my balance and land on the toilet seat. Lights go on and off in my vision.

He follows and looms over me with clenched fists, his muscular body trembling and ready to give me some more.

Regaining my cool, I palm my sore jaw and grin in pure admiration. The nerve! He fucking punched me, the son of a bitch. Who would've thought!

And to be very honest … I gotta admit I like it. The pain radiating from my bruised jaw and this punk's insanely bold act have my dick stirring in my pants.

Chapter Three

Practice time. Heavily protected hockey players glide across the ice, chasing the puck and clashing into each other and the tall Plexiglas fence with loud *bangs* that resonate under my feet. The sounds of shredding skates and sticks colliding and tapping on the frozen surface echo between rink walls. There is shouting, too, but not the angry kind. The team has agreed to behave, with Smith and Greg in black coach helmets pirouetting between players and giving orders.

I follow the training itself from behind the tribune fence, having eyes only for the club's new addition and approved fighter. From Smith's addressing him, his name is Ricky, and he's one mean motherfucker on the ice. With an incredible balance, swiftness, and speed, he outsmarts the other players and sends puck after puck between their legs and into the net—each time throwing *me* a glance as if to check my reaction.

I don't give him what he wants. No recognition. No flattery. But inside I'm grinning and my heart is palpitating. The kid is experiencing the dream I lived years ago, and nothing pleases me more than to see him reenact my role of hockey superstar.

Surpassed by his obvious talent, his co-players now seem to tolerate his presence despite their previous indifferences. Or maybe it's his rough, unforgiving playing style that forces them to cooperate with him…

When Smith raises a hand and blows his whistle to announce practice is over, the team leaves the field in a slow duck walk, hunching and complaining about the exhausting workout.

It's time for me to go bring the two goal nets to the equipment room, then jump into the ice-resurfacing machine and wipe all traces from the training session.

I'm about to put my skates on, when a familiar stick-tapping sounds out on the ice. I look up—Ricky stands in the middle gazing at me. What does he want?

Again, he taps his stick, the players' signal for *"Send me the puck!"*

A game with me? Why not—I don't get invitations like this very often. Excitement fluttering in my stomach, I send him a grin. "Lemme get my gear."

He nods agreement with his helmet and swivels to skate away at full speed alongside the ellipse-shaped rink, shredding the ice with each step. *Ha,* the nerve of that kid!

****

Competing with Ricky is fucking awesome. I had no idea another person could make me feel so alive, so heady, and bring a boost of pure, unfiltered exhilaration into my monotonous life.

He's worn-out from the first practice, but keeps the intensity on a high level. I'm really impressed by his endurance. Over and over, we run across the ice chasing the puck, clash, and send one another colliding into the Plexiglas fence. My head spins and my lungs burn from the efforts, but I fucking love every bit of our fight. Though we're padded—too much for my taste—this teeth shattering competition of the champions is brutal enough to make the impacted parts of my body throb and heat. What a turn-on! I'm thrilled and horny as hell, my cock pulsing.

This feeling is quite recent. I haven't always enjoyed rough handling—it's a dark urge that developed after the loss of my family. I bet a shrink would have a field day analyzing the mechanisms in me. Maybe it's my subconscious way of telling life, *"Fuck you,"* since everything good I had was taken away from me, I play it

223

by the bad rules. Or no rules at all. It's my dark secret, and though I'd love to share it with a girl, I'll never find the right one. Too bad Ricky is a guy.

We take a break to have some water.

Chest heaving, I put the drinking tube through my face mask and gulp down half the bottle. So refreshing.

Since he stands near me for a quiet moment, I'll seize the opportunity to apologize for my behavior in the men's room. While I was busy coming to my senses on the toilet seat, he bolted out the door and never gave me the chance to explain. I seldom apologize for anything, but from his violent reaction, I must really have hurt him. It wasn't my intention.

I clear my throat. "Hey, about earlier. I wanted to say I'm sorry."

"Oh, that." He nods.

"Never meant to hurt your feelings."

"Okay."

"I don't have anything against gays, ya know."

"Don't worry 'bout it. I was a little worked up, that's all." His brown eyes glimmer through the wires of his visor. Is he telling the truth?

"Yeah, well, I wanted to make sure you knew that."

"It's okay."

"All right." I down some more water and wait a bit before raising another subject. "Are you aware of who I am?"

He smiles for the first time. I don't know why, but it embellishes his face and warms my cold bastard heart. "I know who you are," he says. "I used to look up to you when you were at the peak of your career. Even had a poster of you on my wall, among other hockey stars."

I widen my eyes at the surprising compliment, and a boost of pride inflates my chest. I've lost all contact with my fans, so it's pretty neat to meet someone who not only knows who I am from back in the day, but actually admired me. "So, today you punched one of your old heroes," I tease, flashing my teeth.

"You can say that. And I don't apologize." He grins and puts his bottle on top of the shoulder-high fence.

I raise a brow and laugh. "You don't?"

Shaking his head, he grabs his stick in one swift move and skates away from me, then swivels to face me with a half-smile and a daring look.

He wants to play some more?

All senses on alert, I drop my bottle to the ice and follow him, my entire body sizzling with excitation for another one-on-one fight.

****

Game over. Breathing fast and sweating gallons, Ricky and I glide toward the fence door while taking our gloves and helmets off. My limbs ache deliciously, and warm perspiration drifts from my chest like a fog. Our skates come to a screeching halt on the ice and we hit the door with a *bang!* We step out onto the thick linoleum mat.

In the narrow hallway, kids and adults come toward us in a long line, heading for a locker room at the other end. Everyone carries or pulls pieces of heavy hockey equipment, making our way down this passage a complicated task.

As always, seeing children gives me images of what my daughter would have been like at their age. Would she have resembled her mother or me? My heart tightens every time I say her name in my mind. Coral. When she came into my life, she filled a hole in me I hadn't known existed. The day she died, that hole became all too apparent, a deep, open-flesh wound. I'll never get

225

used to the emptiness.

Uh-oh. One of the parents, a gorgeous long-haired female, locks eyes with me. For a moment, we stare at each other, gazes gleaming. She bumps me ever so innocently as we pass.

Talk about mood change. My curiosity piqued, I turn to watch her over the kids' heads. *Damn!* Would you believe that hot thing is wiggling her ass? For me?

I grin and continue down the hall, searching for Ricky's reaction so I can make a smart comment about her. But he's ahead of me, and by the time I catch up with him, he has reached the locker room.

He tears the door open, steps inside, and throws his sweaty equipment to the floor, stripping off the parts one after the other with grunts of annoyance. From the lines in his forehead and slowness of his movements, he's drained.

I can't help bringing forth our battle on the rink as I close the door behind me. The sounds of our heavily padded bodies slamming into each other still resonate in my ears, and I remember the raw force with which we wrestled. My cock springs to life again.

The kid attracts me, there's no denying it, and I'm okay with it as long as we keep things at this superficial buddy level. I would never engage in a sexual relationship—that's what chicks are for.

Hot and excited, I sit on a bench opposite him and undress. Every piece of equipment hits the floor with a thud—shoulder pads, chest protector, shin and elbow guards, mouthpiece, the heavy girdle … and, finally, my sticky shirt. The soaked socks take an eternity to peel off my skin. You'd think I'd taken a swim with all the gear on.

Of course, my hard-on tents my boxers. There is no way Ricky was going to miss that detail. In order for him not to think *he* is the cause of my arousal, I make a point of rubbing my cock and exclaiming, "Whoa, did you see that hot piece of ass in the hall?"

"No," he grumbles, looking down as he rips off his last sock. In the buff, he's a sight of colorful, intricate tattoos from head to toe, pumped-up, shivering muscles, and full veins stretching his flushed skin. When he moves, the deep ridges between his brick-like abs make straight lines. Why is he so moody? With looks that amazing, the stud can have anyone he wants.

I continue playing with my cock through my boxers. "Man, she had a pair of tits beggin' to jump out of that tight shirt. I'm tellin' ya, I'd sacrifice my left arm to have her give me one of those titties to suck on."

"Pfft." He shakes his head, stands with a groan, and goes to the showers. I can't help noticing the firmness of his butt cheeks as he spins, and the red bruises here and there from our clashing together.

He disappears, and a waterfall sounds from the open entrance.

I strip off my boxers, cover my erection with a towel, and follow him.

In the white-tiled showers, he stands underneath the farthest showerhead with his back to me, water gliding down his hair and hard, bruised limbs in rivulets reflecting the light. Damp heat oozes from him to the ceiling.

I stop in my tracks and stare for a moment. I used to have a body like that. Though I try to stay in shape and am still surprisingly fit for a thirty-three-year-old drunk, no one will ever look at me the way I look at him now: with admiration. Those days are over.

He turns his face to me, away from the spray, and eyes me. What is he thinking?

I came in here to shower, not to stand around

naked with a raging hard-on in front of a gay man. Even though I tried making clear I was aroused by the hot chick in the hall, he could get ideas and make advances, and I'm having none of that.

Truth is the chick has nothing to do with it. Neither does Ricky, despite my deeming him a nice-looking tough guy. It's what we did together on the ice that turned me on. The roughness of our handling, his hard punches making my body jolt with energy, and our fierce sense of competitiveness. A combination of mental determination and physical interaction making all my senses beg for more. It feels better than booze. Better than sex, even. But I so want a sexual climax.

I can't get a release with a gay man staring at me like he's going to eat me up right here in the shower room.

I send him a man-to-man wink. "Damn, that female has me undone. I'll be right back." Not wanting to see his reaction, I go to the small bathroom next door, lock myself in, and hang the towel on a hook.

Whew, finally alone. I grab my stiff rod, close my eyes, and conjure up the episodes that kicked my brain into dark-sex mode. Jerking off with quick strokes and trying not to moan too loud, I replay my desire to connect brutally with Ricky's firm mass of muscles, the hard collisions that punched the air out of my lungs, and the fire in his savage eyes.

Moments later, my body tenses. I explode, searing heat spreading out from my balls. I swallow a groan deep in my throat while long rushes of cum shoot out of me, again and again.

Chapter Four

A rap sounds on the office door, bringing me out of my whiskey-induced reverie.

It's evening... I was with my daughter, for once allowing myself to think of her and some of the good times we had. It's fucking hard to ignore the sharp pain that comes hand in hand with the memories. A minute ago, I managed to push it aside. I wanted to focus on Coral's beautiful smile on her chubby baby face and keep her alive, flesh and bone, as though she'd never left.

A muffled voice sounds through the door. "Slay?" A male voice.

Yeah. Drawing a deep breath, I get up from my chair and, a bit unsteady, walk to the door and press the handle.

Ricky stands on the landing dressed in sportswear and a cap, brown eyes indecipherable. What does he want?

"Hey." I move back and let his big frame in. "Who told you I'm here?"

"Veronica." A whiff of cologne reaches my nostrils as he passes me, drowning my booze breath for a second. He stops in the middle of the low-lit room and looks around.

I'm not sure I like him seeing the kind of life I lead. Then again, why do I care what he thinks of me? It's not like we're buddies.

I close the door and point to the couch. "Have a seat."

"Thanks."

"Sure." How mighty formal we are being. I sit in my office chair, cross my legs on top of the desk, and eye him.

Seated on the couch, he folds his hands and nods to the whiskey bottle beside me. "Why do you have that?"

"Why are you asking?"

"Veronica says she brings you groceries, but I don't think—"

"Veronica talks too much."

His eyes widen. "I asked her about you. It's not her fault."

"Why?"

"Why what?"

I slip my legs down and lean forward to stress my seriousness. "Why are you putting your nose in my business?"

"I told you, I used to look up to you. Now I'm wondering what happened to you, why you—"

"It's my father's Christmas present. We don't talk, but once in a while he'll send me a bottle. Keeps me down in my misery. Nice, huh?"

Ricky blinks.

"He could've visited me and talked to me, tried to help me recover."

"I don't understand why a father would—"

"He's ashamed of me. Probably thinks I'm a lost cause."

"I still don't understand."

I shrug. "It is what it is. I'm happy to have the booze."

Eyes shiny, he leans forward. "What happened? Why did you drop out?"

"I don't wanna talk about it."

"Will you tell me, someday?"

"I don't know."

"Jesus." Before I realize his intentions, he gets up, moves over to me, bends, and puts a hand behind my head while pressing his lips to mine.

Ugh. On instinct, I lift my hands and push him away.

He stumbles back a few steps and stops to stare at me, wetness in his eyes.

I shake my head. *No.*

"Why? 'Cause I'm a guy?" he asks, voice choked.

How weird to see such a mentally and physically strong guy become so emotional. Every time he does this, I'm surprised. "Yeah, 'cause you're a guy." I feel his sincerity and don't want to hurt him, but he can't just kiss me and think—

"Fuck!" He steps forward hands first and pushes at my shoulders, destabilizing me.

I regain my balance and face him.

"It's not fair," he wheezes. "I don't deserve your shit."

"My shit?" What a bold prick. In other circumstances, I'd put him in his place.

He splays his hands. "I'm a healthy, normal guy."

"I never said you weren't."

"So, what's wrong with me?"

"I prefer women, that's all. Nothing against you personally."

He lowers his voice. "You have any idea how hard it is to be rejected because of my sexuality?"

"No. But I do know how hard it is to be rejected, period."

"I know you do. And maybe that's why I'm drawn to you. I wanna see how you deal with it."

"I don't. I drink and hide." I shake my head again, these outspoken words reminding me of how truly alone I am. Which is why I need physical pain to forget.

He sits back on the couch and hunches. "After my family learned I was gay, they threw me out. My friends dropped me, too. In the other club, I was a top scorer, like you, but someone caught wind of my sexuality and ruined everything. Thankfully, the manager traded me into this club here. He said he hoped I would blossom, that I'd be happy."

I nod.

"So, I play hockey 'cause I'm damn good at it and it makes me feel worthy. I lift weights and cover my bod with ink 'cause it makes me feel like I'm one of the guys. But the truth is I'm on my fucking own. The only people I have left are my grandparents. They send me money so I can have a"—he makes quote marks in the air—"*nice* apartment."

"The club don't pay you enough?"

He shrugs and lifts his sweatshirt to display the colorful tattoos covering his chiseled chest and stomach. "I've been getting these, and I'm goin' to a private fitness gym."

"Well… At least you have your grandparents. You're not alone."

He grimaces. "They don't call me. They just send money."

I raise a brow.

"They hate that I spend *their money* getting the tats instead of finding that nice apartment. But I don't care. I do what I want with my life. I'll spend the dough on whatever I want and use what's left to rent a dirty room somewhere. I really don't fuckin' care."

Uh-oh, I don't like the sound of this. "Don't be like me." I roll my chair over to him so we're face-to-face.

His eyes ping-pong between mine. "What do you mean?"

"Don't become a bum like me. Don't lower yourself to living in a small, dirty place in a dangerous neighborhood just so you can afford to be this tough guy and compensate for your sexuality."

"*What?*" His face scrunches in anger. "Fuck you!" He reaches out and gives my shoulders a shove so hard, my chair tips over.

"Ah!" I flap with my arms but can't avoid being propelled backward. My chair skids and lands on the floor with a shattering noise. The back of my skull hits and bounces off the hard surface. A sharp pain shoots outward before reds and blacks invade my brain, but I fight to stay awake, don't want to go away. This is too good, the hurt so intense I'm feeling alive for once, really motherfucking alive, tenfold what I experienced on the ice earlier. All the nerves in my head are on fire, sending sizzling darts of heat down my body, all the way to my groin.

"Slay," a distant voice says to my buzzing ear. Hot breaths brush the side of my face. "Slay, come back."

I croak, "I'm here." Floating in a euphoria of pain and digging it. The air was punched out of my lungs, but I catch my breath slowly. I fix my eyes to the ceiling above while endorphins circulate my body and blood inflates my cock. This sharp pain pulsating in the back of my head gives me the hard-on of the century. *Ha ha,* I feel so good! I'm laughing at life and kicking it in its face. This feeling is my fantasy, the condition I try to reach in the gym while hitting myself like crazy.

I reach for my throbbing cock and palm it through my jeans to ease the pressure.

An intake of breath sounds in the silence, almost a gasp.

Vision dancing, I gaze at Ricky.

He's at my side, on his knees, twining his hands, looking bothered. Not exactly sheepish, for his dark eyes glow with their usual fieriness and I read no apology in them, but he clearly doesn't like the situation.

Well, fuck him. I didn't go over the line addressing his issues, but this young bull has a way of taking everything personally.

He shifts. "Why in the hell aren't you pissed off?"

"Pissed off?"

"Yeah, you're lying there with a big grin on your face. If I were you and someone did this to me, I'd jump up and—"

I lift a hand. "I have a fairly good idea of what you'd do."

"You're not answering my question."

"And you're an arrogant asshole." I eye him and fight to stay calm. "I'm not angry, 'cause what you did makes me feel…" I don't know how to put it without making the message too blunt. Maybe he'll condemn me, like society would, if I tell him I get off on pain.

I catch him glancing at the bulging erection in my pants. Part of me is so turned on, I want to tear my zipper down and ask this stud to do whatever the fuck he wants to with my cock. No doubt he's good at this, better than a chick, even. But for me to allow it, I need to get past the fact he's a guy and accept he has a cock, too. What am I supposed to do with that? I've never touched another guy's dick. That's always been totally out of the question.

Maybe the booze can loosen me up. If I drink myself senseless, I won't be conscious of what I'm doing. Or accountable.

I raise my head, ignore the dots dancing before my eyes, and point to the whiskey on the desk. "Gimme me the bottle."

"Okay. But first…" He leans over me and lingers for a second, a big mass of heat and masculine strength hovering over me with cologne sneaking into my nostrils and deep, brown pupils staring into mine. What is he up to? Is he going to kiss me again? Will I allow him this time?

Heart beating out of tune, I gaze at his full, parted lips and wait. Trapped by the fallen chair underneath me, I can't escape. Not sure I want to. Some crazy part of me gets a kick out of the red-black crack in his lip, and I want to lick it, suckle it. Definitely crazy. Must be the blow to my head.

Before I have the time to do anything, he slides his hands underneath my armpits, pulls me up from my chair with surprising ease, and helps me over to the couch.

Ugh. I grimace from the pain in the back of my skull and slump on the soft cushions with a breath of relief. My brain swims and my cock throbs worse than ever, threatening to burst my fly open. It takes all my will power not to rub it. I don't know what I'm waiting for. Maybe for the nice, hot liquor, so I can let consciousness slip out the drain and let the young bull fester on me. Having a homo suck on me can't be all that bad. I could think of far worse things happening.

Ricky grabs the whiskey, turns back to me, and sits on the couch. He makes an effort not to sit too close, doesn't even glance at my crotch, probably wary after my previous rejection. The punk is too proud to be burned twice.

He takes a sip, swallows with a grimace, and passes me the bottle. I have a few harsh gulps, too, and close my eyes while the liquid torches my throat and stomach.

An uncomfortable silence settles between us.

The bottle slips out of my hand. A gulp sounds at my side, followed by a pained gasp. Then more, and again. He coughs. Is he drinking to drown his pain?

I open my eyes and take the bottle from him,

swallowing some of the burning drink.

The kid looks lost as he chews on his lower lip and keeps his gaze straight ahead, fixed at some point on the wall across from us.

I want to move my hand to his nearest thigh and squeeze these nice, firm muscles, tell him I'm here and not such a bastard he can't give me another try.

After a long silence, I ask him, voice low, "You're not saying much."

He sighs. "I'm tired. Long day, new faces, new fucking challenges." Wetness grows in his eyes and he turns aside so I can't see him.

"Hey, have some more." I reach out and tap the whisky on top of his thigh.

Not looking at me, he accepts the bottle and lifts it to his lips, then secures it between his thighs.

With the booze sloshing in my veins and deliciously numbing the pain in the back of my head, it's time to consider whether I can accept having a sexual relationship with this guy or not. Can I put aside the fact Ricky is a male and just see the great person he is? I like him, so why is that such a big deal?

His head slumps backward, eyes closed and mouth half-open. Has he fallen asleep? *Man,* he must be drained.

Regular breaths heave his chest. I pinch his arm, but he doesn't react.

Okay. I grab the bottle from between his legs and put it on the floor. I've had enough, too.

I study him, this young, brave stud who hides his fragility beneath a tough layer of boldness and arrogance. The more we are together, the more I realize he's just like me. A younger me. He has the same courage, determination, and want to push himself harder, and the same sense of competitiveness and killer instinct on the ice. Like me, he has a strong personality with a dark side he feeds on to be the person he is on the outside. But how twisted is his inner darkness? How far is he willing to push it? Can he combine his inner pain with a physical one to obtain relief?

Everything about him tells me he might to be the one I'm waiting for—a very special kind of person with whom I can have a sexual, strictly casual relationship with no emotional strings attached.

He himself has apparently fallen for the rugged ex-champ turned recluse that I am and doesn't mind my dirty ways or low spirts. He accepts me and doesn't condemn me or advise me to change.

The question is, can I accept him, too? Can I make up my mind to choose *him* to play with? And will he be up for my hard, mean sex games? Will he enjoy them as much as I do?

There's only way to find out, and that is to test him.

Not in my office. We need more room to move about and loud music to drown the sounds. The gym is a more fitting place. I'll have to carry him, then. Best do it before he wakes because I'll have to lock him in to make sure I have time to show him everything and test his bad-boy playing ability.

I bend near his chest, place his arms and large chest over my shoulder, and lift him. *Whew,* he weighs a goddamn ton, but I've learned to handle this kind of dead weight from years of hockey, trying to knock players out and carry them off the ice.

The gym is two floors down. I can take the elevator. It's late and there shouldn't be anybody in the hall. With luck on my side, I should be able to bring him there unseen, then lock the door and hide the key.

Yes, that's what I'm going to do.

My heart beats faster and adrenaline kicks my nerves alive. I'm sizzling with a weird mix of nervousness and anticipation. It takes some kind of balls to abduct someone and keep him imprisoned within the confines of a public building, but … just the thought of the twisted things we can do together makes me even harder.

Chapter Five

For about a half hour, I've sat with my back to the wall watching Ricky. Lying on a gym mat in his alcohol-induced sleep, he hasn't stirred once. If he doesn't wake soon, I'll have blue balls for the rest of my life...

The building is about my age and it shows in the way humidity crawls up the grayish, flaking walls. To make our rendezvous more intimate, I keep only a couple spotlights lit. They cast tortured shadows from the various gym equipment machines. A horror movie could easily be set here.

Black metal music blasts from a speaker in a corner. I've chosen one of my favorite bands in the genre, *Satyricon*. Their dark, heavy guitar riffs, doomsday lyrics, and the vocalist's growl-like voice trigger the darker sides of my mind and keep me focused on the task at hand—testing Ricky's ability to become a playmate.

Sadly, no woman has titillated me enough to go this far, neither has any man before Ricky. This young, arrogant stud is the first one with the right combination of fighting instinct, will power, bodily strength, mental resistance, and rebellion. The big question is, does he have it in him to mix sex with pain?

C'mon! I grab a water bottle and spray some cool drops on his face.

He grimaces, sucks in a breath, and opens his eyes wide. "What the—" He lifts his head, losing his cap in the movement, and scans the four corners of the room. "What the fuck!" Bewilderment on his face, he blinks and turns to me. "Did I pass out here? No..."

I don't reply, and keep my features placid. In time, he will answer his questions and discover my plan on his own. Only then can his reaction be genuine and I find out whether he's the right person to play with or not.

So much at stake. A rapid pulse beats in my neck; the only thing he sees that betrays my inner excitement. I'm tense. If this experiment goes badly, there's a possibility he'll press charges for abducting him, and the legal system will certainly have a heyday with that... Then again, I'm already locked up, with no perspective for the future. Prison here or prison there, what's the difference?

He rolls over to a side, gets up on his knees, and scrambles to his feet. Swaying, he waits a minute before going to the door and pressing the handle. It clonks, but nothing happens. Slowly, he turns back to me. "Why is it locked?"

Without a word, I get up and face him. The next moments will be crucial.

He squints, his eyes darkening. "Where's the key?" He doesn't look scared, but pissed.

I don't answer.

He closes the distance between us and does his usual push-my-shoulders thing, shoving me backward. "Slay, where did you put the fucking key?"

Good, we're getting somewhere, and his rough reaction turns me on. I'm so ready for this!

He gives me another push, harder this time. I stumble back a few steps, but find my balance. Thank fuck the fitness room is large enough for us to play our little game without bumping into all the equipment laying around.

"Unlock it!" He sneers. "Now!"

I meet him face-to-face with a grin.

His eyes slit. "You sick fuck. What the hell are you doing?"

From the escalation of things, he will find out soon enough.

Nostrils flaring, he shakes his head and gives me a look of contempt. "I always knew something was wrong with you."

These words sting a little, but I keep my cool.

"You gonna open that door, or I have to make you do it?"

I shrug.

His response comes hard and fast: a punch to my stomach, knocking the air out of me.

Damn, the kid is a born boxer. I'm not going to fight back. Yet. Instead, I double over and lean my forehead against his chest to recover, but he sends me a new punch with the other fist.

My stomach cramps and burns, forcing me to draw deep breaths to regain my composure. *Okay, enough.* My turn. With a growl, I take a step back and head-butt him in the chest with all of my strength, sending him flying backward.

He loses his balance and lands ass first on the floor. "Fuck!"

I won't give him time to move. I jump on top of him, straddle him, and press his spread arms down. Can he feel my hard-on pushing into his belly?

Face flushed and contracted with anger, he wheezes, voice barely audible above the music, "You really are sick."

If you only knew… I lift my brows with a pleased grin that only enrages him more.

Somehow, he manages to roll me over. We tumble sideways, two big bodies still enlaced, and wrestle. I don't know exactly what we're trying for, but we hold each other down before rolling around again, one the stronger man a minute then the other taking over. It's all about physical strength, endurance, and a good dose of shrewdness.

I dig such an aggressive handling, it's in my fucking blood, and this is how I want to die—fighting with a worthy opponent and donning the biggest hard-on ever.

He sends a mean fist to my jaw so my head bounces aside and my ear hits a square, metallic object, maybe a rack. The sudden, extremely sharp pain in my ear is barely tolerable.

All fired up, I bring my knees up to my chest and shove Ricky away as hard as I can. He lands on his back with a loud *thud*, and I jump up again and sit across him. He has woken the dark beast in me. Now he'll see what I have in mind. Pinning him to the floor with all the force I have in my arms, I lean over him and put my lips to his, clashing our teeth together and seeking a way to enter my tongue into his mouth.

He groans and writhes underneath me, but eventually relents. Is he sensing the meaning of my actions?

Breathing fast, I let go of his mouth and stare at him. In the low-lit room, he returns the stare calmly but with eyes dark and holding a gleam I seldom see in a man. It's no longer anger—I recognize the cocky stubbornness, pride, and self-confidence of the superstar I once was.

His chest heaves for air, firm muscles pushing into me. "You're one mean motherfucker, you know that?" he asks, voice close to a growl. So fucking rousing.

I grin. "Question is, do you like it?" Before he gets to answer, I catch his half-open lips again and bite the lower one, right where his cut has begun to heal, then suck on the crusted crack 'till it opens and a drop of blood reaches my tongue. The coppery taste ensnares me, urges me on. I rub my swollen dick against his belly to stress what I want to obtain from all of this and to let him know what my goal is.

He lets out a gasp and jerks underneath me.

This is the moment of truth—what if he tells me to fuck off?

"Jesus, do that again," he groans, eyes closed.

What?

As if succumbing to a strong need, he lifts his pelvis with a long, hard rod pressing against mine.

My fucking God, I can't believe he's up for this game. Oh, but he is. Sizzling with lust, I release his arms, reach for his ruffled hair and stick my tongue into his open mouth. I lick him all over, explore every part, roam deeply. Drawing back a little, I bite his cracked lip again and suck his wound dry.

A low groan erupts from his throat. He not only lets me fester on him, he sneaks a hand to the erection tenting my pants between us and fondles it. Heat envelops me and sweet darts of pleasure shoot outward. It's the first time a guy touches me down there, but it's strangely okay.

He must be thinking the same thing. When I withdraw from his mouth to catch my breath, he opens his eyes and stares, his gaze feverish. "Uhm, what's the big change? You said you didn't like guys, but you—"

"I like *you,* you little punk." My heart stills. This is more than I've ever said to a man, and now, in my life as a bum, there is no other soul but Ricky that deserves my affection.

Ricky flashes me a warm smile, before his eyes move to the side of my face that is swollen. "Hey, you're bleeding!"

Frowning, I reach for my ear, which still throbs, and bring my hand between our faces. Blood. The rack I hit must have cut my ear. "I don't care. Slap me there."

His brows furrow. "Huh?"

"I said, slap my ear. Hard."

"Why?"

"Because I *feed* on it."

"That's perverted."

"Like when you enjoyed me biting your lip."

He grins. "Okay. You asked for it." He sucks in air and sends a flat hand to my wounded ear, the contact shockingly painful and the ringing inside overwhelming.

I wince and close my eyes. My head spins and it takes me a while to recover. Black and white dots swim in my inner vision. The good thing is the pulsating hurt almost has me ejaculate. Keeping my eyes closed, I demand, "More," and wait. My whole body tenses with anticipation and the need to climax.

"Okay."

I don't see the next blow coming. When Ricky's iron-like palm hits my ear, the pain is so surprisingly sharp I have to drop my ringing head to his forehead with a grimace. "Aww, fuck." Heat traverses my cock and drips out of its tip. Pre-cum. All hell is about to break loose. I growl a warning. "I'm gonna come."

Warm puffs of breath from Ricky's mouth brush my lips. "Wait. Get up." He pushes my chest and stomach up above him. Once I remain in that position, he moves the waistband of his sweatpants down to his ankles.

Shit, this is for real. I'm in a sexual situation with a guy. Though I've arranged for it to happen, it's still mind-boggling, challenging everything I've believed about me and my maleness, and forcing me to face this innate unease about homosexuality. But there's no backing out. Especially not for a fucked-up brawler like me. Trembling with the feral desire to explode, I open my eyes and glance down.

Ricky's thick, purplish erection stretches from a mass of black hair to the lower tattoos of his firm stomach. So manly.

I blow out air. I don't want to give too much thought to the fact that my transition from straight to bi happened so fast, or the reason why such a morph was even possible. Moving back onto my calves, I spread his legs and lift his ass to rest on my thighs for better access. I unzip my pants, fist my pulsating and very needy cock, and point its tip to Ricky's butt crack. No reason to wait.

He gazes at me with his lips parted and eyes hooded.

A thought pops into my mind. "You got a rubber?"

"No, but I'm clean."

"Me too. Haven't screwed anyone in like a century." Since my wife. My breathing erratic, sweat rolling down my chest, I try to stall my impending orgasm by reaching for his butt cheeks and giving each a hard slap.

"Ouch!" He grimaces. "Take it easy, BDSM man."

"What's BDS-something?"

"Bondage and shit."

I raise a brow. "I don't see how bondage has anything to do with this."

"Well, you get off on pain, so that qualifies as sadomasochism. Spit on your cock."

"*What?*"

"Use your spit to lube your dick. I like my ring muscle the way it is, intact."

Ring muscle? I chuckle. New terminology for me.

I gather some spittle in my mouth, drop it on my length, and smear my thick penis head with a couple fingers. I'm more in control now. Our talk has lessened the need to come.

With both of his big, muscular thighs spread on

my lap, I ease into his crack. I look too big to penetrate that tiny hole, but bore fast anyway and past the hindrance, burying myself balls deep inside his hot, super-tight tunnel in one single thrust. *Fuck,* this new feel is heavenly, the friction much better than with a pussy.

"*Ow!*" he complains, arching his back, "too fast." But his cock jerks, revealing he must enjoy the combination of sex and pain. So my suspicion was correct—he has the potential to be a playmate.

"You like when it hurts?" Pumping inside of him, gliding in and out, I chase my orgasm. Ricky's tightness is so perfect, the gliding of my dick past his ring so good, I'm high again, my climax just within reach. The rhythmic sounds of flesh slapping flesh fill the room.

"I've only…" he groans with ragged intakes of air, "been with someone a few times … it was a *nice* kind of approach, while what you're doing is kinda dark… But I … but I like it. Every sensation feels stronger, sharper."

Exactly. His words make my brain spin. Like a rocket, my hovering orgasm crashes down on me, sending me into a complete, overpowering bliss. I cry out loud while long rushes of searing hot cum shoot out from the deepest of me, over and over, and into him. *Fuck me,* this is the wildest … ever…

It takes a long time for me to recover. I catch my lost breath and come back to Earth. My thighs trembling as if I'd run a marathon and my head still in a daze, I slowly pull out of Ricky with a thankful, "Whoo!" and meet his ecstatic gaze.

The gorgeous kid grins. "That was fucking awesome." Beneath his short-cut hair, sweat pearls on his face and throat, giving them a shiny glow in the low light.

"Yeah. Awesome and…" *Crazy.* I've just had sex with a guy. I don't want to tell him how shocking that is to me. It would hurt his feelings. On the contrary, I want to comfort him and make him feel good. "You deserve a release, too." I push his sweatshirt up to his ribs and stroke the tight, warm muscles of his stomach, draw the contour of their neatly sculpted shape. It's the first time I caress a man's body, but it's no different than caressing a woman—except he sports a furious boner begging for my attention. Can I give him what he wants?

I need to think. Buying time, I lift Ricky's sweatshirt farther up his heaving chest. A thin coat of perspiration covers the tight skin of his pumped-up pectorals, defining the ridges between them. Short, ragged puffs of air escape his parted lips. I focus on those fleshy things and want to bite them again, but choose one of his nipples instead.

As I approach my teeth to the erect bud, the musky scent of maleness fills my nostrils, and it's surprisingly all right—ensnaring, even. How can it be? The smell of other men have always repulsed me. I put my mouth over his nipple and suck it in. His skin tastes the same, and it hits me: I like this scent and taste *because they're Ricky's*. The kid is growing on me.

Stunned, I give the nipple's surrounding flesh a bite so sharp the flavor of blood bursts onto my tongue, like juice of a ripe fruit.

"Aww!" He jerks and groans. His hands shoot to my head and fist my hair in an attempt to pull me away.

After letting a few seconds pass to tease him, I release the bruised piece of skin and allow him to lift my head. Glancing at him, I lick my copper-tasting lips.

He grimaces and disentangles his fingers from my hair. "It's my first time, Slay. You wanna take it a little easy. Like, alternate the pain and the pleasure. Some pain, some pleasure."

I sit back on my calves and let him speak.

His eyes shine. "Give me time to adjust. Like

now, you could…" He reaches for his erection, pushes it to stand between us, and holds it at the base while sending me a questioning look.

That, I can do. I grab his cock—a first for me, but nothing different than holding my own—and stroke the firm, velvety shaft up to its thick mushroom head and down.

A gasp escapes him. Face flushing, he stares at my caresses.

I smile. "You like it?"

"Fuck, yeah."

While I pump him the same way I'm used to doing myself, images from the past flash in my mind. My wife, Ella, bending in front of me and taking my cock in her mouth, her long hair sliding alongside a shoulder like a golden waterfall. The tip of her hot, wet tongue easing into the hole at the tip of my cock then deliciously licking around my veined length in a slow dance, each stroke leaving a wet trace on my stretched skin.

As if reading me, Ricky asks, voice raucous, "You wanna taste it?"

The vision of Ella evaporates, and it doesn't make me sad. I'm over her.

Ricky watches me.

Well, to put his dick in my mouth would be like sucking my own dick. How can any man do that? Damn, it's against my nature.

"It's okay," he says. "You don't have to."

"Hey." I wink, swallowing my discomfort. "Give me time to adjust, right?"

"Yeah."

"Maybe next time."

"There's gonna be a…?"

I flash him a grin. "Sure."

We hold each other's looks. Desire burns in his

eyes, and confidence. He trusts me. Of course there will be other times. The way we connect and enjoy the same things, I see many experiences ahead. But that will include fucking—not just me doing him, but him doing me, too. I stare at his cock in my hand. Would I be willing to try … impaling myself with him?

"What are you thinking?" he asks.

The black metal music stops, as if on cue. The sudden silence in the room accentuates the eerie sense of suspense.

I never thought I'd do it, but why not? I'm so full of endorphins and adrenaline and pain from my still-aching ear, sticking something up my butt can't be that bad.

"Hey, Slay, you can hurt me now if you want to." Concern in his tone. He must be sensing a shift in my attitude and worrying that I change my mind.

Without a word, I rest his cock on his stomach, reach for the nipple I bit earlier, and pinch the bud until its skin turns a furious red and droplets of blood prickle out of my tooth marks.

He writhes like a worm and gasps.

Now, to act. I get up on shaking legs.

His eyes widen. "What are you doing?"

"Close your legs." I slap the sides of his thighs and wait for him to obey so I can pull my pants down and straddle him.

"Do you wanna…?" The astonishment in his voice has me grinning again.

On my knees above his crotch, I grab his cock again, lube it with semen leaking from my still-hard cock, and direct it to the sensitive hole in my ass.

"Wow, you're amazing." Admiration lathers his voice.

I don't reply. I'm so fucking nervous my pulse

beats out of control and sweat runs down my temples, but I've got this. I'm Slay, and I don't cower.

"Take it slow the first time."

I throw my head back and swallow a deep breath. "But you know I'm a sucker for pain."

He chuckles.

The firm tip of his cock pokes at my entrance. Everything in me says it's not natural, I'm not supposed to stick anything up my ass. Still, it's what gays do, and more importantly, it's what Ricky wants, what he needs me to do. We're playmates, he's given me a mind-blowing orgasm, and I owe him one in return. I may be a bastard, but I have honor codes.

One, two... Fixing my gaze on a spot in the ceiling, I lower myself onto him and … accept … the intrusion, the invasion of his thick shaft inside me. *Owww.* When the hard tip passes my ring, all the nerve endings at that tiny hole come alive, a fire raging right there with flames shooting outward. *Fuck,* it hurts so bad I grind my teeth and hold my breath, focusing on the burn and ignoring everything else. That's what I chase when I hurt myself: a physical pain so consuming I forget about the torturous ones plaguing my mind.

After what feels like minutes but is probably seconds, I've gotten used to the searing pressure and glance at Ricky.

Eyes closed, he arches his back and lifts his pelvis to press more of him inside me. "Don't stop," he groans. "Please."

I release a breath. "Yeah." Large beads of sweat roll down my abs. Too hot. I pull my sticky t-shirt over my head and toss it aside.

Then farther down Ricky's cock I glide, until all of it has slid in and I'm sitting across his hips. He fills me so well, and the sensation of fullness mixed with the constant burn of my asshole makes my cock twitch. I dig this, want more. It's like an itch I can't help but scratch. I raise my hips with slow, calculated moves, enjoying the renewed pain sending darts of pleasure to my brain, and almost have him slip out of me before I descend again.

He opens his brown eyes wide. "Holy fuck, you're hot!" Mouth agape, he lets his gaze roam all over my naked body, from the point where we're connected at our inner thighs, up my abs, crossing my chest from one shoulder to another, and ending at my face.

What an amazing feeling to be eaten up like this.

"A dream come true," he whispers, shaking his head, before giving me a loaded stare.

Beside admiration, I read respect, honesty, and something I haven't seen much in the past years—affection. The kid actually makes me feel good. About myself, about sex, about being with *him*. Warmth fills me, inflating my chest and making me light-headed. Strangely, right now I don't need pain to be alive, don't need it to drown anything inside.

Content, I rest my hands on my hips and let his thick cock glide in and out of me at a quick, controlled pace, pumping him over and over.

He groans with each thrust. Soon, he will come like crazy.

Look who's talking… With the intense burn and fullness in my ass—and the look of unfiltered desire in Ricky's eyes—my dick stiffens to an intolerable level again. *Fucking hell.* I'll just have to fist it between our glistening stomachs and give it what it wants.

"Wait, let me." With ragged breaths, he snatches my cock from me and pulls on it, stroking the length of my shaft with expert moves.

Oh! The tug from another guy is a complete surprise. This is insanity. But he knows what he's doing.

While I ride him, making him thrust in and out of my tunnel at a steady rhythm, he grabs my sack with his free hand and squeezes each sensitive nut tight, oh so tight, and tighter still, until they're small and hard like golf balls. The sharp pain has me seeing fucking stars.

"Shiiiiiit." Heat rushes through me. Am I capable of having another release so soon after the first one? Arching my spine, I reach for the back of my head and fasten my hands there. My body trembles.

The more I increase the speed and friction inside my ass, the more Ricky pulls at my cock and squeezes my jewels. The combination of pain and my renewed arousal is so intense and similar, I can no longer tell what is what.

Epilogue

"Bring your skates," Ricky said in my office door the next morning, radiant, before pulling me out with him. And I mean out, as in *outdoors*. A place I have rarely visited in the past years. So, after donning my winter jacket and gloves, I followed him to the skating rink outside, which is right next door to the indoors one I have hibernated in.

It's sunny and chilly, the sky a clear, bright blue. I squint from the unusual light stinging my eyes. The crisp air bites the skin of my face.

Kids and adults alike glide and pirouette around on the ice, some showing their figure-skating skills. Squeals of joy and applause fill the open area. They are all so busy having fun, they don't notice the couple of guys walking in their direction.

Well, I say "couple," but not in the sense that Ricky and I are engaged or anything. Which brings me back to yesterday. The last thing he said as we prepared to sleep on my couch back in the office was, "Is there any place for love in all of this?"

"Love?" I asked, my body bruised and my mind high on the best, darkest sex ever.

"Yeah. What we did in the gym was amazing. It was wicked in many ways, but I digged every bit of it."

"So if I'm understanding you correctly, you wanna know if love stands a chance when the sex is so bad and dirty?"

"Uh-huh."

I honestly didn't know what to reply to that and told him so, whereupon we fell asleep in each other's arms.

A ringing tone brings me back to the present. My

phone.

Sending Ricky a questioning look, I take off my gloves and fish the phone out of my pocket. The screen says, "Sampson."

"Hello?"

"Slay?"

"Yes."

"How are you?"

"Very good, and you?"

Laughter sounds at the other end of the line. "Excellent. Where are you?"

"Outside." I omit being with Ricky, for fear Sampson will deduce we're being more than buddies.

"Outside? Well, that's … unusual."

Yes.

"Listen, I have good news for you."

"Yeah?"

"Smith was very impressed with the way you handled the fight yesterday, and he saw you skating with Ricky after practice. He says you have *major* potential and it's a shame the club isn't using you for other tasks than … you know."

"Oh. Well. Thank you." What does this mean? I glance at Ricky, who leans against my shoulder and eavesdrops on my conversation. Heat oozes from his ear, thankfully warming my bare fingers in the cold. The only bit of him I can see is the red tip of his nose and the damp puffs of breath he exhales. I smile.

Sampson's voice comes through again. "So, I talked with the board members, and listen to this—"

"I'm all ears."

"The chairman suggested we hire you as a coach. You and Smith will have the same status. He's getting old, and between us, Greg isn't really up to the task, so we would've been looking for new blood soon anyway."

My heart makes a triple flip, and I widen my eyes in surprise and awe. "Oh. That's very kind of you. I didn't expect—"

"If you accept, we'll discuss the details when you're back at the rink."

"Of course."

"I'll see you later, then."

"Yeah. Thank you, Sampson."

The line cuts.

I suck in a long, deep breath, filling my lungs with chilly air and feeling as though I haven't breathed right in many, many years. Then, eyes blinking with astonishment, I turn to Ricky. "Did you hear that?"

The young stud grins from ear to ear. "Congrats, coach. You'll be able to afford a decent place to live now."

I smile back and resist adding, "With you". One day into our relationship is way too early to invite another person to live with me. On the other hand, Ricky isn't just "another person." He's my embodiment, fitting me and my bad ways like a glove sex-wise—quite literally—and earlier, as we passed the Plexiglas wall encircling the indoors ice rink, he promised he was going to get me back on my feet. "You'll see, the champ will make a comeback," he said, and apparently, he was right.

Wow. I still can't believe this is happening. Having a steady income means I won't need Veronica to bring me food anymore. I'll be able to buy new clothes, and I won't be so reluctant to going out and facing the big world. I'll probably put that whiskey bottle away in a desk drawer, too, only savoring once in a while when I want to celebrate with the new … *man* … of my life. I might even open up about what happened to my baby doll and explain how finding her dead in her crib sucked all spirit out of her mother and me, like a bath draining of water.

Ricky comes closer and wraps his strong arms around me, not afraid of showing his feelings in public. Maybe someday, I'll work up the balls to do the same. In just a few hours, he has become a guidance, a rock to hold onto.

Our intimacy and complicity send jolts of heat to my groin, hardening my cock in seconds, but I try not to think of sex.

He inches into me, the devil, igniting more fire. "You have a dirty mind, but—"

"I'll show you how dirty later," I growl.

He grins and says to my mouth, "But I do believe we'll find a place for love."

Love?

Fuck, my heart hurts in my chest. But it's a good hurt, the kind I felt on my wedding day when Ella and I vowed to love each other until death do us part. Which it did, the damned beast. But that's in the past now. I must look forward. From the conversation with Sampson, I have a lot awaiting me, and it boggles my mind. As for Ricky, he is a definite rising hockey star.

I gaze straight into his beautiful soul. "You have any idea how awesome you are?"

"You have any idea how *handsome* you are?" he quips, grinning, and raises a hand to ruffle my hair and stroke my unshaven jaw.

"No?" I laugh, but accept the compliment. Such a strange feeling to see my heart come alive. Me … the one who thought I'd buried love years ago and would never have the courage to look it in the eye again. How did it happen?

Well, there's a simple answer to that. My amazing new playmate has dug my withered heart out of its hiding place in the cold, hard dirt, dusted it, and kick-started it back to life.

Not sure what the future holds for us, but embracing it nonetheless, I slide my hands underneath Ricky's jacket and circle his hot and very firm waist. He jerks and laughs from the cold feel, but when I put my lips on his soft, delicious ones, he closes his eyes and returns a kiss of unimaginable fervor.

The End

www.leabronsen.com

UNINVITED LOVE

L.J. Longo

Copyright © 2016

Chapter One

Even the snow in Galway City was dirty. If it started the fall pure, the pointed skyline corrupted it. By the time it settled, it was only gray slush and black ice.

Next time take a cab, Sal Hughes thought. He shifted the duffel bag that contained everything he owned, and then stuffed his hands into the pockets of his worn leather jacket.

Next time get a warmer coat. Next time keep your apartment.

In the summer, Sal walked the two miles between Galway University and the shelter easily, but in the winter, every step was bitter. Especially over the icy bridge where nothing sheltered him from the salty wind. Sal put a hand on the frozen metal to steady himself.

What are the warning signs of frostbite?

A violent shiver shook him. Sal had the somewhat romantic and very unhelpful image of the wind as a demon lover. A flurry of snow and ice would manifest into a winged thing and spirit him away to a sunken castle in the nearby ocean. In the demon's icy embrace, Sal could just let go and—

An approaching car—clean, sleek, black, and a

fucking jaguar—slowed and stopped.

"Thank God." Sal jogged to the car and smiled his broadest most innocent grin.

The window rolled down.

"Hi, I'm headed to the Cathedral. Big green dome right ahead. Not even two miles—"

The driver pulled down the green scarf wrapped around his wolf's smile.

Sal stepped back and glanced around to see if he could run. "Vade…"

****

A few days before Halloween, when Sal first met Vade, a smoke and latte could beat the chill.

To afford these vices, Sal leaned under the overpass at Hill's Palm Park. Somewhere in the dark, a man needed a blowjob more than twenty dollars. East Quay, the local gay bar and male revue, teemed with potential clients just over the hill. Sal never figured out how they knew to come here when their future boyfriends chickened out or their ex-boyfriends failed to deliver. He knew because his mother taught him the ins-and-outs of the oldest profession before he turned thirteen. By now, in his twenties, he'd made the decision to get clean, stop selling himself. But student loans didn't cover cigarettes and lattes, so these days he drew the line at oral sex.

A man stalked toward the underpass, an animal in a tailored suit. The streetlight shone in his coat's sleek, warm lining. Strong arms, meaty thighs. Dark face and eyes, darker even than Sal. He couldn't be too far past thirty and too solemn for the business Sal had in mind.

So Sal was surprised when the man stopped at the edge of the overpass, just outside the shadow.

"Are you one of the bridge boys?" he demanded.

"I didn't know we had a name." Sal smiled.

The man didn't return his smile. "How much does

irrumation cost?"

Sal leaned against the wall again. He didn't know the word or care for the tone. "I only give head."

The man pulled out a smart-phone wallet. The thin case bulged in the middle. "How much?"

"I let the client bid first."

The man's gaze dropped. The look-over. Sal smirked. If the guy shopped the market for good-looking twinks, he couldn't do better than Sal.

The man drew a hundred dollar bill.

Jesus Christ! Sal didn't to react to the extremely generous offer. He just stepped away from the wall. "That'll do it. What's irrumation?"

"More forceful than fellatio." Big Spender didn't extend the bill, luring Sal closer.

Fancy word for face fucking. Nice. "Swallow or spray?"

Big Spender finally showed some hesitation. Sal trusted it when the men felt the dirt. "Sounds messy…"

"Swallow it is." Sal plucked the bill, stuffed it into his pocket, and dropped to his knees.

"Here?" The man jolted when Sal loosened the lowest buttons on his coat.

"It's safe."

With the coat out of the way, the bulge in Big Spender's crotch rose as prominent as the one in his wallet. Sal fondled the boulder through the trousers. Soft expensive fabric. Hard cock. This wouldn't take long.

Sal leered up at him. "I see the East Quay Cuties put on a good show tonight."

"Yes. Very stimulating." The man watched Sal unzip his trousers.

"You want to tell me about your favorite?"

"No."

Sal didn't continue the conversation. Normally,

Sal went straight to work when men showed up ready to go, but a hundred dollars ought to buy a little finesse. This cock deserved it. Nice defined head, stretched foreskin, dark as chocolate. Sal kept a hand between the man's legs, fondled his balls, and enjoyed the warmth.

He ran his tongue around the tip, under the foreskin, teased the excess flesh, and tickled the sensitive skin underneath. Then he popped the head between his lips and gave it a good hard suck.

Big Spender released a guttural rumbling groan. His gloved hands clenched near Sal's head. Sal expected him to grab his hair and thrust. Instead, Big Spender played the gentleman for now.

Sal wet the man's shaft with his tongue, pinched his lips, and angled his head so that the tip rubbed the roof of his mouth.

The gloves crinkled as the man gripped Sal's hair. Sal hollowed his throat, waited for the cock to ram. Then the other hand lifted Sal's chin.

Big Spender's cock slipped slowly past his lips as Sal's face tilted up. The man's panting breath clouded the air. "I want to take you to my house."

The standard script ran, "You can't afford me," but Sal had never seen a hundred dollars so effortlessly change hands. So he repeated. "I only give head."

"How much?"

Sal had boundaries, limits to what he would do for cash. "No."

The man's eyes narrowed. He didn't like to be told "no" but he wouldn't stop now. "Go on."

Sal obeyed. He left the finesse and swallowed Big Spender's cock. He bobbed and sucked as deep and fast as he could. Until the man groaned with lust and gloved fingers tightened in Sal's hair.

Big Spender jerked him closer and pumped his

hips forward. Sal gripped the man's thighs to steady himself as the man fucked his face—beg his pardon, irummated. He kept his lips tight and his throat hollow, but generally kept out of the man's way.

Cum flooded his mouth, spicier than most. Sal swallowed, breathless when the deluge stopped.

Big Spender wasn't so solemn now. "I want to take you home."

His insistence thrilled and frightened Sal. Most of the men who wandered down here couldn't compare to Big Spender's appeal. Nice face, great body, and that intensity was a turn-on. Sal had never been so tempted to break his rule.

"Sorry. I only give head." Tempted, not convinced.

Big Spender zipped up and fixed his coat.

When Sal stood and rubbed the grit from his knees, the man extended a personal business card. His name—Vade Chadrah—and his cell number.

"For when you change your mind."

Later that night, sitting in the shelter, with his hands around a cardboard cup and a fresh pack of cigarettes in his jacket, Sal stared at the card.

Not even "if" but "when."

****

"Hello, Salvatore." Vade crooked an arm out the window like a motorist on a balmy summer ride. A handsome man who drove a jaguar and handed out hundreds like nothing remembered his name. Sal didn't know if he should be thrilled or fleeing.

They'd met a few more times. But blowing a guy for cash had an entirely different vibe than hitching a ride. For one thing there was the jag, sleek and luxurious.

"Fancy meeting you here." Sal rolled the duffel off his shoulder.

"Must be providence. You're going to the Cathedral? I didn't take you for a Catholic."

A dozen of his own half-formed poems about worshiping at altars of sex to appease the gods of poverty swept through Sal's mind, but he answered, "I thought I was your angel."

"Angels fall."

Fleeing. I should be fleeing. Sal thought.

"Are you heading for the homeless shelter next to the Cathedral, Salvatore?"

"How's a guy like you know about a place like that?" The heat rolled out of the open window and Sal resisted the desire to plunge his hands into the warmth.

"My family believes it is the *dharma* of the wealthy to give. I like to confound them by giving to shelters for queer youth," Vade answered.

Sal couldn't unpack that sentence. Something vaguely religious and too smug. He didn't trust it. He tapped the car and walked away. "Generous of you."

The jag trolled beside him.

Sal looked over and smirked. "You'll cause an accident."

"Get in the car, angel. There's no reason for you to suffer."

Sal studied the man's dark eyes, his smile, not exactly friendly, not exactly cruel. "I'm not dumb, Vade."

"I wouldn't want you if you were."

"You're not a nice man."

"So you said the last time we encountered each other."

The last time... East Quay's dance floor where Vade had promised to worship, kiss, and conquer if Sal relented and went home with him. Then the public bathroom, the taste of Vade's cum on his tongue, and Vade promised not to ask again.

A car beeped behind the jag. Vade didn't care. "Maybe I want to change your mind, Salvatore. Show you I can be nice."

A sharp wind whipped around the bridge so cold it nearly brought Sal to his knees.

Vade mimed an exaggerated shiver. "Bit nippy?"

The cathedral glowered miles away half-hidden by the snow and the advancing darkness. The wreaths and pine boughs that decked the lampposts writhed and pitched as the bitter wind ravished them. Vade was right. Too cold. Too far. He didn't deserve to suffer.

"Okay, Vade, what's the deal?"

Vade held up a fifty. "Plus the ride, of course. Call it a holiday discount."

Sal hated that he wanted the money, the ride, and when he let his guard down this man. But he took the bill. "Fair enough."

"Just get in the back. No need to chance the traffic."

Sal obeyed. The interior's black leather, cleaner and softer than his aged coat, practically vibrated against his hand. It was the biggest backseat Sal had ever crawled into and in the old days, there had been more than a few. "Nice car, by the way."

"Of course, it is." Vade reentered the flow of traffic and spoke conversationally. "So, Salvatore, is it rude to guess how you became homeless?"

"Most people just call me Sal."

"Good for them. Is it rude, Salvatore?"

"My guess is you'll do it anyway." Sal chuckled.

"Thrown out by your parents for coming out?" Vade guessed.

"Nope," Sal answered. His mom knew when she found magazine clippings of naked men he stored in his social studies book. Half paralyzed by Valium maybe, she mentioned some "friends" and how he'd make more money doing them than his paper route. The backseats of their cars weren't luxurious. "Mom was very supportive."

"And father?"

"Never knew him." Sal put his hands into his pocket and touched the fifty-dollar bill. His mom got fifteen dollars, twenty pills, and a coupon to McDonalds for his first time.

Vade hummed. "Drug problem?"

"No." Sal answered at once. He didn't like these personal questions, but he answered honestly. "My mom was a junkie. I don't make her mistakes."

Getting into a car with a stranger is absolutely her kind of mistake. Sal leaned into the front seat. "The shelter is—"

"I'm headed to the park. More privacy. Will that do?"

Don't forget you have to earn kindness. Sal blew into his hands and rubbed them together.

"Park is great." Sal answered brighter than his dour thoughts. Then because the looming silence hurt worse than honesty, he said, "I'm actually in university. I lost my housing at the last minute when my roommate decided—"

"At Galway University?"

Sal nodded. "Yeah. Full scholarship."

Vade looked over his shoulder with new admiration. "I'll be damned. What do you study?"

"It's a toss-up between literature and media sciences. The goal is to end up in a cubicle in a big office tower," Sal answered, thawed a bit with Vade's esteem.

"My angel aspires to be a zippy."

"A what?"

Vade didn't answer. "I admire your education. Sorry to interrupt. At the last minute your roommate…"

"We decided not to be roommates. See Mark was—" closeted. He'd wanted to keep Sal and his girlfriend. Sal didn't like either but it was being the secret, not being kept that drove Sal away. There was no wisdom in telling Vade that. "Mark had to move back home. I couldn't afford the fees on my own."

"Pity."

"I'll get a new roommate next term." No, he wouldn't. He'd stay in the shelter. "How about you?"

"Me?" Vade startled, as if no one had ever asked him a personal question. "Oh, I... What about me?"

"Where are you from?"

"Vizag. I mean, um, Visakhapatnam. Vizag is a … a nickname like … Frisco." Vade found his ground and regained his formality. "India. I'm from India."

Sal had not expected shyness. It was sweet. "Is that a small town?"

Vade laughed. "Sure. Like San Francisco is a small town."

"What brought you to the States?"

"My parents sent me to live with my uncle when I was … sixteen or so."

"Oh … to go to school?"

"To avoid prison. Homosexuality was illegal until … well I was in my twenties and already established here. Besides, the government waffles back and forth on the issue."

"What a nightmare."

"My parents knew they couldn't control me. So I was sent to work for my grandfather's company."

"While you were in high school?"

"No reason for high school. I studied hard for the equivalency test."

Sal reconsidered the car and his evaluations of Vade. "So is this Uncle's car?"

Vade chuckled and looked over his shoulder. "Uncle works for me now. I run the three offices in Galway City."

"Damn." Sal glanced over at him. "You're only, what early thirties?"

"Twenty eight."

"Wow."

"It's not that impressive," Vade said. "Considering all the advantages I've had. The grooming I received. You're accomplishing far more with far less."

Before Sal could sort out if the remark offended or pleased him, Vade ended the topic. "I've never seen this park so deserted."

"Winter." The loneliness of the dirty snow and gray sky chilled Sal's bones.

****

Like a warrior waging war against the winter winds, Vade's big body blocked most of the cold when he stood outside the backseat. One arm crooked over the door and his hand pressed on the roof of the car. Trousers pulled down just far enough to expose his cock to the backseat where Sal sat and studied it in the daylight.

From the defined head, down the thick shaft, Vade possessed an enviable cock. The foreskin was exotic, but Sal realized as he took it into his mouth, familiar now. Vade's happy moan brought a low sexual rumble to Sal's spine and reminded him of Vade's words in East Quay. Worship, kiss, and conquer. Vade danced so close, he'd practically fucked him through their clothes.

Now, as Sal fondled the big man's balls and did his best to deep-throat, Sal imagined stripping Vade from this winter coat and fashionable green scarf. He'd reveal a thick mat of dark wiry hair, shaggier than his well-trimmed beard. Unleash the powerful muscles confined by his tailored clothes. Peel away layers, expose rich dark skin. Sal would offer his body entirely to the beast's mercy.

Sal shivered and his cock swelled. This wasn't helpful. *Stop daydreaming. Make this fast.*

Vade gripped his neck, possessive. "Trying to finish me quickly, angel?"

Bastard. Sal slowed his ministrations, teased the ridge of Vade's cock-head with his teeth, and savored the shaft with his tongue.

Vade groaned. His fingers tightened. "Angel, I promised I wouldn't ask you to go home with me."

Please don't. Sal wanted to beg, but gagged by the beautiful cock he said nothing. *It'd hurt me so much to go home with you. To let you worship, kiss, and conquer. To let you pay for that. But I'd go.*

Vade squeezed his neck and gently stroked his hair. "But … I want to see you masturbate. Will you do that for me, angel?"

Vade's deep voice rumbled down Sal's spine and launched an avalanche of lust that thundered to his cock.

Fuck it.

Sal opened his jeans before the better parts of his brain could reject the idea. He stroked his cock and sucked on Vade's and wanted more. Sal moaned. He'd be a whore for this cock. He'd do anything for Vade.

Before Sal allowed Vade's cock to slip out of his mouth, Vade had to push him away. Vade wanted the unobstructed view of Sal's hand on his dick and the knowledge made Sal jerk faster. Sal licked his lips, empty and useless without Vade's shaft between them. He kept his eyes closed and his head tipped back. An orgasm raced to his cock.

"Magnificent." Vade's low voice hit Sal like a drug, and sent shards of pleasure through his veins.

When Vade stroked his own shaft, sharp occasional tugs, Sal moaned and opened his mouth to take his cock back where it belonged. Vade teased him. Traced the tip over his lips, pulled away when Sal sucked. Tormenting himself as much as Sal, Vade gradually gave him the tip, the head, half his shaft, and finally the whole thing.

Then Vade thrust in and fucked his mouth. Sal hollowed his throat and melted with pleasure and gratitude.

The words of a poem slipped into Sal's mind. "Bend your force to break, blow, burn, and make me new." A John Dunne verse about God and it startled Sal that he applied it to Vade.

Too far. You've let this go way too far.

If Vade asked now...

Go on and ask. Fuck me. Worship, kiss, and conquer. Just ask. Ask now. Before I remember how to say no.

With no warning, Vade jerked his cock back and erupted. Thick spurts of cum landed on Sal's cheek and hair. The endless stream drizzled down his chin onto his shirt and only ceased when Vade rubbed his cock against Sal's neck, leaving a trail there.

"Thought you didn't like messes?" Sal's hands trembled on his shaft. He wanted so badly to finish himself. Instead he pushed his erection back into his jeans.

Come on, Sal. Get control of yourself or he'll—

Vade kissed him, pushed a knee between Sal's legs on the seat, and bent his big body to fit in the car. He bowed Sal down with the kiss. As Vade crawled over him, Sal unfolded smoothly into the car. His body remembered how to curl for a backseat fuck.

Sal moaned as Vade kissed his face, chin, and

cheek. Vade licked his neck and Sal realized Vade had cleaned the cum off his face.

Fucking hot.

Vade's fingers fumbled at his jeans. He kissed Sal's stomach, headed toward his heart.

"No!" Sal jolted back. He pressed against the door. "I can't…"

Vade knelt with one leg on the seat, body cramped, arms braced on either side of Sal, a beast too confined to pounce. His breath came as ragged and raw as his expression of desperate rage. His cock swayed under his coat already hard again. The man wanted so much he was dangerous.

That fierce power aroused Sal so damned much. It took everything in Sal's power to say, "Sorry. I got carried away."

It hurt to reject him, damned cruel to Vade and certainly not what his own cock wanted. But Sal had his line. If he crossed it, he'd slip back to easy money, violent men, and used needles. If he wanted a normal life, he couldn't go this far, not for money. He wouldn't go under the overpass again.

Vade's nostrils flared as he grabbed Sal's shirt and jerked him close.

Shit.

Vade had the power to force him. Even if Sal had the will to scream and he wasn't sure he did, no one was near this isolated park. Powerless before the man's strength, he shut his eyes and shuddered with desire, eagerly awaiting the violence.

Then Vade's hands trembled. "Sorry… Boundaries."

The big man's fist uncurled, strong enough to shatter those boundaries, but stronger than his lust. Sal sucked in a breath, only half-relieved as Vade slid away.

Vade stood and zipped his trousers. His voice was stony. "Nothing can change your mind?"

"No."

When he got back to the shelter, Sal would bolt for one of the private showers. He'd stand under the lukewarm water and stroke his cock. He'd imagine Vade hadn't stopped, but had pinned him in this backseat and fucked him. He'd decide later whether he fought in vain or begged for more.

"I'll walk to the shelter, thanks."

"Don't be ridiculous. You're nearly as far as the bridge."

Vade closed the door.

Right, but on the bridge I wasn't ready to throw away all self-respect and be your slave forever.

Chapter Two

Vade Chadrah gripped the steering wheel and focused hard on the icy road to save himself from his rage and lust.

The man in the backseat of his car—if Vade looked he'd certainly go mad—had haunted him for weeks. On a dark whim, Vade investigated the underpass where cheap whores and drunken queers were rumored to linger. From the moment he caught sight of Salvatore leaning in the shadows, he'd wanted him. The creamy olive of his skin, the huge honey-brown eyes, the hard smirk on his soft lips, everything about the man plagued him with desire.

Vade replayed each encounter, considered alternative scripts. A more soothing tone, softer words, and the angel relented to Vade's demands. In his fantasies, "please" or "five hundred" bought the rest of his lean body. "Strip" or "bend over" granted the forbidden pleasures still un-tasted for all the time he'd been banished to this cold country. Vade blamed shyness and fear of the very rejection he battled now.

It shouldn't be so difficult. Not with men who sold themselves.

Salvatore was different, special, and worth the effort. Angels were.

Vade glanced to the rear-view. Salvatore's honey-brown eyes gazed out the window. His cheeks blushed, maybe not with cold.

Vade snapped his vision forward, already painfully hard. He didn't like this lust-filled rage. He'd never been this uncontrolled before Salvatore, and he didn't like where this desperation had led him already.

****

That last time in East Quay, lust and loneliness had driven Vade to the only gay bar and nightclub he dared visit. He'd never been approached and never dared approach another man. But maybe one day.

The men on the dance floor looked half-dressed and later they would be undressed with each other. Mouths that laughed and spoke now would kiss and suck. Hands that barely brushed would boldly stroke. Bulges leashed in tight jeans waited to be sheathed in flesh.

Then, providence. Vade nearly dropped his tumbler. There on the dance floor, his angel brought light and life to the darkness as he swayed.

The music owned him and he danced for himself. Eyes closed. Hands raised. Hips unashamed. He wore his leather jacket. Beautiful and daunting, he lured Vade as flame entices a moth.

Vade set the tumbler hard on the bar. He braced himself to stand, to speak to him, to buy him a drink, to ask him home.

Then another man, a college boy, brushed against his angel. Lanky and lacking, this intruder wore the Fitch logo like a branded man. They both laughed when Fitch whispered in his angel's ear.

"Another?" The bartender was far too cheerful.

Vade nodded without looking away. He couldn't stand the idea of this other man touching his angel, possessing him. Fitch, close enough to kiss the angel's cheek, instead, wandered off with a phone in his hand. His opportunity squandered.

Vade downed the second bourbon. The roar of the alcohol burned down his throat and lit a fire in his cock. Fortified, he strode into the mob. Dancing was expected.

Eyes flitted up as he passed, but Vade honed in on his angel. Angry because he was afraid. Aggressive because he was angry.

"I find your partner lacking. He's unfinished, immature, and unworthy of you." Vade put his hands on the angel's waist and swayed behind him an imitation of the couples surrounding him and he hoped a preview of what they would do later.

The angel jolted to find someone pressed so close. His wide-eyed fear hardened immediately into a haughty smirk.

"Yeah, but he's sweet," the angel replied. "And he talks like a normal person, Vade."

Vade's heart fluttered whenever this man said his name. "I didn't get the pleasure of your name when we last encountered each other."

The man smiled broadly and danced some distance between them. "You forgot to ask."

Vade jerked him back and ground his cock into that wonderfully taut ass. "I'm asking now."

The angel only smirked.

Damn it. He won't tell.

Then the man leaned his shoulders into Vade's chest and tilted his head back against Vade's neck. His lips, so close to Vade's ear, burned his name into Vade's memory. "Salvatore."

"Is it presumptuous to assume I can beat his price and steal you?"

"He wouldn't be hard to beat. He's not paying. He's a friend. Do you have those, Vade? You go to night clubs and dance with them." Salvatore demonstrated, lifting his arms and swaying back into Vade.

"Will your friend understand if you slip away?" Vade slid his hands slowly up the angel's sides and rubbed the hardness of his cock against his body. The technical term was frottage and he'd go mad soon.

"You gonna ask me to go home with you again?" Salvatore sounded breathless. Fear or lust?

"I don't think you appreciate what I plan to do when I take you home." Vade dared to touch his lips against Salvatore's neck. His angel smelled musky and sweet. His fingers grazed under Salvatore's shirt and found hot skin.

"Tell me." Salvatore slithered with the melody, the snake charming the man.

"I will worship, angel. I will kiss and touch and experience every inch of this lovely body." Vade thrilled with desire and victory. His left hand slipped higher, delighted in hot smooth skin. His right dipped precariously low and gently squeezed Salvatore's crotch. "I will conquer."

Salvatore took Vade's hands, but lost the will to pry him away. "I... I don't—"

Vade would not beg. He jerked his angel around and kissed him hard. He'd never kissed anyone before. Salvatore opened his mouth and returned the kiss. Vade relented to a heady molestation of sweet lips and talented tongue.

Please hung in Vade's mind, when he broke the kiss. His lips brushed over Salvatore's forehead. "Will you come home with me?"

"No."

The unbearable heaviness of defeat.

"Restroom then? Usual price?"

****

East Quay's restrooms were no place for an angel, but Vade was in Heaven. The stall didn't reach the ceiling, but if someone entered he'd only see a man escaping the heat and boom of the club. He wouldn't know about the angel perched before Vade, tongue hard at work.

Vade watched the dark flesh of his cock disappear past red lips. Salvatore was a wonder with his mouth.

And that swell in Salvatore's well-worn jeans offered so much promise. Was his angel as tormented by lust as Vade?

The bathroom door opened and let in an explosion of noise. The sound startled Salvatore, as if he knew he'd been found. In a way, he had.

Fitch, the "friend" entered, lost and alone.

Vade put his hand in Salvatore's hair to soothe him, but he glared at Fitch until the man recoiled. Pathetic. He deserved to be robbed. He wore the symbols of a wealth and power, but he hadn't earned them. He couldn't keep an angel.

Fitch called, "Sal? Are you in here?"

Salvatore froze with his lips tight around Vade's cock. His eyes lifted to see what Vade would do. How did he manage to look so innocent with a man's cock stuffed in his mouth?

Vade groaned with lust, louder than he needed, and thrust his cock hard and fast. The unmistakable sound of a forceful cock plundering a wet mouth filled the stall.

Deliberately, Vade leered at Fitch while Salvatore slurped his cock. *Yes, you found him, but you've lost him. He's mine. Right here, right now, sucking my cock like it's my God-given right.*

Vade ran his hands through Salvatore's sleek hair and groaned. "Take that cock, angel. Take it all."

Predictably scandalized, Fitch stumbled and escaped into the heat and roar of the club.

Salvatore drew off Vade's cock. "You're not a nice man."

"It was an easy victory, but a satisfying one," Vade answered.

Salvatore smiled at him, then his eyes slipped closed and his lips parted asking for more.

Vade didn't disappoint. He pounded his cock

between his angel's lips. Vade's mind whirled with images and connotations. He imagined Fitch, weak and startled, under his angel's ministrations, too afraid to touch the hair on his head. Vade gripped Salvatore's hair tightly and thrust his hips against his face. The ancient Greeks thought of oral sex as degrading as anal. One silenced a man with one's cock, stole his voice, and violated his humanity. Salvatore hummed and gripped Vade's thighs. Rush of lust. If he came in his mouth again, if Salvatore kissed his "friend" on the dance floor, would Fitch taste Vade's cum? The way Salvatore twisted his tongue, the pressure of his lips, the perfect resistance and compliance. Salvatore's legs brushed his and Vade remembered the cock in that worn denim. That cock should be liberated. This angel should be in Vade's bed, legs spread wide. Salvatore should be straddling him, riding his cock and moaning. Or tied down.

Bliss whited out the whirl of thoughts as Vade orgasmed, his mind quiet. He savored the pure pleasure of release.

Salvatore continued to suckle. The angel wanted more. He had to want more.

"Come home with me." Vade didn't have proper control over his voice yet. The words were hoarse, demanding, lacking charm and gentleness.

Salvatore tucked Vade's cock away. "No."

Vade swam with frustrated helplessness. He slammed his hand on Salvatore's shoulder. He needed more. "Why not?"

"I have boundaries. I don't sell that." Salvatore never flinched. Vade admired his firmness.

The angel had boundaries. Of course, he did. There were limits to what money could buy. Heaven could not be bought.

But it could be stolen.

Salvatore was thin and lean, much smaller. Vade could yank him to his feet in this stall, right now, tear down those jeans, turn him to the wall, and force him.

No. Not here. Too many people.

"The answer will always be no," Salvatore said. Infuriating, alluring, and ignorant to how he taunted fate.

Maybe he wouldn't scream. Maybe if his mouth was covered, no one would hear. Maybe they would hear and they wouldn't help.

Have you lost your mind? A moment of sanity broke through the violent lust.

"All right." Vade repressed the need that nearly overpowered him.

Vade unlocked the stall and backed out, shaken by his barbaric desire, afraid to stay near Salvatore's damned beauty. "I won't ask again."

****

So Vade had avoided East Quay, afraid of himself. He didn't like what he'd nearly done then in that filthy bathroom. What he'd nearly done just now in that deserted park. If Salvatore's shudder of terror hadn't stopped—

The shelter. A small yellow-brick building with a rainbow flag. Vade stopped along the curb. How many men in there had seen Salvatore naked in the showers? Or lain next to his body in the darkness?

"Thanks for the ride." Salvatore pulled on the door handle.

"No worries."

The door didn't open.

Vade glanced at the driver-side door panel. The car had child locks. He'd noticed then before but never had a passenger to test them. The door wouldn't open from the inside unless he pressed that button.

Salvatore was trapped.

Vade's left hand moved instinctively to the panel to release his captive, but he paused. Providence, over and over. He hadn't intended to imprison his angel, but then he hadn't expected to find him wandering homeless in the dead of winter.

A weird calm descended. Vade watched Salvatore. He wasn't hard-hearted enough to keep a man against his will. Not if he cried or begged.

Salvatore laughed. "I think you have to let me out, Vade."

I don't have to do anything. Vade put the car in drive.

"Vade?"

Stop this. Turn in the church parking lot, you fool.

The cathedral slipped past on the left and he didn't turn.

"Holy shit." Salvatore leaned forward. "Are you actually kidnapping me?"

Yes I am. Insane and morally repugnant, isn't it? But I can stop. Turn left and go around the block.

Vade's heart hammered. He turned right toward the bridge, heading to the highway. "I said I wouldn't ask."

"Fuck." Salvatore threw himself against the seat.

In the rear-view, Vade spied the phone. "Salvatore, if your friends couldn't spare the time to drive you to a homeless shelter when it's below freezing, will they really chase my car around the city?"

Salvatore snorted and returned the phone, the cheap kind that ran on gas station minutes, to his pocket.

Still time. Turn at University Drive.

Vade watched the road. "I'm not interested in hurting you."

"I know what you're interested in," Sal said, his voice diamond-hard and angry. "This is severely fucked up, man."

Vade watched him in the rear-view in short bursts.

He could attack. Strangle me with my own scarf. Stab me with a pen. But, Salvatore only hugged his arms and stared out the window.

University Drive slipped by.

"I won't damage you. Too many consequences," Vade promised.

"Kidnapping has consequences," Salvatore answered.

"So does rape."

If he mentions the police, I'll turn back. Vade decided.

The highway neared quickly, so Vade prompted him. "Why not try the police?"

Salvatore growled. "You're a respected business man who donates to charity and drives a god-damned jag. The police don't give a shit what you do to a homeless prostitute."

Excellent point.

"Very dangerous business you're in, Salvatore. You should consider a career change."

"I'll get right on that."

Salvatore wouldn't show fear. He'd sit angry and motionless.

He wasn't motionless in the park, stroking his cock. Then he'd been unhinged with lust. He'd wanted it when Vade kissed him. He didn't want to submit, but he would. He'd do it happily, and he'd do it soon.

Vade turned onto the highway.

Chapter Three

When the road sloped upward, Sal knew Vade lived on The Ridge. If Hill's Palm Park was the cup of the city's giant hand, The Ridge was the wrist. The mansions overlooked Galway on one end and beaches on the other.

Can't walk home.

The garage was sterile, cleaner than the shelter. Vade stood outside the door and beckoned him nearer. Sal answered with the middle finger.

"Stop acting like a caged animal, Salvatore." Vade opened the door.

Sal didn't move until Vade leaned into the car. Then Sal kicked at his head, but Vade caught his foot. Before Sal's wild jab came close to Vade's face, Vade clamped his other hand on Sal's wrist. Vade dragged him out of the car and dropped him onto the clean concrete.

That didn't go as planned.

Before Sal could recover, Vade grabbed his neck, lifted him, and pressed his face into the hood of the jag.

Christ, he's strong.

Rather than relent to his helplessness, Sal got angrier. He screamed and kicked, thrashed and swore.

Vade calmly pinned him and rifled through his pockets. He took his phone and his cigarettes.

"Nasty habit. You ought to quit," Vade said.

Sal lurched, twisted his own arm.

"You'll only hurt yourself, angel."

Sal was out of breath, his shoulder hurt, and his heart could punch a hole in his chest. Meanwhile, Vade held him without effort, his sheer mass doing most of the work. Vade's cock pressed hard against his ass and it scared and aroused Sal.

He dropped his head to the car's hood and groaned. "I'm so fucked."

Vade chuckled. "I'm afraid I must agree."

Then, for a long moment, Vade stood still.

Sal glanced over his shoulder to see those dark eyes flit around the garage. "Did you forget your handcuffs?"

"Well, it's all so sudden. I left my other toys in the bedroom."

Other toys.

Sal thrashed again. Vade gripped his hair and held him down. Sal breathed in the scent of the metal, leather, and sweat.

"I'd hate to damage your jacket. It completes your rough-and-tumble ethos." Vade rubbed his nose in Sal's hair. "Besides I have the strong suspicion it's your only coat."

"Let me go and I'll take it off."

Vade chuckled again and ruffled Sal's hair, then clamped those fingers on Sal's balls. Hard. Sal gloried in that strong grip. If Vade twisted the pain would be crippling, but for now, it was possessive and sexy as hell. Sal hated that he liked it.

Vade released his arms. "Take it off."

Sal removed the leather jacket without a fight and hated it.

"Now your shirt," Vade said and Sal hated him.

Still, Sal tore the t-shirt over his head. Before Vade commanded him, he unbuttoned his jeans, knocked Vade's hand away, and shoved them down. He didn't own underwear. He'd been bought for the fifty in his jacket pocket. He wanted to be worth more. At least, it wasn't fifteen dollars, twenty pills, and a coupon to McDonalds.

"You truly are an angel." Vade's hands traveled

over Sal's bare ass then around to his stomach and his chest. Sal groaned with the soft caresses and didn't fight as Vade pulled him against his chest. The man's lips brushed his neck.

"So beautiful," Vade whispered.

Sal felt dirtier than before. Shakespeare's *Rape of Lucretia* contained a meticulous description of the woman's beauty as her attacker stared as a "grim lion fawneth o'er his prey." Sal doubted the doomed lady had given the man blowjobs for cash. She certainly hadn't been half-crazed with lust in the backseat of the guy's jag either. This situation was fucked up. He shouldn't be this aroused. He'd never been more aroused.

Vade nipped his ear. "Shall I fuck you right here?"

Yes. Fuck me now. Please. He wanted to say, but he answered, "Do I really get that choice?"

Vade kissed his neck and rubbed his hands over Sal's sides, choosing no answer. Vade stroked the globes of Sal's ass. He fondled Sal's cock as if it belonged to him. His mouth traveled from shoulder to neck to ear.

Sal bent over the car and gave up. Mom always said he was lucky people would pay.

Vade unzipped his trousers.

Sal braced for pain.

Instead of a cock, a finger pushed inside.

The last time anyone fucked Sal, it was in an abandoned building permeated with the stench of alcohol and weed. College boys, too many. They had tricked him, held him down, and when they finished left him tied up in the empty house. They'd never aroused him, though.

Two fingers. They flexed and twisted and Sal groaned, and hated the pleasure burning his skin. He wondered if even the cold wind on the bridge could cool the desire in him.

Three fingers. Vade got rough and fucked him with those fingers. His other hand squeezed, pinched, stroked Sal's cock. Vade wanted a whimper, a moan, any noise to indicate Sal experienced this. Pain might make Vade soften. Pleasure would be Sal's defeat. So he clenched his jaw in silence.

Vade pressed his dick between Sal's legs. Bareback.

"No protection?" Sal flinched.

"Do I need it?"

"I'm a whore, aren't I? You don't know where I've been."

Sal was clean, but maybe given the chance Vade would take him to the bedroom. Maybe in the bedroom, Vade would keep his promise to worship and kiss, not just conquer.

Vade tugged Sal's jeans up and found his wallet. A rip of Velcro and he had the condom Sal kept inside.

"You seem like the type to be prepared." Vade opened the condom.

"We rough-and-tumble angels always are."

Vade cupped Sal's cock and rubbed his face into Sal's shoulder. He stalled because he wanted permission that Sal wouldn't give. No matter how much Sal wanted this.

"You know this is my first time…" Vade stroked his cock through the condom, a slippery plastic sound. "Kidnapping someone, that is. I wish you'd come willingly."

Sal scoffed. "Am I here talk or to fuck?"

Vade answered with one jarring stab and buried his cock completely.

Sal gasped, shocked by the pain. Vade groaned over him, his full weight bearing down. Sal inched forward to relieve the pressure of so much cock stuffed so deep, to give his chest room to expand, but Vade growled and ground harder.

Finally, Sal whimpered.

As if he'd waited for that sound his entire adult life, Vade moaned with pleasure. He slowly withdrew. Sal gulped air. Before Sal could take another breath, Vade thrust back in and crushed him again.

Sal winced from the unexpected force. Again Vade withdrew slowly. And again, just before Sal could fill his lungs, the cock slammed in.

This time Sal clenched his teeth and bore the pain in silence. He refused to moan, to speak, to indicate how god-damn wonderful it felt to finally have that monster buried inside.

Vade kissed his neck and ran his hands over Sal's sides. Then his hand circled Sal's cock and stroked with gentle easy glides.

Sal needed to come so badly. Vade withdrew slowly again and when he slammed back in, he squeezed Sal's cock. Sweat poured down Sal's face. He'd shoot before Vade even started. Five thrusts and he doubted he'd make it past ten. Still, Sal kept his mouth pressed into his arms so Vade didn't know.

A sixth hard thrust. Sal stubbornly remained silent. Vade withdrew until only the tip throbbed inside. Sal resisted his desire to wiggle back, to nudge Vade's cock into his emptied insides.

"Enjoy this, angel."

That name, so inappropriate, so sweet, so wrong filled Sal with delight. Vade licked a trail from Sal's mid-back along his spine until his tongue lapped at Sal's hair. Sal gasped, surprised by the high-pitched, desperate sound of his own voice. A shock wave of lust quaked straight to his cock. His brain teetered, light-headed. He was coming.

When Vade slammed in the seventh time, a thick stream of cum rocketed out of Sal's cock and hit the car. Then, in case Vade missed the first splat, three more came. Sal groaned, more breath than voice. The release overwhelmed him and the residual throes shook his body.

Vade fucked in earnest then. Eight thrusts rapidly multiplied, sixteen, sixty-four, eighty. The car rocked as Vade rammed. The coat's belt slapped against Sal's leg. Vade grunted words so low and frantic that language was lost entirely. His rumble grew louder until the garage echoed with the roar of his orgasm.

Then silence. Except for Vade's belt tapping against Sal's leg.

Slowly, Vade's cock slithered out. The burden of the man's weight lifted and Sal sucked in breath.

It was done.

Vade would take him to the shelter. Sal tugged up his jeans, buttoned them. Tomorrow he'd put Vade's money in the bank. Tomorrow, he'd sort out what he felt, what it meant. Or not. Repression worked.

Something sleek wrapped around his neck. The belt. It tightened and cut off his breath. The metal buckle scraped his chin.

When Vade kicked his knees, Sal dropped. He clawed the belt to loosen it, to breathe. He turned his eyes to his captor, pleading.

Vade loomed, the belt in his fist like a leash. His fancy coat and green scarf looked tidy and sane, but his smile was wicked.

Vade wasn't finished with his angel. Not yet.

Chapter Four

"And to conclude our tour … the master suite." Vade hurled Salvatore into his dark bedroom.

His green scarf bound his angry angel's arms behind his back. He'd forced Salvatore to march through each room of the house and he'd reveled as the inherently graceful man struggled to keep his balance, his naked torso wrenching and twisting.

This final push, however, was well calculated to make his angel fall. Salvatore landed on his side with a grunt. He scrambled on the floor and desperately fought the scarf and belt.

Vade shut off the hallway light and plunged the room into darkness. Careful of his captive lover, Vade crossed the room and pulled the curtain cord on the huge picture window.

This view had sold the house. Galway City twinkled below. Little cars flashed like fish in white-blue pools of streetlights. The office buildings sparkled and reflected red and green decorative light. Small amber boxes beamed from apartment buildings. At the center of the small city, the cathedral's dome glowed a soft green.

"Oh." Salvatore ceased his struggle, perhaps stunned by the sight, perhaps understanding the distance he needed to cross to return to his normal life.

"Lovely view, isn't it?" Vade walked behind him. The city burned brighter than moonlight and Salvatore looked good in the city glow.

Vade pulled the man to his feet in front of him. Then hugged him from behind. His hand ran over Salvatore's naked chest. He kissed his shoulder. A sweet gesture, except of course, Salvatore was bound and completely at his mercy.

Vade kissed his neck, sucked the skin. Salvatore trembled, so Vade tightened his grip in case he wrenched away again.

"We're near the beach," Salvatore whispered.

"Of course, angel." Vade unbuttoned Salvatore's jeans and reached his hand inside to fondle his cock. "Half of Galway is near the beach. In the summer, you can lie naked in the widow's watch and sunbathe."

Salvatore squirmed. "I won't be here in the summer."

Vade threw him on the bed.

He intended for his captive to land facedown, ass-up, but Salvatore twisted and landed on his back. He slid to the floor at the foot of the bed.

"This is fucked up, Vade."

Vade knelt beside him and carefully removed Salvatore's canvas sneakers and socks. There were soaked through and still cold from his long walk. Vade's heart wept with pity. He rubbed his hands over Salvatore's bare toes and ankles until the man drew them away.

Unapologetic, Vade came nearer. He touched what he wanted, ran his hands over Salvatore's bare chest, the beautiful half-defined muscles of his stomach. His jeans had a gap at the waist where Salvatore's thin body didn't fill them. Vade parted the unbuttoned jeans and removed them.

At last, the sight of his angel naked. The beauty of his long legs and lovely lean chest were finally exposed to the open air and glorious. Salvatore's cock, steel-hard, shone with precum.

Vade sucked in a breath surprised. He rubbed a hand on Salvatore's thigh. "You enjoy this more than you let on, angel."

Salvatore said nothing.

Vade stroked his lover's cock, kissed his cheek. Salvatore twisted his face away when Vade came to kiss his mouth. Vade gripped his chin and held him still so he could press his mouth over stiff lips. Vade massaged his angel's cock.

Half a kiss turned to a whole one, as Salvatore gradually relented. Tongues mingled, tip touched tip. Salvatore moaned, arched into Vade's hands.

Until he pulled away.

"Vade … you can't keep me here like this," Salvatore meant it as a statement, but the crack in his voice made it a question. The first real fear Vade had detected.

"I know," Vade answered kindly and stroked his face. This was so incredibly wrong. In the morning he'd face so much shame and regret, but the damage was done. He'd enjoy his angel while he had him. "I'll need chains to hold you in the long run."

As he stood and went to the nightstand, Vade delighted in the fear and shock on Salvatore's face. If he'd seen that fear in the backseat of the car, he would have turned around, but it didn't stop him now. He opened the nightstand and took out the pack of condoms he'd bought when he first met Salvatore. About time he used them.

"Vade, I'll be sore. I mean, you just fucked me really hard and I … why don't you let me use my mouth this time?"

Vade hesitated holding the condom. Salvatore's lips looked so plump and wet. It was probably the kind thing to do. A gesture of good faith.

Vade ran his thumb over Salvatore's lips. "You like to suck cock?"

The belt around his neck bobbed as he nodded. "Yeah."

289

"You like sucking my cock?" Vade opened his trousers.

"Vade, I love sucking your cock," Salvatore answered.

It thrilled Vade with a mind-stealing lust, but still he opened the condom. "You like teasing my cock and denying me. You're done doing that."

Vade sank the condom onto his dick and stroked it. Salvatore exhaled with ragged breaths. Fear or lust? Did it matter?

"You're a fucking bastard." Anger.

Vade used the belt to drag Salvatore to his feet again, turned him, and pushed him onto his knees on the bed.

"This is wrong." Salvatore insisted. He grunted when Vade pressed his shoulder down, forced his ass into the air and his face into the bed.

"I understand your hesitations." Vade knelt on the bed behind Salvatore. "I choose to ignore them."

He licked Salvatore's neck. His reward: a breathless gasp and renewed thrashing.

Vade jerked the belt and forced his bound lover to lift his torso and balance on his knees or be strangled. He held the green scarf to steady his poor captive.

"Don't struggle, angel. You'll strangle yourself."

"Fuckin' sadist."

Vade had never thought of himself that way, but the evidence was overwhelming. He hugged their bodies tight together and kissed Salvatore's ear. Then reached into his nightstand, opened the tub of lotion and soaked his fingers. He wet his cock.

Sal moaned and squirmed helplessly.

Another gob of the lotion and as he kissed his angel's neck. He eased a finger into Salvatore's entrance. He was fairly confident he had this part right. He'd read about this, but he'd never used the lotion except for masturbation.

Salvatore bit his mouth to be as silent as possible. So Vade added a second finger and moved them in and out quickly until Salvatore whimpered from the stabbing duet.

Vade kissed him. Distracted by pain, Salvatore forgot to resist and his mouth opened.

Then Salvatore twisted away. "Don't do that."

"Kiss you or finger you?" Vade added a third, probably sooner than he ought.

Salvatore squeezed his eyes shut and arched deliciously away from the pain. He twitched around the thick triangle of fingers and when his breath came evenly again and his back relaxed, Vade withdrew.

Salvatore's breath hitched. "How long are you gonna keep me?"

"As long as I damn well please," Vade answered and rammed in his cock.

"Fuck!"

So good to be inside him. Hot. Tight. The way it should be. Perfect Salvatore. Vade took him slowly. Easier this time to move, to thrust, to possess his captive lover.

Salvatore moaned and Vade kissed his ear and whispered, "are you sure you don't enjoy this, angel?"

His silent defiance was unmistakable, but when Vade stroked Salvatore's cock, he found his desire was unmistakable, too.

Vade shifted his grip and held Sal only by the belt around his neck. To avoid falling forward, Salvatore was forced to arch back. Sal whimpered as Vade thrust, but the sound transformed to pleasure as Vade stroked his cock. Soon it had morphed entirely and Salvatore was desperate with lust.

"Tell me you want this, angel."

"Yeah. Mmm… Yeah."

"Say the words."

"I fucking want this, Vade." He grunted. "I want it so much it's sick."

So Vade stopped. He pulled Salvatore tight against his body, wrapped his arms around Salvatore's throat and his stomach.

"Oh Christ, Vade." Salvatore writhed in his arms and squirmed his hips desperate for Vade's thrusts. "What do you want, Vade?"

"If I untie you—"

"Yes. I'll do anything."

"Tell me what you'll do?" Vade twitched his cock inside Salvatore.

Salvatore moaned and licked his lips. The belt hung loose. The breathless hesitation was his own. "I… I'll ride you."

"Oh, you're not too sore?"

"Don't be a bastard. Untie me and let me ride you, Vade."

"Say—"

"Please…" He begged.

Vade withdrew his cock, dropped Salvatore onto his face and untied the scarf. Vade lay down on his back and waited.

His angel rolled his shoulders when he had freedom to move them, but wasted no time. He straddled Vade and lowered himself back onto Vade's cock.

"Is this what you wanted?" Salvatore braced his hands on Vade's chest, bucked, and slid on the slippery fabric of Vade's suit.

Thrilled, Vade nodded and ran fingers over Salvatore's nipples and his long lean sides. Salvatore gripped the bars of Vade's headboard and fucked himself deep and hard.

Vade groaned with lust, about to lose control and come again. He grabbed Salvatore's hips first to slow him, then to steady him as Vade thrust up.

"Masturbate for me, angel."

In his state of liquid lust, Salvatore complied. A soft small hand gripped that perfect cock. Glorious. The sight made Vade light-headed.

"Tell me before you come." Vade demanded.

Salvatore moaned and nodded. He ground his hips, pleasured himself with Vade's cock as much as his own fingers. His hand moved faster and he bent over Vade, gripped his suit, wrinkled the soft cloth, and madly gyrated his hips.

"Okay." Salvatore gasped. "I'm ... almost there."

Vade grabbed his shoulders and threw him onto his back. He pinned Salvatore's hands.

Salvatore made noises like swearing, but no actual words made it through his rage. Vade twined the scarf around his hands, bound him again. Salvatore freed one hand and punched him. Vade took the first few hits gamely, and then rose on his knees over Salvatore to put his head out of reach. He wrestled his angel's hands to the headboard.

"Oh come on, you asshole!" Salvatore fought hard with Vade, then with the scarf, but lost the fight.

Vade tied the belt around the bars. Then he sank back and gave Salvatore room to fight. He watched the muscles work as his naked body braced and bucked. The bars shook, the bed rattled, but the headboard held out longer than Salvatore's strength.

"Fuck..." Salvatore surrendered and was still, his eyes shut, his breathing hard. "I could kill you right now."

Vade smirked and rose on his knees again. He

held Salvatore's ankles together over his shoulder. As Vade eased his cock back inside, Salvatore glared up at him, dark eyes shadowed in the night. How long for Salvatore to be reduced to that state of intoxicated compliance again?

Vade kissed his arms, his neck, his chest, everywhere he could reach as he thrust into his lover. He ran his fingers over the straining muscles of the man's body, delighting in his heat and flesh.

Then Salvatore released a full-throated moan. The first he hadn't stifled.

The sound infected Vade like a musical drug. He gripped Salvatore's legs and hammered harder.

"Vade, please…"

No. Don't beg now, angel. It's too late for that.

"Please … take…" Salvatore struggled to speak between Vade's deep thrusts, "your clothes off."

Vade paused and shuddered with desire. "Goddamned tease."

"Please," Salvatore begged. "I want to see you naked."

Vade threw down Salvatore's legs and got out of the bed. He hadn't even thought of his own clothing. He tore off the suit. He didn't care about neatness, or the price of the thing, just to get it off and get back inside Salvatore.

"Slower," Salvatore commanded.

Vade understood the danger of his lover's heavy-lidded eyes, the power of his sensual gaze. Slowly, Vade divested his suit until he was naked.

"Oh, Christ…" Salvatore moaned, watching him. His cock twitched.

No one had ever looked at Vade with that much lust. No one had ever seen him naked. It thrilled him. He ran a hand over his chest, drew it through the narrow strip of dark hair between his pectorals and down to his cock still glistening with lube.

"You like what you see, angel?"

"Yeah. Since that first time under the bridge… I knew you were a beast in a tailored suit and I wanted … well, you're not the only one with fantasies, Vade."

Vade snorted, partly believing him, but mostly not.

"Vade, will you make me come?"

There were precious few times in his life when Vade was struck dumb and obedient. When his parents had gotten him out of jail and asked him to live in America for his own safety. When his uncle asked him to forgo school and work at the company. Nightmares and dreams mingled to suck choice away. So in the face of Salvatore's desire, Vade fell back on the response he had given them. "I'll do what you ask. Thank you."

"What?"

Vade had spoken in Hindi, but he didn't bother to translate. Powerful in his nakedness, powerless under Salvatore's eyes, he returned to the bed. Salvatore made no protest when Vade parted his thighs and climbed between them again. He sank back where he belonged easily and his cock twitched with pleasure inside his angel.

Then Vade gathered Salvatore in his arms and kissed him. He delighted in the tongue that tangled with his as he thrust his aching cock slowly back and forth. This time Salvatore hummed, moaned, and rocked with him.

Vade took Salvatore's cock in his hand and stroked until his lover squirmed with breathless pleasure. Salvatore frantically bucked, then spasmed. A rich white cream erupted from his cock and coated his belly and Vade's hand.

"Go on, Vade." Salvatore panted, stared up at him through half-closed eyes. Angelic permission. "I know you need to fuck me hard. Do it."

Vade lost control again. He slammed into Salvatore, pounded him hard into the bed, and rattled the headboard himself. He grunted and growled, tore into his bound lover until his own back hurt from the effort and sweat slicked his body. No matter how he howled or how hard he thrust, that anger never returned to Salvatore's eyes. He watched Vade with a sad longing, took the abuse, until his cries of pain and moans of pleasure were indistinguishable.

Before he came, Vade pulled out and ripped off the condom. He slammed his fist along his cock and Salvatore fell quiet and watched him.

Vade howled. A rush of bliss, a splintering joy, and a warm wet explosion. His cum coated Salvatore's belly and chest. The sight satisfied Vade.

Light-headed with release, he collapsed. He hugged Salvatore close, then loosened the belt around his neck, the scarf from his hands. Sal sighed, freed.

Vade lowered his head to his lover's shoulder and wrapped him tight in his arms. "Mine."

"Yeah," Salvatore agreed. He stroked Vade's back and drifted toward sleep. "For a little while."

Chapter Five

Sal thought of his childhood as Dante's tenth circle of Hell. Fear ran through his life like an underground river, but he'd learned how to navigate. Fear of violent men. Fear of drug-addicts' desperation. Fear of his mother's depression. He'd found corpses. He'd starved. He'd been deathly sick. But Sal had never been more afraid, than right now lying naked beside Vade.

Fear came in waves as he listened to Vade breathe. Tides pulled by warring emotions.

Some moments, Sal would feel the soreness of his wrists from being bound, the ache in his shoulders. The city stretched out of the huge window like a toy and he resented the man's wealth and privilege. Vade was a spoiled brat who'd gotten his way and could skirt out of trouble with enough money. Or worse find a more permanent trap. A pair of good handcuffs would do it, since no police officer would search the mansion's closets for a homeless queer.

Sal would spend the rest of his life in sexual servitude. Just a toy and whether he was treated roughly or with love depended on his owner's mood.

Then Sal would need to escape—now before he lost the will to fight for a freedom that meant starving, sleeping on floors, and wandering in the cold. The need for freedom would suffocate him.

So Sal would steel himself to get out of the bed, but when he shifted, Vade would hum or place his hand on Sal's arm half-waking, or smile at him.

Then the need for freedom would pass, as Sal's misplaced affection sucked away the strength in his legs.

He stayed with his head on the pillow surrounded by warmth and comfort. Vade was sweet and lonely—

confused and aggressive certainly—but he hadn't hurt him. Consent was a commodity Vade could afford. If Sal was unwilling, Vade would have released him. If Sal was not exactly the right person to take this abuse, Vade would have backed off. Sal was absolutely certain.

Why so much trust? This lead to a fear so deep Sal couldn't touch it without trembling.

It was more than the attraction, though Vade was goddamned handsome especially out of his suit and asleep. More than the man's money and the sex, Sal wanted… Sal was not the type to fall in love, certainly not so quickly.

The fear of that feeling threatened to drown him. If Vade cheerfully handed him an envelope of cash and sent him away, Sal would break.

But if Vade offered to extend this arrangement, to keep Sal, sex in return for housing, his consent surrendered for comfort and warmth, and if Sal agreed… He was just as broken.

No way to come out of this night safely.

Except maybe to disappear.

Vade's hand slipped away when Sal slowly put one foot on the ground. With a ghost's stealth, Sal stood. For a long moment, he gazed at the dark sky and the city below. He had no idea how he'd get back to it, but he still had that fifty dollars. The edge of the sky grayed with dawn. He'd hire a cab.

His shirt and jacket were in the garage, but his jeans and shoes were somewhere in here. What had Vade done with his phone and his wallet? The shelter would help get replacement IDs.

Vade knew where he lived. Would Vade find him again? What the hell then? And where were his clothes?

Sal dropped to his hands and knees and groped on the floor. Vade took them off near the bed.

"When you fell asleep, I put your clothes in the wash." Vade's voice rumbled even deeper with sleepiness. "Everything and the duffel. They'll be clean and dry tomorrow."

"Oh." Sal stood.

In the darkness, Vade shifted. Could Vade see his silhouette against the window? "I'll pay you then as well."

"I don't want your money, Vade."

"If I don't warrant a proper good-bye, you deserve to be paid."

Sal didn't know how to respond to that, but it cut deeper than he expected.

The hurt wasn't soothed when Vade said, sweetly, "Will you come back to bed, angel? It's very early and you deserve rest."

Sal didn't know what else to do. He was tired. Nothing in his life had ever been as comfortable and as warm as Vade's bed. So he relented and crawled back. He curled on his side to look at the city and face away from Vade.

Vade wrapped an arm around him. An undemanding embrace. His hand drifted lazily over Sal's arm, his side, his thigh. Sal shivered when Vade kissed the back of his shoulder.

Slow and leisurely, the gentle caresses and kisses continued. The sky brightened with the first light of dawn and Sal's body tingled. Sleepy, soothing, more tender than anyone had ever touched him. When the soft strokes stopped, Vade's hand rested on his stomach. Sal expected that Vade had fallen asleep and turned to glance at him. Instead, he found Vade sadly gazing at him. He looked surprised Sal was awake.

Sal smiled and turned, stayed beneath Vade's protective arm. His knee brushed against Vade's thigh.

He kissed Vade's lips, a tiny close-mouthed peck, and stroked Vade's cheek. These tiny gestures took Vade's breath away, and the hand on his back tensed, then relaxed.

Little kisses grew longer and smoldered without igniting into violent passions. Whispered sighs and moans passed between them. The slightest ripple could break the moment.

When Vade lifted his body and the blankets, Sal thought it was over. The gentle touches would crash into hard hands groping, tongues clashing, frantic grunts and growls. Instead, Vade caressed Sal, large dry hands tingling over Sal's skin. He moved, soft and boneless, were Vade led. Vade kissed as if he were unspeakably precious.

The tender touches broke Sal's inward battle. The warring desires for independence and for raw sex were drowned by that deeper thing, the thing he most feared, that uninvited love. No one had ever kissed him that way.

He squeezed his eyes shut and forced his breathing to stay slow and calm, even as the tears stung. He lifted his arms around Vade, and held him close.

Sal loved him and it terrified him.

Chapter Six

Vade, terrified he'd destroy the precious moment with his clumsy hands, and his inexpert lips, moved his kisses from Salvatore's mouth to his neck. Salvatore shivered and Vade relished in it, in all the little signs and signals from Salvatore's body. He wanted to touch every part of his angel before the day arrived, to discover every single erogenous zone. His hands roved on their tender mission brushing over Salvatore's abdomen, chest, shoulder, elbow, and hand.

Salvatore's hands reflexively gripped his. So Vade sent his mouth on the same expedition. His lips followed the path to Salvatore's shoulder, and then diverged at his collarbone, to the nipple.

Salvatore sighed, a sweet, sad sound. Vade ached for him, for more than possession of him. He wanted to alleviate that sadness, to shield and protect, to love. What a fanciful notion—that he could share his life with another man. If Vade opened himself to the impossible dream, he'd like that man to be Salvatore.

"God, Vade." Salvatore moaned and wove their fingers together.

His voice rippled like fire through Vade. He'd love it to be Salvatore.

Vade kissed lower, his hands happily bound up in Salvatore's. His angel had the lightest dusting of hair over his abdomen, a thin trail that spread and thickened into his pubic hair, then disappeared at his cock, lean and long. The tip begged to be licked.

Vade glanced up at Salvatore's face, hoping for a smile and nod. Instead, his angel's head tilted back, his chin jutted forward, braced for pain.

Quelling his own nerves and praying to any God

who wouldn't be offended, Vade took Salvatore's cock into his mouth. Technical term: fellatio.

The moment shattered. Salvatore jolted away and Vade tightened his grip, pinned his arms down. His angel settled, unable to fight.

"Did I hurt you?" Vade had not seen that kind of fear before.

"No, you didn't." With a shrug and a smile, Salvatore pulled his hands out of Vade's fingers. "You don't have to do that."

"Suppose I want to."

"Well … you know, no one's ever, um…" Salvatore's fingers ran through Vade's hair, ready to push, or pull, debating. "You know, for me."

Vade pressed a kiss to the tip of his cock. "May I?"

"I…" The question caught Salvatore off guard. "Yeah. Please."

At least, Salvatore wouldn't know if he did it wrong. But how could he do it wrong? He'd learned from the man himself. Vade practiced the techniques Salvatore used on him, ran his tongue around the head, licked the shaft, and slowly teased the tip past his teeth.

Salvatore's narrow cock slid easily into his throat and Salvatore moaned and clenched his hands in Vade's hair. Vade sucked and bobbed, tongued at the crown of his cock, and then swallowed him down.

Vade was amazed at how arousing it was to pleasure his angel. Not subjugated at all, rather empowered. Each sigh and moan a reward, the stroke of his lover's fingers proof Salvatore needed him.

"That's good, Vade," Salvatore struggled to speak. His words fought past the pleasure. "Yeah… Like that."

Obediently, Vade continued. Soon, Salvatore

rolled his hips into Vade's mouth. Vade scooped his hands under his ass to grope and thrust his cock deeper. The scent of his body, the taste of his flesh intoxicated Vade. He'd crawl through Hell to have this again.

"I'm gonna…" Salvatore tried to push him away.

Vade sucked harder unrelenting. Salvatore's cock twitched and a rich cream erupted into his mouth. Vade, surprised, pulled away and the rest of Salvatore's cum ended up on his own belly.

His angel sank into the sheets and pillows, eyes half-closed. He stared at Vade a long moment, and then commanded, softly. "Come here."

Vade crawled over him. Salvatore wrapped his arms around him and drew him down for another kiss. Vade surrendered to Salvatore's mouth. His lover's legs lifted around his waist and his fingers wrapped around his cock to draw him inside.

Vade reached to the condoms in the side drawer. "What about—"

"The shelter makes sure we're clean. If you say you are…"

"I am."

"I trust you." Salvatore guided him inside.

Vade fell into the tight warmth. The heat and pulse of Salvatore's body engulfed him. He groaned to contain his lust, buried his face in Salvatore's neck, and shuddered at this final gate of Heaven.

Vade dragged his face away from Salvatore's shoulder. He wanted to see his lover's face as he took him, slowly, gently, closer than he'd ever been to any living thing. They shared a breath and a heartbeat.

Still, Vade only knew Salvatore was crying when he kissed his cheek and tasted the salt. Salvatore's eyes shone in the faint light.

"I didn't mean—" Vade pulled away.

"No." Salvatore wrapped his arms and legs tighter and nuzzled his face into Vade's shoulder. "Keep going, please."

Vade obeyed, slowly possessing the tremble and tightness of his lover's body. He thrust carefully, deliberately, uncertain if he could hold his lust in check. Salvatore's soft breaths panted in his ear, the little catches and moans that his force had drowned out earlier. Each exhale was a musical note of pleasure and want, and as Vade moved inside, he knew he conducted the symphony.

Then Salvatore rocked into him, urged him faster, deeper. His lover moaned loudly in his ear, clung to him, and bucked with abandon. Vade was out of his mind with lust and he couldn't think of when the change had happened.

Vade stared into Salvatore's eyes. The dawn light illuminated his sated face with perfect clarity. Bliss overwhelmed Vade. He emptied himself into his angel, poured out heart and soul with a kiss and a whimper. Vade clung to Salvatore. A wave of desperate terror washed over him. He'd done everything wrong. Until just now. But now was too late. He'd never earn his angel's forgiveness. He'd never convince Salvatore that he loved him.

Vade slipped onto his back and tried to sort the roil of emotions into compartments, to understand when lust had become love and what the hell he was going to do about it.

Salvatore curled into his chest, sighed contentedly. "You went backward Vade. You said you'd worship, kiss, and conquer."

Vade kissed his cheek. Tasted the wet and the salt. "Why were you crying?"

"How about I tell you in the morning?"

"Because you won't." The light of day would be too harsh for this sweetness.

Salvatore hummed and acknowledged the truth. Vade didn't press the issue, just kissed Salvatore's hair and rubbed his back.

His lover trembled. "I knew this would happen."

Vade stung with shame, but didn't loosen his embrace. "That'd I'd kidnap you?"

"No. The rest. That I'd want you. That I'm someone you can buy and I'd still want you."

"Salvatore…"

"Just let me—" Salvatore tried to move away, but Vade wouldn't let him. Instead, he curled back and shuddered. "When I was twelve, my mom sold my virginity for fifteen dollars, twenty pills, and a coupon to McDonalds. I lost count of the men who've fucked me since. If I ever bothered to keep track."

Another violent shudder. Vade kissed him, held him tight, didn't interrupt.

"You're not the first to drag me off someplace remote when I didn't want to go…" Salvatore paused on some memory. Something he didn't want to share yet. Vade did not pry. "No … not even the most violent. Not nearly. But Vade…"

Salvatore lifted his eyes. "You're the first to call me angel. The first to…"

Then Salvatore pressed his lips tight together. Finished. He didn't say what he wanted, but Vade understood his shiver. Salvatore had never made love.

Vade folded him close and Salvatore melted into his arms, tension drained from him. Very quietly, Vade confessed, "You're the first."

Salvatore looked up at him, waited for more.

Vade looked back, added nothing.

"Oh," Salvatore said.

"The closest I ever came to another boy was in the yoga camps designed to cleanse us of our homosexual habits in Vizag." Vade, aware how silly that must sound to an American, added, "Religious healing. I kissed his cheek and he ran away. His family prosecuted me for attempted rape. My family had the money to save me a long imprisonment. I came to America later that year, had my own house by eighteen, but I … I never dared."

"Why?"

Vade shook his head, then remembered Salvatore's confession, and continued. "Fear, I suspect. I … I don't like not knowing what I'm doing. I don't take rejection well, I'm sure you noticed. And the … the flamboyance, the pride scares me. The dancing and the openness… I feel unworthy, lumbering, and stupid."

Salvatore kissed his forehead, a gentle brush of dry lips and soft breath. "You don't come off that way."

It soothed him. Vade caressed his lover until they both drifted off to sleep.

Chapter Seven

Sal woke confused by the quiet around him, the softness beneath him, and the sheer amount of light in the room. The panorama of Galway City reminded him.

"Fuck."

When Sal sat up in the bed, his ass, wrists, and legs ached. A residual tingle buzzed on his skin, as if the previous night had marked every part of his body. Vade Chadrah had conquered, kissed, and worshiped.

What the hell now?

Sal imagined Vade installing a human-sized cage in the basement. Handcuffs for the short term. He'd be allowed to sun on the widow's watch as a reward for good behavior.

No, that wasn't fair. Vade was a lonely, confused man, but he wasn't cruel.

Sal stroked his shoulder and thought of Vade's kisses as they'd made love—no, fucked. Men pay to fuck.

His clothes, all of them, were neatly folded and freshly laundered on a chair in the corner. The duffel had also been cleaned. Men who pay to fuck don't usually do laundry. Then again, men who pay to fuck don't usually kidnap, either.

Sal dressed, packed, and headed out of the room. He expected Vade to be in the home office, on the phone conducting his business. Vade would wave him over, hand him an envelope, and put a hand over the phone to thank him for his time and understanding. Ask for his number to arrange another tryst. Sal would take the envelope and give his number. He didn't have the strength to fight his poverty and his feelings for the man at the same time.

Instead, Vade sat at the dining room table.

Pancakes and peaches, strawberries, bananas, and whipped cream all surrounded the empty plate at the unoccupied end of the table. Next to that plate lay a beige folder, a white envelope, and a small, delicate book.

Vade sat at the far end of the table, and the sight of him distracted Sal's thoughts from the breakfast or the objects. His hands were folded on the table. He looked serious and stern, like a man who belonged in a boardroom, not the man he'd met in the bedroom. Though instead of a suit, he wore a white knitted sweater which set off his rich dark skin and made Sal's heart ache and stomach clench with desire.

"Salvatore." Vade noticed him and rose with a smile. Then Vade cleared his throat, wiped away his smile, and corrected his weak start. "If you'll come down. I believe we have three possible courses of action to discuss."

Sal tilted his head. He'd never been to a business meeting before. He came down the stairs, his duffel over his shoulder, and his jacket under his arm.

Vade continued. "I will abide with whichever you choose without question. I've made an irreparable mistake and I … I don't know if there's a way I can … apologize for it."

Sal put his duffel down near the empty place setting. The envelope contained cash. He peered in, then picked it up and counted, just to be sure. Hundred dollar bills. At least twenty. "Jesus Christ."

"That was a Christmas Bonus. I always spend it … frivolously." Vade could not look at him. "The folder is a typed out and signed confession. I'll bring you to the police station. It details how I abducted you and … and forced you. My attempt to bribe you with a few thousand dollars is included in the report. No mention of your… employment, shall we say?"

Sal flipped through the confession, the dry and accurate account reminded him of the explicit details, until the memory made him blush with desire. He shut the folder and wondered if Vade would go through with it. Not that a good lawyer wouldn't talk him out of jail and into some kind of clinic.

"Did you sleep at all last night, Vade?"

"No." Vade sounded annoyed that Sal lacked the proper sense of gravity. He softened at once. "After we … I had a lot on my mind."

"This police thing is stupid." Sal dropped the confession onto the table.

"I absolutely mean it."

Sal studied him. "Yeah, I think you do."

"I'm sorry and I don't know a better way to express my regret than to pay for what I've done."

"Which you could also do with 2K?" Sal picked up the envelope again, just to check his math. Then set it down. "Or a new book. What's that supposed to mean?"

"Well, Rumi is … a romantic poet and it's one of my … it's an old book. It's a … very precious … not in monetary value I mean, but in … personal … and such …um."

Vade ran a hand over his forehead, furious with himself. Then paused, took a breath, and started over.

"It's the first book I ever read in English and it has a great deal of sentimental value. I'd hoped what it represents would be obvious."

Sal crossed his arms and leaned over the chair. "It's not."

Vade narrowed his eyes, but his annoyance immediately turned to fear. Sal wanted him to speak it out loud.

"The book is… It's meant to represent… I mean, obviously … you have breakfast with me and we discuss, well … future relations … relationship."

As Vade's ability to communicate broke down entirely, Sal understood. Vade only knew business words, predatory talk. He could sell, verbally spar, and command, but if he needed to express more he struggled for language. He'd never learned the words to be vulnerable. Except perhaps what he could learn from a slim book of translated poems.

"Damn it." Too soon, Vade surrendered. He sat and bowed his head nearly to the table, hands buried in his hair. "Just take the money and … I hope it makes your living situation easier and you can think fondly of me. There's train station at the foot of the hill. You're a five minute ride from the college."

Vade was right. It would be easier to take the money. Sometimes the easy thing to do cost too much. Sal wouldn't take the money. He knew when Vade … made love to him. Vade's attempt to break through the barrier of language with tender touches had worked. Sal had always been good enough to fuck, but that was the first time he'd been good enough to love. He wasn't going to accept payment for that.

So Sal put the book into his back-pocket and sat down at the empty place.

Vade lifted his head, shocked and afraid.

"You know I memorized some Rumi once. Libraries don't kick you out if you sit in there too long and I have a good head for words."

Sal paused and licked his lips. "I think my favorite is: Your task is not to seek for love, but merely to seek and find all the barriers within yourself that you have built against it."

Vade smiled. Then asked, hesitantly. "Do you…" Then he shook his head, decided to save that question for another time. "Do you want some orange juice?"

"Sure." Sal held out his cup and let Vade serve him. "And yes I think I do love you. It scares me, but I probably do."

"Probably too soon to talk about such things." Vade trembled as he poured the juice. "But if it makes you feel less scared ... I do, too."

The End

www.gracefulindecency.wordpress.com

RUNNER

Kai Tyler

Copyright © 2016

Chapter One

The main door to my building slammed behind me as I jogged down the short steps to the paved walkway. The sky was gray, neither dark nor light at this time of the morning. My running shoes pounded the tarmac as I headed across the road, squeezing between parked cars to go toward the park.

Behind me a car started up—one of my neighbors who worked in a bakery—the only other person who got out of bed as early as I did.

Ahead, trees stood as unmoving sentries and bushes demarcated the shadows of the adventure playground from the ghost mist hovering over the glittering large pond.

Keeping to the open space, I completed two laps before the regulars appeared: dog walkers, joggers, or just people using the park as a cut-through on their way to their destinations.

With a wave here and a shout-out there in greetings, I paused to stretch my warmed muscles before carrying on with the third lap.

The skin on my neck prickled, and I glanced back.

My heart took up a sudden staccato beat.

A man in an all-black outfit ran behind me, about eighty yards away and made no effort to close the distance between us. I'd never seen him in the park before, and he appeared strange because he wore a long-sleeve jersey with a hood and full-length track bottom.

Strange as although it was still early morning, we'd been experiencing a hot season. Sometimes I came out in long sleeves, but once I'd warmed up, I would store my sweatshirt in my pack or loop it around my waist.

He covered his entire body aside from his face.

And what a striking face—tanned skin, rugged features, salt and pepper stubble on his chin. Piercing eyes intent on me, like a predator tracking prey. He exuded dominance and danger.

A shiver of pleasure ran down my spine as my cock twitched. The man could be an axe-murderer and I found him attractive. What the fuck!

Heat streaked my cheeks. I turned away, fiddled with the volume of my music player app, so I could hear if someone came up close and increased my speed. I did another set of laps, avoiding the dark, dense foliage of trees.

The prickling on my nape indicated the man still trailed close. I refused to glance at him, worried about my body's response to his presence. Granted, my sex life sat in the doldrums at the moment due to schoolwork and training schedule. But picking up strange men in the park had never been my thing and I wouldn't start now.

After a while, I slowed down, pulled my water bottle from the latch of the little pack on my back, and took a drink. The cold water refreshed and boosted my energy levels, ready for me to do the last batch of laps. Putting the bottle away, I took a couple of steps and stumbled.

The man in black sprinted in front of me, heading in my direction. He had the most entrancing fluid stride possible.

Frozen to the spot, I stared at him with open appreciation until he stopped beside me.

"Are you okay?" he asked in a guttural voice tinged with an accent I couldn't place immediately. His sharp black eyes searched my face.

Swallowing hard, I bobbed my head, unable to work saliva into my dry mouth. He had to be the best-looking man I'd ever seen. He appeared older, somewhere in his late thirties, perhaps early forties. Tall, wide, and well-built from what I could see outlined in his sports kit. Beneath the black hood, a hardened face with asymmetrical features loomed over me. He had straight, thick brows over those striking eyes. And sensuous lips that made me think of fallen angels.

He reached for me, hand sliding from my shoulder to my neck.

My breath stayed trapped in my throat and for a few seconds, I couldn't breathe. Couldn't move. There was something compelling about him, especially now he stroked me. His touch was gentle yet possessive. He smelled like a crisp, spring morning in the woods. Locking my knees, I resisted the urge to lean in and sniff him. My skin heated up, and I shivered, my cock pulsing to life.

"You don't look too good. Have a drink." He stepped close, reached for my pack and withdrew the bottle of water. His actions were without timidity or uneasiness, his motion decisive and dominant, seeking no permission.

"I'm all right." Coming to my senses, I took the bottle off him and stepped away. How could I permit him to touch me like this? Like he had a right to. Like I belonged to him.

Rob, one of my neighbors slowed his jogging and marked time on a spot beside us.

"Ash, are you all right," he asked, staring at me and then to the stranger.

"Yes, Rob. I'm okay," I replied after drawing in a shaky breath. I glanced at the man in black and said. "I have to go."

His expression remained inscrutable, but he nodded as if giving me permission to leave. A part of me felt as if he could've detained me. This had to be a ridiculous notion as the park lay busy with people and Rob still stood waiting.

Shaking my head to dispel the fuzzy sensation, I jogged off in the direction of home. My hands trembled, and my heart pounded. But that could've been just the rush of going home to grab a shower.

****

Buzz. Buzz.

The phone in the back pocket of my jeans vibrated as I inserted the key in the lock of my apartment door. My hands were already full with grocery bags, so I couldn't reach the cell immediately.

Once the lock clicked, I shoved the slab with my shoulders, stepped across the threshold, kicked the door shut, and hurried inside my one-bed studio. I expected a call from the manager of the pub I worked in. We'd discussed me doing extra shifts, and he said he'd call if anything came up.

Dumping the bag on the table, I reached for the phone and pulled it straight to my ear as I clicked to answer.

As soon as I heard the voice on the other end, I wished I'd checked the caller ID first.

"Hey Ash," the male voice crackled a little.

315

Closing my eyes, I tilted my head back against the high cupboard. I didn't need this right now. My life was stressful enough without having to deal with my half-brother's shit. He rarely ever called me, and when he did, trouble always came next.

"Ash, are you there?"

I coughed and cleared my voice. "Yes, I'm here. Donny, is everything okay?"

It was hardly a welcoming response. But I knew him too well. He was always involved in some scheme or hustle. They were never good news. It still amazed me how he'd managed to stay out of jail or even alive during the twenty-six years of his life.

"Can't I call you anymore without you asking if everything is okay?" He sounded irritated.

Our father divorced his mother and married mine. We all lived together until he moved out to go to college. Then he dropped out. I was determined to graduate.

I puffed out a breath and tried to appease him. He was still my brother no matter what. "I'm sorry, Don. It's just that I don't hear from you often enough."

He sighed. "It's okay, Ash. I should keep in contact and call you more often."

He paused, and I nodded my head. I knew he couldn't see me. But I didn't say anything.

"So how are your studies going? Do you have any upcoming meets?"

"Good, thanks," I replied, grabbing a tea towel and rubbing the coffee stain off the kitchen counter. I was at university on a track and field scholarship based on my athletic prowess. "We have the qualifier for the Nationals coming up."

Being an athlete wasn't easy. My life at the moment consisted of school, homework, training, working—when I was needed at the bar—and sleeping.

My stomach growled as if to remind me there was another activity I omitted. Of course, I ate somewhere in between all the other things going on. But sometimes in the rush to get about I survived on energy bars.

I couldn't remember the last time I'd just chilled out or even partied.

"That's cool," Donny said.

"Will you be able to come and watch me at the Nationals?" I hadn't qualified yet, but I had every intention of being part of the team. My body was in peak condition.

He never came to my meets, but there was always the first time and hope.

"Maybe," he said in a grave voice. "I have a job for you."

I twisted my mouth. Donny fancied himself as my agent, booking me for gigs. He'd gotten me a modeling shoot once. The money had been good, but I felt uncomfortable about using my body in that way. The poses had been more glamour than fashion. "What kind of job? Modeling?"

"Yes, just like the last time except this one pays better."

"How much better?" I couldn't help asking.

"Ten grand for you."

That was more money than I earned a year with the bar job. "Are you sure? What exactly would I have to do?"

"Nothing too difficult. I'll explain when I see you."

My throat clogged and I couldn't shake the feeling that something was wrong. But I'd wait until I saw him to get the full details. "Okay."

"Great. I'll call you soon. I've got to go. Bye, Ash."

"Bye, Don."

He hung up, and I stared at my phone blankly unable to shift the heaviness settling like stones in my gut. I turned around and routinely stored away the groceries before making a quick bite to eat. I then settled down to work on my homework. Afterward, I showered and got into bed. I'd be doing the same routine again tomorrow.

****

Something woke me in the middle of the night. I didn't dream a lot when I slept, and I rarely had nightmares.

Opening my eyes, I stared up at the ceiling in the gloom. Yellow light from the street lamp streaked in weakly. The current heat wave meant I kept the window open to get as much air in as possible. It didn't help. The cotton t-shirt I slept in clung damply to my chest.

"Hello, Ashley," a rumbling voice spoke in the darkness.

I bolted upright, heart thudding, my eyes scanning the dark room. Nobody used my full name except my parents. They'd been expecting a girl before I was born but I turned up instead. And since I didn't believe in ghosts, it ruled them out. "Who's that?"

A shadow moved forward at the foot of the bed, and I reached for the light switch. "Don't do that."

My hand froze midair, and I pulled it back. I couldn't miss the threat in his voice. In any case, did it matter if I saw the face of the person who was about to murder me in my bed or something worse?

I couldn't see his features except that he was a tall, broad man in dark clothing. The cut and shimmer of his jacket identified that he wore a suit.

"Who are you?" I swallowed between the words. My throat had gone dry, and my voice sounded sharp.

"My name is Sergei but that doesn't matter at this moment," he replied. Something in his deep voice had a weirdly calming effect, considering the situation.

I should've been freaking out at having a stranger in my room in the middle of the night. Instead, the almost familiar, rich quality of his voice and his mysterious presence fascinated me.

What the fuck was wrong with me?

"What matters is what I want," he continued.

A cold finger of fear slithered down my spine. I dreaded asking the question, but the words came out of my lips anyway. "What is it you want?"

"You." He stepped forward so that the weak light from the window hit one side of his face.

Recognition dawned on me. I'd seen that face before. Seen him. This morning.

Mr. Sexy and Dangerous.

The man in black.

Now as I stared at the same man who stood in my bedroom looking as menacing as ever, my muscles went rigid as I realized that the look I'd seen in his eyes this morning had been a veiled promise—he'd see me again.

He'd come here for me. A stalker.

Shit! The hairs on my nape and arms lifted. My gaze bounced around the room and my mind worked fast calculating how to get away.

"Are you going to hurt me?" It seemed a silly question to ask when a strange man had broken into my apartment, but I had to ask.

"No one has to get hurt if you do as I say," he replied in a smooth voice, lacking any inflections.

The words didn't reassure me and galvanized me into action. I bolted off the bed, heading for the door. I was an athlete and running was my specialty. I couldn't fight him. He was bigger, taller, and wider. Still, I could outrun him.

Lie here quietly for him to rape and murder me or whatever else he'd planned? No way.

I sprinted down the hallway. It didn't matter that I was barefooted and in my sleep shorts and shirt. If I could get out of the front door, there stood a chance of one of my neighbors overhearing the noise and intervening. Or at least, someone would call the police.

Reaching the entrance, I clicked the lock, and twisted the handle in my hand.

Arms banded around me, imprisoning me. There was a second man. How many others were there?

I kicked out and screamed just as hands covered my mouth. A needle pricked my neck. Dizziness overcame me.

"Be careful with him."

I heard the warning from Sergei before I blanked out.

Chapter Two

Light hurt my eyes when I opened them. Feeling disorientated, I squeezed them shut, and let out a groan. A marching band seemed to be having a festival in my head.

Did I drink last night? I didn't imbibe alcohol when I worked and I hadn't been partying in ages. Not with Nationals coming up in only weeks.

Snatches of yesterday flashed through my mind.

Donny's call. The man in black. In the park. In my room.

Sergei.

My eyes flew open and I sat upright in bed. Not my bed.

I glanced around the space. Not my apartment.

Light from the rising sun beamed through floor-to-ceiling windows into what could only be described as minimalist heaven—white walls and doors and large bed with luxurious, soft, white sheets, the only furniture.

Did Sergei abduct me?

What matters is what I want ... you.

Remembering his words made me shiver. I rubbed my arms as my feet hit the thick-piled carpet. I still wore the clothes from last night. Had it been last night?

With quick steps, I reached the first door and turned the handle. It didn't budge. I repeated the action with the other doors. One was a closet filled with men's clothes. The other was a bathroom with a sophisticated shower unit, light gray limestone tiles covered the walls and floor, a white sink, and a glass shelf with a plastic toothbrush and tube of toothpaste.

Locked in. I had no obvious way of getting out.

Blinking rapidly, I walked stiffly over to the window. At the edge, a wave of dizziness hit me and I stumbled back.

Mouth agape, I stared over the city from several floors high. My hands turned clammy, and my knees weakened.

I had mild vertigo, a fear of heights. Even if I didn't, I couldn't very well climb out of this window. There were no obvious ledges to hang onto. Imagining the drop turned my gut into stone. I turned my back to the bright view of sprawling metropolis.

I wasn't chained up and locked away in a dingy dungeon. Still this ivory tower stood as my prison. I couldn't escape it.

Who was Sergei and why had he abducted me? The place reeked of money. A man who could afford high rise penthouses would have a pick of beautiful people.

This situation made no sense.

A clicking sound made me stiffen and turn to the locked door. It swung inward. A huge man in a black suit, tie, and white shirt stood there. With an aluminum tray in his large hands he could've been a butler. But no butler I knew packed as much muscles as he did. He strode in and placed the tray on the bed.

"Good morning," he said in a heavy Slavic accent. "I brought your breakfast."

I stared from him to the tray and back again. They'd drugged me to get me here. I wasn't going to risk the chance of being sedated again.

"What am I doing here?" I asked, crossing my hands over my chest as I tried to look past him through the open door.

His massive frame blocked the view. "You're Mr. Petrichenko's guest."

"Guest?" I snorted with disdain. "I don't remember accepting an invitation and who the hell is Mr.

Petrichenko?"

His bullish expression didn't change. "You know him as Sergei."

My skin prickled at the mention of the man-in-black's name. A picture of him in the park, his sharp eyes holding me captive, swam in my mind. I shook my head, wadding off the uneasy feeling.

Sweat broke on my forehead and I paced the floor, rubbing my hand on the back of my neck. I needed to get out of here.

"Look, I'm sure Sergei—Mr. Petrichenko is a nice man and all, but I have to get home. I have lectures and practice." Not to mention a part-time job I didn't want to lose.

"You can't go home. You are to stay in this room, eat you food, and Sergei will come to you when he's ready."

The way he said that made me imagine medieval brides waiting for their new husbands to visit them in their bed chambers. My spine stiffened, and my anger rose. I wasn't going to become anyone's fucking "bride" or whatever.

"Didn't you hear me? I don't want to be here. Or don't you know it's illegal to detain someone against their wish." My body shook, and I sucked in a deep breath. "Look, if you let me go, I won't tell anyone about what's happened. I just want to go back to my life."

The man just shook his head and walked out the door, closing it behind him.

Rushing over, I tried the handle again. Like before it didn't budge. Frustrated, I kicked it, stubbing my big toe.

"Ouch." I hobbled over to the bed and sat on it, rubbing my injured foot. The door was made of metal or something unyielding.

When the pain eased a little, I took the fork from the tray and hid it in the closet. I might need it later as a weapon. Then I showered and got dressed. It'd be better to be fully clothed when I escaped. The expensive clothes in the closet all seemed to be exact fits as if Sergei had stocked them in readiness for my arrival.

Shuddering, I tugged a gray t-shirt over my head and pulled on the dark blue denim trousers. I sat on the bed and slipped my feet into white socks and a pair of leather and suede sneakers. I could never afford them, but it seemed Sergei was a generous kidnapper. They weren't exactly my trusted comfortable running shoes, but they were luxurious, and they'd have to do.

The large windows and sparkling cerulean sky gave an illusion of limitless space from the bed. It was just that—a deception. I was caged by the windows and walls and doors. By the entire building.

I hated it.

Tugging at the V-neck of the t-shirt, I sat on the bed. There wasn't much else to do while I waited for Sergei or the other man to return.

Would anyone notice that I wasn't in class today? The coach would notice my absence from training, and some of my friends would miss me. They probably wouldn't raise an alarm for another day or so.

By then wouldn't it be too late? I was intact for the moment. But I didn't know what Sergei planned for me? Was he into human trafficking? I'd read horror stories about people who went missing. I didn't have any surviving family aside from my brother. So perhaps I was a perfect candidate for abduction.

The thought unsettled me more and my gut knotted.

Chapter Three

Lying on the bed, I drifted in and out of a restless sleep. Later, probably late afternoon by the position of the sun and the lengthening shadows, the door lock clicked and I sat up in bed.

The butler-slash-bodyguard returned. The man was built like an armored tank, he had to be security. He picked up the tray and stared at it.

I pretended to be more interested in the lettering on my t-shirt so he wouldn't notice that I was eyeing him with my peripheral vision.

"Give me the fork," he said.

I feigned ignorance and shrugged. "What fork?"

"The one you hid in the closet."

Damn. He'd seen it. They had a camera in this room. I glanced around but didn't notice anything like the gadget.

"If you know where it is, then get it yourself."

I eyed the entrance as he walked around the bed. The door stood open, and I could see a well-lit hallway, more panoramic views of the city, and the intricate black metal spikes of a balustrade. Did that lead downstairs? The idea of freedom made me sit up and swing my feet over the bed.

"Don't even think about leaving this room," he said as if reading my thoughts.

I glanced behind as he reached the closet door. I'd be out of here before he could reach me. I was faster. His bulk would hinder him in a race. But I hesitated. I didn't know who else was in this apartment, and I didn't want to be sedated again. I had to bide my time.

He returned with the fork, and placed it on the tray.

When he stepped out of the door, it didn't close as

I expected.

Instead, someone else stood there, blocking it.

Sergei.

Without the hooded outfit, he was stunning. Like a dark angel. His hair was jet black and longish, turning into curls around his neck, softening the perfect hardness of his face. His gaze settled on me and his lips curved into a half smile.

My breath caught, heart thumping against my chest. I couldn't look away from him.

"Hello again, Ashley."

The soft way he said my name made tingles travel down my spine. My mouth dried out as I watched him stride across the room like a tiger stalking deer.

I shuffled across the bed to the other side of the room, but he didn't stop his advance.

"You didn't eat breakfast. Tut. Tut. Tut. As an athlete, you should know the importance of every meal."

My cheeks heated as if I were a little child he'd just told off. I really should've eaten. I didn't have enough body fat for my body to utilize. It would start breaking down muscles if I didn't eat soon. And that wasn't good.

"I'm not going to allow you to drug me again," I said in an annoyed voice.

He stood a few feet away and tilted his head to look at me.

"I won't drug you again unless you make me do it," he said in a low voice that almost sounded reassuring aside from the hidden threat. "You can eat dinner with me this evening."

Hope fluttered in my chest. "You mean you're going to let me out of this room?"

"Of course." He took a couple of steps forward.

I did the opposite. Backing away until my back hit

the wall and there was nowhere for me to run. My heart hammered in my chest, and my gut tightened.

"I know you like the outdoors," he continued. "So in a few days, I'm going to take you to my country home. You'll have all the space and freedom to run."

That sounded great, running out in the countryside. In open space. I imagined the greenery and trees and nature. No skyscrapers. No exhaust fumes. Heaven.

He raised his hand and his fingers stroked my cheek, trailing down to my neck like feathers. Strangely enough, I didn't move, didn't try to avoid his touch. I felt disorientated. Confused.

His hands caressed my skin, burning me, making my breath come out choppy.

He smiled as if in response to my reaction. How could someone be so stunning and so terrifying at the same time?

"Why am I here?" I asked in a breathy voice.

He leaned forward and inhaled deeply as if taking in my scent.

My body heated up, and my cock stirred.

His hand slid under my t-shirt scorching my skin as he pushed the shirt up. "I want you, and now I'm going to have you."

His words brought me back to reality. Okay. He hadn't hurt me yet, but his intentions lay stark in his dark, heated gaze. It didn't matter that his closeness made me want to rub up against him and feel his hardness inside me.

"No," I said more to myself than to him. "I don't want you."

"You don't?" he said in an amused voice as his thumb stroked over my left nipple.

I barely stifled a gasp as a bolt of heat rushed to

my groin.

"I saw the way you looked at me in the park and saw the way you responded when I touched you."

"No. That was just because of Rob—"

Before I could finish his hand wrapped around my neck, hefty and menacing. He tightened it, crushing the breath out of me. I could see the threat of violence darkening his eyes, feel it in the press of his hand.

Sweat broke out on my top lip and my forehead. I couldn't speak, couldn't move.

"Never mention his name again. Unless you want him dead. Do you understand me?"

I swallowed and nodded.

He squeezed his hand around my throat for a couple of seconds before releasing me and stepping back.

My body shook, and my legs felt as if they would give way. Only held up by the wall.

"Get undressed."

My eyes widened as more shock ran through me. I knew what he wanted but I just couldn't. Not after the warning he'd just made.

"No." I shook my head.

"Don't make this harder than it needs to be." he said in a voice hardened to steel. "Take your clothes off now."

Without thinking, I feigned to the right to distract him and ran across the room. I heard his curse behind me, but I didn't stop as I ran into the hallway, my heart pounding so loud and strong it could've punched a hole in my chest.

Sergei's racing feet thudded behind me.

I was nearly at the top of the stairs. Just two more strides and I'd be lopping over the steps.

A hard body hit my back, tackling me to the floor. I struggled, kicking, wriggling. He didn't let go, just gripped me tighter.

It didn't help that I was face down on solid wooden floor. Sweat dripped down, making me slip and slide all over unable to get a proper grip.

He pinned me with his weight, straddling me. His breath fanned my nape.

"You like running," he said in a husky voice. "Guess what? I love chasing."

He lowered his head and nipped the section where my neck met my shoulder.

I couldn't help my response. I groaned, arching my neck as if giving him more room just as a spike of heat shot to my balls. The denim suddenly felt very tight as I got hard. Fucking hard.

Heat streaked my cheeks, a mixture of shame and desire. How could I practically roll over for him like this?

There was something about having his body covering me as he caged me with an arm around my neck, the weight of his rigid cock grinding against my butt. His teeth grazed my sensitive neck again.

Intense heat flared in my veins. I rocked my hips, my hole clenching.

Fuck! I wanted him inside me. This made the whole situation worse. He'd taken me by force. He was keeping me here by force. How could I feel any attraction to such a man?

My body responded to the kisses he peppered my shoulder, and I didn't notice that he'd taken his tie off until it was too late.

He grabbed my hands and wound the silk around them before securing it to the balustrade.

"Let me go!" I tugged and bucked, but the knot only seemed to tighten around my wrists.

My body sagged as I finally accepted defeat. I couldn't get out of the tie. To be fair, he hadn't done anything violent to me. I'd been expecting him to hit me for running. Instead, he kissed my body, caressing it as if it were precious. As if I was important.

Something sharp and pointed poked my lower back. Then a ripping sound.

I froze, my heart nearly exploding in my chest. He had a knife in his hand. Was he going to stab me?

Perhaps I shouldn't have run. He'd only wanted sex. Now he was going to kill me.

"Please." I swallowed the lump in my throat. "Please don't hurt me."

Fingers stroked my neck.

I jerked on reflex, fear making my body tremble. "Shhh. Don't move."

I did as he commanded, holding my breath.

The hand on my neck, held the collar of my shirt as he cut it with the knife in the other, pushing the torn sides apart until I felt the chilled air on my skin. Then he reached for the fly of my denim.

I stiffened, knowing that as soon as he touched me he'd know I was turned on, and I didn't want him to know how much he affected me because that would just be sick.

"Lift your hips for me," he said in a low voice.

Instinctively I did as he asked before I could stop myself. Why was I so quick to obey? Why was my body betraying me this way?

He unhooked the button and tugged the zip. If he felt my aching cock or the pre-cum dampening the briefs, he didn't say anything as he tugged my jeans off, pulling off my shoes and socks on the way.

For a few seconds, nothing happened.

I turned my head to see what was going on and found him staring at me with appreciation and hunger.

I'd never known anyone to look at me in that way

before. It was an all-consuming gaze.

It made me yearn to lift my hips up and spread my cheeks for him to take me. Pre-cum dripped onto the floor as I hardened even further.

"You are so fucking beautiful," he said in a thick voice.

He started taking his clothes off. I couldn't keep my gaze away.

He wore a charcoal suit and gray shirt. He took the jacket off and tossed it aside before unbuttoning his shirt and removing his cufflinks.

As his shirt opened up, I got a glimpse of dark ink against tanned skin.

My breath caught as he shoved the shirt off revealing skin covered in tattoos. They were everywhere on his torso. Chest, stomach, arms, back—a mixture of Russian text that I couldn't understand, tribal art, and a dragon whose tail went down one arm and the body wrapped around Sergei's back with its head on the right side of his chest.

I thought he'd been stunning before. Now he stood like an exhibition, an impressive work of art.

I understood why he'd been fully covered in the park. The distinguishing ink on his body would've attracted a lot of attention.

I'd been so distracted with studying his tattoos I didn't notice as he removed his trousers and shoes until he stood naked.

Gloriously naked. Broad shoulders. Compact muscles. Sturdy legs. Erect cock.

I was speechless, just watching him. My body shook, and my heart felt like it would explode.

He moved, disappearing into a room behind me and came out too quickly for me to make use of his absence.

He held something in his hand that I couldn't quite see and lowered onto his knees.

I finally found my voice as I realized what was going to happen. We were in the hallway overlooking the mezzanine level. Anyone down there could see us. "Don't do this. Not here."

"I wanted our first time to be on the bed so that you could be comfortable," he said as he caressed my body. "But you have to learn that you belong to me now. And I'll take you wherever I desire."

The mix of threat and promise in his voice made me shiver. I was so fucking screwed up.

I had a healthy sex life when I got time in between everything else. But I'd never even fantasized about being taken like this. So why was I responding to Sergei? What was going on in my mind? Was I losing it? Was this Stockholm syndrome?

He parted my ass cheeks and pressed a finger against my hole. It wasn't forceful, just a presence.

I clenched and bucked.

His lubed finger pushed past the ring of muscles easily, his touch exploratory.

I gasped. The pain I'd been expecting didn't materialize. He prepped me properly. Not taking me dry like I'd worried he'd rip me open.

Sighing with pleasure, I relaxed, enjoying his questing fingers, sliding in and out, loosening me up.

When he brought me up to my knees, I didn't resist. But I wasn't expecting what he did next.

He played with my sacs as his tongue stroked the spot between my balls and ass. I nearly came on the spot and whimpered. I fucking whimpered. Then he was tonguing my ass. No one had ever done that for me before.

Heat flushed my body, and I shuddered with

pleasure. I wanted him inside him. I was going to start begging if he didn't do something soon. And I didn't wish to do that, so I clamped my lips together.

He shifted, and I missed his touch immediately. I heard the crackle of a condom wrapper as he tore it open and sheathed himself before he was nudging my hole with the broad head. With a push, he was in. It was still only the head, and I was in agony wanting all of him inside me.

My grip on the bottom of the balustrade tightened, and I jerked my hips backward just as he rammed all the way in.

Gasping, I cried out in pain.

He didn't move, his hips pressed against my butt cheeks, his grip on my hips tight.

I needed him to move. "Please…" I begged.

His right hand stroked down my clammy spine in a caress. "Tell me what you want, *lyubimaya veshch.*"

I didn't know the words in Russian were, but they made me feel special, and I lost my inhibition. My shame. "Fuck me … please," I said, feeling breathless.

He leaned over me, tugged my head to the side and kissed me, taking more of my breath away with the passion he unleashed inside me. It was like having a drug. I couldn't believe my response to his kiss. I shouldn't welcome his kiss, but I did. He took his time, stroking his tongue against mine before sucking my lower lip into his mouth.

His mouth felt so good. He felt so good. I forgot where I was and instead felt as if a lover was making love to me.

My body was ablaze as he gentled the hand in my hair, cradling it.

Breaking the kiss, he stared down at me. His eyes gleamed with desire. His lips were wet and shiny and swollen from our kiss. They curled into a lopsided smile that made him look like an angel.

He pulled out a little and stroked back, pegging my sweet spot.

Yes!

He did it again, harder this time. I moaned out loud, arching my back and presenting my ass to him.

He took what I gave and rammed into me again and again. Soon we were both grunting and groaning, the sound bouncing off the high ceilings, echoing in the apartment. Whoever else was here would hear us.

My cock ached, dripped. I just needed friction on my dick, and I would come.

As if he knew what I was thinking, he wrapped his hand around my erection. The lube made his grip glide wonderfully over me from head to the base. One pump. Two. My body arched as I hit climax. Cum rushed out of me, splattering onto the wood panels.

My pleasure didn't ease though, as he gripped my hips with both hands and fucked me forcefully until he came with a grunt and a jerk.

I lay there panting, trying to catch my breath while he untied my hands and slid his arm around my back and the other under my knees, lifting me up. I was five foot eleven and weighed one hundred and sixty pounds, so I wasn't light. But he looked totally at ease as he carried me without effort to the bedroom.

Chapter Four

A few days later I sat in a car with the butler. I'd since found out his name was Ivan. I'd made a joke about Ivan the Terrible when he'd told me, and he'd laughed it off.

Sergei had business keeping him away for a few days so Ivan was driving me to the country villa. I hadn't left the apartment for five days so I had to admit I was excited about seeing something other than walls, windows, and sky. And of course the prospect of running with the wind whipping my face made me tingle all over.

The plan had been to fly out in Sergei's helicopter but my fear of heights meant I would've been sedated. I begged Sergei to let us drive instead. He'd relented and warned that I had to behave while in the car with Ivan.

On his part, Sergei had kept his promise not to hurt me if I behaved. Of course he took me whenever and wherever he wanted. Sometimes he fucked me rough and hard. Other times, he stroked me slow and tender. Each time he left me breathless and sated. Each time it felt as if he made love to me.

How could it be love? I wasn't here of my volition, was I?

So why hadn't I fought him each time he'd taken me to his bedroom? Why hadn't I resisted when he'd pulled me into the humongous shower stall and cleaned me up with such tenderness? Why didn't I turn away when he kissed me or caressed my body, his touch gentle and firm, leaving me in a fog of lust? Why didn't I struggle when he took my cock in his mouth or when he fucked me in the shower stall or when he took me back to his bed every night, cradling me?

I couldn't explain my instinct to submit to him.

I guess a part of me still hoped for an opportunity

to escape. So why was I in a car heading to his home in the middle of nowhere where help would be further away?

All the thoughts in my head were making me a little crazy, and I decided to have a conversation with Ivan to distract myself.

"How do you know Sergei?" I asked, wanting to find out more about their relationship.

"I've known him for many years. He saved my life once, and now I work for him." Ivan shrugged. His strong accent made w sound like v.

"Oh, so what does he do?"

He looked at me and flashed crooked white teeth. "He's business man."

"What kind of business?"

His gaze remained through the windscreen on the road ahead. "I'm sure when he wants you to know, he'll tell you."

That sounded ominous and made Sergei even more enigmatic.

"So why is he keeping me. I mean a man like him can have anyone he wants. Why me?"

He glanced at me, looking a little uncomfortable. "Yes, he can have anyone. But you're special."

I laughed at the implication of his words. "Special? Is he in love with me?" I asked jokingly. A man like Sergei didn't know love. A man who took whatever he wanted. Who had no qualms about breaking into my apartment, drugging me, and taking me against my wish. He might be obsessed with me—a sinister obsession—but it wasn't love.

Ivan stared at me with an expression I couldn't decipher. "You think being with him is bad? Trust me. There are worse things than being with Sergei."

I bet there were people in worse situations, but

this wasn't the life I wanted for myself. My ambition lay in sports medals and Olympic glory. I hadn't pictured I'd become someone's prized pet. No matter how stunning or generous they were.

I didn't want this at all. I wanted to go back to my life and I had the perfect opportunity to get away.

I watched the road. It wasn't busy. We barely went past another car in the past hour since we left the city. Greenery and tall trees lined either side and stretched out as far as the eyes could see.

I calculated that if I started running, I'd be back in the city within a few hours as long as I kept close to the road. Ivan would never catch me if he chased me on foot. Today I was in warm clothes and comfortable sneakers.

"I need to pee," I said as the idea got into my head.

"What?" He glanced at me.

"I need to have a pee, you know, a slash."

"Can't you wait until we get there?"

"Not unless you want me to do it in here."

He grunted. "Hold on."

He pulled to the side of the road and killed the engine. "You're not going to try anything, are you?"

I stared at the gun visible under his jacket and up to his face. "I wouldn't dare, would I? Not when you're likely to shoot me in the back."

He didn't say anything and undid the leather cuff around my wrist, releasing my right hand. Then he clicked the button to unlock the doors.

When he nodded at me, I pushed the door open and got out. He came around and leaned on the bonnet of the car.

I walked to the grass verge and glanced back. "Are you just going to stand there and watch me?"

"Yes," he replied without moving.

I scanned the line of trees. "I'm going to go a little deeper, so no one sees me from the road."

From the corner of my eyes, I saw him straighten up and match my steps. As soon as I crossed the tree line and felt there was enough of a gap between us, I took off running.

"Stop! Ashley!"

I heard him shouting for me as his footsteps crashed through the undergrowth behind me.

Heart thumping violently, I didn't look back, and I didn't stop. Twigs crunched beneath my sneakers. Leaves whipped my clothes and exposed skin. I ran until I couldn't hear him anymore. Panting, I leaned against a tree to catch my breath and looked back. I couldn't see him or hear him. I'd bet he wasn't built for distance running, and I'd been right.

But it didn't mean I was safe yet. I had to make my way to civilization and get help, and that was still miles away. I resumed running, heading in the direction of the road. When I saw the black asphalt surface, I ran parallel to it. I didn't want to risk that Ivan was still out there patrolling the road.

I didn't see anyone else, and I wasn't brave enough to run out on the tarmac when the occasional car drove past. By the time, I saw what seemed like a farmhouse in the distance the sky had already turned purplish orange. I was tired and hungry. I needed to rest. Hopefully, there was a phone in the house I could use.

A man sat on a tractor. I ran toward him, hoping he'd see me among the tall wheat.

"Excuse me, sir!" I waved my hand in the air. "I need help, please."

He stopped the tractor and studied my appearance. "Are you lost?"

Panting to catch my breath, I eyed him. He

appeared harmless enough. I explained that I'd been abducted, that I escaped and needed the police. He said there was a phone in the house I could use. I hopped on the tractor, and he drove back toward the house. The sun had set by the time we arrived at the farmhouse. I got off the tractor, and he led the way.

Just as we got toward the front verandah, a beam of lights hit us. I held my hand up to shield from the glare.

A man got out of a black car. In the gloom, I hadn't noticed it parked to the side of the house. As soon as I saw his silhouette I knew who he was before he spoke. He looked menacing and unforgiving, a dark angel on a mission.

I'd thought he'd travelled on business. How had he gotten back so quickly?

My mouth dried out and I froze.

"Get in the car, Ashley." The grim tone of his voice didn't inspire challenge.

Breath bursting out of me, I felt rooted to the spot as my shoulders tightened. What would he do to me if I go into the car? He'd promised not to hurt me. That was before I ran away.

"You're trespassing. Get off my land," the farmer said in an annoyed voice.

Crack.

I flinched, body trembling, leg muscles tightening. I was ready to run again.

The farmer cried out and crumpled to the ground.

"He didn't do anything. Why did you shoot him?" I cried, ready to heave out whatever was left in my empty stomach.

"I told you no one needed to get hurt as long as you do what I say. If you don't want me to put a bullet through his head, get in the car. Now." Sergei pointed the glinting weapon at the farmer who lay on the dirt of the front lawn, clutching his arm where blood seeped through his fingers.

"I'm sorry," I muttered to the prone man and walked to the car with stiff legs and locked knees. I'd condemned the man by coming here. By running away.

Ivan held the door open. Feeling numb and tired, I climbed into the back seat. I'd been running away from Sergei for hours. No food. No water. Just when freedom seemed within reach, he'd recaptured me.

He'd already shot the farmer. What would he do to me?

Sergei got into the back seat beside me. He didn't say anything as Ivan drove down a windy, dusty lane back onto the highway.

Hands jammed into my armpits, I sat huddled in the corner afraid he'd kill me.

Chapter Five

There were worse things than death.

I found out when we got back to the city. Instead of heading to Sergei's penthouse, we drove to a building I didn't recognize.

Ivan parked in an underground car park and opened the door for me. Sergei walked ahead as if he didn't want to look at me, his disappointment evident in his stony expression.

Shoulders sagging, my gut twisted as I walked beside Ivan. Why did I feel as if I'd let Sergei down? Why did I feel hollow inside? What was going on with me?

He'd taken me away from my life. I'd watched him shoot an innocent man. He'd made me get into the car tonight?

Still, I couldn't help the hollowness in my chest at the hurt look in his eyes just now.

Swallowing the big lump in my throat, I focused blankly on the gray metal as we got into a service lift.

Ivan pulled down the grill. It went up, and we got out into a large space displayed like a warehouse.

We walked through a corridor, our footsteps echoing off the concrete surface. On either side were rooms with glass doors.

In one, a naked man was on his knees while another face-fucked him.

My cheeks heated, and I stared in the other direction only to watch two men spit-roasting another over a bench.

My body flushed. What the hell was this place? I hurried along and all through the hallway each room had some sexual action going on.

We rounded the corner into an open space where

my brother sat at a table with another man.

My brows arched. What was Donny doing here?

Sergei grabbed my arm. It was the first time he'd touched me since he'd found me at the farmhouse. Strangely I didn't feel repelled.

"Roger, here's your star attraction."

He shoved me forward, and I stumbled but righted myself before I face-planted on the floor.

"Donny, what's going on?" I asked, my mouth dry, my heart racing.

My brother appeared as if someone had dragged him out of bed, hair disheveled, clothes askew and sweat dripping from his forehead as he shifted uncomfortably, foot bouncing on the floor.

The man next to him who I presumed was Roger, leered at me and licked his lips as if I were a meal he was going to enjoy eating.

My stomach lurched and bile rose in my throat.

I turned back to Sergei, who'd already turned to walk away.

Was he going to leave me here? I panicked. "Sergei, please, what's going on?"

He swiveled and shoved his hands into his pockets. "Your brother owes me a hundred grand, and he offered you as the payment to work here as one of the sex slaves for a year."

It couldn't be. My head whipped around in my brother's direction as my heart froze. "Donny? Is this true?"

Donny avoided my gaze. "Mr. Petrichenko was going to kill me. I had no choice. I'm sorry."

"You're fucking sorry?" I rushed at him, but Ivan grabbed me from behind, pulling me back.

My head spun. Donny had sold me to pay his goddamned debts. What kind of brother did that? As I struggled, it finally hit me that Sergei had taken me for himself instead of bringing me here. He'd been trying to save me in a twisted kind of way.

"He's a feisty one," Roger said. "I'm going to enjoy taming him."

I saw Sergei stiffen, and his face was an implacable mask. Shit. Was he going to leave me here with these men?

"Please, don't leave me here," I begged, shaking myself from Ivan and rushing to kneel at Sergei's feet. Tears fell from my face. If he left me here, I'd never get out. "I want to go with you."

Sighing heavily, Sergei's palm settled at the back of my neck. He gripped my head, tilting it back, so I looked up at his hardened face. "How can I trust you? How do I know you won't run away again?"

"I won't. I promise. I'll do whatever you want me to do." I sniffed, hoping I could reach the compassionate part of him if there was one.

A bitter smile curled his lips and his dark brow rose. "You will?"

"Yes."

"Prove it." Gripping my neck, he dragged me up to my feet.

I stared at him, knowing I'd do whatever he asked just to get out of this place giving me the creeps.

He put his hand inside his jacket, pulled out his handgun and placed it into my palm. I nearly dropped it from the shock and weight.

Sergei still held onto the gun in my hand. "Shoot your brother."

"What? No!" I'd never held a gun before let alone kill anything.

"You've got to be shitting me," my brother said in a shaking jokey voice. His eyes darted around the space and landed on me, his mouth in a half-smile half-grimace.

Sergei tilted my head and held my gaze with an intense look. No amusement tinged his expression. "Prove that I can trust you. Show me where your loyalties lie. Me or your brother."

Fuck! The whoosh of rushing blood sounded so loud in my ears, and my vision blurred a little.

Sergei turned the gun in my hand toward his chest. Licking my lips, I stared from Sergei to Donny. I swear I must have been delirious or something. It had to be because I was tired, my body sore and I needed a drink of water. I wasn't thinking rationally.

I had a gun in my hand pointed at the man who had abducted me. I could pull the trigger and kill him.

Still, I couldn't do it. Couldn't hurt him. I cared for him.

I was in love with him. My abductor. A warped kind of love.

He'd taken care of me, in his dark, peculiar way. In Sergei's own way. It made no sense to ordinary people. But I stood as far away from ordinary as I'd ever done.

I could trust Sergei to protect me. He'd done so already.

My brother, however, I couldn't trust.

It all happened as if I floated in the air, watching myself. I twisted the gun around, aimed it at my brother.

He scrambled up from the chair. "Ash, no!"

I pulled the trigger.

Crack!

The sound echoed in my head. I jerked backward into hard muscles, holding me upright.

"You fucking shot me!" Wide-eyed with shock, my brother clutched his shoulder, a red stain spreading through his shirt.

Sergei took the gun from me and shot Donny again. Blood splattered the chair as he slumped to the floor.

Surprisingly I didn't scream. Didn't cry. My legs gave way, though.

"Clean this place up," Sergei instructed as he scooped me up and carried me back down to the car.

I couldn't remember much of the drive back aside from when he offered me a drink of water. My mind was numb, and my body shook. The image of Donny lying on the cold concrete floor played in my head on a loop. Sergei held me all the way.

At home—this was now home, wasn't it? I couldn't go back to my old life. Not after what I'd just done—he took me straight into the kitchen and sat me on a high stool while he went about frying eggs and bacon.

"It's a new day," he said in the deep sensual voice I'd fallen for. He took his jacket off, hung it on another chair and rolled up the sleeves of his shirt, revealing the artful ink I loved so much. "And we're going to start afresh."

I couldn't help gazing at him as the muscles moved beneath his shirt. He really was striking and sexy. Hot.

And he was mine. For now at least. I didn't know how long he was going to keep me. Something twisted in my chest at the idea that he'd send me away when he got bored with me.

My exhaustion seemed to depart as I watched the rising sun stroke his body through the floor-to-ceiling window. Perhaps I was going crazy, but I wanted him. Right here. Right now.

He had other ideas as he put the plates of fried breakfast on the table. I wouldn't usually eat this kind of food, but right now I didn't care. I was famished. I tucked in and barely tasted it.

He sat beside me, eating a little but mainly studying me.

I lifted the glass of fresh orange juice he'd just squeezed and practically gulped it down. Some of it dripped down my chin.

Sergei leaned forward and licked the drop off my face.

My breath caught. I placed the glass on the counter and turned into him.

He captured my mouth with his, kissing me the way only he did, with passion and tenderness that I'd never expected from a ruthless man like him.

He was such a ball of contradictions, and he unbalanced me. I loved him regardless.

I reached for his shirt and started unbuttoning it. I wanted to see him in all his glory again.

He broke the kiss and straightened, letting me carry on as he tugged the shirt out of the trousers.

I brushed my hands over his skin as I pushed his shirt aside. "You have the most incredible body I've ever seen. I love touching it." I couldn't help the awe in my voice.

His lips curled into the skewed grin that I loved so much. "Not as amazing as you. The minute I saw you I knew you were for me."

He said that with such reverence, stroking his palm down my cheek to my chin. He made me feel fantastic. Made me feel special when he spoke like that.

I went down on my knees as I undid his belt buckle. He let me push his trousers down, setting his magnificent cock free. I held it, stroked it with my palm before licking it with my tongue. I worked down to his sacs, nuzzling the short hairs at the base, inhaling his manly scent.

He didn't try to take over, just let me do whatever I pleased.

I glanced up at him, my brows raised in a query.

"You mouth is wonderful, but I want your tight ass."

He gripped my shoulders and pulled me up, then proceeded to divest me of my clothing before lifting me onto the table.

"Pull up and hold your knees."

I did as he instructed as he went on his knees, rimming my ass and pumping my cock. Pleasure shot through me, and I moaned, arching my body to his rhythm. Fever rushed through me.

He stood up and reached for a bottle of olive oil. It wasn't the best lube, but I couldn't wait, and I didn't want him to leave me alone even for one second. He drizzled some down my crack and breached me with his fingers.

My body rocked as I cried out. Then he was there, his cock head at my hole.

We both groaned as he pushed in. I closed my eyes and breathed heavily, and he pulled out a little and then slammed all the way into me.

He took me roughly, as if re-establishing his control over me. I cried out as pain swirled into pleasure. He began rocking in and out. I opened my eyes and stared at him.

His expression was fierce as he stared down at me, his grip tight on my thighs.

My heart expanded in my chest as I watched him. I knew at this very moment that I didn't want to be apart from this man. I didn't care about how I got here or what he'd done. I'd shot my brother. I was an accomplice in Donny's death. So perhaps I was no better than Sergei.

After my parents died in a car crash, I drifted,

never belonging anywhere. Running and school had provided me with focus, a distraction from my loneliness.

Now, I had Sergei. He'd become a part of my life as much as I was in his.

"You are beautiful, and you're mine." His words echoed my thoughts as he rammed into me again and again, sweat coating both our bodies. "Don't ever forget it."

"I won't," I replied, my body arching as my orgasm rose, my balls tightening. "I'm yours."

I cried out as cum spurted from my cock onto my stomach.

He leaned over, gripped my head and kissed me almost savagely. Then he pulled out, bent me over the table, and took me from behind.

The table felt cool under my face as I turned to watch this dark angel that had entered my life take me the way I wanted him to. He fucked me, possessed not just my body but my heart too, and I knew I wouldn't change it for anything. I would give up running for him.

"*Lyubimaya veshch,* I'm never letting you go," he said as he body froze and he came inside me.

I made one stunning realization: I didn't want him to ever let me go.

The End

www.kaityler.com

EVERNIGHT PUBLISHING ®

www.evernightpublishing.com